Choose your Lane to love!

Readers love
AMY LANE

School of Fish

"...for fans of the series this is a must!"
—Open Skye Book Reviews

Safe Heart

"Cash impressed me and I was happy to see that he went beyond the call of duty to show he was not only serious but ready to be a part of all of Glen's life. In any way possible."
—Love Bytes Reviews

Silent Heart

"...lots of action, nail-biting rescues, and a nicely building romance between the two men."
—Joyfully Jay

By Amy Lane

All the Rules of Heaven
An Amy Lane Christmas
Behind the Curtain
Bewitched by Bella's Brother
Bolt-hole
Christmas Kitsch
Christmas with Danny Fit
Clear Water
Do-over
Food for Thought
Freckles
Gambling Men
Going Up
Hammer & Air
Homebird
If I Must
Immortal
It's Not Shakespeare
Left on St. Truth-be-Well
The Locker Room
Mourning Heaven
Phonebook
Puppy, Car, and Snow
Racing for the Sun • Hiding
the Moon
Raising the Stakes
Regret Me Not
Shiny!
Shirt
Sidecar
Slow Pitch
String Boys
A Solid Core of Alpha
Three Fates
Truth in the Dark
Turkey in the Snow
Under the Rushes
Wishing on a Blue Star

BENEATH THE STAIN
Beneath the Stain • Paint It Black

BONFIRES
Bonfires • Crocus

CANDY MAN
Candy Man • Bitter Taffy
Lollipop • Tart and Sweet

DREAMSPUN BEYOND
HEDGE WITCHES LONELY
HEARTS CLUB
Shortbread and Shadows
Portals and Puppy Dogs

DREAMSPUN DESIRES
THE MANNIES
The Virgin Manny
Manny Get Your Guy
Stand by Your Manny
A Fool and His Manny
SEARCH AND RESCUE
Warm Heart
Silent Heart
Safe Heart

FAMILIAR LOVE
Familiar Angel • Familiar Demon

FISH OUT OF WATER
Fish Out of Water
Red Fish, Dead Fish
A Few Good Fish
Hiding the Moon
Fish on a Bicycle
School of Fish

FLOPHOUSE
The Muscle

Published by Dreamspinner Press
www.dreamspinnerpress.com

By Amy Lane (cont.)

GRANBY KNITTING
The Winter Courtship Rituals
of Fur-Bearing Critters
How to Raise an Honest Rabbit
Knitter in His Natural Habitat
Blackbird Knitting in a Bunny's
Lair
The Granby Knitting Menagerie
Anthology

JOHNNIES
Chase in Shadow • Dex in Blue
Ethan in Gold • Black John
Bobby Green
Super Sock Man

KEEPING PROMISE ROCK
Keeping Promise Rock
Making Promises
Living Promises
Forever Promised

**LONG CON
ADVENTURES**
The Mastermind

TALKER
Talker • Talker's Redemption
Talker's Graduation
The Talker Collection
Anthology

WINTER BALL
Winter Ball • Summer Lessons
Fall Through Spring

Published by Harmony Ink Press
BITTER MOON SAGA
Triane's Son Rising
Triane's Son Learning
Triane's Son Fighting
Triane's Son Reigning

Published by Dreamspinner Press
www.dreamspinnerpress.com

The Mastermind

AMY LANE

Published by
DREAMSPINNER PRESS
5032 Capital Circle SW, Suite 2, PMB# 279, Tallahassee, FL 32305-
7886 USA
www.dreamspinnerpress.com

This is a work of fiction. Names, characters, places, and incidents either are the product of author imagination or are used fictitiously, and any resemblance to actual persons, living or dead, business establishments, events, or locales is entirely coincidental.

The Mastermind
© 2021 Amy Lane

Cover Art
© 2021 Tiferet Design
http://www.tiferetdesign.com/
Cover content is for illustrative purposes only and any person depicted on the cover is a model.

Mass Market Paperback ISBN: 978-1-64108-235-8
Trade Paperback ISBN: 978-1-64405-873-2
Digital ISBN: 978-1-64405-872-5
Mass Market Paperback published July 2021
First Edition
v. 1.0

Printed in the United States of America
∞
This paper meets the requirements of
ANSI/NISO Z39.48-1992 (Permanence of Paper).

Mary and Rayna for being my buddies always—
but also Elizabeth, forever, and Damon
and anyone who has ever needed a hero to beat the odds.
And Mate for being mine.

Coming Up Close

DANNY LOVED and hated Chicago. Loved it because it was his hometown, and if he wore the black overcoat and the natty little fedora, he had just enough gray at his temples to look like he owned the place, particularly when he walked down La Salle toward the river.

Something about the way the wind gusted, as if it was trying to carve out his entrails, made him feel a little like a warrior—and he liked that. He'd take any help he could get feeling young these days.

He'd been happy here once.

In the past.

That's why he hated it.

He paused at the corner, looking to his right. The ..st floor of the polished gray granite building was a .obby, but the second floor held a bank of very exclusive PO Boxes where he had his mail forwarded.

Every three months, Danny checked the box, even if he had to fly in from somewhere to do it.

He'd promised. Yeah, the promise had been over twenty years ago, but dammit, *he* kept his word.

And even if he didn't usually, he would have kept to his self-imposed schedule this time. Too much history, no matter how painful, was calling his name.

He waved to the receptionist, then took the palm-print-operated elevator up to the second floor and emerged into a vault of a room surrounded on all sides by PO Boxes that required a key, a code, and a thumbprint.

Of course, Danny's thumbprint wasn't associated with his real name—he was too smart for that—but it was his real thumb, of course, and that always made him uneasy. Still, he paid a great deal of money for the privacy and discretion of this hidden floor of this particularly notable building, and he liked to think that his pricy Italian snow boots made pricy Italian clicking noises as he crossed the polished granite floor.

"Mr. Biondi!" said Carina Weiss, the sleek and chic mother of three who sat at the reception podium in the middle of the room. "So good to see you. Would you like your usual booth?"

"Indeed." He gave a gracious nod.

"Your young protégé is already ahead of you," she said with a knowing smile, nodding at the lockbox on the stand in front of her.

Danny's eyes widened. "Indeed?" Protégé? Uhm, no. Ten years of boy toys and no-strings-attached liaisons, maybe, but nobody worth a title—certainly not a "protégé." And a protégé worthy of the woman's arched eyebrows and a catlike smile?

Definitely not.

But in order to get into this room and retrieve his mailbox, his "protégé" must have had the requisite ID. His palm print and his signature must have been in the system, and Mr. Protégé must have known Danny's keycodes as well. Still, even if he'd been able to access the PO Box, only Danny could get into the locked container that held the mail.

Danny was very interested to see who this man must be.

He followed Carina to the row of bare, sound-proofed rooms, wondering what was in his mail that warranted this interesting new development.

"Here you go," Carina said cheerfully. "Mr. Biondi, Mr. Contrell, I hope your business proceeds smoothly."

And with that, she set the box on the table for Danny to open with his own key and departed, leaving Danny and the very familiar stranger in the room together.

Danny managed to keep his professional, silk-smooth smile on until the door closed and the click of Carina's heels could no longer be heard.

Then he let his delight show through.

"Josh! Oh my God, look at you. You're practically grown."

The slender, stylish young man with the expensively cut hair, black leather topcoat, and black cashmere turtleneck and slacks, hopped up from his calculated sprawl at the table and rushed into Danny's arms for a warm, hard, and *very* filial hug.

"Uncle Danny!" he cried. "Oh my God, he told me you'd be here, probably today, and I barely had time to prepare."

Danny pulled back and gave him the gimlet eye. "You got access to my mailbox? How in the world—" This was supposed to be an absolutely unhackable PO Box—a thieves' Casablanca of mail, as it were.

Josh grinned, his brown eyes sparkling. "Oh, I was taught by the best. Between you and the Fox, this place didn't stand a chance."

Danny tried to look disapproving. "Did you do the hacking or—"

"I got a friend to do the hacking," Josh admitted. "And what about the look? Do you like it?"

Josh spread his arms and did a slick pirouette, his black half boots complementing the entire ensemble.

"Did Fox help you with that?" he asked fondly, suppressing the inevitable pang in his chest whenever Felix "the Fox" Salinger was mentioned. He'd damn the man for making Josh a part of his life, but God, Josh had just been such a joy. Seeing his "nephew" once every three months had been one of the driving forces bringing him back to this room four times a year—but Danny was usually the one doing the sneaking. Josh wasn't even supposed to know where he got his mail.

"No." Josh sobered. "He's been… busy."

Danny swallowed against the lump in his throat. "Yeah. I've seen the news." A blaze of fury—tamped down for the last week since the story had broken—tried to leap from his chest. "Josh, look. Whatever they say in the news, you mustn't believe it. Felix isn't capable of any of those things. You know that, right?"

Josh nodded, sober as a judge. "Yeah. That's why I'm here, actually." He glanced around the soundproofed room. "I figure this place is safe, and I stopped off at a department store, so the clothes are clean right down to the boots. I changed out my wallet and activated a new credit card. My friend's brother even swept me for bugs." He paused. "I need to talk to you about something."

Danny sank into one of the black leather chairs, puzzled. "Well, if I'd known we were going to get serious, I would have eaten beforehand," he said, his stomach rumbling.

Josh laughed softly. "I'll take you out afterward, and you can meet all my friends. We'll have pizza."

"Deep dish?" Danny asked, mostly to buy time.

"In Chicago? Is there any other kind?"

Danny shook his head. "He's... he's okay, isn't he? Your father?"

Josh's expression turned suddenly very adult. "I've known for quite some time that he's not my father—and you're not my uncle. It's okay, Uncle Danny. Mom explained it to me when I was twelve. That doesn't mean I love him any less. Or you."

Danny's eyebrows went up. That hadn't made the letters. "You've been keeping that secret since you were twelve? And you never once mentioned it to *me*?" Josh's correspondence—and his own furtive visits to see the young man do things like perform in plays and graduate from school—had been his link to the city and the life he'd once known. Josh confided almost everything to his Uncle Danny, but this was one hell of a secret.

"I was dumb," Josh said frankly. "I thought... I thought if you and Fox knew I knew, you'd come and take him away from me—and Fox is the only dad I've ever known. But when Grandpa finally died, and Mom and Fox divorced, Fox stayed in our lives—hell, he and Mom still live in the house in Glencoe. And it suddenly hit me that they'd both been having discreet affairs, probably since I was born." He met Danny's eyes squarely. "Or for him, one long hidden affair—with you."

Danny had thought he was beyond shame, but the heat that swept his neck and cheeks certainly had that flavor, didn't it?

"Ten years," Danny said, his throat dry. He wondered if he could get Carina to bring him some water. Some pizza. A time machine. "Ten. I couldn't… I couldn't…." He looked away. "I just couldn't."

"I know," Josh said softly. "But you didn't leave my life either, and eventually that penetrated my thick skull, you know?"

Danny's mouth twisted, and he tasted bitterness. "You… you're the best thing he and I ever did together."

"You can have more time to do better," Josh said soberly. "But first we need to get him out of the mess he's in. I've got some ideas, but I haven't been doing this for twenty years like you have."

"Almost thirty," Danny corrected grimly. "I started when I was twelve, you know."

Josh's eyes lit up. "No, really? How?"

"I told a bully that he'd be cursed with bugs in his pockets if he kept stealing our lunch money. Then I got the kid who liked bugs to bring me a box of them, and me and my friends took turns sneaking them into the pockets of his coat whenever he wasn't looking." They'd tripped him in hallways, dropped them in his hair when he was concentrating on classwork—whatever it took. "For a week that kid couldn't sit down to eat without a worm falling out of his sleeve or a cockroach crawling out of his pocket. He finally broke in math class one day, confessed everything, and started throwing money on the ground to pay us back."

Danny gave a smile that Fox had always called "predatory" but Danny had always felt was more "self-satisfied."

"Poor kid. I understand he grew up with anxiety issues. Unfortunate."

Josh snorted softly. "Yeah, that's a real fuckin' tragedy, Uncle Danny. But however you started, you were an expert at it by the time you met Fox, and you've made a living on the grift for your entire adult life. And now we can use it to help the only dad I've ever known. Are you game?"

Danny nodded. "But first you have to tell me what happened—what *really* happened—okay?"

Danny knew what really happened. Anybody with half a brain who knew Felix could figure out that what happened in the press was all spin. A woman who'd worked for Felix had accused him of discriminating against her because she was female, of using her work and calling it his own—and she'd done it in tears, on television. The outrageous lies and blatant spin that resulted in his spectacularly painful flameout in the press had been played over and over again on the news. But while Josh covered the basics, he let his mind wander, just a bit. An indulgence, really.

An image.

Two boys grifting through Europe, absolutely sure the world would never tear them apart.

Two boys madly in love.

Past

FELIX, TALL, lithe, blond as a god, running down the cobblestone streets in Rome, one step ahead of the mark he'd just pickpocketed, his red scarf streaming behind him like a banner.

Danny had been pocketing his breakfast as he'd watched the boy tear-assing down the road, and he'd been so delighted watching an amateur thief in his brazen glory that he'd forgotten himself and actually paid for the pastry he'd grabbed before he realized he could have simply walked away.

Oh no. The boy was fast—no doubt about that—and nimble. He dodged a family with cameras, and a clowder of cats, and didn't crash into a single tourist. This close to the Coliseum, there were plenty, but they were on a side street, and Danny was pretty sure if the kid kept running like that, he was going to hit a cross street against the green light and die messily in traffic.

Even running full tilt, Danny had seen the pale, aristocratic features, the hectic flush across his cheeks, the flyaway blond hair. As he'd sprinted past Danny's café, the scarf had fluttered from around his neck to the ground, a slash of crimson against the tan bricks.

It would be a *shame* if that kid died on the streets of Rome.

Before he even knew what he was doing, he'd walked out of the café and was surveying the Vespas, bicycles, and Fiats parked on the street. He chose a Vespa without pausing in his step and used a small metal bar to unlock the ignition while he kickstarted the thing. It was easier for him to steal a vehicle than to actually own one, and he took off down the street before the owner could spot him from the café.

It wasn't like Danny wasn't going to abandon the mini-motorcycle a couple of blocks away, right?

He stepped on the pedal hard, listening to the engine buzzing like a laboring mosquito. It didn't bother him; they always sounded like that, and no matter how slow the Vespa *felt* like it was going, the truth was, he was going faster than the boy who had dropped his scarf in the street and, even more importantly, faster than the big angry tourist shouting obscenities as he chased the boy who had dropped his scarf in the street.

In fact, Danny was going fast enough that he felt compelled to use the little motorcycle's quick start and stop capabilities to pick up the scarf.

. He easily passed the tourist, who ignored him because the mosquito cycles were all over Rome. When he drew abreast of the boy, he slowed down a bit and called to him.

"I see you have lost your scarf!"

The boy shot him a look that was part annoyance and part amusement. "How inconvenient," he shouted, still running. "How nice of you to return it."

"But if I return it," Danny hollered, "you will only get yourself killed!"

"Then," the boy said, pulling in a breath, "you may keep it."

"If you come with me, you might not die," Danny said, turning his head enough to flash his dimples. At twenty, that was all he needed to do to a lot of boys. This one was no exception.

"Then I shall have to come with you!" the boy told him. Behind them they heard a shout as the tourist picked up speed. Danny stopped the motorcycle just long enough for the boy to hop on behind him, taking the scarf so Danny might better drive the little mosquito cycle along the crowded streets.

Danny gassed the thing as he headed for a tight left turn, and behind him he heard his passenger cry, "Let go!" The tourist had nearly caught up and had grabbed the scarf. Danny grinned as his passenger ripped the scarf—a fine cashmere; Danny had felt it—right out of the man's hands.

Even the gods probably heard them laughing as Danny gunned the Vespa and powered the thing toward a far corner of the city, where the cafés weren't quite so crowded and he might get to know the boy with the red scarf a little better.

"UNCLE DANNY?"

Danny pulled himself back to the here and now, to the sterile, gray, soundproof room with the boy he loved like a son sitting across from him.

"Sorry," he said with a faint smile. "Lost in the past. But don't worry, I heard what you were saying."

"Prove it," Josh said skeptically.

"Felix was grooming this Marnie Courtland woman to take over his news programs," Danny said, although that was common knowledge. When Josh's grandfather had passed away, he'd left his cable affiliates to Felix to run—Felix had been doing it anyway. Hell, it's why Felix and Julia had kept up the pretense of the marriage. Not for Josh, obviously. He was fine. But Felix had worked hard to make a life for Julia, and the old man had been set in his ways. He wouldn't leave the station to Julia, so Felix had earned it by virtue of hard work, charm, and that certain lack of scruples that had made him and Danny so compatible in the first place. Once the old man had gone, about two years after Felix and Danny's final, horrible breakup, Felix had taken the little group of cable network stations—a news station, a movie station, a cable action show station—and built an empire.

An empire Marnie Courtland was about to bring toppling down on his head.

"She was the principle news anchor of his highest rated news show," Josh said, the loathing dripping from his voice. "Progressive, tough, fair-minded—she had the perfect reputation. Dad taught her everything he'd learned working his way up and then gave her free rein. Only he started to get complaints."

Danny's eyebrows went up. "Explain?"

"Well, she apparently skipped that ethics class that journalists are supposed to take. She pressured sources, threatened to blackmail the people who had evidence that disproved her story, and left a paper trail of some truly batshit, unhinged emails and direct messages that people brought to Dad because he was the man in charge of the network."

"His circus," Danny said, because that's how Felix had referred to it during those covert, hidden, lost years when they met once every couple of months for the weekends that kept Danny barely fed enough on Felix's presence, his love, his skin. The years of being a dirty little secret and of drinking to cover the pain.

"Yes, and his monkeys." Josh's lips twisted sardonically. "He said that a lot. But he had proof—has proof—that she's a freakshow nightmare of bad behavior and bullying."

"But he'd mentored her from the beginning," Danny said. "So he felt responsible." Just because he'd broken up with Felix hadn't meant he'd stopped watching him work. Marnie Courtland's onscreen presence, her turns of phrase, her woman-on-the-street approach, all of it had the earmarks of Felix's time in the anchor's seat. Fox had spent a good ten years there, and had made the news station particularly his own by hard work and by learning a trade he'd only pretended to have in order to land the job. Bitterly, Danny remembered how they'd laughed while planning the original grift on Josh's mom. They'd tell her Felix was a journalism major. All the rich Americans in Europe were journalism majors: lots of syllables, not a lot of job opportunities. It was perfect.

Little did they know the grift would put Felix in a position with Josh's grandfather that would let him work his way through the ranks as a junior reporter and then an anchor and then a program director, turning Hiram Dormer's most neglected businesses into a Chicago entertainment staple.

"Yeah," Josh said, his betrayal palpable. "He did. Like he'd made this monster, so it was up to him to sort of gentle it into the real world."

"*Un*like the original *Frankenstein*," Danny said, lips twisting. It had been their only paperback that first summer, and sometimes he wished they'd had something longer—hell, *Pride and Prejudice* would have at least made them laugh. But *Frankenstein* it had been, and apparently Felix had learned the lesson too well.

"I hate that fuckin' book," Josh said brutally. "Anyway, so Dad pulls her into his office, tells her straight up that people have the goods on her and she might want to get ahead of the situation, issue apologies, call in a lawyer, and she says, 'You mean you're not going to back me?'"

Danny's eyes went wide. "That's… ovarian. Very, very ovarian."

Josh smirked. "Well, I hope I can be that ovarian if I ever get busted, because my balls would have been shriveling into little hairy raisins at that point. But not her. Dad said, 'Marnie, what you were doing was illegal!'" Josh scrubbed his face with his hands. "You have to hear him tell this story," he said brokenly, "because I've heard it a dozen times. He told Mom, me, his lawyers, friends. And every time he tells it, his voice just… wobbles, and he's surprised. Every damned time he tells it. He tells her she was wrong—she'd been caught blackmailing people, bullying them, *threatening* them with her social media platform, and he doesn't want that behavior representing his news network or his company as a whole. And she looks him dead in the eye, musses up her hair, and screams, 'Harassment!' Then she runs through the newsroom screaming, 'Felix Salinger threatened my job if I told the truth! He's been plagiarizing my work for years—he uses and harasses every woman who works for him.'"

Danny snorted, hating to even hear it, because it was so antithetical to everything Felix had ever stood for.

"Yeah, I know," Josh muttered. "She was standing right on the soundstage where they were filming live. She finished it up by sobbing, 'I just couldn't take the lies anymore.'"

"I saw that part," Danny said, his voice hard. "Just like the rest of the world. Sixty thousand times. Didn't believe it once."

Josh's face crumpled a little, and he almost wrecked his perfect outfit by wiping his eyes on his sleeve. Danny produced a handkerchief from one of his pockets and handed it over, his own eyes burning.

The story had broken two weeks ago, and the media frenzy had only gotten worse. Marnie had gotten up in front of national TV and told the world that Felix Salinger was a backbiting misogynist, a harasser, a bully, and Felix—Felix had twenty-year-old secrets to hide, including the biggest one of all.

He wasn't Josh's father.

Josh's entire inheritance—and all of his and Julia's social standing—would come into question if that came out, and Danny knew Felix. Just because he was a criminal didn't mean he was a bad man. And he'd do *anything* to ensure Josh's future and protect Julia's good name.

"He can't go up against her," Danny said, massaging his temples with his fingertips. "If people look into his past, before his interaction with Marnie, they'd find… oh so many things."

"I'd give up everything," Josh said, looking miserable. "I'd give up the money, the property, the house. But… but it's not even mine to give up."

"It's your mother's," Danny said softly. Even when things had been at their worst—when Danny had felt like every breath filled his lungs with broken glass— he'd never blamed Julia Dormer-Salinger. Her father had been a monster—he'd left the works to Felix, who had turned the three stations into a network empire and insured her fortune for life. But if Felix lost *his* money and prestige, so did Julia. They could lose everything. "She doesn't deserve to lose her home." And even if she could keep the house, the things in Chicago that made it home—her work with the businesses, her work with charity foundations, her friends and acquaintances—those things would be gone.

"No," Josh said. "She's offered. She's gathered her lawyers together—they have all Dad's evidence, by the way. He's got a rock-solid case for slander, malicious mischief, filing a false report. But Marnie's created such a… a media juggernaut. It's going to take a doomsday device to blow her up before she takes out the entire network. But her story was her *only* story.

Now that Dad's no longer running things at the stati⚊ they've got nobody bringing in contacts, and noboo⚊ will work with her—they all know she's poison. The network is going to go bankrupt, and my parents are going to lose—"

"Everything," Danny said.

"Dad already lost you," Josh told him. "I… I don't want him to lose what he's worked so hard to build."

"Me neither." God, Danny didn't. Felix. That bright, laughing boy with the sense of mischief and the champagne tastes. He'd given up so much for Josh's legacy.

He'd given up Danny.

Danny had wanted him to have the world. The least he could do was help him out of a jam.

"What do you want to do about it?" Danny asked, because it was obviously what Josh needed to hear.

Josh's face lit up like Times Square.

"I've got a plan," he said eagerly.

Danny raised an eyebrow. This was the child who had once left their hotel room in Prague when he'd been seven, panhandled for bus fair, and spent a day at a museum while Danny, Felix, and Julia had been having heart attacks trying to find him.

"Of course you do."

The Pines of Rome

FELIX SIPPED his Macallan moodily, staring out the second-floor window of his Glencoe mansion, noting that the outside lights were still on. The comforting yellow glow illuminated the slashing silver of an early spring storm. Locals were probably just glad it wasn't snow, but Felix didn't mind the snow.

He minded that this day wasn't over yet.

Wasn't it nine o'clock yet? Wasn't it ten? Wasn't it tomorrow yet? Next week? Next month? Sometime when he could recover and didn't have to see his face splashed across every news network on the planet as the world's biggest misogynist?

His neck muscles started cranking tightly, and he took a bigger swig of the scotch, trying to relax.

"You know what you need?" Julia asked, padding into his bedroom uninvited. Well, they'd lived like brother and sister for over twenty years. She slept in this house when she was in Chicago, the same way he slept in her townhouse when he was in New York.

"A time machine?" he asked bitterly.

"Sex," she said frankly. "You haven't had a lover in a really long time."

Ten years, he wanted to say. Physically it wasn't true, but emotionally?

"Now is not the time," he said softly, taking another sip of his scotch.

"He's in town, Felix. You should ask him."

"No," Felix said.

"Felix—"

He yanked his attention from the rain. "How do you want me to start that conversation, Jules? 'Hey, remember how I wouldn't walk away from my sham marriage because I wanted to run an empire? Well, the whole thing got yanked around my ears in a colossal act of karma, and now I'm fucked. Want to come commit some illegal acts to prove I'm innocent of harassing every woman I've come in contact with? It won't fix the last ten years, but *I* can get some fucking retribution.'" He killed the rest of the tumbler and poured himself another healthy dose from the decanter at his dressing table. "I think no."

"Well your pitch is terrible," Julia said. She was dressed simply in off-the-rack flannel pajamas with an oversized sweatshirt—one of his—down to her knees. Her feet were bare except for bright pink polish on each toe and a whimsical little jewel in the center of the first little piggy. She looked hardly out of college, someone in their salad days, not like a mother about to pass forty.

Not like someone who could have bought and sold this pricy house ten or twenty times with just one bank account—if Marnie didn't take it all, damn her. Not like a ruthless businesswoman who had taken her father's holdings and—against the old man's wishes half the time—expanded them.

Not like an heiress.

Like a friend.

His friend walked up to him and put her arm around his waist and leaned her head on his shoulder.

"You need to work on your pitch," she prompted again.

"Yeah? What would you suggest?" God, he missed Danny.

"How about 'Hey—I know we ended things badly, and that was my fault. But I've never stopped loving you after all these years, and I'd love to be back in your life. But I've got this pesky legal situation that's haunting me, and I'd appreciate your help.'"

Felix swallowed. "You really think that would work?"

"It's Danny," she said softly. "I watched him come back to you again and again. He's never left our son's life. Danny's a good man."

Felix snorted. Danny was a thief and a con man and would have laughed uproariously at that last statement.

But that didn't change the fact that it was true.

IMMEDIATELY AFTER saving Felix's bacon on the streets of Rome, Danny took Felix on a tour of Rome's poorest neighborhood—and saved his soul.

Felix had been bored. His parents were wealthy but indifferent, and Felix had gone to Europe for an adventure. The dickwad American tourist stalk along the streets yelling at people who didn't speak En glish had appealed to his sense of fun.

Felix didn't need the money, but boy that asshole sure did need the setdown.

Danny pulled the Vespa into a tiny corner street and left it, tugging on Felix's hand.

"Where are we going?" Felix asked. "And who are you?"

Danny turned to him with a gamine smile. He had a little gap between his front two teeth, but that didn't stop the entire smile from lighting up his narrow face. His chin was pointed like a fox's, and his eyebrows—which he'd later pluck and groom extensively—arched with wicked intent.

"I'm Danny. Who're you?"

"Felix Salinger," Felix said hesitantly.

"Like the writer?" To his credit, the boy looked suitably impressed.

"No." Felix shook his head. "Like the Salingers from LA, who have a lot of money and let me take a vacation to Europe."

Danny wrinkled his nose. "That's a lousy pitch. No, if you get busted, you gotta be like 'Yeah, like the writer's great-grandson. I love that book, don't you?'"

Felix let out a bark of laughter and tried not to twist his ankle on the broken pavement. "Where are we go-ing?" He felt a yank on his back pocket and whirled around to grab an urchin—complete with lice and a sour smell—by the shoulder. "Give that back!" he snapped, reaching for the wallet he'd rightfully stolen.

The kid jabbered at him in Italian, and to his surprise, Danny answered. The kid argued for a moment, and then Danny shouted, "Enough, Berto, or I tell your mama!"

The kid recoiled, wounded. "No fair," he replied in ~~ck~~ English. "Is no fair you tell my mama!"

"This one, he's under my protection, okay?"

Berto gave a disgusted sniff and leveled a look of pure bathos at Felix. "Not even his wallet."

Danny snorted and turned to Felix. "It's only fair he shares the spoils, then, okay?"

Felix was about to argue. This kid wasn't getting what he'd worked for! Then he got a look at the kid—a good look. Yeah, the little beggar was crafty, and he was a thief. But his clothes were threadbare, and as Felix watched, Danny pulled a loaf of bread from the front of his oversized sweater, ripped it in half, and offered the other half of it to Berto… who practically tore it out of his hand.

"*Grazie*!" Berto mumbled through a full mouth.

Felix let go of the wallet. "Keep it," he grumbled. "But be careful. The asshole who used to own it is mean."

Berto nodded and gulped down an enormous mouthful. "He'll never know where it went," he said, eyes big.

"Berto," Danny said sternly as the kid turned to take off.

Berto stopped as though shot. "Sorry, Lightfingers," he mumbled. Like Danny, he was wearing an oversized sweater, and from the folds of the front, he pulled out Felix's *actual* wallet.

"You dropped it," Berto said through another mouthful, sputtering crumbs.

"Of course I did," Felix murmured. "Thank you so much for returning it."

"Berto?" Danny repeated.

Berto scowled and pulled the cash and credit cards out of the pocket of his ragged jeans. "You also dropped these," he said, with admirable dignity for a kid who looked about seven and smelled like pee.

"Indebted," Felix ground out from between his teeth.

Berto gave him an unrepentant grin and skipped off into the crowd, and Danny shook his head. "God, you're an easy mark. I can't believe you had the balls to lift a wallet when you're such a sitting duck."

Felix might have been stung by the words, but this guy had not only saved his wallet—and his money—but he'd also been kind to the street urchin who'd stolen it in the first place. Felix had spent his whole life being told how to act like he had money—and now this adorable pixieish boy was showing him how to act like he had *class*.

Besides, he had no room to throw a hissy fit when he'd almost been left in a foreign country with no money and no ID.

"What would you suggest?" Felix asked. "I stole that wallet because the guy was an ass, grabbing girls' butts, talking about all the foreign tits for sale. He was gross. I don't plan to make a living at it."

"Good, because you're shitty at it," Danny said, rolling his eyes. He grabbed Felix's hand again and pulled him through the crowd. "But you're not completely useless. Okay, do you know where we are?"

Felix looked around. "Not the tourist part of the city?" he hazarded, realizing they were toward the outskirts, near the hills.

"Nope. Now something super interesting happens here. You saw Berto? See all these kids around here?"

Felix glanced around and noticed that a lot of them were staring at him with a predatory gleam in their eyes—right up until they saw Danny.

"Yeah?"

"Their parents all work for those people." Danny gestured with his chin to a series of opulent villas about half a mile up the road from the street they were wandering. The road itself was lined with umbrella pine trees, and the scent of pine nuts was sharp and mouthwatering. "Those people are very rich. And you, it appears, are also very rich."

Felix eyed the closest mansion, which would probably house the entire block of big houses he'd grown up on. "Not that rich," he said honestly. "I'm like… less rich."

Danny snorted. "Yeah, but they don't know that. Now hurry!"

"Where are we going?"

"Well, one of those rich bastards comes down that hill about once a day to drop his spoiled kid off in the shopping district."

"So?"

Danny rolled his eyes like Felix was almost too brain-dead to breathe. "So! 'Gee, mister, I'm so glad I saw you. I lost my wallet and all my money. My parents live in a ritzy place in the States, and if you give me some cash, I can have them wire you a refund.'"

"I'm not going to do that!" Felix protested, repelled.

Danny sighed, his shoulders slumping. "Yeah, I figured. Whatever." He turned away then and stalked through the crowds of children and residents, and Felix had the sudden fear he might lose this new and interesting person right when he'd found him.

"Hey, wait!" Felix caught up with him and tried not to flinch from Danny's reproachful look as he drew alongside.

"Why's it so important? That you screw this rich bastard with the spoiled kid?"

Danny shrugged. "It's not," he said. "Forget I mentioned it. Come on, though; there's a café down by the corner that's not nearly as crowded as the ones in the shopping district, and the food's better." His grin came back then, brilliant and enticing. "Trust me!"

Felix would find out later why Danny hated Julia's father—"that rich bastard"—so much, and the reason hadn't been pretty.

But not that day.

That day, Danny bought him a meal of pesto bread and sweet wine, and the two of them sat in the shade of some rich people's mountain and looked out onto the bustling ancient city. Felix told Danny everything he knew about Rome's history, and Danny told Felix everything he knew about how to make enough money to live.

"But why don't you… I don't know? Get a job?" Felix asked, as Danny explained the finer points of a short sting. "Wouldn't it be easier?"

Danny's eyes—hazel, almond shaped, with just the slightest upward tilt at the ends—lit with unholy fire. "Yeah, but it's not as fun."

Felix fell into that fire so willingly and quickly he wasn't aware he'd even stepped into the pit.

That evening, Danny pulled him into a tiny garret apartment that held a twin-sized bed with a plain linen duvet that was mostly clean, a chest of drawers that appeared to hold most of Danny's possessions, and a bathroom.

"What are we doing here?" Felix asked, although he thought he knew. His experience so far had been with girls—and it had been disappointing in the extreme.

But every time Danny's pointed features lit with that puckish joy, Felix found himself more and more wanting to taste his full mouth, wanting to run his hands under that loose sweatshirt to feel the lean body beneath.

And Danny hadn't let go of his hand since they'd left the café.

He wasn't just holding Felix's hand to direct him. Their fingers were entwined, and every now and then, during a still moment as they were waiting to cross a street, Danny would rub Felix's knuckles with his thumb.

And the shiver in Felix's belly would resonate a little bit harder. At this moment, it was an avalanche in his chest.

No, Felix may have been a little naïve, but he wasn't entirely unaware of what was going to happen.

Danny closed the door behind them and turned the lock, then spun around to Felix with dancing eyes.

"You tell me," Danny said breathlessly. "You just followed a thief into his bedroom. What do you think he's going to steal?"

Felix's eyes felt heavy, his breath quickened, and he thought of all the things he wanted to do with this wiry little thief and all of the places he wanted to put his mouth. But at the same time, he knew that once he tasted Danny, once they'd put their hands on each other, what had started as a morning's adventure and turned into an afternoon's interlude would suddenly be something much bigger than that.

The stirring in his stomach was nothing less than extraordinary.

"Everything," Felix whispered, taking a step closer to Danny, then another. "You're going to take everything."

Danny reached out and tugged on his belt, pulling him close until they were groin-to-groin. Felix let out a whimper as he realized he and Danny had both gone half-hard under their zippers.

His entire body ached, and there wasn't enough air in the world.

"If you're sweet to me," Danny said, leaning forward until their mouths almost touched, "I'll give it back again."

Felix wrapped his arms around Danny's shoulders and hauled him in for a kiss, hard and hungry, more passion than he'd ever shown another partner, more desire than he knew existed in the world.

Danny's hands slid beneath the waistband of Felix's slacks, and Danny kneaded his ass, fearless and without mercy.

"Don't want it back," Felix gasped, shaking. He slid his hands up Danny's cheeks and scraped his fingers through thick handfuls of curly chestnut hair. "It's all yours. Take it."

Danny kissed him again, the thread of the conversation lost. He whirled Felix around until his back was against the door and dropped to his knees, pulling Felix's pants down as he went. Felix's cock flopped forward gracelessly, and Felix could do nothing but stare as Danny opened his mouth and engulfed it without finesse.

Later they would learn to tease, to play, to edge, even. They'd learn the finer points of making love. But in this moment, Danny's mouth on Felix's cock was everything, and he couldn't imagine improving on the moment in any possible way.

He cried out, cracking his head back against the door, and knotted his fingers in Danny's hair, not so much to control Danny but to anchor himself. Danny grasped Felix's hips and thrust forward, taking Felix's cock to the back of his throat, and then slid backward, using his lips and tongue to make the journey excruciating. Forward and back, forward and back, and Felix's body dropped away, along with his past history and the morals he'd thought he had, until all that was left was Danny's touch, his breath, the way he'd dropped to his knees with generosity and abandon.

His mouth on Felix's cock became the end and beginning of Felix's world.

It seemed like forever—though it was probably minutes—before Felix convulsed and came, crying out as Danny swallowed all of him down. When his body was done, he slid down the back of the door and welcomed Danny's kiss, the way Danny sprawled on top of him happily, as if this moment, Felix's come dripping down his chin, was the best possible outcome he could have imagined for his day.

"You like that?" Danny asked, those Peter Pan eyes alight and glowing.

"Does anybody say no after that?" Felix mumbled, a little dazed.

"Not so far." Danny's grin cranked up a notch or two. "But your answer matters most."

Felix smoothed Danny's hair back from his face and kissed the corner of his mouth, licked off the come. "Why?"

That grin faded, but the eyes—their intensity—remained. "Because you know my name is Danny," he said soberly. "Danny Michael Mitchell. Everyone else here thinks I'm Lightfingers. I made that name up. You know my name."

Felix's mouth parted in wonder. He still planned to ravish Daniel Michael Mitchell until he was made of spunk, but in that moment, with his name, with his honesty, Felix realized that while he'd given this boy everything, Danny really had given it back.

Danny had given him the world.

FELIX DRAINED his second glass of scotch and made a hurt sound as he looked at the tumbler. Julia took it gently from his fingertips and poured some more, taking a sip before handing it back.

"He'll help you," she said softly.

"How do you know?" he asked.

"Because he's here," Danny said behind them. Felix's heart stopped, but Julia laughed.

"The front door was locked," she chided.

"Really?" Danny asked, ingenuousness dripping from his voice.

"The alarm was set," she said.

"Imagine that."

She hugged him fondly. "But some people you just can't keep out," she said and kissed his cheek. He hugged her back, and Felix grimaced. No, they hadn't always gotten along—but in the end, Julia, Felix, and Danny had all wanted the same thing: what was best for Josh.

It had made them unlikely allies.

It might even have made them family.

But it didn't make it any easier for Felix to face Danny now.

"Scotch?" he asked, because looking at the decanter and glasses would be easier than looking into those fox-light eyes.

"No," Danny said. "Thank you."

Felix's eyes widened, and he actually saw Danny. Oh God, same guy. Same Peter Pan eyes, same chestnut curls and pointed chin. Some gray in the hair now, some wisdom lines around the eyes, but he still looked—Felix swallowed—so good.

"You used to love scotch," he rasped.

Danny—*Danny*—turned his head and glanced away. "Well, I drank a lot of it ten years ago, and now I don't drink anymore."

Felix dropped his own tumbler onto the tray with a clatter, Macallan sloshing over the side. "I…." Danny. "I'm sorry." So inadequate. Ten years ago… and that dreadful, dreadful fight.

"It was not your doing," Danny said, with that abundance of kindness he'd always shown. "And definitely not why I'm here today."

Felix ran his hand through his hair, reached for the half-full tumbler, then let his hand drop. "Why… why?"

"Drink the scotch, Fox," Danny said gently. "I'd be falling off the wagon too, if I'd had the month you've had." Oh, that nickname! Danny had given it to him, because in their grifting days, he'd said nobody evaded capture like Felix the Fox.

Felix tossed the scotch down, and the burn finally penetrated the numbness that had overtaken him during that terrible moment when Marnie had mussed her hair and screamed, "You're a harasser and a bully, and I'll make sure everyone knows it!" and Felix had guessed her endgame. He started to cough like a novice, and Danny's hand thumping on his back was actually a comfort.

"Didn't expect a con in an honest man's business, did you?" Danny asked softly.

Felix closed his eyes, remembering how Marnie had played him, flattered him, told him that she owed her success all to him. Felix had remembered when he'd felt like leading this network into success had meant everything, and he'd bought her lies because he missed the days when he'd had that kind of confidence, the kind of chutzpah she'd exuded. But then, when he'd realized that she'd been posting stories in bad faith, she had turned on him on a dime.

"No," he whispered. He turned and sank down on the bed, his knees not holding him anymore. An insidious voice whispered that it was weak to let Danny see him like this, that Danny had left him and Felix couldn't trust him anymore.

The creak of the bedsprings next to him drowned out that little voice, and Danny's arm around his shoulders was the solace he hadn't dared ask for.

"I'm sorry," he said, and while it wasn't an apology for ten years ago—or the ten years before that—it didn't seem to matter to Danny. He tightened that hold until Felix had no choice but to lay his head against Danny's shoulder and cry.

Grazie

FELIX MUST have been drinking for some time, because he fell asleep on Danny's shoulder, and Danny was grateful. Felix was a light sleeper on the best of days, and when he was stressed or upset, he would go for a week without lying down and shutting his eyes.

He'd done that when his parents had threatened to disown him if he didn't leave Danny and come home from Europe to go back to school.

He hadn't slept, he hadn't eaten. Danny had finally gotten him drunk on a bottle of the cheapest wine he could find, just so he would shut his eyes.

When Felix had awakened, he'd been dehydrated and headachy—and absolutely lucid.

He'd written his parents and told them that he'd rather make his own way in the world than be dependent on their judgment for a dime. Danny had been so proud of him then; his lover was confident, independent, wouldn't let money ever dictate what he did with his life.

His disappointment when that had proved to be something of an overstatement had been… acute.

But when a guy is young, it's harder to forgive people for just being human. Felix's basic qualities—kindness, intelligence, decisiveness, seeing the big picture—had remained. The fact that Danny was the one without the strength to put up with being the hidden mistress didn't change that. It had taken Danny a long time to come to that conclusion—and even longer to forgive Felix.

And longest of all to forgive himself.

He scooted sideways on the bed to help Felix find the pillow, then stripped off Felix's loafers and pants. He was going to flip the duvet over the top of Felix like a man burrito, but Felix surprised him by half opening his eyes.

"If I get under the covers, will you turn out the lights and lie down with me?"

Danny couldn't have stopped the wounded sound that came out of his throat if they'd been in the middle of a game and their lives had hung on him being silent as stone.

"Just to sleep, Danny," Felix murmured. "I wouldn't hurt you like that."

"Didn't hurt the way we did it," Danny replied lightly, playing for time. He wandered around the room, turning off the lights, closing the door enough that the light from the hallway didn't slice through the room.

"No. It was the other stuff that hurt."

Danny couldn't argue with him there. He finished his round and paused, watching as Felix rolled under the covers and snuggled down. God, he looked so innocent like that, hands under his cheeks like a choirboy. It was easy to forget that he was as wild in bed as Danny was, so single-minded in passion that he could block out the sun and make you think he was the thing around which the world revolved.

He'd been Danny's sun for eleven years, hadn't he?

"Please," Felix whispered, and Danny let out a sigh. He shed his topcoat and suitcoat and hung them over the chair by the old-style oak dressing table, then stripped down to his T-shirt and silk boxers. He wasn't planning to sleep, but he'd left his clothes at his apartment before he'd decided to come visit Felix, and he hated being rumpled. When he was done, he grabbed the throw—red cashmere, because Felix loved it so—from the top of the bed and went to lie down on top of the covers, using the throw for warmth.

"Thank you," Felix said as Danny wrapped the throw around his shoulders.

"I'm sorry this happened to your legacy," Danny told him soberly. "Don't worry. Josh and I have some plans to get it back."

Felix struggled to open his eyes wider, but Danny chuckled and passed his hand over them.

He gasped when Felix grabbed his wrist and pulled his hand in to kiss his palm.

"Fox—"

Felix released his hand and closed his eyes. "Don't game her, Lightfingers. She'll… she'll expose you. She'll figure out who you are and spread your real name across the internet. Lots of people still want your head on a platter. I need you alive, Danny. Just… don't cross her."

"We will talk about this in the morning," Danny said, yawning. That morning he'd stepped off an international flight, dropped his luggage at his Chicago condo, and gone to check his mail.

It was nearing ten o'clock in Chicago now, he'd been up for nearly thirty-six hours, and his head was starting to pound with jet lag. He'd close his eyes for a minute here—an hour, maybe—before he went downstairs and spoke to Julia, told her what he and Josh had talked about, made more plans with Josh to see the people he'd lined up.

But first he'd watch Felix sleep for a moment, see the rise and fall of his chest. He'd kept himself in tiptop shape—had eaten well and walked daily, even on the streets of Rome when they'd been too young to diet.

Felix had aged well. He had only a few strands of silver in his blond hair, blending in like they were supposed to be there. His blue eyes were just as striking in his tanned face, his jaw as square and masculine as it had been even when it held the softness of youth.

It wasn't soft anymore, was it?

It was hard and decisive, the jaw of a man used to making tough decisions.

Julia's father had put him in charge of a growing cable network and made Julia's and Josh's fortunes dependent on Felix making it work. Danny had chosen the worst time in the world to go off the rails. He hadn't known it then, but he knew it now.

A couple more years. Felix had begged for a couple more years. But Danny had spent a decade playing the mistress, being "Uncle Danny" to Josh and a ghost to

Hiram Dormer, and he'd needed more, so much more than what Felix could give him.

He'd picked that fight, and he knew it. But he'd had to get roaring drunk to do it. In those days, it hadn't been much of a stretch; he'd been drunk most of the time anyway. But he'd needed to be extra-strength Macallan-scotch drunk to give Felix an ultimatum, because it was the only way to forget the way Felix's eyes had looked in the moonlight when they were making love. The only way to forget the touch of Felix's skin or the whispered promises of "someday" he'd been giving since Danny and Felix had decided to try that long con on Hiram Dormer and his spoiled daughter in the first place, before really knowing what poor Julia's life was like.

Danny watched Felix sleep and wished for those ten years back, wished he could undo the hateful things he'd said, wished he had a time machine so they could travel back to Rome and leave Julia Dormer and her snake-mean father alone.

Except—oh God—then Josh would have had another stepfather, one probably more like Julia's old man and less like Felix.

The idea of it made Danny's head throb with exhaustion, and he couldn't stay awake for another minute, even to watch his Fox sleep. Instead, he closed his eyes and breathed in, smelling wine and pine nuts, hot dusty roads, and olive trees in the sun.

Danny didn't dream of their final fight. Maybe his heart was too sore, but more likely he was too soothed by having Felix next to him again. Instead he dreamed of their last perfect day in Rome, before they decided to take on Hiram Dormer, before they got taught a real lesson about who was innocent and who was just in it to hurt.

Past

IT STARTED with a day so perfectly hot that even the thought of pickpocketing a rent boy in an igloo couldn't cool their skin, and doing Danny's regular hustle in the tourist quarter was unbearable.

They went up into the hills to a swimming hole Danny's friend Berto had shown him. The trek along the small footpaths that led there was exhausting, and Danny and Felix had been the only ones braving the savagery of the midday sun. They swam naked until they cooled off enough to rest in the shade.

To make love in the shade.

Was it the coolness of the water after the hotness of the sun that made Felix's mouth so exquisite on his skin? They'd spent the past months learning everything they could about each other's bodies. Felix loved to top, but he loved to rim too, and having his face buried between Danny's asscheeks while Danny moaned and pounded the ground beneath them with his fist was one of Danny's favorite things.

Followed by Felix, coated in olive oil, thrusting into him, taking his body over from the inside out. Danny's restless brain, the constant processing of angles, of ways to take advantage, ways to be had, found rest when Felix possessed him. It was over; he was taken, abandoned to the dark pleasure, the high, of giving himself to someone else and letting them take charge.

It was a high he'd only had with Felix, a need he didn't like to admit consumed him.

He thought about those moments, Felix's cock thrusting into his asshole, nearly every waking moment of every day, but he only yielded once in a while because Danny didn't like to be weak.

Today the heat, the cool, the decadence of lounging naked in the shade, even the taste of the apples and bread they'd lugged up into the hills with them—all of it spoke to the abandonment of the careful habits of guarding his heart Danny had learned in order to survive.

Danny lay on his back, the better to see Felix, spine arched, face turned toward the sun, thrusting hard enough that their flesh smacked together like clapping hands. White light, tinged with the red of dark pleasure, consumed his body, and his orgasm rolled over him like the bright sky—inevitable, powerful, beautiful. His back arched, and his cry of climax echoed over the hills as Felix pumped inside him, come scalding across his belly, his chest, inside his clenched ass.

The final convulsion rocked him, and he fell back against the blanket, unable to see, unable to *breathe*. His body felt captured in that moment of sunshine and savage completion, and to his shame, his eyes burned.

Oh God, Felix was looking at him, watching him come completely undone. Danny turned his head, more afraid of being raw and vulnerable in that moment than he'd been afraid of anything since he was fifteen.

"Hey," Felix said gently, fingers grasping his chin. "Don't hide from me. That was beautiful." He slid out and stretched gracefully on his side, his arm under his head. With gentle fingers he traced the line of Danny's jaw and the curve of his ear. "That... us. We just get better every time."

Danny closed his eyes, enjoying the touch. "We do. You sound surprised."

Felix leaned close enough to lick a trail of sweat down Danny's neck. "Everything about you surprises me. What's our next adventure?"

Danny loved the way he called them "adventures," not "cons" or "jobs." When Danny taught him the finer points of pickpocketing, Felix thought of it as an adventure. When Danny taught him the basic lost tourist panhandle, Felix thought of it as an adventure. By now they were both pros at spotting someone who needed a ride to the bus station or train depot, and Danny had actually *bought* a Vespa with a cart on the back so they could take turns ferrying tourists to their destinations in a hurry—either accepting a tip or helping themselves to one when they got their passenger where they wanted to go.

And Felix had watched Danny help genuinely lost people—secretaries or poor students who'd saved their pennies and slept in hostels so they could see a little bit of the world, or natives who needed a break, please God, a ride to work, just this once—when he felt called to give them a hand.

Felix neither judged him a bad con man when he chose not to fleece people, nor as a bad man when he targeted a mark. And Felix's kindness—as awkward as it could be—was incredibly endearing.

THEY HAD talked about doing some longer cons with bigger payouts. When he'd first met Felix, Danny had spent a few hours each week writing to "pen pals" he'd met in the city who wanted to "keep in touch" after they went home. These people—mostly rich young men who went to Europe to play away from their parents' eyes and wanted the promise of a playmate next time they had a chance to return—were willing to send Danny an astonishing amount of cash to keep him from being evicted.

He didn't tell any of them when he moved into a better apartment than the shithole they'd seen, which he could afford to do because Felix had arrived to help with the rent. Danny and Felix moved out of that original garret and into a townhouse a little closer to the tourist center. Together, they were unstoppable.

They were still flush after Felix made him break it off with his pen pals because, in Felix's words, "That's not a game you run when you're with someone for real." Felix kept reminding him of that: no matter how many games they ran, this thing between them, this was for *real.* And as much as Felix seemed to enjoy grifting, there was something about him that screamed solid. Real. Responsible. Something Danny couldn't help but crave in his bones.

The interlude that day by the swimming hole made it even more so, and Danny was... terrified. He'd had so very little in his life that was real. His mother had tried. She'd loved him, but she'd struggled with money, with her health. She'd been hospitalized when he was twelve, and he'd spent the next three years in foster care. When she finally died, on his fifteenth birthday, he ran away for the first time. By the time he was seventeen, he'd learned enough about lying, running, hiding, hustling, and stealing to be okay on his own. He'd caught a bus from Des Moines to the Jersey shore and got into the game for real. He'd lucked out two years before he met Felix and found a much older sugar daddy who'd wanted to take Danny to Europe with him.

After three days on the streets of Rome, with its different smells, different foods, and different *people*, Danny had gathered his possessions—and the gentleman's spare cash—and slipped away. The man hadn't been awful. Not cruel, just… proprietary. Danny had been his whore and his property, and he'd needed to know his place.

Because he hadn't been cruel, Danny had left him his passport and two credit cards.

Because he'd been sort of a dick, Danny drained one of his bank accounts before he'd even awakened the morning Danny left and had spent a good three months living off that money while he taught himself the finer points of his trade.

To have Felix here, touching him, sexing him, *making love* to him, willing to follow wherever Danny led, that was a kind of fear Danny had never known.

Which was probably why he hadn't shut down what Felix said next.

"I think we should do that long con," he said. "The one you were talking about. The old guy with the daughter."

Danny caught his breath and turned to meet Felix's eyes. Not much put the sky in Italy to shame, but those blue, blue eyes did it.

"Why?" he asked, afraid in his bones. The girl was spoiled but innocent; he'd always gone out of his way to shield the innocent.

"Why do you want to do it?" Felix asked soberly.

Danny grimaced. "He…. You know Berto?"

"Yeah." Felix seemed to bear the kid no ill will from their first meeting, and Berto had been a willing helper when Danny had trained Felix in the finer points of picking pockets.

"Hiram's Berto's father."

Felix's mouth dropped open—innocence was one of his qualities too. "No!"

"There's more than one kid in that pack who was fathered by Hiram. They know one another. Their mothers are coerced. They will do anything to keep their jobs, and he may—*may*, mind you—hire them back after they have their babies. It's… it's fucking medieval. The women can't get jobs in other places if the owners find out, like it's their fault this guy can't keep his dick to himself." Danny's voice grew low and ugly, his secret resentment out into the brutal sunshine at last.

"That's… that's awful," Felix said. Felix wasn't blind, though. "But why? Why is it so personal to you?"

Danny kept his face turned away. "My father was like that," he said. "I… I never met him. I heard most of the story from my mother's friends, who were all stupid young, like she was, and didn't think twice about telling me. I had a stepfather for a couple of years, but he died because of another asshole who thought it was okay to take whatever he wanted. It's a cycle of use. Of abuse. I hate it. I just think Hiram needs payback."

"Okay," Felix said, so readily Danny actually turned to look him in the eyes.

"Okay?" Felix had hated the idea so much in the beginning.

"One condition," Felix said soberly.

"It's your con," Danny said generously. "What's our hard limit?"

"We can't hurt the girl. She never asked for this. All we know about her is she likes to go shopping. So do we. I can't hold it against her."

Danny had no problem with that. He didn't give her a second thought. The idea of this—a longer, more complicated adventure—lit him up inside. The sex had been better, but Danny was afraid of that. He wasn't afraid of the game; he'd been practicing the game since he'd gone into care and had worked his first foster mother for more cookies.

They could deal with the girl. Whatever it was, they could deal.

And this way, Danny had a reason to hold on to Felix Salinger through another adventure. Maybe after this one, there'd be another. And another.

All the adventures they could have together. Danny could get excited about that. The low rumble in his gut that told him how much he needed Felix's touch— that could go to hell.

But then Felix kissed him again in the glorious sun, and his body sang some more, and not even that resolve could stick.

Present

DANNY WOKE up to sunlight streaming through the big bay window in Felix's room, deeply entrenched in the duvet.

He flailed for a moment, because it was morning, and someone had covered him with more than that cashmere throw, and—

"Easy," Julia said softly, coming to sit by his side. "You're here at Felix's house. You're fine. But I think you were jet-lagged as hell. I've never seen you sleep like that."

Shit. He'd slept the whole night there. That had *not* been his intention. The plan? To come in, do the job, leave. He was good at going ghost like tha—

"And don't even think about disappearing," Julia said frankly, and he glared at her.

"I don't even know what you're talking about."

Her laugh was charming, and Danny had always known she did a lot more of it since Felix had come into her life.

"You were going to come in, do your job or whatever to save him, and disappear," she said, close enough to feather a touch down his temple, as if they were friends.

They *were* friends. Coconspirators for over ten years. Danny had learned more about breaking and entering by spiriting in and out of Julia's and her father's homes to see Felix than he'd ever learned on the streets. And they'd all learned more about doing long con jobs—setting up business events to lure Hiram away from Chicago so they could have their household to themselves.

"Well, what?" he said, trying hard to leech the defensiveness out of his voice. "I put him back in charge of his media empire and where does that leave me?"

She snorted. "He never wanted the media empire," she said, lifting a shoulder. "Leave the media empire to me." Her eyes grew wistful. "Take him on adventures. Take him to Italy again, and stay in the villa legitimately instead of breaking in. Break the law a little—gently, and with good intentions." She patted his cheek. "Get a tan. My goodness, Danny, where have you been doing business?"

Danny grunted. "England. There's this whole… political thing."

"Lots of targets," she agreed.

He tried to look modest. "And plenty of people in need of a setdown."

Her eyes sharpened. "That anti-Muslim politician who lost her home to tax fraud…?"

"Horrible person," Danny agreed. "I'd feel sorry for her, but, you know, reaping, sowing…."

"All very biblical, I can tell." Her soft laughter faded. "We need you in our lives. Me, Fox, Josh—we miss you, Danny. Come home."

"I don't even know if he wants—"

"He's making waffles," she said bluntly.

"I beg your pardon?" Felix didn't cook. Ever. In Italy he'd once gone for three days without food because Danny was on a job and nobody had made him anything to eat. They'd been in the middle of making love when he'd gotten a nosebleed and passed out. Danny hadn't spoken to him for three days after that, he'd been so worried.

"For you. He ran downstairs almost frantic, asked Phyllis for a recipe—"

"Have you called the fire department? Poison control? Dancers with restraints?" Danny was sitting up in alarm, his T-shirt rucking up above his waistline. She'd seen him in his boxers before, and neither of them had ever made note of it.

Until now. "Danny!"

He covered his ribs where the scars still lingered. "Shit."

"Danny, what in the hell—"

"They're old, Julia," he said practically. Then, because maybe she'd leave him alone, "About ten years old."

She met his eyes. "You… you crashed pretty hard back then," she said delicately.

"Con men who crash get caught," he agreed.

Her eyes—big and green and lovely—glittered suddenly with tears. "What I made Felix do to you, it wasn't fair. I'm so sorry, Danny."

He tried to shrug her off, let it roll off his back like he'd tried to do all those years ago back in Italy when things had gone so wildly south. "I agreed," he said, and his grifter's smile—that easy devil-may-care weapon in his arsenal—finally graced his mouth, but it fought him every step of the way. "You were in a tight spot. Water under the bridge, over the shore, what—"

But she launched herself into his arms, sobbing, and it was all he could do to calm her before the smoke alarm started beeping downstairs and all hell broke loose.

Dawn at the Horizon

FELIX SAT glumly at the counter of the giant open-air kitchen, feeling affronted, while Phyllis scolded him within an inch of his life. The remains of her best waffle iron, covered in fire-retardant foam, had been hauled outside and disposed of by the local fire department, the kitchen smelled like smoke, and Danny…

Danny was probably out the window, over the roof, and far, far away by now.

"I don't even know why I'm bothering to yell at you," Phyllis muttered. "You look like I kicked your puppy. *You set my kitchen on fire!*"

Squat, sixtyish, Phyllis had been hired when Julia and Felix had returned from Italy after their "whirlwind courtship and secret wedding." Julia had been the one

"Are you fucking kidding me?" he gasped as he barreled into the room. "You can't even stay for breakfast?"

Danny whirled to scowl at him. "Are the firemen gone yet?"

"Yes!" Felix snapped. "And Phyllis is all excited about cooking for you, so don't even think about leaving."

"I was supposed to be gone last night, remember? You, me, Josh… we were all going to have a civilized conversation this morning. Then you were going to let me do my thing, and—"

"Danny, it's freezing outside. You're barefoot in sweats. You were, what? Going to run across the lawn like that? There's still frost on it, for Christ's sake!"

Danny leaned his head against the window pane, face contorted in a miserable scowl. He scanned the lawn like he could see real freedom from this prison he found himself in. He was wearing an old pair of Felix's sweats and a tattered sweatshirt from a thousand years ago.

Over ten years ago, actually, and a sweatshirt that Danny had given Felix on a long-ago birthday. Well played, Julia! But now it was Felix's turn to seal the deal.

"I…." Danny swallowed. "This was supposed to go so differently," he said. "Last night I was supposed to explain the con, let you think about it, and this morning Josh and I were going to meet, work out the finer points. We had a schedule."

Felix looked at Julia, and she bit her lip. There was something here nobody had told him. Danny didn't look vulnerable like this very often, not even when it had been just the two of them.

Felix advanced carefully, not putting it past Danny to leap out the window and onto the well-manicured lawn. He placed a gentle hand on the nape of Danny's neck and began to massage it. Danny's tense body gave a shudder, and he sagged, more of his weight on the window, some of it still in his tensely held shoulders.

"C'mon, Danny," he said softly. "Is it so bad, seeing me again?"

Danny shook his head, closing his eyes against the freedom beyond. "It's fine," he said, voice cracking. "It's... I...."

Felix lowered his mouth to Danny's ear. "I missed you like I'd miss a lung, a kidney, and my right hand. Can't you come down to breakfast? We'll call Josh. It'll be like old times."

"Sure," Danny said tonelessly. "Whatever."

That wasn't promising. Felix looked at Julia, and she turned away. What was going on here?

Felix took advantage—it was what he did. Twenty years of running Hiram's businesses had brought out the confidence that Danny had depended upon back in Rome, and the stakes were much higher now. He slid behind Danny's back and wrapped his arms around his waist, burying his nose against Danny's neck. It was intimate, and it was a liberty. But Felix was damned if Danny was going to come back here to Chicago on some sort of rescue mission without Felix making some sort of move.

Danny stiffened in his arms but didn't pull away.

"What're you doing, Fox?"

"I'm declaring my intentions." Felix ran his lips along the neck of the old sweatshirt. "You showed up and said, 'I'm going to fix your life!' I'm letting you know that you won't get away that easy."

A fine tremble rattled up Danny's spine.

"I literally almost died the last time we did this," he rasped. "I... I... I left here after that fight and woke up in a casino in Monaco owing a small country to a mobster after we did this last time."

Felix frowned. "Did you pay him the small country?" Never get in over your head, especially when you didn't have backup. Wasn't that what Danny had drilled into him?

"He took it out of my flesh," Danny said shortly, but his body was relaxing, and Felix kept playing dirty pool. "And I went into rehab. Don't... don't fuck with my head here, Fox—"

"You didn't show up," Felix said, frowning. He'd been drunk a lot too after that fight. "I went to your PO Box, and you didn't show up. Four months later I got a postcard with a new address on it. I... I just assumed you didn't want to see me, so I had Josh write you."

"I didn't want to see you," Danny said, and Felix had to hold fast to his heart or it would have crumbled. Then Danny's voice wobbled. "I spent a month in the hospital, trying to pay back a small country. And another two months in rehab. I wasn't in any shape to be seen."

Felix's eyes were burning, but he didn't let go. He wiped his face against the skin of Danny's neck so Danny would know what this did to him.

"Is that why you wanted to leave?" he croaked. "So you didn't have to tell us that?"

Danny grunted and leaned back against him, and for a sweet moment, Felix bore his weight. Then Danny took Felix's hand and placed it under the sweatshirt, and Felix frowned. A network of scars crossed the flesh there, bumps and gashes that hadn't been there before.

"What the—"

"Doesn't feel like a small country, does it," Danny asked bitterly, and Felix gave up and let the tears fall.

"I would have come to get you," he whispered. "I would have sold everything. I would have... I would have kidnapped Julia's fucking father and ransomed him from his bankers. I would have—"

"Done nothing of the sort," Danny said harshly, and Felix captured his hand as he tried to pull it away. "I was a falling-down drunk, Felix. I wasn't worth it."

"I thought you were," Felix rasped. "I still do. Please don't go, Danny. Stay for breakfast. Stay for lunch. Run the damned op out of here. Julia will help. God, don't you see? We've needed you. This whole time we've needed you. Please stay."

An eternity passed, Danny's body still tense in his arms while Felix refused to give way. Patience, he'd learned. Sticking to your guns. Finally Danny relaxed infinitesimally, and Felix could have fallen to his knees and wept.

"For the job," Danny said heavily. "For the job only."

But he didn't move out of Felix's arms, and Felix didn't let him go.

Phyllis's call for them to come downstairs was almost a relief—almost. Felix's arms, full of a warm, if resistant, Danny, ached to just keep him there. Almost as much as his heart ached to know the cost of his coming back.

Because there *was* a cost to Danny. Danny had a core of pride. Felix may not have known that when they were younger—he'd thought the grift was a lark, for fun, something to do before a better game came along.

For Danny, though, it was a way to never be dependent on the cruel whim of fate. Danny was in charge.

He was manipulating the people, the transaction, the money, to *his* specifications. No more families that didn't care, no more sugar daddies that treated him like property, no more waiting for someone to get better when they were just going to die on him. With the grift, he was in charge.

Until he'd trusted Felix to do one lousy thing.

Past

THE ROPER had an important job in a longer con. He was the person who put all the players together. Felix's job was to rope Hiram Dormer's daughter into a position to trust Felix. He'd infiltrate their home, get a bead on the material objects that Dormer loved, and then, when Felix was accounted for, Danny would steal the one he loved most.

And then pose as a buyer on the black market and sell it back.

Of course, any money they could get from Julia Dormer was a plus, but Felix had been adamant about one thing. He'd been a rich kid who had more expectations than affection. He wouldn't take things with Julia beyond friendship. He'd just be a fun companion. Someone to dance with at the local discos. Someone to escort her to dinner when she was bored.

It had gone perfectly, in the beginning.

Danny spent a week getting Felix's wardrobe ready. He watched the young American tourists; he paid one off for his jeans, one off for his T-shirt, and one for his shoes. He stole the windbreaker from one who tried to run his Vespa off the road and an entire suitcase from an asshole who didn't tip en route to the airport.

He'd done all of that so he could leave Felix in a cloud of dust on the long road up to the villas, just in time for Hiram Dormer's town car to come into view.

Felix stepped out, flagging it down with a wide-eyed expectation that of course they'd stop, and to his surprise—he almost expected the monstrous vehicle to crush him flat—Dormer did.

"Can I help you?" Dormer had rolled down the tinted window to scowl at him, and Felix gave his best, widest California boy smile.

"Yeah, hi! I'm so, like, sorry to bother you, but I was on my way to visit my uncle's villa, and the guy giving me a ride was, like, all sorts of shady."

"Shady." Dormer was a fiftyish man with a square face and no lips to speak of. He had tiny eyes, like gray pinpricks in leather.

"Yeah, he got tired halfway up and just bailed!" Felix put all the earnestness he could into that, because the truth was, Danny was down the road, hiding behind a tree in case this didn't work.

"Where you headed, kid?"

This part had required homework. Danny and Berto had spent the better part of two weeks asking around for which villas were empty and which families would be the most likely to have family in California.

"The Koehlers. They should be up toward the top of the hill."

Dormer grimaced. "Hell, kid, did you even talk to them and ask?"

"Yessir. They gave me this date, I swear! My dad made the plane reservations himself."

"Well, those people just left yesterday. They must have had an emergency or something."

They had. They'd won an emergency yacht trip. Danny knew a guy.

"Oh, well shoot. Do you know when they'll be back?" Felix made his eyes big and let his lower lip wobble. Dormer blew out a breath, and Felix could see the wheels turning. If it was up to this asshole, Felix would be sleeping on the street—or in a shitty hotel. But the community of Americans who vacationed in those villas was small. If news got out that Dormer had turned away someone's relative when he could have offered the kid a place to sleep for a few days…? Well, he'd find himself on the receiving end of a lot of unfriendly glares and possibly some lost business deals.

Dormer knew this. "Get in the back," he muttered. "Julia, get back there and talk to him. Keep it down."

Without a word, the quiet, willowy girl next to him got out of the front seat. She paused for a moment, letting the dusty breeze blow at her ocean-blue sundress, and Felix was caught by the yearning in her eyes as she scanned the city from the road.

She wanted to be free.

He could sense that in her, much like he could feel Danny's underlying fear of being pinned down. Like Danny, this girl had been hurt, again and again. Like Danny, she'd damn near gnaw off her leg at the ankle to get out of the prison she found herself in.

Felix slid into the seat, keeping his idiot farm-boy grin in place with an effort. Once he'd belted in, he gave her an eager puppy-dog smile.

She glanced at him and then away, like she was afraid to even make contact.

"Don't you just love the smell around here?" he asked, because it was one of his favorite things about the hills. "The pine and the olives?"

She glanced at him again, surprised. "I like the smell of the ocean," she said softly. "I miss it."

Oh. Oh, that was real.

Felix's heart twisted. "The beaches in San Diego are the best," he said fervently, and she relaxed enough to shake her head.

"The ocean in Ireland is part of the heartbeat."

Poetry. Felix's heart gave another vicious twist. He'd never fall in love with this girl—not like he loved Danny—but dammit, he had better not hurt her either. As they passed the hedges behind which Danny crouched, Felix looked out his window searchingly, hoping for something, anything, that would tell him what to do.

Present

"HE'S HERE," Julia said in Felix's ear while Danny gave Phyllis an enthusiastic greeting. Felix marveled. It had taken less than a breath, less than a heartbeat, really, for Danny to put a happy face on the broken, miserable part of himself he'd let Felix see.

With a swallow, he gave Julia a weak smile. "Most of him," he said.

"You can't hold yourself accountable for that," Julia murmured. "It was all—"

"I can and I will." Felix had to turn away. "Julia, what we asked him to do twenty years ago…."

"I was going to say it was all my fault," she said, her voice toneless. "You start something to get you out of a bind in the short term and—"

"And you find yourself trapped." Felix closed his eyes. "Ten years we trapped him into being the dirty secret. It wasn't fair."

"And he keeps thanking us for Josh," she muttered. "I could weep."

Danny turned from Phyllis and pinned them with a bored gaze. "You two—out of the guilt pool," he demanded. "Phyllis has made me chicken and waffles and bacon, and look! It's cold as fuck outside, but the sun is shining. I'm calling it a win."

But Felix saw Julia shake her head, and he knew what she was feeling.

If Danny hadn't been blackmailed by bacon, he would have been out the door before they could stop him.

Because they didn't deserve absolution. They hadn't earned it yet, either of them. Not if they wanted Danny back in their lives free and clear. Not if Felix ever wanted to hold him again.

And Felix did. More than anything, Felix wanted a future with this man who held the keys to his past.

"What are you doing?" Julia asked softly, looking over his shoulder as he pulled out his phone.

"Texting," he said, keeping his voice innocent.

"Texting who?"

"Our son."

"You really *are* a con man," she said, voice full of admiration. "I thought you'd forgotten."

"Never."

Danny's here, but if you don't get your ass over right now, he'll be in the wind.

Shit. We're on our way. Tell Phyllis to make lots of food.

Deal.

"Better make it a buffet," Felix said, his voice jovial, like butter wouldn't melt in his mouth. "Seems Josh and his friends are on their way over."

Phyllis looked up and caught his eye, then slid a look at Danny. Felix nodded back.

"Excellent," she said, as though cooking hadn't been a thing she'd had to learn or Julia's father would have fired her. "Can't ever fry enough chicken."

Felix and Julia made themselves busy setting the table, while Danny regaled Phyllis with stories of a glamorous Monaco that featured no mobsters, no failed cons, no rehab, and no scars.

Since he wasn't going to get the details from Danny—not now—Felix instead allowed himself to fall back into the past. That had been harsh enough.

Past

LIVING UNDER Hiram Dormer's thumb turned out to be harder than Felix had anticipated. The man didn't like noise, he didn't like Felix and Julia talking, and he didn't like Julia going places unescorted.

But he was also in Italy to do business. Felix could never fathom *what* business because his portfolio in the US was so incredibly diverse. It wasn't until he eventually took over part of that portfolio that he realized Dormer had gotten most of his first cash investments from the mob.

But in that first week, it was just him and Julia, knocking around the big house, trying to be nice to each other during meals and not get caught talking to each other at other times.

It was rough because old Hiram—in addition to wanting to know where she was every minute of every day—had ears like a bat. Felix had started asking her for walks in the garden more for his own sanity than as any part of the con. While there, he'd talk—tell her stories about feeding the cats by the Coliseum, watching the sunset from the bridge at Fiumicino, and how the smell of pine nuts made him wake up hungry every morning.

She listened to his rambles without responding for so long that Felix wondered, was there something he was missing? Did she have difficulties communicating? Did she *ever* talk?

Until one night, at the end of his first week, she looked up at the sky and said, "Do you think your young man minds you being out here under the stars with me?"

Felix gaped at her. "My… I, uh, don't know…."

"My father drives down that street all the time. I spotted the two of you a couple of weeks ago."

Felix's stomach twisted, and he wondered if he had time to throw up and collect his things before he vaulted the garden walls of the Dormer villa and made a break for it.

"Has your father…?"

She shook her head. "He knows nothing." There was a viciousness to the way she said it. Felix, who had heard Hiram scream at her for being thirty seconds late for dinner and then seen him throw salad at her from across the table when she wouldn't eat, could understand the viciousness.

"He's pretty awful," he said candidly, admitting nothing.

"Whatever you and your friend want to do to him, he deserves it," she said bitterly.

Felix had no answer to that. It was true. He paused for a moment, head tilted back, and wondered at the smell of olive trees. It was like olive oil. You didn't think it added anything to the flavor of your food, but then it would hit you—life was just better because it was there.

"Do you want to help?" he asked, hoping Danny would forgive him. She seemed so lost here. Lost and alone. And Hiram Dormer deserved a chainsaw up his ass more than he deserved kindness from his one living relative.

She made a sound he was not expecting, something choked and awful that seemed ripped out of her heart.

"I'm sorry," he said in a panic. "I'm sorry. We can just forget I even mentioned it. I didn't mean to make you cry. That was one of the conditions, you see, that you not get hurt."

"Get hurt?" she said, voice broken with tears. "I'm going to be worse than hurt. Do you have any idea what he'll do to me? Any at all? He pushed my mother down the stairs. She barely recovered after I was born. She managed to get away, but she had to leave me, and every letter she writes is 'Please come! Please!' But I mentioned it to him once, and...." She shuddered. "So you're likely here to steal from my family, and all I can do is beg you to take me with you!"

Felix's heart beat unsteadily in his throat. "I can't!" he gasped. "We have no place to put you. Danny would get busted. Me and him, we're practically invisible, but you? You'd be like a signal flare."

"But...." She caught her breath. "God, please. You're the first real human I've talked to since he brought us here. Everyone's so afraid of him. He's going to marry me off to one of his business contacts and… and they'll kill me. They'll have to, because…." He couldn't follow what she said next in the flurry of weeping. He asked again and again, but all he got was "I didn't know him, but he was sweet, and I didn't see him afterward and… and… and…."

And then he got it. Got *it*. Got why she was so afraid, so desperate that she'd run off with a con man and his lover, just to get away.

"Shh," he soothed, holding her head to his chest like he'd seen people in the movies do. "Shh. We'll fix it. Danny's smart. He can fix anything. He's street smart. He knows how to survive."

She nodded against him, calming down. He finally took her to her room, afraid her father would get there and find they'd actually communicated. He kissed her on the forehead and grimaced.

"You'll ask him?" she whispered.

"I'll ask him."

The next morning he slipped a note to Berto's mother. She was their prearranged contact in case the plan changed. Felix remembered that it rained that night—a terrible storm—and he and Julia stood out under the veranda near the garden, waiting for the slight figure to come trudging up the hill, leaning against the wind.

When he finally got to them, Felix practically melted into his arms. He was *so* glad to see Danny. Couldn't they just go back to the apartment? God, they'd even go back to the garret if they had to. Where things were simple. They could pick all the pockets and fleece all the tourists and nobody would ever care.

"Felix?" Danny mumbled against his neck. "Felix, there's a girl here."

Felix pulled back and nodded at her. "She'd seen us in town," he admitted. "She's apparently not blind."

Danny's eyes went wide. "So, uh… no adventures tonight?"

Julia shrugged, looking pale in the rain, and held out a small parcel. "It's an ivory snuff box," she said, "with a painted miniature of a young noblewoman. Said to be painted by Rosalba Carriera. She painted—"

"In the early 1700s," Danny murmured. "Was said to have been the face behind the miniatures of the rococo movement. Favored pastels and may have sacrificed her eyesight for little goodies like this." He took the parcel with reverence. "You want us to fence it or arrange to have your father buy it back from a fence?"

Her eyes sharpened. "That would—" Her mouth flattened, corners twisted up. "—irritate him to no end."

Danny gave her an equally devious smile. "It would," he said. Then he took in the two of them. "But that's not why I'm here, is it?"

Felix told him then about Julia's pregnancy— probably four months along—and about her father. And her fear.

"He'll hurt you?" Danny asked, while the olive trees raged around them. The rain poured off the sloped roof of the porch, leaving them alone in the faint glow of the lamp inside. Everything around the three of them was chaos.

"Yes," Felix said, while Julia nodded. "He's… he's more of a bastard than we thought, Danny. She asked to run away with us, but—"

"We don't have the resources," Danny said, shaking his head without ego or conceit. He looked at

Julia apologetically. "It was one thing for me," he said, shrugging. "When I started, I could give a blowjob and not give a fuck. You can't do that."

Felix remembered breathing in and out hard. He'd suspected. Things Danny had said about using condoms with every guy he'd ever been with until Felix. Things he'd said during lovemaking, when Felix wanted to be sweet. Until that moment, watching Danny assess Julia's odds of staying alive if she ran away with them right now, tonight, it hadn't hit him how hard his lover's life had truly been.

Which made what Danny proposed next both ruthlessly practical and one of the most selfless things Felix had ever seen.

Present

JULIA TOUCHED his elbow, and for a moment, he was still back there in the storm, while the olive trees raged and the rain dripped steadily from the eaves and Danny proposed the salvation and destruction of the three of them.

It took him a moment to put himself back into his Chicago mansion, twenty years later, with the older, wiser, sadder man in front of him as his young and beautiful lover.

No longer young. Still beautiful.

Danny glanced up in the middle of regaling Phyllis with another story—this one about returning a rare miniature of Micaela Almonester to her tiny museum in New Orleans after "liberating" it from her husband's estate in France. "After all," he said, finishing the story as he looked Felix in the eyes, "New Orleans was ever her home."

Felix opened his mouth to say, "And I am always yours," but at that moment, there was a rattle at the door and Josh walked in, followed by what appeared to be the junior college mafia. At that moment, Felix's life took a left turn at Albuquerque, fell down the rabbit hole, and ended up in an Elmore Leonard book.

Well, he'd promised himself he'd do anything to get Danny back this summer. It was time to pony up.

Saddle Up

DANNY HAD never been so grateful for any-body's entrance—not even the copper in Monaco who had taken him to the hospital and saved his life after Kadjic, that bastard, had left him bleeding in an alley for trying to cheat him out of that small country.

For a moment, he'd been lost in Felix's eyes, sur-rounded by chaos and blowing olive trees, safe in the circle of his arms as Danny planned to save Julia Dor-mer just because Felix thought she was worth saving. The moment had spiraled out around them, become every decision thereafter: Felix and Julia's hasty mar-riage, their travel back to the States, and ultimately, the thieves' training ground of a lifetime.

Everything Danny learned about getting in and out of secure buildings, about manipulating businessmen to do what he wanted, about milking a mean-spirited stone for money and making it feel like it had won something, he'd learned by sneaking in and out of Felix's bed after Felix married Julia Dormer.

He, Felix, and Julia had once manipulated a media market in China to lure Hiram there for six months so they could have some alone time—Felix with Danny, Julia with her lover of the moment. She'd had a few over the years, but nobody she'd ever cared enough about to introduce to Josh. The three of them had taken Josh out of school—he'd been six or seven at the time—and had run him around Europe and taught him math and spelling and how to sneak in and out of a museum with a first-rate alarm system because they wanted to see what was inside and they really didn't like crowds.

They'd practiced fleecing tourists outside a pub in Ireland—Josh was great for that; he could pick up on an accent in a heartbeat, and he'd had the most preciously large eyes as a child—and had spent a week running an adoption scam on a pair of really obnoxious Americans who wanted "a cute little Italian kid to take home for their daughter."

They'd given the money to the local orphanage and disappeared into the night, on to the next adventure.

Julia had been part of some of them. Within the small circle of her family, she'd blossomed, come alive. She, Felix, and Danny had Joshua to raise, to teach, to play with, to love. The three of them had given him security because Danny had known what it was like to have none, and attention because Felix had missed that growing up, and kindness because Julia knew what it was to need it desperately.

But eventually, Hiram had returned, Felix had gone back to running the old man's media companies pretty much singlehandedly, and behind his back, saving them from being run into the ground. And Danny?

Danny had gone back to Europe for a couple of months and had used all those skills he'd learned over the past year to rob rather a lot of museums and bankrupt a small, corrupt city.

Until the urge to see Felix again had become too strong and he'd learned to sneak into a whole new security system, and the circle started again.

But every time he left, he'd spend a little more time drinking, and every time he came back, he'd have to spend a few more days in Felix's bed crying, sleeping, detoxing his body from the feeling of living on the grift, remembering what the world was like again when you were safe and had a home.

Standing here in Felix's kitchen, Phyllis cheerfully cooking for him, Felix and Julia watching him like he was their long-lost brother—it all had such a terrible ring of familiarity to it.

His stomach churned. It was so seductive, such an easy trap to fall into. But the hope that it would last, would be real—that would eat away at him. He knew that now. It would eat away at him until the only way he could face it was with a flask of something expensive and mind-numbing, something that would let him forget the screaming of his heart.

So when the door burst open and Josh and his crew barreled in, Danny could have cried. This was different. This was a job. He was here to do a job, and then he'd be on his way, only to visit Chicago once a quarter so he could check his mail and see Josh.

"Uncle Danny!" Josh's embrace was tight and excited, and Danny responded without reservation. Unlike with Felix, Josh's embrace was as whole and without pain as it had been the first time Danny had held him as an infant. To Danny, Josh was all that was good in the world.

"You brought your friends." Danny pulled back and smiled at the young people he'd had pizza with the day before, and they all greeted him warmly, but as with Josh, he was a favorite uncle, not a buddy.

They were kind, but they still made him feel old.

As the young people assembled in the kitchen, Phyllis put them to work setting the grand table in the dining room, transforming what had looked to be a simple breakfast into a brunch, made official when Julia disappeared for a moment and returned with two bottles of champagne and one of sparkling cider.

Danny smiled at her as she arrived and then resumed his probing conversation with Charlie Calder about his days in the military. Charlie—Chuck to his friends—was satisfyingly cagey about his job as a "specialist in assorted trades." Danny had worked with enough munitions and transport guys to know that the same guy who blew the safe—or the building—could also be an outstanding candidate to drive the getaway vehicle. Chuck had signed on to be "you know, whatever Josh needs" for this mission, and while he was older than most of the kids, his clean-cut, square-jawed intensity was offset by the widest, prettiest green eyes Danny had ever seen.

He was muscle, he was a driver, he was an ingenue. Danny couldn't believe he'd never worked with a
Good Luck Chuck before.

"Danny?"

"Yeah?" Danny turned toward Felix but watched
over his shoulder as Dylan Li—called Grace by his
friends—practically danced around the table as he set
cloth napkins at every plate. Willowy as a blade of
grass, strong as tensile steel, he was a ballet dancer and
gymnast in a rather prestigious uptown theater company—and had been Josh's best friend since grade school.
He had tip-tilted brown eyes, a narrow, puckish face,
and straight black hair cut into wispy bangs and tinted
pale blue in strands.

As he'd revealed to Danny the day before, over
pizza, he also had a 175 IQ and got bored easily. He
liked doing things like tightrope walking, base jump-
ing, and climbing in and out of ventilation systems in
local high rises.

Sometimes he came out with small items of great
value that just slipped into his pockets. Josh had been
helping him find buyers for these items—often they
were previously stolen, so the risk of reporting was
minimal—and somehow all of the proceeds ended up
in the coffers of the dance studio that had taken Dylan
in when his parents had been too busy climbing social
rungs in Taiwan.

"Danny, who are these people?"

Danny gaped at Felix. "These are Josh's friends!
You don't know them?"

Felix looked around the table. "Okay Grace, obviously—he lives here, when he and Josh aren't dorming
together for school. And Stirling and Molly I know."
His mouth flattened with sadness. "Their parents died

overseas, I guess, but… I don't know. Something about that sounded fishy to me."

Danny glanced over at Stirling, their computer ops guy. Slight and quick-fingered, Stirling had sharp cheekbones, gray-green eyes, and skin the color of pale bronze. His sister, Molly, was Irish-pale, with blue-green eyes, and the wildly curly hair that sprang from her crown and fell to her waist was dyed in spirals, from aqua blue to neon pink to bright yellow, but a random half of it was left the brilliant sunset orange that was probably her natural color.

"They're pissed," Danny agreed. "I take it they'd both been in the foster system before the Christophers took them in."

"They were ten, twelve. It was right after—" Felix swallowed. "—right after I let you slip away."

Danny's jaw hardened. "I left, Fox. My doing. Don't take that away from me."

"I was dumb enough to not see that fight for what it was," Felix said. "I was dumb enough to drive you to it."

"That's not what we're doing here." God, this conversation hurt. "Tell me more about Stirling and Molly."

Felix shook his head. "Later, Danny. But sure, Stirling and Molly I know. They're good kids. Their parents died last year. Molly had just turned twenty. Stirling's still nineteen, but the Christophers had written iron-clad provisions for both kids, including college funds and trust funds and the house. They have an older brother whose wife wasn't too excited—all three of them got about the same amount of money. But I had my lawyer advocate for them, and they kept to the spirit of the will. Stirling's in electronics. Molly's in theater, sometimes front of the house, sometimes behind the scenes. See that outfit?"

Danny did; very college student, with an over-sized jacket over tight slacks and ballet slippers. The fabrics weren't run-of-the-mill colors, though. He may have recognized the cut of the brilliant green jacket and the peacock-blue slacks, and even the bright peach handbag had a familiar shape, but the silks and wools and textures she'd used were... unusual.

"Yes?"

"She's been picking out and sewing her own clothes since she arrived on Stella and Fred's door-step." He made a hurt sound. "She and Stella used to go through catalogs of fabrics every season, and Molly would make her the most fabulous dresses. It was something that kept them close, even when Molly went through the hard years."

"What about the boy?" Stirling met nobody's eyes, kept his body very self-contained, and answered people's questions with abrupt nods. He was dressed entirely in black, but his vest was done in black brocade, and his long-sleeved button-down was silk.

"He's a different fish," Felix admitted. "Everyone thought Fred and Stella would just toss him back into the system because he's so not good with people. But they worked at it. They knew *one* of them would find a way to connect. He's not in his comfort zone here. But you should have seen him in the living room on his keyboard when Fred was watching sports. Stirling would be rattling off betting statistics and player stats, and Fred would be switching from screen to screen to keep up with him. Fred liked action—within reason. He and Stirling used to make a bundle every weekend, and they'd spend it on tickets to see the games in real time."

Felix let out a sigh. "I wish every kid like Stirling and Molly got to have parents like Fred and Stella. It really hurt when they died."

Oh fuck. Danny had gotten a little bit of that vibe from Molly, but Stirling? Oh man, that kid was going to look at Danny and see a father figure.

And Danny was going to leave?

Dammit.

"You haven't taken over?" Danny asked.

Felix shrugged. "I'm not his person. I'm not everybody's."

"You're the roper, Fox. Everybody likes you."

"Not everybody."

"Shut up."

Felix snorted. "Fine. So much we have to talk about later. I'm loving this. Now who's the guy in the corner who thinks we're not going to see him?" He had shoulder-length brown hair, gray eyes, and a lean mouth. Wasn't tall, wasn't short, and had a way of melting into the background Danny entirely approved of.

Danny chuckled. "That is a guy who's invested a lot in learning fighting techniques. See the way he's put his back to the wall?"

"Oh yeah." Felix nodded. "I take it you've seen him move?"

"He was last to the pizza place yesterday," Danny said, remembering. "Warded off a pickpocket with a shrug of his shoulders. Left the would-be thief out cold as Hunter just kept walking."

Felix suppressed a smirk. "You've got a muscle man named Hunter?"

Danny let himself grin. "Who else would he be?"

"Right. So who was the cowboy you were talking to?"

"Good Luck Chuck and Grace," Danny told him. "Chuck's ex-military. Grace is... well, his real name is Dylan, but—"

"Dylan I know—he lives here, remember? And he's been stealing mine and Julia's jewelry for years, holding it for a few months, and then replacing it. He's your grease man," Felix said. "I hear you. This is a very impressive crew you've got here. Most of them are even over twenty-one. What are they doing in my dining room, again?"

"You can feel free to run along and not worry your pretty little head about it," Danny told him mildly, half hoping he'd do it.

Felix's snort was his only answer. "Please. Molly's your roper? I don't think so. Losing your touch, Lightfingers?"

"I thought you had an empire to run," Danny shot back. Sure, Felix had been asked not to run things at the station as the program director, but he was still technically part of the board, right?

Felix looked pained. "The board of directors asked me to step down temporarily. It's being run by a proxy."

Danny grunted, hurt for him. "Not for fucking long."

"Sit down, Uncle Danny," Josh urged, patting the seat next to him.

Danny complied, greeting the others before filling his plate and urging Julia and Phyllis to join him. Felix practically booty-bumped them out of the way to take the seat on Danny's other side, and Danny gave him a droll look.

"Not. Over," Felix said.

"You're not making staying look any more attractive," Danny lied.

Felix arched one eyebrow, showing that he knew the statement for what it was. "Me making you a priority is what we needed all along," he said, just low enough for Danny to hear it.

Danny tried to turn away before Felix could see his expression, but Felix's hand on his knee told him he'd failed.

Damn, Felix always could read him like a book.

This isn't going to work, this isn't going to work, this isn't going to—

"So, Uncle Danny," Josh said brightly. "How's this going to work?"

Danny took a breath and focused on the task at hand.

"Well," he said softly, surprised when the table quieted down. "The way I see it, we need to decide what we want from this. Do we want to blackmail her, get her to recant her statement, or—"

"Publicly humiliate her until she has to move to another country and can't breathe without hearing the jeers of her enemy," Molly said promptly.

Danny's eyebrows shot up. "That's a little, uh, bloodth—"

"Destroy every shred of reputation she's ever had until she has to buy a new face just to go out to dinner," Chuck said, and he and Molly shared a fist bump.

"Bankrupt her until she has to sell her shoes for food," Stirling added.

"Good one," Chuck told him approvingly, and Stirling studied his frittata and waffles with terrifying intensity.

"Steal something she's not supposed to have and taunt her with it," Grace murmured, a dreamy smile on his face.

"Uh… wow."

Molly made a sound like a feral cat. "My parents voted red when they were just out of college, and she did a piece on bandwagon progressives that featured them front and center. The week after they'd died."

"Oh dear God."

"She's a twat-shaped virtue signal, and she needs to be smashed," Molly said, eyes narrow and spitting fire.

"Praises veterans in one show and talks about the one guy who's maybe been convicted of welfare fraud in the next," Hunter snarled. "Because welfare is such a fucking free ride as it is."

Danny knew about state assistance. When his mother had first gotten sick, she'd tried to feed the two of them on it for a while. Powdered milk and ramen noodles for months at a time. Fun times. He and the "kids" hadn't talked about the job the day before. They'd just talked about their qualifications. "That's a little…." He thought about how hard Felix had worked to create a small, independent cable network that told the truth, that supported the arts, that showed old movies and new with an eye to the ones that made people the happiest. Yes, he'd inherited the job from Hiram Dormer, but Felix—he had such power. He hadn't been able to stand watching Dormer buy and sell the network like a commodity without even exploring its potential, so he'd taken over the running, had made it profitable. While Hiram had run his businesses into the ground, practically bankrupting himself, Felix had made the network the centerpiece of the family fortune. He'd become so damned legitimate that when Danny had begged him to give up the job, to divorce Julia so they could be together, he'd been unable to abandon the work he'd done to make something productive out of Hiram Dormer's castoffs.

Danny couldn't forget that image of Felix trying to explain this to him during their last dreadful fight.

Nor that clip of Marnie Courtland screaming into the news studio words that would never be unheard, either.

"A little what?" Josh asked, apprehensive, as always, for Danny's good opinion.

"A little bit of a start," Danny said, remembering the cold precision he and Felix had used to lure Hiram away from Chicago time and time again. It hadn't been good for the old man's heart. But then, that organ had only really been used to pump blood anyway. "So, here's what we need to do—and what we need to decide."

"What?" Chuck asked. "I mean, we're all in. You know that."

Danny nodded. "I gathered that yesterday. I'm not going to ask if you want to back out. I'm taking your word for it. But if we want her humiliation to be public—and we want it to stick—we're going to need to do some research and some reconnaissance. Stirling, you know where to find the dirty, right?"

"Bank records, social media, school records, recommendations—"

"Yes," Danny said, nodding. "But don't forget, it's not what's said about them or what they say about others. It's the inconsistencies. Did she get a recommendation from a teacher she talked shit about? What's the body language in the photos? Are people looking at her like they'd like to kill her while they're singing her praises? She considers herself a social media influencer. Who's on her side now who talked trash about her a year ago? In a week, I want to know who's most likely to poison her coffee and who's most likely to take a bullet for her. Can we do that?"

There was an agonizing pause, and Danny remembered what Felix had said about Stirling's people skills. "Don't worry, Stirling. You get the info, and we'll have a meeting once a day to hash out your findings. Feel free to ask me, Josh, Julia, or Chuck—"

"Or me," Felix inserted.

"Or anyone you're comfortable with who's good at reading social cues," Danny said blandly. "You get the info, you grab one of us to help you analyze it, okay?"

Stirling's eyes lit up, and the smile he gave Danny was almost transcendently grateful. "Thanks, Uncle Danny."

Danny screwed up his face, and Felix laughed softly next to him.

"Hush," Danny murmured and then continued, "Chuck and Hunter? You need to look at where she lives and works. Josh's dad can help you with the printouts of the studio, but we need to know her house or apartment—"

"Apartment," Grace said, looking smug. "Those modern ones by North and Vine."

Danny made another face. "Gah. Okay. Remind me to give you guys a key. That's my digs too. You can use it as a base in the city."

"Eww," Felix said, giving him a pitying look.

"They're very upscale," Danny said with dignity.

"Yeah, but Danny, they're not really homey," Julia said. Then she brightened. "Josh, you and your friends can bring Danny's stuff here. We have his old room all ready."

Danny had to blink to make sure his eyes would close. "My old room—"

"We've changed it a bit, but it's still yours." Julia's smile was so warm these days. "Same furniture, different curtains. Felix wanted to make sure you felt welcome when you came back."

"You didn't know," Danny said, rolling his eyes in disgust.

Felix tightened his hand on Danny's knee. "Josh was waiting for you this quarter," Felix murmured. "Guess who was going to be waiting for you in the summer?"

"Easy to say," Danny murmured before raising his voice. "Grace, Hunter, Good Luck Chuck, you're on recon. We need to know her travel routes, where she goes for coffee, who she sees, who hates her, and who she overtips. Grace, get a look at her apartment. What are her tastes in art, furniture, fashion? Is there anything in her personal space that we can use to get her to compromise herself?"

He took a breath. "Okay, folks, here's the hard part. We can't call her a liar to her face. All of the people who have ever reported sexual assault, harassment, or discrimination are going to be in her camp. She's going to be their hero. Calling her a liar to her face will only hurt the people who have already been victimized."

"It's one of the things that makes me really want to strangle her with her own entrails," Julia said viciously, and Danny nodded. Julia had spent her entire childhood living a bullied nightmare—and Marnie Courtland had just used stories like Julia's to hurt an innocent man.

"Alas, that punishment is off the table, pet, but we'll try to do something that will hurt even worse."

"You're too good to me," Julia said with a grim smile, and Danny winked before getting back to the matter at hand.

"If we can get her talking into a microphone about setting Felix up, that'll be great. I'll take it. Merry Christmas to us. But we can't count on it. What we need is an established pattern of unethical behavior in other areas. She needs to get busted kicking puppies, firing the maid, giving to white supremacist charities— something that will make her a pariah in every community she's affiliated with that does *not* touch on sexual assault."

"But—"

Danny looked at Josh with compassion. "We want your dad to have his day," he said to Josh. "But we can't sink to her level, and we can't make it she said/ he said. We need to show she's an unscrupulous person who will do anything for a story. Then we want to make it clear what she *did* do."

"What kind of plan do you have?" Molly asked eagerly.

"Felix, what does she want more than anything else in the world?" Danny asked.

Felix answered like he'd studied the test. "A network job. Not a small cable network. She wants to be the next Barbara Walters, not the next Rachel Maddow."

Danny cringed. "She thinks she's better than Rachel? That's unlikely."

"I'm just telling you," Felix said with a laugh. "She'll take anything. Even the network whose name we don't speak, if you know what I mean."

Danny grinned. "Then I may have the right con for her. That's... well, she doesn't know her market well, does she? Or her fans. That's good. She's greedy, and she's not particularly loyal." He frowned. "How is it you didn't see all this when you hired her?"

Josh spoke up first. "She was really good at sucking up. Mom even liked her at first."

Julia let out a sigh. "Yes. And then the stories kept getting more and more lurid—but her ratings were good, and Felix had to find a real reason to let her go."

Felix took up the thread, and Danny listened avidly. He'd wondered how Fox—who'd always been such a solid, decent man, even when on the grift—had gotten snowed by someone who now seemed so monstrous. "I mentored her," he said. "And I remember steering her towards more ethical behavior, but once she got the anchors' seat—and two shows of her own—she seemed to get more and more corrosive."

"Absolute power?" Danny asked delicately, thinking that Felix had never succumbed.

"Yes," Felix agreed. "And she thought nobody could bring her down. Her online presence is huge—and she's really good at bullying people with much smaller platforms. But that's not something that shows up immediately, and not something that people look at. And you know what an echo chamber those places are like. If you scream 'misogynist' in a crowd of Twitter users, they won't see what your ulterior motives are, they'll just parrot it back to you. But she was leaving a paper trail—the station started getting complaint after complaint. Normally that sort of thing is handled by HR, but after the piece that featured Stirling and Molly's parents, I started to investigate." He shuddered. "It was like unearthing a mass grave of people's careers, many of them she seems to have smashed just for spite."

Danny nodded, chilled. "Such an easy thing to happen in this age of instant outrage." In spite of himself, he found himself patting Felix's knee in comfort. He snatched his hand away and pulled himself back to the task at hand. "But the paper trail is good. That will show up in her history, in the skeletons she stuffed in the closet, and in the bodies she walked on trying to get here. We just need to show her trading loyalties and show the world her trail of carnage, with you as the cherry on the sundae. We can do this, you guys think?"

"What am I doing?" Josh asked anxiously.

Danny had chewed on that for much of the previous afternoon as he'd walked his pizza off in the streets of his favorite city. "Here's the thing, Josh. Whether this job works or it goes tits up, you are going to have to deal with these people for almost all of your adult life."

"I don't care," Josh snarled. "I hate them. What they did to Dad…."

"Yes, son," Danny said, keeping his voice firm. "But you can't screw over all your father's old business associates now if you hope to keep milking them as contacts later. So what I want you to do is find out who's still on your father's side and see who is reporting directly to Marnie. We need to know how people feel. Map their reactions. Who wants to be Marnie Courtland's pet, and who just wants to stick it to Felix? Who might be afraid of her and feels like they're protecting their job or their family? We need to know who can help us—deliberately or inadvertently—before we even start."

Danny turned back to the rest of the crew. "I get the impression you all want to find a way to give Marnie an allover screwing."

"I would like to see her have to move back in with her mother," Grace said happily. "She ran a story on Aether Conservatory that made it look like a low-rent alternative to—her words—'more polished and up-scale' dance troupes. It was demeaning. Like a pat on the head. I want her to move in with her mother and have 'You should find a nice man and have babies' written on her wall in Sharpie. Can we arrange that?"

"No," Danny said, wishing he could. "But we could make her think that would be the best thing to ever happen to her. Take a look at her apartment and tell me what she values—and what's easy to slip out in your pocket."

Grace's smile was pixilated and sublimely happy. "Excellent. Right after my brunch nap."

"We can start tomorrow," Danny conceded. "Josh, whatever your crew had in mind for today—"

"We'll get equipment for Stirling," Josh said. "Dad, can we set the downstairs den up as an op center?"

"Course," Felix said, nodding.

"Chuck, that means today you and Hunter need to be on security for *this* house and for my apartment. Can you upgrade the systems?" Danny asked.

"We just got new security for this place!" Felix protested.

Danny cocked his head and sent Felix a level look.

"Anybody else would have had a problem," Felix said with dignity.

"Until it can keep *me* out, it's not good enough," Danny told him. He raised his voice. "That goes for everyone. I know you all have your own places, pets, whatever. If you visit them, visit with another member of the team. If you have a cat, bring it here. If you have a roommate, you now have a new boyfriend or girlfriend."

"Boyfriend," Josh said, not surprising him.

"Boyfriend," Chuck said.

"Boyfriend," Stirling muttered.

"Boyfriend," Hunter snapped out.

"I am in *luck*!" Grace gasped happily.

"I have got to find a new peer group," Molly muttered. "For the record, it's boyfriend, but I guess we're all trading off."

Danny tried not to laugh and failed. "I'll leave it to you all to work out." He sobered. "But make this place your base of operations. Josh?"

"Yes, sir?"

"Try to find some straight friends for Molly. This is no fair at all."

Molly grinned at him. "Thanks, Uncle Danny. You're the best."

He winked at her. "I do try, sweetheart."

Everyone at the table laughed then, and Phyllis and Julia surprised him.

"I can keep you all fed," Phyllis said. "But Grace?"

Grace looked at her in surprise. "Yes, ma'am?"

"Try to find out where her housekeeper shops. Domestic workers socialize—I can be more use than you think."

Grace's smile went wide and beatific. "You're amazing. I shall wash your dishes out of gratitude."

Phyllis sent him a look that was clearly unimpressed. "You can wash my dishes anyway. You live here."

"We'll all wash her dishes," Josh said, his tone brooking no argument, then gave Felix an arch look of pride.

Felix shrugged and mouthed, "That's our boy" before Julia spoke.

"I can do some charity dinners," she said. "I'll fish for information too. You said we have a week, Danny?"

"Two at the outside," Danny told her. "At least to gather information. News cycles move so quickly. In two weeks, people will have forgotten why they're glad she got taken out."

"With Phyllis talking to the housekeepers and me talking to the employers, we can make it three days," Julia told him.

Danny nodded. "Everyone who's free meets tomorrow morning, and we'll hone our approach. Family dinner in two days. Everyone have reports ready, and we'll flesh out a plan."

Parenting Fails

FELIX PULLED his son away from the cleanup hubbub with a touch on the shoulder, and together they retreated to the den.

"I know what you're going to say," Josh told him, sounding bored.

Felix's mouth twitched, and he bravely contained his smirk. Josh had always been precocious, but he so rarely played the put-out teenager card—even when he'd been one.

"Are you sure?" Felix grinned tightly. "Are you *sure* you know what I'm going to say?"

Josh pretended to think about it. "Let's start with 'How could you bother Danny like that' and move on to 'Please don't put yourself at risk fighting my battles.' And maybe 'We don't do that anymore, Josh—you have too much to lose if we jump back into the game now.'"

Felix shook his head. "I'm glad you bothered Danny like this. I wasn't kidding about doing it in the summer." He swallowed, his stomach knotting. "I just had to build up my courage." If he'd known about the scars, the trip to rehab, the mobsters in Monaco, he might have found his courage ten years ago. But maybe not. Josh had been so young then, and Danny was painfully right about his drinking. Felix and Julia had loved him—and he'd never put Josh in danger—but Felix hadn't been able to trust if what came out of his mouth was Danny or Crown Royal.

Of course some of that had been because what *was* Danny was so painfully lost and hurt, and that had been Felix's fault, but he'd been all about dodging that responsibility then.

"He seems to be doing well," Josh said hopefully. "No boy toy in his life. He would have said something."

"Have there been many?" Ten years, and Felix had refused to ask. But they'd seen each other, they'd touched, and now he allowed it to matter.

"Not really," Josh said, eyes gentle. "Dad, you know he's never gotten over you."

Felix tried to shrug, but he pulled in a hard breath instead. "I...." *I'll never be over him.* "I shouldn't have asked," he said with dignity and ignored his son's smirk. "But about fighting my battles—"

"It wasn't fair," Josh said, and his big, precious brown eyes were suddenly narrow and hard. "You built that network. I know Grandpa bought it, but you turned it around and made it profitable and made it popular. You—" He bit his lip and turned away, uncharacteristically evasive. "Never mind. Yes, I'm going to fight in this. Because we're family, and you've been a super decent father, and—"

Felix scowled. "It is not like you to not say exactly what you mean, Josh. Remember when you bought me the ultra-expensive moisturizer for my birthday so my laugh lines wouldn't be so prominent? You were seven."

Josh's shoulders hunched, and he hid his face in an uncharacteristic show of mortification. "Aw, Dad! Why you gotta tell that story." And before Felix could answer him, he straightened, his face growing adult and hard again. "In fact, you *don't* tell that story, do you? And do you know why?"

Felix sucked in a breath. His son was playing hardball.

"I, uh, it was a long time ag—"

"Because you've been passing for straight for twenty years, and that story would show this family to be as wonderfully bent as it actually is. You all made sacrifices so I could grow up happy. I didn't know it at ten, but I know it now. So yes, I'm going to fight for you. Because you and Danny stepped up to fight for me and Mom before I was even born, back when Mom wasn't in any position to stand up for herself."

"You know, I really wish your mother had never had that conversation with you!" Two years after Danny left, Josh had wanted to know why. He'd been old enough then, but Felix had put him off, still unable to even talk about Danny. So Julia had been the one to have the conversation with Josh, and she'd revealed far more than Felix would have.

"Why?" Josh gestured broadly. "What's wrong with knowing I was raised by good men? What's wrong with knowing that people in my life stepped up for me?"

Felix grimaced. "We spent your entire life trying to give you things we didn't have when we were growing up," he said, "because we didn't want you to have to break laws and steal to get by. How did you even end up with a crew like this, Josh? Dylan, Stirling, and Molly I knew, but I didn't know about the rest!"

Josh gave a wicked smile. "Well, you know Grace likes to walk off with our jewelry—that can't be much of a surprise. And I know how to spot someone boosting a car from fifty feet away, even if they're Chuck. I was trying to bust a mugger in a parking garage when I saw Hunter do it first. Let's face it, Dad, you gave me a very select set of skills that made regular friends at school a little... boring."

"Regular people aren't boring!" Felix muttered, but the words even *tasted* like hypocrisy.

"You mean like the guys you've dated over the past few years?" Josh pointed out, his eyes flat. "They weren't boring?"

Felix opened his mouth and then closed it again. "Owen Harding played polo," he said.

"Polo." Josh crossed his arms.

"Horses." Felix shuddered. "They're terrifying."

"So was watching you try to look excited about your dates," Josh told him, lifting a corner of his mouth in irritation.

"Josh!" Felix pinched the bridge of his nose. "There were reasons for what we did. We... we stopped playing games when you were younger so you could have a normal life."

"You stopped running cons when Danny left because it was no fun without him," Josh said.

"That's not entirely the way of it," Felix said, his heart aching.

"Then what was?"

"Danny…. Keeping him in the closet when your grandfather was alive—that was hard," Felix said, hating having to say this.

"You guys always made a game out of it," Josh said, thinking about it. "Don't mention Uncle Danny. I never did. He was like the family imaginary friend."

Felix swallowed. "He was the love of my life, and you weren't allowed to say his name." It was hard to even say the words past the lump in his throat. "He loved you like a son, and you couldn't tell your friends at school. We couldn't so much as walk out the door and hold hands." Gah! All those things Felix had told Danny hadn't mattered because they could be together behind closed doors, and now they were things Felix wanted for his family the most. "All those games we ran—those were so we could have Danny in our lives." He let out a sigh and his shoulders slumped. "Once he wasn't here anymore—"

"All the fun went out of the world," Josh said, and Felix looked away. "Well, he's here, Dad. He's *here*. And he's running a game to save your ass. So don't worry about me."

"If I have to bail you out of jail, you can be damned sure I'll worry about you!"

Josh shook his head. "You and Danny taught me better than that. Hell, even *Mom* taught me better. Remember when she showed me how to cheat at poker?"

Felix let out a soft snort. "She used to have to play cribbage with your grandfather," he said. "Hiram got cranky when she won." She'd learned how to lose—but how to do it cannily, the better to make her humiliation complete. Julia had learned very early on that if Hiram got to humiliate her in something small, like a card game or a word game, he would be a lot easier to deal with. Less yelling, more disgusted silences were a good thing sometimes.

Josh nodded. "Dad, I have no regrets about knowing the things I do, growing up the way I did. Why do you seem to?"

Felix looked at him helplessly. "There are risks, Josh. Getting busted by the police is just one of them." He bit his lip, feeling vulnerable in front of his son in ways nobody had told him about when he'd signed on to be Julia's husband in name only. "When you were a kid, Danny would leave town to dodge your grandfather and come back with bruises and scrapes and 'near miss' written all over his body, his face, his... his heart." Just the memory of the scars on Danny's ribs burned Felix's palm like fire. "The fear of being pulled away from your people—that's a real thing. That leaves scars you can't see. And we gave you these skills, this feeling that it's all a game." He rubbed his chest. "We didn't let you feel the dangers, and that's our bad. But that doesn't mean we want you exposed to them now."

Josh paused, and enough of the brightness faded from his eyes that Felix knew he was taking this seriously.

"Dad?"

"Yes?"

"This is Danny. This is you. You haven't been happy since he left. And he needs us. All of us. You'd better believe I take this seriously." He paused. "And he's not the only one who needs us. My friends, uhm, seem to need him too."

Felix let out a breath. "Yes, I noticed that." He chuckled, resigned. "You know, when Danny and I started, we were broke, living on the streets of Rome.

If we'd gotten arrested then, that would have been it: five year minimum in a real shithole. But now?" He shrugged. "Stockbroker prison. I hear there are golf courses and massage therapy. Those could be rumors, but you never know."

Josh rolled his eyes. "Chuck knows how to blow shit up. Even if you went to prison, it wouldn't be for long. Is there anything else?"

"Be careful." Felix sighed unhappily. "We never wanted you to grow up like us, you know?"

"Then you shouldn't have been so much fun." Josh winked and left the study, leaving Felix wishing for a drink.

But he'd been drinking for the past two weeks, and looking at Danny sitting next to him at the breakfast table, trying so hard to keep his distance, had warned Felix he'd better be on his toes.

He could lose his company; he could lose his place in society. But that didn't bother him because those things had felt like the biggest scam of all in the end. But he couldn't lose Danny—not again. He'd play this game, but he had to remember what was at stake.

It wasn't revenge on Marnie Courtland, although he had to admit that was a bonus.

BY THE time he emerged from the study, the house had mostly cleared out. Julia was sitting at a corner of the clean table, having an in-depth conversation with Phyllis. Felix wouldn't have interrupted, but Julia saw him and gestured him over.

"Where's Danny?" he asked, and to her credit, she didn't roll her eyes at his transparency.

"He left with Josh and Grace to show them around his building and get his things." She gave a thoughtful tilt to her head. "I think he needed his space."

Felix nodded. "I would imagine."

"Sit down," she said, patting the chair next to her. "We're trying to decide how best to dig for information."

Felix sat. "Well, the housekeeper thing was inspired, Phyllis. Too bad we can't smuggle one of the others in as help."

Julia cocked her head and batted her eyelashes. "Actually, darling, Marnie is throwing a dinner party in the next couple of days. I would imagine she'll need a little extra help."

Felix's eyebrows hit his hairline so hard it probably receded. "She's what?"

"She is a shameless whore," Phyllis said without remorse. "She's throwing a dinner party. I didn't give Julia the invite when I first got it because…." She grimaced.

"Because you didn't want me to break anything," Julia said, her social smile grafted onto her face. Felix had learned that smile within their first month together. It meant her dentist was going to have to fill in cracks in her molars again. He took her hand and massaged the palm, waiting until the smile faded and the scowl she'd always wanted to wear had taken its place. They had never been lovers, but they had been friends living in the same house, and particularly in the last ten years, they had both been lonely. Sex they would never have, but the physical closeness that helped all human beings find some measure of peace was something they'd developed over the years.

"What would you have broken, dearest?" he asked her lightly.

"One of my father's humanitarian awards," she replied promptly. Then she smiled—a real smile, but feral and catlike and fierce. "If there were any left."

Felix kissed her knuckles. "That's my darling. Why would she have sent you an invitation anyway?"

"Because she thinks you two despise each other," Phyllis supplied promptly, and Felix stared at her in surprise.

"I know the divorce was public, but we've never shown any animosity. I don't understand why she'd think that. We've shared the same address for the past eight years!"

Phyllis nodded. "What I've gotten from the other housekeepers is that not everybody buys the happy divorce thing, particularly after Marnie did her cry-wolf bit on national television. The gossip is—and it's getting stronger—that you two hate each other's guts, and you're sticking it out in the mansion to keep control of the company."

Felix couldn't help it. He was catching flies. "But... but, Julia! You and I have been running the place since Hiram kicked off, God rot his soul."

"I know." She pecked him on the cheek. "And we've done a wonderful job, if I say so myself. But sometimes people want to believe the worst. And you've never been public with your affairs—nor have I—so the assumption is we're living here bitter, celibate, and seething with acrimony."

Felix couldn't help it; he was both appalled and fascinated. "That's... that's the most marvelous thing I've ever heard!"

"I know, right?" Julia laughed. "It's like an eight-year con we didn't mean to pull off!" She sobered. "But now it can get us something. Marnie invited me, probably because she thinks we're sisters and I'm going to spill some tea."

"She's going to milk you as a source," Felix said in wonder.

"Oh yes. And Phyllis and I were just thinking…. What would be the best story we could sell her that she could use to hang herself with?"

Felix raised his hand to tug on his ear and then dropped it. It was a habit he had from his teenaged years—one of the first things Danny had broken him of when they went on the grift, and one of the first things to return when Danny had left.

"I have an idea," he said, pondering slowly. "But you'd have to be all for it."

Julia and Phyllis had a brief meeting of gazes. "Does it involve Danny?" Julia asked after a moment.

"Yes," Felix said, meeting her eyes.

Julia smiled happily. "It's about time." She leaned her head on his shoulder like a little girl. "Can I still live in this house with you when it's all done? Can we still go on adventures together?"

He kissed the top of her head. "Of course," he said fondly. "I don't think Danny would want our lives any other way."

A COUPLE of hours later, Felix was working in his study, pulling up profiles about the higher levels of society for the crew. On his computer, he started color coding them.

Walt Chandler—Marnie's biggest fan. Also known to "audition" interns in his office, both male and female, because Me Too meant he wanted part of the exploitation action as well.

"Did he take any of his stuff?"

There was a pause that indicated Josh was looking around. "No. His suitcase was inside the door anyway. He hadn't even unpacked."

"Yeah. He just needed some air. I'll go get him."

"You'll go where? Dad, I don't even know where he went."

"I do," Felix said, but he wasn't telling Josh. It felt like a violation. "Don't worry, we'll be by for his things later."

"Dad, he could be—"

"Yeah, he could be, but he won't."

"But Dad—"

Felix sighed. "Josh, do you trust me?"

He didn't even take a breath. "Yeah. Course."

"Do you trust Danny?"

This time he did pause. But then Danny had been the one forced to come and go, forced to treat "home" like an Airbnb—great place to stay, but you had to make your time slots.

"Yeah."

"He wouldn't leave you, son. He didn't the first time. He won't now."

Josh blew out a breath. "I didn't even hear the door close."

"This is not your fault. It's not even Danny's."

"Yeah? Well, whose is it?"

"Mine."

Past

AT FIRST Felix thought Danny's attraction to the big tourist places was purely venal. The bigger the attraction, the more tourists. The more tourists, the more pockets to pick, the more scams, the more money. It hadn't been until their first day in Chicago together that Felix had figured it out.

They'd been walking in front of Buckingham Fountain, and Danny had tilted his head. "I know this," he'd said. "I've seen it on television. That old show…?"

Felix had named it, liking the innocent way Danny's eyes crinkled. They hadn't seen each other in three months. Felix and Julia had gotten engaged and dropped the baby bomb, plane tickets at the ready. They'd been in a car and on their way to the airport before Hiram had truly begun to rage. Danny had been there, hiding in the kitchen. He'd spirited Berto's mother out when the marble objets d'art had started hitting the wall.

Julia had a trust fund, activated when Felix put the ring on her finger, and they'd bought the house and were well settled in before Hiram caught up with them. By then all of his business partners had gotten their wedding announcements, and there was nothing he could do.

That had been Danny's idea, sending the announcements out, having the travel arrangements made, setting up housekeeping before the old man even had his feet under him.

But with Hiram's scrutiny, it had been months before they could see each other again, and when Hiram had gone off for a three-month sojourn in Hong Kong, Felix had written, sending him plane tickets and a meeting place. Julia had shown him the city while he'd chafed at not seeing Danny, and now it was his turn.

It hadn't been until Felix had seen him from afar, smiling at a child who was running in delighted circles around the famous landmark, that Felix felt nerves creep into his belly.

He'd gotten used to Danny's clever mind, his quick fingers, his cunning.

He'd forgotten the boy who had merely wanted revenge on an abusive boss, or the composed young man who had assessed Julia Dormer and had seen a frightened young woman instead of a spoiled heiress. He'd forgotten the boy who had picked his red scarf up off the cobblestones and ridden to his rescue on a stolen Vespa.

This Danny—the one who ignored the wallet sticking out of the harried young mother's purse for the billfold hidden in the tight fist of the perpetually angry businessman—didn't go to public landmarks just to steal.

He went there because he'd heard about them, and they were glamorous, and he enjoyed being a part of something larger than himself.

He used to take Felix to the Coliseum at sunset and say, "Look at that sky. I bet there were thieves in the crowds back in the day, do you think?"

Felix had actually learned about Rome in school— he'd been rather good at history—while Danny was staying home trying to take care of a mother who'd grown increasingly too ill to take care of him. "There were, and did you know the gladiators used to be on billboards? Like here? They advertised things like hair oil!"

Danny's laughter rang through his bones, and then, standing at the Buckingham Fountain that spring day long ago, seeing Danny—in jeans and a T-shirt—gnaw on his thumb as he waited for Felix to show, Felix had his first inkling of how very vulnerable Danny "Lightfingers" really was.

Unfortunately it hadn't been enough to prepare them for the next twenty years. But on that day, they'd had all the optimism, all the hope, that their little deception would allow Julia some freedom and Felix and Danny all the scratch they'd ever need to game their way through life.

Present

TODAY, FELIX took a moment approaching the glittering water and iconic copper metalwork to appreciate another rare glimpse of Danny Mitchell unguarded.

He was still wearing Felix's sweats under his topcoat, and Felix's heart lurched. He must have felt trapped indeed. He stood, arms crossed, surveying the Chicago skyline over the rainbow arcs of the fountain, gnawing on his thumbnail. The wind was coming fierce off the lake, as it did in late March, and Danny didn't have a hat or gloves—just that absurdly rich coat and the dress shoes he'd worn when he'd broken into the house. Felix wanted to rush up and rescue him, gather him in his arms and wrap him in a cashmere blanket, take him to his bed and never let him go.

But Danny wasn't that man—hadn't been that boy—and if Felix wanted him to stay, he had to respect Danny's space.

Instead he strode up to Danny with purpose, allowing his loafers to scuff on the rose-colored paving stones around the fountain, letting Danny know he was there.

Danny looked at him sideways as he drew near, and grunted, but he continued gnawing on that already bloody thumbnail.

"Pretty day," Felix said, keeping his voice neutral.

"Very." Danny scanned the horizon. "I love this view."

"Well, you know Chicago. No view is a—"

"—bad view." Danny let out a breath that should have been laughter. "I remember."

"Josh was worried about you."

Danny grimaced. "I didn't mean to make him worry. You know that, Fox. I just…."

Felix heard him swallow and gently tugged at the hand near his mouth. Danny was reluctant at first, until Felix took his knuckles to his lips and brushed a kiss against them.

"You got scared," he whispered.

"I didn't realize we'd trained him so well," Danny said, apology in his voice. "Did you see that? He has his own crew!"

"I don't think that's what he planned for it to be," Felix said. "I mean, we tried to send him away to school—he's not bad at computers, really—but he wanted to go to Columbia, because dramatic arts. And look who he hooked up with."

"Criminals," Danny said. "Just like his parents."

"Well, we're criminals, but we're not bad people really." Felix tried his most winning smile, and he managed to win a smirk from Danny before he looked away.

It felt like a badge of honor.

"I… I thought by going away, by letting you and Julia raise him normally, we could maybe nip that in the bud, you know?"

Felix snorted. "After he'd spent his first ten years idolizing his Uncle Danny, are you kidding me?

Remember that private collector in France? The one with the stolen Renoir?"

Danny snorted. "Pig. Son of a pig. He was keeping it in his *wine cellar*, Felix. We were doing the art world a favor. You know that."

"I do." Danny had always known his art. Like the big tourist attractions, to Danny a good piece of art was a piece of history. A thing larger than himself.

Back in the day, Felix had agreed with him, but maybe those sorts of ideals were for young men. Now, pushing forty, Danny loomed larger than the urgency of freeing a Renoir from a wine cellar.

"So what about it? The Renoir, I mean?" Danny glanced at him, and Felix appreciated the way his eyes lingered on Felix's profile. All of that vanity about moisturizer, and it all came down to a warm glance on a cold spring day.

"So the year after you left, when we were trying to cheer Josh up because his Uncle Danny had left so suddenly and we weren't sure when you'd be back, we took him to the Art Institute of Chicago. And we rounded a corner of the impressionist display, and boom! There's our Renoir. The one you literally dug a tunnel into a wine cellar to steal back and donate."

Danny rubbed the back of his neck. "We scammed that man out of a lot of money," he said.

"I remember."

"And while he was writing you the check—"

"You stole the painting. I was there, Lightfingers. You showed up at the hotel looking like you'd swum half the Seine, with a waterproof tube strapped to your back, telling us all that we'd never seen you."

"We caught up again in Spain that year," Danny said mildly.

"And spent the next two months on the beach. I was *there*, Danny. I remember. But you're not hearing the story."

Danny swallowed. "The part where I broke our son's heart by trying to drink myself to death in Monaco? Yeah, that's a fun story. Let's hear that one."

"We missed you," Felix said, voice raw. With his free hand, he rubbed the sandpapered empty space Danny had left when he'd taken off. "But you kept sending Josh postcards. Do you remember?"

Danny shrugged. "I... I mean, of course I do because I kept visiting the PO Box. But...." He let out a breath. "So much about that time was hazy. I really was sort of hoping to die of cirrhosis in a windmill, like Mimi in *La Boheme*. Yes. I... it's a good thing I wasn't doing anything besides the damned mobster, or I would have led the authorities right to you."

Felix's heart clenched. "Those postcards became our world." Oh, they had. Josh had kept them—there'd been nearly fifty over the next ten years. Josh would write back, every time, the special PO Box in Chicago giving them all hope. He still had a connection to their city, to *them*. About a year after the breakup, Danny started showing up at school performances and birthday parties. Felix and Julia never saw him, but Josh did. Danny's greatest grift was once again sneaking in and out to see his family.

"I.... Does this story have a point?" Danny asked, voice breaking a little.

"The point is, you were right. We ran into that Renoir, and Josh started to cry right there in the museum. And as Julia held him, calming him down, Josh started to hiccup. He was trying so hard to say something. It took us forever to sort it out, but what he was saying was that your heart lived in that painting. Your heart lived in every job you'd done. He knew you were coming back to see him because your heart was there for everybody to see."

"Aw, Felix, fuck you. Like this isn't hard enough already."

Danny made to wipe his face on the shoulder of his once immaculate topcoat, but Felix beat him to it with a handkerchief pulled out of his coat pocket with his free hand—a nicety he'd learned from Danny, who had probably learned it from television, but it didn't erase the fact that Danny's heart made him more of a gentleman than Felix's family wealth had ever made Felix. Still keeping their fingers twined, he turned to face the man he'd never stopped loving and carefully swiped under his red-rimmed eyes, then folded the handkerchief over his nose and let him blow.

"Your heart has always been there for us to see, sweetheart," Felix said, his voice so low not even the fierce Chicago wind could blow it anywhere. "And so is Josh's. So's his crew. They're good kids—and probably fantastic thieves—but they need you." Felix swallowed, forced into honesty way too early in the game. "*I* need you. Come home, Danny."

"Just for the—"

"No. I mean, fine, if that's what you want to tell yourself now. But come home. Let's run this game, let's finish this. Let me prove to you that this *is* your home. It will be forever. You'll never have to run a game or a grift to be with your family again." His mouth twitched. "Unless you're trying to sneak into a hotel room with a stolen painting on your back. That might be an exception."

Danny shook his head, as if he was trying to break out of Felix's spell, and Felix captured his chin between gentle fingers.

"I can't do this," Danny said finally, squeezing his eyes shut. "It almost killed me—"

"Because I thought you were invincible. I never saw that we didn't have to worry about the police or Interpol. I was killing you slowly the entire time by making you be a secret, when family was the only thing of value you ever wanted." A tear tracked its way down Danny's cheek, and Felix swiped at it with his thumb. "Julia and I are officially divorced now. There's no scary father-in-law in the picture. We can't lose custody of Josh. We can't even keep him from doing his laundry at our house on the weekend." Danny's mouth twisted, and more tears slipped by. "My reputation is already crap, and if that means I can get you back, good riddance! You're not coming back to the same home. The same people are there—and they love you more than ever—but there's no reason to hide anymore. We don't have to grift to keep you in my bed. There's no scam in the two of us being together. There's just the two of us together, and the people we love around us all the time."

Danny's shoulders were shaking, and Felix let go of his chin and kissed his forehead, drawing him in against his chest.

"I can't," Danny whispered. "I can't do this again, Fox. I can't… I can't…."

"You don't have to," Felix murmured in his ear. "You don't have to leave. Ever again."

Danny didn't answer. Felix just held him, warm and shaking in the circle of his arms, until the resistance trembled out of him and he was left pliant and quiet and ready to come home.

The Plan

FELIX STOPPED by Danny's apartment building for his suitcase, dragging Danny upstairs with him so he could reassure Josh with his presence.

"How's it going?" Danny asked, trying to pretend to be a grown-up and not the lost child who had broken down at the fountain.

"Great." Josh all but rubbed his hands together like a cartoon villain before gesturing to the laptop setup with six screens of video feed. "We've got sound and picture in every room."

"The bathroom?" Danny asked, hating the ethics of that.

Felix shook his head and let out a breath. "Nothing. Nothing but that you're very self-sufficient, and it irritates me. I wouldn't be nearly so good on my own."

Danny rolled his eyes. "Please. Have you seen your house? I've seen your house. It's stunning. You must have remodeled twice in the last ten years. The furniture is new; even the art is new." There had been a cityscape of Chicago by the river, done in stained-glass colors, on the back wall of the living room. If it hadn't been six feet tall and ten feet wide, he would have stolen it on principle.

"We rotate it in from the smaller collections," Felix said. "New local artists. We show it at our house, hold a few meetings there, let people know the art is for sale, and return it to the galleries to be sold."

"It's almost like a scam," Danny said with admiration as he hopped into the SUV. Felix had always been clever like that. He could do legal things for money that made Danny's skill at thievery look like small potatoes. "Except straight. It's… it's…."

"Good business," Felix said, sounding like his temper was short. "In ten years, you must have heard me say good business was a lot like grifting, but good business—"

"Gets you the better lawyers," Danny supplied dryly. Yes, he and Felix had learned a lot about being rich for that ten years, and most of it involved how very little held the two worlds apart.

"And apparently the interior decorators," Felix muttered, backing out of the space and pulling forward into the garage.

"I'm sorry?"

"You should be. Danny, that apartment looked like a grifter lived there!"

"Well…."

"Except you're too good to let your place look like that. No art on the walls, no pictures. It was… a rental property!" Felix pulled one hand off the wheel and flailed.

"Well, yes, Felix, I am a renter. And I do let the apartment sit vacant when I'm not there."

"It wasn't personal," Felix told him, sounding hostile, and Danny tried to think. The apartment had a great window view of the city, which was primarily why Danny had rented it. But the apartment itself was pretty utilitarian. The furniture was black leather, the tile was white. He'd chosen an area rug in varying shades of red because the high contrast gave visual interest without a lot of clutter.

In the past ten years, he hadn't been a fan of clutter.

"Why would it be?" Danny asked, hurt.

"Where do you live?"

Danny opened his mouth to say "Tuscany!" or "Dublin!" or "Prague!" because he had apartments there too (well, in Tuscany it was a villa, but it was the same idea), but then he closed it again, because all of them were like this huge sterile apartment in Chicago.

He'd called ahead to have the housecleaning service purchase new linens and make the bed. He had no idea what color anything was.

"You know where I live," he said sullenly. "You just shoved my house in the back of your car."

"Remember the garret?" Felix asked, because apparently his goal was to make Danny feel as naked as possible today.

"No," he lied, and Felix ignored him, as he should have.

"Art books everywhere. You once robbed a librarian—left her the cash and the credit cards but stole her goddamned art books. Weighed a fucking ton. Where are your goddamned art books?"

"Dublin!" Danny shot back. Then he sighed because he knew where this was going. "The tchotchkes are in Tuscany. The picture albums are in a safe deposit box in Prague." He hadn't wanted anybody to be able to trace Danny Lightfingers back to Danny Mitchell, Felix Salinger's dirty little secret. "I kept you safe, Felix."

"Fuck my safety, Danny." Felix's voice was broken, and the jagged edges opened all the fissures from the bad patch-up job Danny had done on his own heart ten years before. "I thought you'd at least had a life these last ten years. God, even if you had another lover, someone who mattered. I thought you'd at least had someone who mattered."

"I did," Danny rasped. "They were all safe here in Chicago." He let out a sigh. "Until some twat-shaped virtue signal ripped a hole in their lives." He'd been impressed by Molly's invective. He was stealing that one.

Felix shook his head, apparently not impressed. "I…. God, I thought if you were staying away for so long, you were at *least* staying away for *something*."

"I was," Danny said crossly. "I was staying away from your pity. And if you don't stop bleeding it all over the place now, I'll go back to my damned apartment and hole up in my room while your son and his friends save your ass."

"*Our* son," Felix snarled. "He's our son, my ass is just fine, and you're coming home with me."

"You didn't used to be this irritating," Danny told him, crossing his arms. "Or this stupid."

"I *should* have been this irritating," Felix retorted. "If I had been this irritating—maybe insisted on a few things, like, say, divorcing Julia and scamming Old Man Dormer out of his fortune instead of waiting for him to die—you might not have left us and we might not have this ten-year hole in our lives." His voice rose at the end, which it had only done once in their entire relationship, on that last horrible day, and Danny gaped at him.

Felix returned his wide-eyed surprise with a scowl. "And what am I stupid about?" he continued after a moment, his voice a little more in control.

"Your ass is better than fine. It's fantastic. Do you, like, live on the StairMaster or something?"

"Yes." And that sounded like it pissed Felix off too. "I actually spend way more time on exercise equipment than I should because I don't have a lover, and I need to work off that energy somehow."

"You…?" Danny couldn't quite say this without sounding interested. "You, uh, don't have a lover?"

Felix rolled his eyes but kept his focus on the late-afternoon weekend traffic. "I tried," he admitted. "The years after you left, I discreetly fucked as many things as possible."

"I fucked many things too," Danny said softly.

"Wasn't the same."

Danny swallowed. "I… no. It wasn't. How were we supposed to know we'd meet our one perfect person learning how to pick pockets by the Coliseum?"

"I should have spent ten years convincing you," Felix said savagely.

"I was the one too drunk to listen."

Felix growled. "I'm done and bored with this argument for the moment. In fact, all I can really concentrate

Danny let out a snort. "Nor should it be. Fox, you're missing the point. She's *on the air*, and she just told anyone with eyes that she's sleeping with the subject of her interview. Do we have any other footage where she's interviewing a lover or a hookup?"

"Yeah." Felix grunted and two-finger typed with amazing speed—but not hacker speed.

"Wow, Grandpa, did they teach you to type like that when the machines were called typewriters and not keyboards?"

"I don't know, Methuselah, is it possible to type by squeezing your ass muscles? Because we could arrange that."

Julia made a contented sound. "Oh, I've missed this. Oh! Talia Clark? Marnie managed to sleep with Talia Clark? That's a shame."

Talia sat like the queen she was, her athlete's body ramrod straight, her muscles revealed by an off-the-shoulder confection of light blue, which shone with lovely radiance against her dark bronze skin. She'd come to the station to be interviewed more than once, and Felix and Julia had fallen a little in love. They still lunched whenever she was in town, and she got them tickets to tennis events other people had to kill to attend.

"Yeah," Felix muttered, starting the clip. "I told my assistant to maybe warn Talia that piranhas don't make good bed partners, but... well, see for yourself."

Marnie was polite. But then, so are glaciers. And Talia, who had started out the interview with a sweet, sort of coltish enthusiasm, managed to trip over her own tongue about twelve times before the interview was over, while Marnie Courtland looked on in sympathy.

"Wow," Danny murmured.

"Yeah." Felix let out a sigh. "That was a shame. Talia went on to lose her next tournament in a crushing first-round defeat. Marnie said, and I quote, 'It's so sad that not all performers can stand the test of time.'"

Danny felt his eyes round in horror. "On the air?"

Felix nodded. "Oh yes."

"Do you think Talia would kill her for us?" Julia asked, also horrified. "I think she's earned first dibs."

"More importantly…." Danny tapped his lower lip. "Fox, I have a plan."

"Of course you do," Felix said, smiling.

"That young man there with the blue border, what's his name?"

"Torrance Grayson," Felix said in surprise. "Why?"

"You think he got an invite to this shindig?"

"Oh yes. His YouTube numbers are really impressive. He's one of the best reporters I've ever seen. Losing him at our station was a huge loss."

"But you like him. Why?"

"Because he left his show the same day she came screaming out of my office. As in, he heard her blubbering, looked at me—and I was still gaping at her in horror—and turned to his producer and said, 'I'm out.' And he walked away from a live taping."

Danny grinned. "So she's running low on contacts, and she wants the world to think she's progressive, and he's on her list. Do you think you could get this Torrance person to bring a date of your choosing?"

Felix wasn't slow. "Talia?"

Danny nodded. "Mm-hmm. And Julia needs to bring someone hot too. Chuck would clean up nicely."

"Good Luck Chuck?" Julia asked in horror. "Are you deranged?"

Danny laughed. God, he'd missed Felix and he'd missed Josh, but he'd missed Julia too. He grabbed her hand as she flailed it in the air and kissed the knuckles, loving the way she grinned back at him. Some women got better and better as they grew older, until they simply glowed, luminescent, like goddesses before they passed. He was pretty sure Julia Dormer, whether she ever found a forever lover or not, would be one such woman.

"My darling, you would be showing up with a young man—"

"A *much* younger man," she protested. "A much younger *gay* man!"

"Nobody knows that," Danny said with a laugh. "And I bet our young Charles can make you look like an adored cougar. He's got that Southern charm down to his toes, yes?"

"He is very sweet," Julia conceded, "but why am I going to Marnie's party with him?"

"Well, it will put her in quite a pickle, won't it? Seduce Torrance, the young reporter she wants very badly to work for her, to get him away from Talia, the woman she publicly rejected, or seduce Chuck, a much younger man, away from a frenemy—you. What to do? What to do?"

"Well, if nothing else," Felix murmured thoughtfully, "we can see what her priorities are and start searching for more skeletons in her closet."

"Exactly," Danny said, the shivers of discovery dancing up his spine. "Her interviews are methodical and agenda driven. She never allows herself to be surprised. But she's floundering now. Her gambit with you put her in a position where she needs to keep her fame ball rolling. So we need to see what we can sell her, what she will grab for. Will she choose Torrance—and her career—at the risk of driving Talia to reveal what a horrible person she is, or will she choose Chuck, because apparently she likes to play with her food."

Felix frowned. "We would need to let Talia and Torrance in on it."

"Can they be trusted?" Danny asked.

"Mm… Talia was really hurt." Felix gave him an apologetic look. "I'd feel as though we were just playing with her feelings again."

Ah, of course. Danny was good at going for the kill, but Felix was good at remembering there was always collateral damage. "Well, if Torrance can be trusted, let's send him. But let's ask Talia, be completely on the level. If she doesn't want any part of it, we can send Molly in. She'd look stunning, and it will be using both types of bait."

"I like how you're not assuming she'll go after me," Julia said archly.

Danny gnawed on his thumbnail. "You're too classy, darling, and too bright. She's pretending to like you to have an ally against Felix, but she's too smart to think that's a real friendship there. Torrance, Talia—they're young and impressionable. Torrance, heaven love him because it was a beautiful gesture, would have been better served to have stayed on set and undermined her until she fell apart. This will give him a chance to get back in and do that, but it will also give us a chance to see what else we can get her on."

"When is Phyllis going shopping?" Felix asked. He caught Danny's eye and explained, "She knows where Marnie's maid shops."

"Ooh, nice," Danny agreed.

"Tomorrow morning."

Felix nodded. "Then I have some phone calls to make."

"Join us for dinner," Julia said, and Danny recognized that tone. It wasn't a question.

"I'll be less than an hour," Felix told her. "Torrance and Talia, I'll ask. If we can get the maid to let Molly and Hunter in as waiters, we could cover that party and walk away with a gold mine of information."

"Danny, you come talk to me," Julia invited, "and then Felix can call Josh and talk about logistics. And Chuck and I should plan our wardrobe, yes?"

"Yes, ma'am," Danny said, knowing he was being manipulated. Julia had learned to do it so gracefully when she was escaping her father's iron fist. He was not surprised when she sat him up at the kitchen counter and poured him an orange juice and seltzer water as she started a simple dinner of grilled chicken and vegetables. He glanced around the kitchen with the modern charcoal-colored tile and black countertops and grimaced. There were bright red accents—the teapot, the color of the spoon and whisk handles, the frames around the food-themed pictures—but otherwise it felt very familiar.

"What?" Julia asked in mid julienne. "What's that look?"

"My apartment is decorated the same way, and Felix had a conniption."

She regarded him from under long naturally-blond lashes. "Well, the kitchen is a very utilitarian space," she said. "We cook here. We clean. I'm not a chef, and Phyllis turns dinner parties over to someone who can do the fancy stuff. The love in this house is at the dining room table, not in the kitchen."

Danny gave a brief smile, remembering those early days when they'd all eaten hot dogs and mac and cheese because that's what they were feeding Josh. Three adults who shouldn't have had a blessed thing in common coming together to be a family for one precocious little boy who thought all families were just like his.

"True," he said.

"So why was Felix upset?"

Danny shook his head. "Didn't like the decorating."

Julia met his eyes, not fooled at all. "Didn't like that you'd been alone all this time is more like it."

Danny turned away. "You know, last night was wonderful— no third degree, no pity, just 'Oh, Danny, we're so glad to see you!' Can we go back to that?"

"Can you promise to stay?" she asked pointedly.

"He doesn't need me," he said, trying to be gentle.

Julia Dormer, heiress, a woman who could have given Grace Kelly lessons in poise, threw a carrot at his head.

"Julia!" He stared at her, genuinely shocked.

"Nobody lies to me when I'm trying to make a healthy goddamned dinner," she said fiercely.

"Oh, fine," Danny conceded. "He needs me to help with the game, but he doesn't—"

She did it again, and this one tagged him in the cheek. "Julia, dammit!" She was running out of carrots. "What's next, a raw chicken breast?"

"No, idiot, the frying pan. I will brain you with a frying pan if you keep saying stupid things."

Danny rubbed the spot where the carrot had struck, and then, because he was a civilized human being, he went and fetched the two carrots from the dining room rug.

"Julia, you know it's—wait!"

She actually picked up the frying pan. "I told you!"

"Give me one reason it's not true that doesn't involve violence!"

She set the frying pan down with a clatter. "Danny, do you see all the middle-aged gay men crawling around my mansion? We've got eight bedrooms and six bath, two dens, a pool, a pool house, and a big bar and an extra den with a big-assed television set downstairs for soccer games and the like, and servants' quarters no servant has ever used. But you know that because half of it is still decorated just for you. Have you seen one extraneous gay man Felix's age around here since last night?"

"Only one," Danny said, and then ducked as she hefted the frying pan again. "No, seriously. No! I get it! He hasn't had any lovers lately. He said he played the field after the divorce."

She snorted. "He tried. Felix has no game. He's never had any. But yes, he woke up in a couple of strange beds. And then he'd come crawling back home, and we'd have breakfast together, and he'd look miserable, and we'd go to the movies or something. We were happier than a lot of married people I know. We still are. But he hasn't done that in quite some time." Her expression softened. "Did you think he was kidding about being there at your supposedly secret post office waiting for you this summer?"

Danny swallowed. "I thought it was a nice story."

She met his eyes and shook her head. "Josh could meet you because he and Felix had already done the groundwork for how to get in. Josh stole his father's con, and the fact that Felix hasn't once taken him to task for it should tell you exactly what it meant to him that you were here last night."

He let out a breath and raked his hands through his hair. "Julia, we'll get closure. That's all I can promise."

"You're still wearing his sweats from this morning," she said deliberately. Danny looked down at himself in surprise, and then his cheeks heated.

"They're very, uh, worn."

"Yes. They're one of the oldest things in his drawer. I suspect you had to dig quite a bit for those."

"I didn't want to wear his new stuff. That would be rude."

One corner of her full mouth lifted, as though she was giving him points for trying. "Feel free to change before dinner," she said. "But you should know, Phyllis took that luggage to Felix's room."

Danny glared at her flatly. "Why on earth would she do that?" he asked, not sure if his heart could take what the next few weeks were going to do to him.

"Because... closure my ass, Danny. One way or another, you are going to end up in his bed, even if I have to have those very muscular young men dump you there. But I don't think it will be necessary."

"Not tonight," he said gruffly. "Tonight I need my space."

She cocked her head. "Move your stuff. I dare you. You can even make your phone calls. Use it as a pretext to go back to the guest bedroom. That's fine. Just don't be surprised if this evening ends up very differently."

He closed his eyes. "Felix doesn't get to feel me up and feel sorry for me—"

This time it *was* the frying pan, and he barely ducked.

"*Jesus Christ*—"

"Go make your calls," she said thickly. "Go move your stuff. If you're going to continue to be stupid, I'm done talking with you. For now, anyway." She passed her hand under her eyes, and it hit him. She felt responsible for this—for the breakup, for everything.

"Honey, this wasn't your fault," he said gently, fetching the frying pan from the carpet, grateful she hadn't added oil to it or started cooking yet.

"Do stop talking," she begged him, her face blotchy. "Just go make your calls and go. But don't pretend—don't ever pretend—that you didn't break all our hearts when you left. Felix doesn't want you back out of pity, Danny. He wants you back because you left a hole in his heart bigger than any mansion or take or haul. You left it in all of us, and we're tired of bleeding. Come back and be a family again, you irritating bastard. Don't just tease us with 'here for a job.' Felix deserves more."

"He always has," Danny said, his own heart doing a fair job of dripping on the carpet. "I'll go change so he can get his sweats back."

"Whatever." Her voice was still thick and full of sadness, and he didn't know what to do about that.

Or he did know what to do, but he wasn't sure if he should do it. Or if he even had the strength.

Chess on Two Fronts

DANNY HAD changed into slacks and a sweater for dinner. It was a classic look, and Felix even approved of the soft blue-green cashmere of the sweater.

But he wished Danny had stayed in his sweats instead.

Still, the sight of Danny, dressed in clothes that fit his lean frame, with his hair water combed and smelling faintly of shower soap and aftershave, was pretty appealing.

Felix could smell him, bury his nose in his neck and breathe him in all night.

They mostly plotted, because that was the language they spoke best. Danny talked about the different angles they could take: getting Marnie to show bad behavior in public, a dramatic reveal, having her vices—whatever they were—catch up with her.

"But what if she doesn't have any vices?" Felix asked seriously. "This could be her big gambit. Some people only do the bad thing once, and that's all they need."

Danny shook his head and wiped a stray bit of pasta sauce from the corner of his mouth. "No, she would have been readier than this. Tomorrow you get on the phone and see which business contacts she's tried to exploit. I need to take a look at her financials, and you already know who's backing her. Let's see what their dirty little secrets are." He smiled at Julia. "This is really wonderful," he said, with the air of someone who was trying to make amends.

Julia gave him a steely-eyed look. "Good. I may need to replace my sauté pan."

"Not a frying pan?"

"No. Ten years and you still haven't learned the difference?" Julia gave the sort of smile that always made Felix think her teeth should have been pointier. "Pity."

In what looked like desperation, Danny turned back to Felix. "Anyway, you sent me plenty of information to study. We've got some late nights ahead of us."

"You must be tired," Felix said instead. "Are you sure you wouldn't like to relax down here with us a bit? We have the big screen downstairs."

"Oh! I've got an adapter. We can turn it into a command center to meet with the kids. Fantastic! That's what we can do tonight before we crash." Danny smiled with forced determination, and Julia gave Felix a kick under the table.

"Sure," Felix muttered. "That'll be a laugh riot. Maybe we should just wait for Josh and Stirling. What would take us hours should take them about five minutes."

Danny grimaced. "Dammit," he muttered under his breath. "I'll be okay up in my room."

Another kick, this one square on his shin, and Felix glared at Julia. "I'm trying!" he mouthed, and she glared back at Danny in a look he interpreted as "Try harder!" Well, he'd worked hard for twenty years to be a captain of industry, a man who wouldn't take no for an answer. It was time to use that skill.

"You've got a desk up there," Felix said, seizing on this, "and an extra chair. Linger for dessert and I'll join you for some brainstorming."

Danny swallowed audibly, and Felix wanted to do a fist pump. *Check and mate, you skinny self-sufficient bastard. Try to avoid private time with Felix, why don't you!*

"Sure," Danny said, his head drooping. "That sounds great."

Julia kicked him again, but Felix was way ahead of her. He placed his hand on the back of Danny's neck and rubbed. "We'll be fine," he said softly. "I only bite on request. And in spite of what you've seen about me on the news, I really don't scream abuse at people unless that's a thing we're doing together."

Danny gave him a small smile. "I know, Fox. Sorry. I don't mean to be so skittish. I am honestly not used to company."

"Well, get used to it. There's a reason we both still live here, you know."

Danny nodded and studied the painting on the other side of the dining room. The room itself was comfortable—a long table, of course, because Felix and Julia still entertained—but the colors were warm: nut browns and pale creams with navy and olive accents. A few traces of mauve showed Julia's touch, but here and in the downstairs entertainment room were the places where they spent the most time, particularly if Josh was in the house with them.

"No red," Danny said, flashing a small smile.

"His red is all downstairs," Julia said, grinning wickedly. "Particularly during basketball season!"

Danny's laugh eased all the iron-tight muscles in Felix's back and neck. Neither of them had been sports enthusiasts before moving to Chicago, but between basketball, football, baseball, and hockey, they'd found themselves getting swept up like pretty much the rest of the citizenry.

"As long as there's some red there for the Cubbies," Danny said.

"You still follow them?" Felix asked hungrily.

Danny nodded and rubbed his chest, unconsciously leaning into the hand Felix had left on the back of his neck. "When I missed… Chicago the most, listening to a game would bring me right back."

"The season starts in a couple of weeks," Felix told him, smiling. "We'll have to see some games."

Danny's face went blank, and Felix's heart stopped beating. Oh no. He could see the whole speech in that expression. Well, bullshit. Felix wouldn't let him leave.

Felix dropped his hand and pretended great interest in Julia's chicken alfredo. "You don't have to look like I kicked your puppy, Danny. If you're not here when they start playing again, that's completely your choice."

Danny grunted and tried to change the subject. "What's for dessert, Julia love?"

"Pie," she said ruthlessly. "Cherry-amaretto. Just extract. Not half a bottle like Phyllis used to use."

Danny's look of betrayal was almost comical. "Vanilla ice cream?"

"Of course," Julia said. "Since Felix isn't saying it, I will. We're going to make it damned hard for you to leave, so you might as well get used to it. Now help me clear the table."

HE RELAXED a little over dessert and talked about his flat in Dublin above an art gallery, and how the apartment in Prague was walking distance from three cathedrals. He'd read every book about the cathedrals, knew every painting, and for a giddy half hour, Felix hung on to his every word about artistic periods and brush strokes and landmark artists and gold filigree work. Just like when they were kids, much of it washed over his head, but listening to Danny had been the whole point then too.

The things that motivated him stirred the passion in Felix's belly, and that hadn't changed one bit.

Finally they moved upstairs into the guest room, and Felix noted that Danny had unpacked—hung his clothes and probably put his underthings in the drawers. This was… promising.

Made it harder to take off in the middle of the night when you had to throw your skivvies in the suitcase, right?

Danny gestured toward the desk that sat to the side of the bed. He'd already set his laptop up there—not your standard piece of equipment.

"Oh my," Felix said, looking at the sleek black carbonite case. "Is that even legal?"

"No," Danny said, grimacing. "It's not cheap either. Once a month I have to take it in to some guy in

Prague who takes it apart and juggles it and scrubs all
the innards out with bleach or whatever, but it's clean.
Nobody can trace my IP address, and if someone tries,
I've got an alarm and a kill switch that will shut down
the signal. Probably not up to Stirling's standards, but
it will work for a bit of research."

"Mm." Felix brandished the Apple he'd snagged
from his desk. "This is your basic laptop. You can buy
it in most of the stores on the planet. There's some porn
there, but so far nobody's come knocking at my door."

Danny's lips twitched. "Now that's a bloody
shame. But if the porn is good enough, why would you
need another hand?"

"My thoughts exactly," Felix said, grinning.

They settled then, on opposite sides of the desk,
Felix looking up business contacts for the people he'd
framed in red and sending the info—and the employ-
ment records—to Danny, who scanned them with that
ferocious intensity he sometimes showed.

For a brief time, Felix lost himself in the rhythm
of the work. Danny would occasionally ask a clarify-
ing question, and Felix would answer briefly, and then
there would be silence. It was comfortable enough that
Danny was on his third yawn before Felix noticed and
called a halt.

"C'mon, Danny. Let's hit the hay."

Danny muffled another yawn behind his hand.
"No, seriously, if you want to go to bed you can—"
Yawn. "—go ahead and—" Yawn. "—go!"

Felix laughed softly, and he realized that if he was
going to take charge, this was the time and place to do
it. He shut his laptop but left it where it was, then stood
and stretched. Danny kept reading until Felix walked

around to the back of his chair and leaned over his shoulder, gently snapping the laptop closed.

"Felix—"

Felix nuzzled him behind the ear. "Come to bed, Danny."

"We're not—"

Felix's body throbbed in a sudden attack of want, but he knew Danny was probably exhausted.

Besides that, sex right now would only make Danny more skittish.

"Come to bed," Felix murmured again. "Let me hold you. You felt so good in my arms last night. Don't tell me we can't do that again."

He kissed the side of Danny's neck, pleased when Danny tilted his head sideways and gave him better access.

"I shouldn't have done that last night," Danny mumbled, and Felix slid his hands down the front of Danny's shoulders.

"I'm so glad you did." Felix nibbled a little at the corner of his jaw. Oh, his face had gotten so much stronger over the years. Felix yearned to taste it all.

"We can't do this." Danny rubbed his cheek against Felix's. "We… we have to work the job."

Felix bit his earlobe very gently, pleased at the whine that came from his throat. "You're good, con man," he whispered, knowing the ears would do it for Danny. "But you're not good enough to convince me you don't need to be touched."

"I don't want to drink again," Danny mumbled, shocking him.

"What?" He pulled back.

"I…." Danny stood up brusquely, not looking at Felix and brushing his hands off on his pants with unnecessary force. "Look, you and I aren't good for each other, and I'm obviously weak. I just don't think I'm made for long-term emotional things, Fox. I don't think—" Felix crowded him until his back was against the wall, cupping his cheeks with hands he kept soft and professional. He only wanted the sweetest touch against Danny's skin.

"Danny," he whispered, touching his lips to his true love's forehead. "I'm going to go back to my room tonight. But when you lay down in bed, I want you to think about something. Think about waking up next to me and showering together and going downstairs for breakfast with Josh, saying hi to Julia, then going out into the city, hand in hand, unafraid of who sees us. Think about having friends at our table who know who we are. Think about living in the sunlight, public kisses on the cheek, the ability to say 'my lover' or 'my husband' whenever you want. Think about you and me together for as long as we both shall live, with everybody's knowledge and approval. Danny…."

The tears started at about the second sentence, and they continued, silent and unaddressed, until Danny wiped his face on his shoulder, eyes averted, his breaths coming shallow so he wouldn't sob.

"I didn't think you'd ever try to con me," he said, and the sob escaped at the last word. "Not me, Felix. Not me."

Felix's chest exploded into hurt like the words had been a blow, and his own eyes burned. "A con?" he choked. "You think this is a con?"

Danny pulled in a shuddering breath and nodded, taking a sideways step that Felix countered.

"You left and my *world* disintegrated," Felix growled. "I couldn't get out of bed for a month! You think this is a *con*? You know what? *Fuck* going to bed alone. *Fuck* giving you your space to think about us! There is no space. There is no con. There is only us. There will only ever be us again!"

And with that his mouth crashed against Danny's, the kiss salty and hot. Danny's lips parted under his reluctantly, but Felix was on a mission. He plundered, he ravished, until Danny's mouth parted willingly, until he curled his fingers in the collar of Felix's shirt and dragged him closer, gulping in their kisses like another man might gulp air.

Felix couldn't stop tasting him, wanting to devour him until Danny was living in his skin, never to be separate again. God! How could he have lived without this? Ten years? He'd been a prisoner of his own longing for ten goddamned years, and Danny held the key.

He tugged at Danny's shirt front until the buttons gave, and Danny held up his hands in front of his chest, his torso—not to hold Felix back, but to protect himself.

Felix pulled back, panting, frustrated, then realized what Danny was doing and swallowed hard.

"We should turn out the lights," Danny whispered, turning his head.

"No. Never. Do you think you have something you need to hide?"

"Just—"

Felix couldn't. Words. They were so good at words. Banter, flip comments, the game. But Danny wasn't listening to his words. Felix's actions, the things he actually did, seemed to be the only things Danny heard. He grabbed Danny's hands, like Danny had done to him that first time, and pinned them to the wall by his head.

Danny pulled weakly, but Felix bit his ear again. "I'm going to see all of you. You didn't think I did back then. Thought I wasn't seeing the good *and* the bad."

Danny went limp against the wall, his body sagging. "There wasn't much good to see," he said, and Felix licked down along his neck.

"All good." He nipped Danny's collarbone, thinking he needed more dinners with Julia, more desserts. He let go of Danny's hands, growling "Stay there" before he shoved Danny's shirt off his shoulders and palmed down the inside of Danny's arms and then along his rib cage.

The scars—bumpy keloid scars, smooth growths of skin over the damage—looked oddly regular.

"Letters?" Felix asked in surprise. "He tried to carve letters on you?"

"Cyrillic," Danny muttered, trying to pull his elbows in out of shame.

"Leave them," Felix all but begged. "What was he—"

"His name. Andre Kadjic. He wanted me to bleed out with his initials carved in my flesh."

Felix pulled back in horror—not at the damage, but the brutality. He covered Danny's body with his own, wrapping Danny's arms around his own back, then leaned his forehead against Danny's to build their bubble, the one with only the two of them, the one that had kept them safe for ten years before Felix had let it fall apart.

"A lover?" he asked, keeping his voice light.

Danny shrugged, looking ashamed. "I figured I was free, I guess. I really could sleep with the mark and leave him with nothing. He… wasn't kind when we were together. I tried to hurt him."

"Like you tried to hurt me," Felix murmured, hearing Danny's words as through a ten-year echo chamber.

Sure, Felix, let's fuck. It's the only thing you ever wanted me for.

Well it's the only thing you're good for now, you fucking alcoholic whore! Get out!

Gah! He hadn't meant it—but he'd been hurt, and angry. Watching Danny sink into the bottle had been hard—and Felix had been so unwilling to see his own part in Danny's misery, kicking him out, blaming him for the whole situation, had been so much easier than owning up.

The next morning, when he'd woken up and realized Danny was gone—every sock, every pair of underwear, every cufflink—it had hit him.

Danny believed that. After ten years of playing Felix's shadow lover, he'd started to drink himself to death because he'd been sure sex was the only appeal he'd ever had.

And Felix had let him feel that way because going against Julia's father had been so formidable, so hard. He and Julia could have divorced then. Hiram had still possessed pull, but Felix was clever. He could have found a way to get the board of directors on his side. He'd spent ten years building up the network—Hiram stood to lose so much more by throwing Felix out than he would have just letting Felix and Julia have an amicable divorce. But God, the old man had been so bitter. And he'd held Josh's custody over their heads like a sword of Damocles.

Julia would have helped. Watching Danny leave had been like watching a brother or an uncle—or a beloved friend—simply walk out of her life.

But Felix had been afraid then. Afraid because the station had been a wedding gift of sorts, and he hadn't felt like he'd earned it yet, in spite of all his work. Afraid for the employees he'd made promises to, the shareholders who thought he was a good man, to find out that he'd been a fraud from the beginning. And he was terrified that if Dormer *did* throw him out, he'd never see Josh again, and that Julia would be at her father's mercy. Only this time she wouldn't have a Felix or a Danny to help shield her.

All of that fear had gotten in the way of Felix realizing that his biggest fear should have been losing Danny. By the time Felix realized who'd *really* been to blame, Danny had been halfway across the world, sleeping with brutal men who would kill him quickly when the scotch was moving so damned slow.

Danny—sober as a judge—was in his arms right now. "I guess I'd gotten better at hurting people back then," he said.

Felix shook his head and then ducked to move his lips over the scars. He knew they often weren't sensitive, but he took his time while Danny threaded increasingly urgent fingers through his hair.

"Felix?"

Felix looked up, finding the more tender, untouched skin of Danny's other side and laving it gently with his tongue. Danny shuddered and sighed, and his fingers in Felix's hair began to sting.

"Felix!" he murmured tightly. "Whatever we're doing…. Oh."

Felix pulled his nipple, small and cinnamon colored, into his mouth, and Danny cried out again.

"God, Felix."

He released it with a pop and moved up to Danny's mouth, possessing him searingly, completely, until they couldn't tell where one breath started and the other ended.

Danny whimpered, clutching at Felix's shoulders, begging for more, and Felix wrapped his arms around that slender waist and pulled him tight.

"You hurt me," he said into Danny's ear. "You pulled my heart out. And I will never touch you like that."

Danny moaned, kneading Felix's backside under his slacks. "It won't matter," he said, a touch of bleakness to his voice. "If this goes south, there won't be enough of me left to carve up."

Touch him? No. Felix planned to *revere* him.

But first he had to take off their pants. He fumbled a bit with Danny's button and zipper, but finally he managed to shove the works down to Danny's knees. Danny helped by kicking off his loafers while Felix stripped in record time. Finally he had Danny up against the wall, gloriously naked.

For a moment Felix flashed to their first time, in the stuffy, sweltering garret, and how Danny had put his mouth on Felix's cock and the world had changed.

For a moment he was possessed by that furor, by that mad lust, and he wanted to jam that cock to the back of his throat and *make* Danny come, *force* him to see reason.

But he looked up into Danny's devastated face and was caught up in a tidal wave. Not of lust, but of tenderness.

He pressed a kiss to Danny's hipbone, smoothing shaking hands down Danny's thighs. He sent a watery smile to Danny and kissed below Danny's navel before pressing his cheek against that lean, concave stomach, wrapping his arms around Danny's thighs, and holding him tight.

Danny stroked his hair, bending forward to drop a kiss to the top of Felix's head.

"I'm older," he said, but the obvious insinuation didn't make Felix want him any less.

"And so much more important," Felix rasped, kissing his stomach again. He slid sideways, nibbling on the other hipbone, coasting his lips down to the crease of Danny's thigh.

"Has it been a while for you, Felix?" Danny taunted, his fingers continuing their massage of Felix's scalp. "Because you keep missing something vital there. Do I have to draw you a map?"

Felix moved to the other thigh, flicking the bell of Danny's foreskin with his tongue as he went. Danny sucked in a breath, and Felix laved the crease right next to Danny's balls, but didn't touch them.

"If you think your cock is my objective here, you haven't been paying attention."

"Fuck, suck, co—oh!" Another quick tongue movement, this one around his cockhead, interrupted that bit of cynicism right quick. "Felix!" Danny begged.

"No," Felix said thickly. "Not quick, not easy. Not fuck, suck, and come." He buried his face against Danny's midsection again, breathing his sex and his sweat, the atoms of scent soaking through him, reminding his cells that Danny was oxygen and he hadn't breathed in ten years.

"Then what—"

Felix took him all the way to the back of his throat, the taste, the fullness, all of it as inevitable as the climax they were building toward, as the emotional cymbal crash that would come with it. He pulled back and gripped Danny's cock in his fist.

"We're not just doing this once," Felix rasped, stroking. "We're not doing it a couple of times and then you're back on a plane. This is us together, Danny. And you may not believe it tonight, or even in a week, or even when we're done, but I'll prove it to you. Somehow. Even if I have to keep you naked and begging to give me time to do it."

"You're going to keep me begging for a week?" Danny squeaked, and the moment was so unguarded, so innocent, that Felix felt his first hope since Danny's first tear.

"Not even for a minute," he said, chuckling. And then he took Danny into his mouth again, this time sucking relentlessly, pressing forward and rocking back, his own nipples hardening in the chill, his own erection going untended. He wanted Danny's taste, his trust, his *come* inside him again, and he would deny himself anything to have it.

He remembered. Oh, he remembered *everything*. The way Danny liked him to swirl his tongue, the way he liked his base squeezed, and the particular cinnamon taste of his skin. Danny leaned his head back against the wall and tugged at Felix's hair, but Felix ignored him, feeling his body bow, his cock and balls tense. He was close, so close.

"Felix," Danny panted. "Felix, I can't—"

Felix stood, the pains of being forty instead of twenty not even registering. He took Danny's mouth, their naked bodies skin-to-skin, the glaze of spit and precome around his lips feeling primal and earthy.

"You can," Felix growled. He reached under Danny's thighs and hefted, and Danny didn't let him down, wrapping wiry legs around Felix's hips so Felix could swing them both to the bed.

"You can," Felix repeated as they landed, Danny on his back, arching feverishly against Felix's swollen groin. Felix reached down to stroke him, holding him firmly and kissing him into submission.

"Felix, I—"

Felix stroked him harder, squeezed, stimulated his head with his thumb until Danny gave a sob and came undone, his come shooting thick, scalding, irrevocable between their heaving bodies and all over Felix's fist.

Felix wanted to taste it, to savor, but Danny gave a little cry and sagged back against the pillows, and Felix wanted to take him even more.

"I still want you," Felix whispered, licking his ear. "I want to fuck you, to be inside you. Are you ready for me?"

"It's… been a while," Danny admitted.

"Me too." Felix kissed him tenderly. "There's lube in the drawer," he murmured, stretching across the bed.

"What's lube doing in the drawer?" Danny asked with suspicion.

Felix turned his head and gave a sheepish grin. "I, uh, ran up here and moved some in when I realized you'd moved your clothes out of my room," he confessed. At Danny's shock, Felix grabbed the lube and some condoms and came back down to feather his lips along Danny's temple. "Did you think I was just going to let you do that? Live here in the same house and not have you in my bed? Not take you? Be near you? Did you really imagine you meant so little to me?"

Danny's averted eyes told Felix everything he'd ever needed to know about how badly he'd fucked up in their past.

"Well, you were wrong," he said, drawing even and kissing Danny again. Danny responded this time, hungrily, and now Felix wanted to cry.

He'd needed this, the eagerness, and he opened and let Danny do the plundering, let Danny do the taking. He handed Danny the lubricant and condom, willing to let Danny make the choice.

Danny pulled away and gave him a quick look from red-streaked eyes. For a moment, his face lit up with desire and play and excitement, and then….

He seemed to get serious, taking the condom and wiggling down until he was even with Felix's groin. He hummed, as though pleased, and took Felix in his mouth with a slow, savoring motion, and Felix moaned.

"Danny," he rasped. "Do whatever you want. Do you want to take me? I'll be taken. Do you want to sit on my cock? Please. Just don't leave me. Not tonight. Not again. Please."

Danny pressed forward, his mouth hot and wonderful, his tongue quick and busy. When he pulled back long enough to unroll the rubber onto Felix's cock, Felix moaned. Danny scooted up and straddled him, his movements fast and needy, and Felix recognized this mood from when Danny wanted to get off but wasn't sure what Felix wanted.

No. They weren't doing this again.

Felix waited, sweating, aroused painfully, while Danny positioned him just… so. Slid down one hot, breathless moment at a time.

Danny's face contorted, head thrown back, as he rose and fell, taking Felix's length and girth in steady increments, until finally—ah, God, finally—he sat flush with Felix's groin, moaning breathlessly as he leaned forward, impaled on Felix's cock.

"You ready?" Danny asked, voice distant.

"Are you?" Felix asked, grabbing his hips. With a mighty thrust—and a prayer of thanks for morning crunches—Felix drove up into him.

"Ah!" Danny's back bowed, and he seemed to lose himself in the pleasure of it. But he was far away from Felix, from his touch, from the two of them, joined in lovemaking.

Felix gave a roar and rolled quickly, like a shark, until Danny was underneath him, staring at him with wide, startled eyes.

"Wha—"

"I. Want. *You*!" Felix kissed him and thrust in even harder as Danny moaned into his mouth. Felix had to pull away then, but he began to fuck, the pace punishing, his hips thrusting hard and without mercy as Danny cried out beneath him.

"You!" Felix breathed, slamming forward.

"Oh wow—"

"You!"

"Felix, I—"

"*You*!" Felix's hips flurried, his want, his need, his desperation, all of it coming to a head as he drilled into Danny again and again, needing not just his body, not just his surrender, but his reciprocation. Ten goddamned years and Felix needed to know he hadn't been suffering alone.

"Oh God!" Danny cried out. Felix could feel his second climax tightening all of his muscles, including his asshole as he clenched tightly around Felix's cock. "Felix, I'm... I'm...."

"I'm right here!" Felix shouted, crashing into his lover again, crashing into orgasm. He groaned from his stomach and collapsed, rutting into Danny's body, into the condom, while he took Danny's mouth again. Danny cried out and spasmed, arms contracting around Felix's shoulders as he held on for dear life.

And Felix kept up the kiss, and more, and more, so Danny would know that he meant it. He wasn't leaving. He wasn't letting Danny leave. Not this time. This time they were in it together. Hearts, bodies, and souls.

Situational Awareness

D ANNY ROLLED over sometime in the middle of the night. He had one foot on the ground before Felix's arm snaked around his middle.

"You'd better just be going to the bathroom," he rumbled.

Danny laughed weakly. "Drink of water," he said, but Felix pulled him back in. That strength Danny had seen in him, the ability to take over, to lead, to make the best things in his heart happen—that had become a real thing in the last ten years. It was like all of Felix's potential to be a fox among coyotes had been unlocked, and as a fox, his entire focus was on Danny.

"Danny?" he said, those blue eyes avid even in the darkened room.

"Yes?"

"For a grifter and a criminal, you're a terrible liar. Now, I can't stay awake all night, and we all need to sleep sometime. If you run right now, you will feel awful, and we'll still take you back, but your window for the con will have closed, and we'll be back to square one."

"Water," he lied, trying to save face. Felix was so strong—always had been. So responsible. Ten years of sobriety, and Danny was afraid his own will would just get mown under, in spite of Felix's promises to the contrary.

Felix kissed his temple in the darkness. "Stay with me. Please. Give me time to prove it'll be different this time. Please, Danny, I'm begging you. Please."

Danny closed his eyes, thinking Felix had never begged him except when they were in the middle of sex, and that was for sport.

"Okay," he said with a sigh, curling up into Felix's chest, which was where he'd dreamed about being for ten years.

Felix bent his head and nuzzled Danny's ear. "Promise, Danny. I believe your promise. Promise you'll stay, see this out, give you and me a chance. Promise me that."

"Sure."

Felix growled, and Danny felt a wave of exhaustion wash over him that had not a thing to do with jet lag or a busy day or even making love to Felix, who was everything he'd ever dreamed about in a lover, but Felix had never been until this night.

He was tired in his bones of being on the run. Tired of floating from apartment to apartment, from game to game. Money, he had, but a reason to stay in any one place overnight?

Not for a decade.

"I promise," he said softly. Instinctively, he burrowed against Felix's bare chest, smiling a little at how much furrier he was than he had been ten years ago.

"Thank you," Felix whispered. "Thank you, Danny. For once I won't let you down."

Danny couldn't let that stand, though. "We let each other down, Fox. Maybe this time we can make it."

"God, I'd sure like the chance to try. Do you still need that drink of water?"

Danny smiled in the dark, a little bit of peace seeping in. He'd made a decision, and those were always good. He wouldn't leave, not lock stock and barrel, not like last time. Felix had been hurt—truly hurt—and Danny believed that now.

"Apparently not," he said, conceding to the inevitable.

"Good."

WHEN HE woke again, it was morning, his second day in Felix's house, born again in Felix's bed.

His body felt used, a little sore but a lot more alive, and as he opened his eyes, he was aware of the softness of Felix's hand as he stroked Danny's cheek.

"Regrets?" Felix asked worriedly.

"Tons," Danny told him, allowing a smile. "But last night isn't one."

Felix's bright and sunny smile was so untouched Danny had to trace the corners of it with his forefinger.

"Good."

For a golden moment, they were lost in each other's eyes, and then the door crashed open and Josh sauntered in.

"Jesus God!" Danny cried and pulled the covers over his head.

Felix thumped him under the covers. "It's not like he didn't do this when he was a kid!"

"But we were a thing then!" Oh God. Danny wasn't ready for Josh to see them, to get his hopes up.

"Don't kid yourself, you're a thing now," Josh said dryly. "Danny, you're a grown-up. Just because you're under the covers, that doesn't mean I can't see you."

"I was so not ready for this," he moaned pitifully, still under the covers. It smelled like sex, and Felix, and... *home.*

"Well, get ready, because Grace and I have lots of good stuff to tell you. Molly and Stirling are at the apartment now, and Hunter and Chuck are going to join us in half an hour. They promised to bring coffee and bagels to give Phyllis a break. I just wanted to give you a heads-up."

Danny groaned and pulled the blankets down past his nose. "Fine. You leave, and I'll get out of bed."

Josh rolled his eyes. "I also wanted to tell you that Grace got light-fingered last night, but I think you're going to enjoy what he grabbed. Mom told us about the dinner in three days. I've got some ideas." He gave a catlike grin, and Danny thought fondly that if they had to bring up a criminal, at least they'd brought up a happy one.

"Excellent," Danny croaked. "Just, you know, don't make any assumptions."

Josh cackled. "Dad?" he said to Felix. "You know he's adorable, right? A laugh a minute. Don't make any assumptions? Is he kidding me?"

Felix sighed and then apparently took pity on Danny. "Son, if you could just, you know, give him some space?"

"No," Josh said without pity, and Danny glared at Felix and then back at Josh.

"No?"

Josh scowled. "We gave you space. We gave you ten years. You came in and out of my life like a ghost. You gave me my first condoms."

"You did?" Felix asked, and Danny started to sink under the covers again.

"And you knew I was gay before my father did."

Felix made another hurt sound. "But why—"

"Because he was my Uncle Danny, and that's who I told things to," Josh said shortly. "And he's belonged here the entire time, but we never had a way to get him here short of putting him in a cage."

Danny sank another couple of inches. "All you had to do was ask," he protested, but the lie fell flat in the room.

"All we had to do was convince you we needed you," Josh said, sounding cranky. "We need you now, but we've needed you this entire time, and we'll need you later. So I know you and Dad finally did the thing, and that's great. Because you can't leave us again if you're doing the thing. Now excuse me. I'm going to go text all my friends that you're doing the thing, because there was some interest expressed last night, and this way shit won't get weird."

And with that Josh turned on his heel, and Danny shoved his head under the pillows and wished for a quick death from asphyxiation.

Felix ruined that by plumping up the pillows and joining him in a little pillow tent.

"We're grown men," he said.

"I know."

"He used to crash in on us when he was a kid."

"Do you think I don't remember?"

Felix's eyes grew somber. "We had to teach him to lie. He'd never seen you, and his mother and father were deeply in love."

Danny closed his eyes. "Not... not the best thing we've ever done."

"Except it was," Felix murmured. "You were younger then than he is now, you know. That night in Rome. You'd never met Julia. You just took my word for it. We told you she was pregnant, and her father might actually kill her, and you... you cooked up a con to save her, to save her child from Hiram. To save him from being alone or poor or ignored or abused. I regret the later years. I regret letting you think you weren't good enough to love in the sunlight. I regret... God, every moment of watching you fall into a bottle because I was too afraid to do the right thing. But I can't regret that night in Rome. Because that thing you started then, that led us to this. That led us to Josh and Julia. You deserve the world for that decision, and I know you've *lived* in the world, but that's not the same."

"I forgot, last night. That us together is so much bigger than us apart. Still." That weighed heavily on him. Julia and Josh were family, and Josh finding them in bed together—that changed their family.

"Yes, but now that's a good thing," Felix whispered. He took Danny's mouth, morning breath and all. "Don't worry so much, Lightfingers. If I can have you right here, every morning, everything is going to be just fine."

Danny closed his eyes and thought, *We are here and happy now. Now is all I have.* The last ten years—that first year, drinking, the second year, recovering, the next eight pretending he could be happy without Felix. Drying out had been the worst. Every moment free and clear, knowing he'd flushed his life with Felix down the drain, had abraded his skin like sandpaper. He'd learned to treasure small things—seeing a sunset, stealing a pretty painting.

"I don't want to hurt them again," he said, because this was the worry that would drop oily paint into the well of happy colors. He smiled faintly at Felix, thinking the spring sunshine must be bright indeed to light the space in their pillow fort. "I don't want to hurt you." He hadn't yearned for a drink in the last eight years, but God, would being with Felix change that?

"I don't want to hurt *you*," Felix said softly. "We know more now." He grimaced. "There has got to be a reason for the gray hair and wrinkles besides funding the beauty industry."

Danny started to laugh, hiding the sound in the mattress. "Oh my God, you're so vain!" And so pretty, still.

Felix kissed his bare shoulder. "And you're disgustingly young-looking for a man who probably doesn't use moisturizer."

"Shut your mouth!" The pillow fort was getting a bit close, so Danny sat up, his earlier embarrassment lightening as his lungs filled with free air. "If you want to sucker the rich—"

"You gotta look like the rich," Felix parroted one of his earliest lessons, sitting up next to him. The covers fell away from their chests, and Felix leaned in and kissed his neck. "Mm, you do taste too rich for my blood."

Danny slid reluctantly away. "Your son—"

"Our son," Felix corrected again, and Danny's chest swelled with pride every time he did.

"Our son is downstairs gathering an army of twentysomethings with bagels. We should greet them and be good role models."

Felix grinned, and the intensity of the night before fell away, their hearts changed but not damaged. "Let's go be con men!"

As THEY gathered in the downstairs media room, Hunter and Chuck wore the hollow-eyed look of men who needed to go sleep, but Josh and Grace were disgustingly bright and perky.

"You get enough sleep last night?" Chuck asked mildly. "You feeling all *chipper*? 'Cause, yanno, I got some chores to do around my house—dry cleaning, watering my plants, feeding my cat. You gonna help with that?"

Josh rolled his eyes. "I *have* to go home with you, remember? Us in pairs? Yesterday's meeting?"

Chuck blew out a breath. "Oh God, Dormer, you're no fun at all."

"He's mad because I wouldn't date him," Josh said, matter-of-factly.

"Why not?" Felix asked. "He's such a charmer." With this, Felix sent Chuck a dark look that suggested that anybody who touched his baby boy should be afraid.

Very afraid.

Chuck laughed roundly, and Danny got a feeling for what Josh's adolescent years had been like. Danny'd had it easy. He'd read Josh's letters and sent replies. Things like "How old is too old to be a virgin?" and "When did you know you were gay?" were so much easier to deal with on pen and paper. And gods, did he bless the fact that they hadn't used the internet or phones to connect. Those things were saved for absolute necessity because they were traceable.

Josh had broken his arm at thirteen in a car-meets-bicycle accident. Danny had been—fortunately—in Ireland at the time, and he'd flown to Chicago and snuck in and out of Josh's hospital room three times with Felix none the wiser. Or at least he hadn't been until Josh told him. But then, that had been the one thing Danny had never tried to do. He'd never told Josh that his visits had to be secret, and that Felix had known had been evident.

Sometimes Josh would give him small packages for Christmas or his birthday—things that only Felix would know he'd love.

He had a pair of art nouveau cufflinks that were said to have belonged to F. Scott Fitzgerald himself and that people thought still resided in a small museum dedicated to the writer.

Only Danny knew that they graced his best tux.

Danny and Felix, who had made Josh carry them for a week when he'd been expecting Danny to visit.

The memory—the full circle of him and Felix and their son—hit him then as Josh blew off this perfectly nice getaway driver with charm and aplomb, and Danny wondered who in the hell he'd been fooling when he'd come back here.

Judging by Felix and Josh, Danny was the only fool there.

"So are we ready?" Danny asked, scanning the slides Josh had put on the laptop. "Julia? You here?"

"Right here, darling," Julia purred. She was curled up in the corner of a leather couch, wearing something too sexy to be a leisure suit, and Danny grinned at her.

"You are looking saucy this morning, my sweet. That new hairstyle becomes you."

She grinned. "I hope so. I've been sleeping with my hairdresser for months."

Felix looked at her, surprised. "And you didn't tell me?"

"Antonio's straight?" Hunter asked, his voice gruff and a little appalled.

Julia winked at him. "They don't all play for your team. And some of them play for both."

Hunter cocked his head, and—tellingly—his eyes darted to Grace, who was standing by the bar. Not because Grace wanted a drink, but because he was wearing some sort of dance slippers and doing slow, deliberate pirouette turns on the tile.

"Huh," Hunter said, letting the syllable sit there uncomfortably.

Danny and Felix had a brief eyeball convo about the vagaries of youth, and Danny put his thoughts in order.

"Josh, are you taking notes for Molly and Stirling?"

"Yessir." Josh nodded at his laptop. "In fact, Molly's online with us. Wave, Molly."

"You all suck, and I want a bagel," Molly said through the computer. Danny grinned and waved at her, then got down to business.

"Okay, so here's our mark. Everybody, you all know Marnie Courtland." He put up a promotional pic of Marnie, her trademark blond updo perfectly coifed, her doe-brown eyes wide and empathetic.

The room erupted into boos.

"Yes, yes, I know. She's a horrible person and needs to be stripped naked, rolled in sugar, and left outside for fire ants and bees. We'll try to oblige. Now here are the things we know about her."

He pulled up another slide, this one from her first year on her show, *Progress is Important*.

"The first thing is she likes to brand herself as a rebellious progressive. Now, this makes her public deflowering harder because, inevitably, when you take down someone in her camp, her entire cause gets blasted. We've seen it happen with politicians—even well-meaning ones—and the same thing would happen here. Every woman ever harmed by harassment in the workplace thinks she's a hero. Calling her out for the lying douchebag she is would hurt them unnecessarily and cause rips in what we all believe should be a united cause. But how do we prove she's a lying douchebag without calling her out? Class?"

"Get her to confess!" Molly called from Josh's computer, and Danny nodded.

"Dr. Evil style?" Danny said, grinning at the screen. "Where she reveals her entire plan at someone's breast because they're wearing a camera?"

There was silence as everyone let that cherished fantasy go.

"Maybe not," Josh grudgingly admitted. "Okay, so, what?"

"We undermine her credibility, for one. We prove that she has a history of dishonesty and bullying, and if we can, we catch her doing something in that vein—but unrelated. We make people ready to *believe* she has no integrity. And then we prove it."

Grace started to laugh and pirouette gracefully. As he spun around the floor, he pulled things from his pockets, setting each one of them down on the top of the wet bar in perfect formation.

"Oh my," Danny said, getting close enough to analyze the jewelry. "Is that snake carved from a giant opal? I've always wanted to steal this piece!"

"Wait, is that a gilt comb?" Julia said, moving behind the bar to avoid Grace, who was still showing off. "Oh my God, Danny. We know this piece!"

Danny took it from her fingers, curious. "We do," he said, squinting. "Somebody get me a magnifying glass."

Grace produced one of those on his next spin.

"He's still…," Hunter said, flailing. "Somebody make him stop!"

Grace laughed, stuck one pointed toe in the air, and reached down to hug his leg while staying *en pointe*. He opened his torso out, literally upside down, and waved cheerily to Hunter, who made a strangled sound.

"Danny!" he complained, pulling a hand through his shoulder-length hair. "Danny, make him stop!"

"Grace, can you come over here," Danny said absently. "I need to know more about these pieces."

"Of course," Grace said. He reached over his head, planted both hands on the bar, and arched, flipping to stand on his hands on the countertop.

He smiled at Danny upside down, and Danny raised an eyebrow. "You are showing off, sweet thing, and while it's very impressive and far better than me in my prime, it is not what we need right now."

Grace sighed, but he pushed up in a spring and landed on his feet next to Danny on the tile. Danny could barely smell sweat on him, which meant that really *had* been for fun and not showing off, and he gave an eye roll for the young.

"You know," he said soberly, making sure he had the attention of those remarkable eyes, "if I'd had half the talent you have when I was your age, I would not have spent my whole life on the grift. Do you understand me? What you do when you do that for real? That is art. Don't let this—" He gestured to the pieces in front of him, all alluring in their own right, and all highly illegally obtained. "—get in the way of that extraordinary being you have crafted yourself into."

Grace had the good sense to look abashed. "I get bored," he complained.

"We'll work on that," Danny said, getting it completely. "Just have a care with yourself, yes?"

Grace smiled again, this time with all his heart and not just in a sly sort of way. The expression transformed him from pretty young man to sublime and ethereal being. To his left, Danny heard Hunter make a strangled, helpless sound, and he almost laughed.

Well, he had no answers for Hunter; he could barely manage his own love life.

"So," Danny prompted, holding up the jewel-encrusted hair comb. "Where did these come from?"

Grace lit up with glee. "She has a *secret* safe!" he said. "It was amazing."

Danny turned to Josh. "Secret?"

"Well, it was inside her wall safe but hidden in a wall inside it. She had a fingerprint plate, and since it was sideways, it was hard to detect. If Grace hadn't printed one of her lamps and used the tape immediately…. This secret safe had two alarms attached." Josh grimaced. "Uncle Danny, she had iron bars set in her ventilation system, set on a timed spring release. Grace saw them before he tripped them and managed to roll clear before they sprang closed, but only because he's quick. If we hadn't been prepared for something unusual, Grace would have been trapped in there." Josh swallowed. "Or, you know. Impaled."

"Impaling is bad," Grace agreed.

"Did you hear that?" Danny called toward the computer. "Stirling, find a way to disable the bars and the alarm systems attached to the second safe. Not a work-around, a complete breakdown. Grace is going to need to get in and out of there a couple of times."

"He's on it, Danny," Molly said from the computer. "He's swearing to himself. I think it's pretty high tech."

"Well, it should be," Danny said irritably. "Because I know these pieces, and two of them are real objets d'art, and they should be in a museum. And three of them are forgeries that she thinks are real."

"Why would she think they're real?" Chuck asked, puzzling over the trinkets.

"Because the people she stole *this* from didn't know it was a forgery." Danny picked up the gilt comb. It was a *very good* forgery. The best materials used: gold, diamonds, and sapphires in prime shape. But the original piece was from the early nineteenth century, commissioned as a wedding gift for Micaela Almonester, the Baroness de Pontalba, for her wedding with her French cousin.

The marriage had been, well, unsuccessful to say the least, given that Micaela's monstrous father-in-law had shot her in the face for defiance. Micaela had lived, but her father-in-law had not survived his own self-inflicted wound, and eventually she'd returned to her home in New Orleans to live a long, productive life and leave her mark—quite literally—in the iron lace-work surrounding Jackson Square.

This comb—or one just like it—had remained in France and should have been in a small private collection owned by one of Micaela's descendants.

And it had been there... before Felix had commissioned the forgery so Danny could replace the original comb, and together they could give the original to Julia on her thirtieth birthday.

It had been one of the last jobs they'd pulled together, but both of them had wanted to remind their girl that she too was a kickass woman who had survived a monstrous, abusive man to find happiness and thrive.

Julia came running back into the room, a small velvet bag in her hand. "Is that the forgery Felix commissioned?" she asked breathlessly.

"It is," Danny said. "Which makes me wonder if there's another forgery in its place. That would be highly amusing, don't you think? A forgery of a forgery? Like a mirror held in front of a mirror?"

"Yeah, Danny," Josh said tightly. "That's really meta and highly postmodern. Do we want to know why Mom has the real thing, again?"

"May I?" Danny asked, taking the velvet bag from her hand.

"Of course," she said.

Deftly, he twisted a bit of Julia's shoulder-length blond hair up to her crown and secured it with the comb. Julia's swanlike neck was revealed, and she inclined her head demurely to the appreciation of everybody in the room.

"Ooh," Felix murmured. "You're still lovelier, my darling, but that really is quite fetching."

Josh grunted. "Okay, so I get it. Mom only deserves the best. And Marnie—who does not—happens to have some stolen art and some forgeries in her safe. What does this mean?"

Danny thought carefully. "Well, for one thing, it means she's acquisitive. Felix, can you think of any other pieces we've kept over the years?"

"Two," Felix replied. "Everything else we've either sold or donated."

"Yes indeed. It's like lovers. She likes to gather them and then leave them in corners," Danny murmured, studying the comb in Julia's hair. "Julia, dearest, have you and Chuck decided on what you're wearing to the party in two days?"

"I'm going to a party?" Chuck said, surprised.

Danny and Felix grimaced. "Well, we've been doing some planning without you," Felix apologized. "But yes. You're going to play the younger swain to Mrs. Salinger's cougar. Are you up for it?"

Chuck grinned at Julia. "Well, ma'am, you are fetching enough to straighten my bent soul."

Julia laughed delightedly. "Why, Charles, I'm just so thrilled to have you accompany me." She sobered in an instant. "You do have a tuxedo, don't you?"

Chuck looked surprised and dismayed. "Why, no, I don't—"

"I'll call Felix's tailor as soon as we're done here," she said. "And I assume you want my dress to match that comb?" she inquired.

Danny and Felix met eyes. "Oh yes. You're going to come in wearing the real thing—and you're going to tell her it's the real thing and you have provenance."

"Do we have provenance?" Josh asked.

"Well, the comb is real," Danny said, "but the provenance not so much." He called to the computer. "Stirling? Molly? If you can, check Marnie's financials and see if she's got provenance online for this." He looked at Grace soberly. "And if you're sure you're not going to get impaled with iron bars, you might want to check her secret safe for actual written papers."

Grace gave a smart salute. "No impalements, sir. Understood."

"Oh dear God. Josh, could you do something about him?"

Grace smiled cheekily. "Hey, he had his chance, but no, he turned me down."

Josh rolled his eyes. "What's that Bob Dylan song? Try and catch the wind?"

Grace laughed, vaulted smoothly over the bar, and was going to do a tuck and roll afterward—it was obvious from his body position—but Hunter stood right in front of him so he came up against Hunter's chest.

"Augh!" Grace hollered, and Hunter, five feet, ten inches of solid muscle, just reached out and steadied him, then regarded him with steely blue eyes.

"No impalements. No showing off."

Grace's tawny skin was swept by dark blotches of crimson, and Danny watched in fascination as the extremely poised dancer lost his cool entirely.

"Okay. Sure. Whatever. Yeah. You're right. So sorry."

Grace backed up a step, and then another. He knocked over a barstool and then ran into the bar and kept backing up, even though he wasn't going anywhere.

"Hunter," Felix said softly, "you're scaring him."

Hunter gave a self-satisfied smirk. "Good. Scared grease men stay alive."

"You'd be surprised," Felix muttered.

"And like a true whore, I need the attention back on me," Danny said, feeling cranky. He was relieved when all the heads in the room turned to him like they were on swivels. "Good. Felix, how rich are you and Julia?"

Felix shrugged. "We won't starve anytime soon. Why?"

Danny rolled his eyes. "Wow. Just, wow. Do you have enough to buy all the pieces here?"

Felix looked at the assortment on the table, his eyes darkening shrewdly. "Four, five, six times over and not blink. Why?"

Danny rolled his eyes again. "Because I was going to offer to do it if you wanted me to, but no, you had to be a dick about it. Since none of these pieces are reported missing, can you spend your day online, buying from museums what Ms. Courtland has rightfully stolen?"

Felix cocked his head. "I can indeed. So I take it Chuck is going to be wearing those cufflinks worn by George the Fifth?"

"Well, it's not like George wore them a lot himself." The monarch had usually been seen in full dress uniform. "And this rather fetching tiara should be in the vaults in Prague. It belonged to the royal family before the revolution, you know."

Delicate as gossamer, strewn with pure white diamonds, with one stunning garnet in the center.

"So where are we going to put them, once we own them?" Felix asked, but Danny caught his eyes; they were twinkling. He knew damned well where this was going.

"Well, I was thinking people we know would be wearing them to Marnie's party. What do you think?"

Julia smiled, catlike. "I think it will make her very nervous."

"Oh God, I hope so." Danny rested his elbow on the bar and his chin on his hand. "You know, it's a shame she's a skank lying whore, this one. She does have good taste in trinkets."

Felix moved in on his left, close enough for Danny to feel his body heat and smell his bodywash from the shower. A memory of the night before hit him, of Felix's eyes boring intensely into Danny's as he fucked Danny into acceptance, into surrender.

His mind wandered, and he wondered how soon before they could be flesh-to-flesh, skin-to-skin again, and it hit him that his desire for Felix had always taken precedence over the game. Other lovers? No, the game was the thing. But Felix?

Felix was the object of the game. He always had been.

"Who did this belong to?" Felix asked, pointing to a striking ring.

Danny leaned quietly back against him and gently stroked the intricately scrolled platinum band. "Francis Douglas," he said. "His lover—Lord Rosebery—made him a Lord in Parliament, and Francis's father was so angry, he hounded Rosebery until he ended the affair. Francis shot himself, and his father went on to imprison Oscar Wilde for being queer."

Felix grunted and edged the ring away from Danny's touch as though it tainted them both. "Do any wedding rings have happy stories?" Felix asked, sounding exasperated.

"Well, yes. But those are the rings that usually end up on the fingers of happy corpses or being willed to happy people who wear them to their own weddings."

"Hmm…." Felix started fondling the tiara next. "Tell me about this piece."

"Well, it's said to be a piece commissioned by Franz Ferdinand for his wife."

"The Franz Ferdinand who was assassinated?"

Danny smiled at him, gratified. "You *do* listen. Yes, that's the one. This was commissioned for his wife, who was so far down the list of noblewomen, he had to proclaim to the world she'd never try to be the queen."

"Nor would her children," Felix said, proud of knowing this.

"Yes!" Danny allowed the pad of his finger to brush against the Bohemian garnet. "Or rather no, they wouldn't. It was quite the scandal at the time." He glanced up and winked.

Felix's mouth parted softly, and Danny returned his attention to the tiara. "See, it was considered a 'morganatic' marriage—when the Grand Duchess made the proclamation and the Archduke's wife agreed—one where the monarchy didn't recognize her or her children. She was just… ignored, forgotten. Except for this tiara, which, you know, I tried to steal."

"I wonder why," Felix said, voice throaty with self-recrimination.

"Well, it wasn't there, but where it was supposed to be was so far back in the vault in the Bohemian Garnet Museum—"

"There's a museum for that?" Josh asked, and Danny gave him an absent smile.

"Careless of them, right? But it's about two blocks from my apartment, so of course I read up on it—"

"I'm stunned," Julia said, leaning over the bar.

"And then I had to see it." Danny shrugged. "And I found where it was *supposed* to be, back in the vault waiting for their month of tiara display, I suppose, but it wasn't there."

"So you just wandered home?" Felix asked, thinking about the lone thief, sneaking back to his apartment, disappointed, in the dark.

"Of course not," Danny shot back, stunned. "There were some garnet ropes worn by the Queen of Bohemia that paid my rent in that apartment for the next five years. Nobody was displaying them, and they were, you know, not very interesting looking, so I figured... why not."

"So are we letting Talia wear this if she's willing?" Felix asked, and Danny nodded, pulling himself back from the fascination of the platinum scrollwork and the dewdrops of diamonds.

"Yes. I think it's only fitting. Marnie tried to delegitimize her, and she's going to show up to Marnie's party on the arm of Marnie's *other* discarded suitor—albeit platonic—looking like the queen she is. We'll put a replica in Marnie's safe, and she'll be both confused *and* embarrassed. It will be great."

"Mm... nice," Felix said. "And as it happens, I know a jeweler who would love to make some forgeries."

"So do I," Danny said mildly. "I know a guy."

Felix smiled. "Of course you do. But you know what would be even nicer?"

"Josh," Molly complained, "move the laptop! Felix and Danny are plotting, and this is just getting good."

"Oh damn," Josh said, "it really is."

Josh moved the computer, and Chuck, Grace, and Hunter gathered around, and between them Felix and Danny spun a web that would destroy a spider.

Spinning

"TALIA, MY darling," Felix said, trying not to sound too jovial. "How are you doing?"

"Felix?" Talia Clark was a stunning athlete and a gorgeous woman, but her low, throaty voice had overtones of shyness that made Felix want to throttle Marnie even more.

"Yes, my sweet. I hope you're doing well?"

"Oh yes. Felix, I'm so glad you called." Talia's voice dropped. "I'm so sorry. What that woman did to you was just… just awful. We all know you're not that guy. I mean, everybody."

"Thank you," Felix said, the well of gratitude in his chest opening wide. "I am so glad to hear you say that. I… I have a sort of favor to ask you."

"Is it revenge?" And the shyness dropped away, leaving nothing but woman scorned. Oh, Felix liked Talia.

"Served cold and bloody," Felix confirmed. "And it requires you to wear red, glorious red. With an updo."

"An updo?" Talia's surprise was as delightful as the rest of her.

"How would you like to wear a tiara, my darling. Like the queen you are."

"Ruby, garnet, or carnelian?" Talia asked, and Felix chuckled.

"Garnet, my sweet."

"Oh, that's my favorite tiara."

"Good."

Felix explained the plan to her while watching Danny work ferociously on his laptop. Danny's back was hunched, his neck sinking into his shoulders, and Felix grunted and moved closer to him so he could cup his spine and rub while they both worked. That didn't look comfortable.

They were in Danny's room again, a breakfast of bagels, lox, and fruit happily tucked away. Chuck and Hunter had each taken a guest room to nap in, and Josh and Grace were busy tracking down provenance for each of Marnie's seven stolen artifacts.

Phyllis was at the grocery store and probably going out to lunch with Marnie Courtland's housekeeper. And Julia? She was shopping.

"So, do you still have Julia's number?" Felix asked.

"I never lost it," Talia said. "Should I send her my measurements?"

"Yes, darling. And don't question her taste. She will make you look fabulous."

"Oh, I know it. It's said that the designers in New York copy *her*!"

Felix chuckled. "Is it?" he asked disingenuously. "I had no idea." He'd planted that rumor and used Torrance to do it, which made the next call a lot easier. "So we'll have the outfit sent to your home, and Torrance Grayson is your date. He'll arrive at seven—will that do?"

"Have him come at six," she said. "Torrance and I are friends. We can have dinner and catch up before we leave."

"You are far too sweet for this caper," Felix told her, meaning it. "But I'm glad to have you aboard."

She made kissy noises at him, and he ended the call, setting the phone aside to rub Danny's shoulders some more.

"Mm… Fox, not that this isn't lovely, but—"

Felix nipped his earlobe, and Danny whimpered.

"We have work to do," he said, pulling gently away.

"I know it," Felix said, moving to his other ear.

"We're on a very strict timeline!" Danny tried again.

Felix nibbled his jawline. "We are."

"Felix—"

Felix turned his head and captured his mouth, gratified when Danny gave up any pretense of resistance and plundered back. Felix pulled away and smiled.

"The hell?"

Felix pecked his lips to silence him. "Incentive," he said. "Get to a good place to quit by lunch and we can take a walk afterward."

"A walk?" Danny rolled his eyes.

"In the sunlight, Danny. To the park and back. Holding hands. We haven't done that for—"

"Twenty years," Danny said, his mouth parting enough to show his surprise. And his vulnerability.

"Yes." Felix kissed him again. "We have work to do, but our lives are not the work. Not anymore."

Danny's swallow was audible. "I thought you were just going to seduce me again."

Felix's chuckle was strained. Danny's taste was still wild, like wind and sea and olive trees and pastries, and as intoxicating as it had ever been. "I am. But first I'm going to show you off."

"To who? The squirrels?"

"To the world. Danny Mitchell—"

Danny grimaced. "Maybe not *that* name."

Felix huffed. "What's on your passport?"

"Daniel Davenport."

"Mm-hmm. Middle name?"

Danny looked away. "Benjamin."

Felix rested his head against Danny's temple. "I'm going to show you off and never let you go. You know that, right? It was inevitable."

"It's just a name," Danny muttered.

"It's *my* middle name. And now it's yours. And you've pretty much sealed your fate." He moved to the side of the chair and closed Danny's laptop softly, set down his phone, and took Danny's face in his hands for another kiss. Tender and carnal, this one was a subtle overlapping of lips and skin, tongue and gentle touches, until Danny growled a little and pressed upward for more.

"I thought," he murmured, taking Felix's mouth again, "that we were waiting for lunch."

Felix returned the plunder, and his heart gave two hard contractions. *You didn't have him for ten years!*

"Turns out—" He sucked on Danny's neck for a moment. "—that I'm starving." He pulled away long enough for Danny to stand up, but the chair shot out behind him and bounced off the wall, and they both ended up on the floor, Felix sprawled on top of him, that still-lithe body hard and trembling underneath his.

"Are you okay?" Felix asked in surprise.

"Peachy," Danny replied, grinning up at him. For a moment, that grin, the laughter, the closeness—he was just as open as he had been when they'd been young, and Felix's heart actually made a tearing sound as he realized how much he'd stolen from the two of them. Danny might blame himself for the drinking, but Felix blamed himself for the blindness. How could he not see that even someone as sturdy as Danny needed a patch of earth and sunlight in which to grow?

Felix captured his mouth and poured his need inside, and Danny gasped, returning kiss for kiss. The kisses were all-consuming—Felix could have done that forever—but his hands roamed Danny's body too: the narrow hips, the definition of the abs and arms. The night before he'd been desperate to capture Danny, to hold him and make him see reason.

Now that Danny was his again, Felix wanted to savor him, to grow accustomed to having him under his hands once more. He could never be bored by Danny's taste, but every kiss flooded his senses, overwhelmed him with gratitude, with desire.

Felix just needed to keep kissing him until he could remember his own goddamned name.

And Danny kept kissing him back. His hands ruched under Felix's button-down and, rougher than Felix's, gently abraded the skin under the shirt. Felix found himself undulating, pressing their groins together, burying his face against Danny's throat and moaning.

He needed more. He needed *all*. In the sunlight, the two of them, he needed to touch all of Danny's body.

"If I get up," he whispered, grinding against Danny helplessly, "to get the lube, will you promise to stay right here?"

"There is a perfectly good bed," Danny reminded him.

"Will you be in it? Naked?" Felix sucked on the collarbone beneath the polo shirt Danny had worn to breakfast, and Danny moaned a little and bucked.

"I'm not going to launch myself out of the window to avoid sleeping with you again," Danny murmured. "Ah! God, Felix, nipples. I have them."

"Promise!" Felix almost sobbed. "I'm going to get lube and get naked, and you will be there to meet me, also naked. And we don't have to ruin the carpet."

"A deal," Danny rasped, sliding his hands under Felix's belt and cupping his backside. "I accept. Two naked men in the middle of a bed in the daytime. What on earth could possibly happen?"

Felix pulled back and pinned him with his gaze. "The earth is going to move, Danny. Make no mistake. It's going to change our lives."

Danny's lashes fluttered shut, and a faint smile pulled up the corners of his full mouth. "Promises, promises," he breathed.

"Meet me naked in the bed and I'll keep them."

Felix pushed up reluctantly and hurried to lock Danny's door. Josh and Hunter may have been in another wing of the house, but it wasn't like Josh hadn't just crashed in on them that morning.

When he got to the end table, he saw with a twist of his mouth that Danny had stripped in record time and was now under the blankets, naked, probably, but not on display. He was regarding Felix soberly over the edge of the comforter, those amber fox-light eyes intent on Felix's face.

"I… my last health screen was clear," he said as Felix rooted in the drawer.

Felix met his eyes and dropped the box of condoms. Danny wouldn't lie to him about this. There was no reason.

"As was mine," he said, tossing the tiny bottle of satiny lubricant on the covers. He met Danny's eyes. "And I've never not used condoms. With everybody but you, Danny."

Danny looked away, his cheeks growing ruddy. "Same."

"Well, then."

"Yes."

It was just the two of them, like they had been. Felix wanted to shout it to the heavens, but he also wanted to cry. He stripped quickly, crawled under the covers, and reveled in Danny's nakedness against his. Their movements were less furious than the night before, but Felix definitely took charge. And this time, Danny folded into his arms effortlessly, fluidly, his own palms tasting Felix's skin like Felix's hands savored Danny's.

Every touch made Felix shiver—partly with the joy of the here and now and partly with the retroactive fear that they might never have had this moment, that they might never have touched like this again.

Felix rolled so he was between Danny's thighs, kissing down his body to capture a nipple in his mouth. So good! He sucked until Danny gasped and kneaded his hair, and then he just kept kissing down. He'd tasted

Danny's cock the night before, had even swallowed his come. But today having it in his mouth, the pressure, the saltiness, drove him almost to the edge.

With a jerk, his movements shaking with want, he let Danny's cock flop out of his mouth and shoved at Danny's thighs until they were raised and spread, and Danny's body, his vulnerable body, was at Felix's mercy.

He plied his tongue without remorse, parting Danny's cheeks, licking him, nuzzling him, sucking delicately on his testicles. This was his playground. Nobody else allowed. Never again. Danny had been out in the world without him and had the scars to prove it. Now he belonged to Felix and only to Felix and that would be how his entire body felt—marked and possessed.

Danny flailed, hands against the pillows, and gave a whimper. "When… do I get… to… oh God! Do that to you?"

Felix came up for air. "When I've had enough," he said, before engulfing Danny's cock and thrusting two fingers inside.

Danny's chest came off the bed, and he buried his fingers in Felix's hair and pushed instinctively. Felix welcomed it, welcomed the assertion, the need. Danny's cock bottomed out in his throat, and before Danny could come, Felix pulled up again. He fumbled for the lubricant next to him on the bed, and as he snicked the cap and dumped some on his fingers, he regarded Danny soberly up his defined torso.

"How you doing?" he panted. He was so primed. So ready. Inside Danny without protection? It's where he most longed to be in the world.

"I'm gonna die," Danny croaked. He reached for his cock as Felix penetrated him, stretching, and Felix batted his hand away. "Ah! You bastard! But I'm gonna die happy."

The thought of that actually happening, of all the near misses—some of them etched right into Danny's flesh—that he'd probably endured in the last ten years without Felix to catch him drove Felix up his body, inside him, without another heartbeat's pause.

"Augh!" Danny, so wonderfully responsive, so joyful in sex, wrapped his legs around Felix's hips and pulled him in.

"Don't you dare die," Felix growled. "Not without me inside you." He punctuated that with a thrust, and another, and another, and Danny matched him in rhythm, reaching up to palm Felix's chest, play with his nipples as he heaved.

"Ack!" Oh, Felix's nipples were sensitive, and Danny's body was *exquisite* wrapped around his cock, and Danny's eyes were half-lidded, his narrow face faintly sheened in sweat. "You're gonna make me—"

"Good," Danny panted. "Stop hogging the foreplay!"

Felix reached between them and stroked, the first spurt of precome a vindication. "You just don't like—" Danny spurted again, and the unguarded ecstasy on his face as he tilted his head back and groaned almost did Felix in. "—coming first."

He stroked again, finding the harp string and flicking it with his thumb. Danny's hands clenched around Felix's biceps, and he cried out, tightening until his fingers bit into Felix's arms.

The pain drove Felix on.

Harder and harder and higher and higher until Danny let out a hoarse scream and convulsed, every inch of his body clenching, every molecule wrung inside out with pleasure and want.

Danny's body went slack against the mattress, his eyes fluttering as he struggled to find purchase, and Felix hit that spot—the sweet spot for both of them. An aftershock took Danny by storm, and Felix let out a gasp and came.

He hated those moments of helplessness in orgasm, hated that his body was pulling him into itself. Hated missing that time inside his lover, the only man he would ever want, when he couldn't be there in his mind to know what he had.

His peak crested, and he fell back into Danny, reveling in Danny's comfort sounds against his ear.

"Shh... hey... you always get so intense," Danny murmured. "I thought sex was fun."

"Only with you," Felix confessed, naked in aftermath.

"You should give me some time on the merry-go-round," Danny said seriously. "I'm a one-man carnival, I swear."

Unexpectedly, Felix's eyes burned. "I'm so afraid you'll disappear," he said. Danny's hands—in his hair, on his neck—stilled.

"I'm not a drunk. Not anymore. Not a sip for ten years. I'm not stupid. You'll know when I'm going, I promise."

Felix nodded, unsure when an afternoon quickie had turned so sober. "Stay," he mumbled, kissing Danny's sweaty forehead. "Just stay."

Danny hummed softly. It wasn't "Yes, beloved, I shall be by your side for always."

But it wasn't no, either.

As aftermath and lassitude stole over Felix's body, he thought he was going to have to take it for the win.

A short nap and a shower later, Felix was back on the phone. He was dressed for the promised walk in sweats and sneakers while Danny showered, trying to get a few more things wedged in before he kept his promises.

"Gray? Yeah, did Talia get hold of you?"

"Yes. So we're going to that bitch's party why?"

Felix chuckled, warmed by Torrance Grayson's loyalty. "Well, as a distraction, sort of. I'm... well, I have something planned," he said after a moment, and his reward was a thoughtful silence on the other end of the line.

"Is it payback?" Torrance asked slowly. Felix could imagine him—thirtyish, cropped dark hair, gray eyes, phenomenal black lashes, and a fireman's chin—as he strode along the river in his signature red topcoat, looking for a story. He even *sounded* cold and out of breath.

"Mm... more like evening the scales," Felix said. "But yes."

"Will I get to talk to Josh again?"

Felix's eyebrows hit his hairline. "Josh is about ten years younger than—"

"He has an old soul," Torrance said with dignity.

"Gray...."

"I'm too old and it's stupid and...." Torrance's voice fell. "So, is he going to be there?"

"He'll be in the, uh, staging area," Felix said, and gave him Danny's apartment number. "We'll be meeting there before the party. Bring Talia."

"Wait, who's 'we'?"

"Uh, some friends. Julia and her date—"

"Wait, *Julia's* going?"

Felix shifted as he stood. The bathroom door opened and Danny emerged, dressed, with his hair wet combed, looking spry and shiny and adorable. He didn't *look* like a thief. He wasn't conventionally handsome enough to be a con man. He was kind to children and animals, and surprisingly diffident at times.

But God, looking at him made Felix's heart hammer in his chest. Every single time.

"Yes," Felix said weakly, trying not to clutch his chest as he found himself falling faster and harder back in love with Danny Lightfingers than he'd fallen in that first moment, twenty years ago. "Yes, we're…. Think of it as undercover. There is going to be some undercover work done there. You and Talia are invited."

"What's our job?" Torrance asked, all business and all suspicion.

"Mm… mostly to play on what Julia says and does. And to react to Marnie as though you enjoy every ounce of her discomfort."

"She's going to be uncomfortable?" Torrance asked, his voice perky.

"If we play our cards right, it will be like watching that politician who called you a—what was it?"

"Overeducated liberal hack taking advantage of his lifestyle for clicks," Torrance recited grimly, and Felix remembered the night Gray had gotten drunk after that had hit the airwaves.

"Yes. That man. It will be like watching him get arrested for drug use while on his knees in a men's lavatory."

"Mm," Gray said, savoring the viciousness of it. "Remind me never to play poker with you," he added gleefully. "But feel free to throw down on her. You know, half the anchors at your network have put in their resignations. So have the segment producers. They're trying to ransom you back."

For a moment, Felix was warmed, but then, as Torrance's words sank in, he swallowed. "You, uhm, realize that Julia and I still own the network, right?" No, he was no longer acting as head of the board of directors or overseeing the station manager, but actual *ownership* was in his and Julia's name. Julia had taken a quieter role in running things. Felix had put his name on the contracts and run the numbers while Julia had visited prospective properties and interviewed assets. Between the two of them, they had such a happy, functional group of programmers, producers, and personalities working for them that apparently without Felix at the head, the whole thing fell the fuck apart.

A leaden silence thumped on the other end. Anchors and personalities and producers were business assets. If they all quit, a generous supplier of Felix and Julia's money simply… dried up, which was the very thing they'd been afraid of when the board of directors had asked Felix to step down.

"Well, *that* was poorly conceived," Torrance said after a moment.

"It was, but let me check my stock portfolio. I have an idea."

Felix had learned a lot in twenty years, and one of the biggest things he'd learned was that diversifying his portfolio would eventually save his life.

"You always have an angle," Torrance said, full of admiration Felix probably didn't deserve.

"Well, right now my angle is to take a walk with my—" Felix watched as Danny pulled on sneakers, as unselfconscious as a kid. "—friend," he finished weakly.

"Friend?" Torrance's voice was arch.

"My everything," Felix said simply. Then before Torrance could ask any more questions, he said, "I've got to go. You call me back with any questions. Oh! And Talia's wearing garnet and Julia's wearing sapphire to the party. If you want to gentleman up accordingly, you know what to do."

"I do indeed," Torrance said, voice smug, and Felix wondered what fashion confection he'd be dressed in Friday night. "I'll see you in your 'staging area' at seven."

"Better make it seven thirty. Talia's got dinner planned for you two. She says she misses talking to you."

Torrance made a happy sound. "Aw! I adore her. I'll call her right now and tell her she's the only woman I could ever love."

"You do that. But if you find some straight men, could you bring them around? I have the feeling we're doing Talia and Julia and Josh's friend a disservice."

"Felix, if I knew any straight men, they wouldn't be straight for very long."

Felix laughed at his outrageousness, and Torrance hung up.

"Are we plotting?" Danny asked, popping up from the bed. "Can I help?"

"Just getting Torrance Grayson to come to our—I mean, Marnie's—little shindig." Felix frowned. "And unsuccessfully batting him away from Josh."

"Don't," Danny said, grabbing a hooded sweatshirt to ward off the early spring chill. Chicago: late March could be sunshine, could be rain—could be snow!

"Torrance Grayson is ten years our son's senior," Felix said, sounding stuffy and unable to help it.

"Yes, but anything has got to be better than his last boyfriend," Danny said practically, pausing at the door. "I still have work to do. Are you sure you want to take a break now?"

"Absolutely," Felix said staunchly. "Clears the head. And how did you know about Sean?"

"Letters, Felix. They're a thing." Danny gave a dismissive sniff. "And Sean was a sniveling weasel who needed to grow a spine and be a vertebrate. This Grayson person sounds like he *has* some spine."

"He does," Felix conceded. "But he's also a slick piece of work who doesn't mind getting into danger for a story." He paused. "I wrote you letters," he said, heart aching. "I even sent a few."

"I know." Danny paused. "Why do you think I kept coming back to Chicago?"

Felix felt anger and grief pushing at his chest. "You couldn't have returned the favor, you bastard?"

"It took a while," Danny said, "before I felt… I don't know. Worthy. I figured after the divorce you would come out and find someone you didn't have to hide."

And there it was. The harpoon lodged solidly in Felix's heart. "You are worth ten of the Torrance Graysons in the world," he said thickly, taking Danny's hand. "I should be flogged for ever letting you believe anything else."

"Al. Co. Hol. Ic." Danny rolled his eyes as though bored. "Not a father figure. Not a husband."

"A good man," Felix said gruffly. He didn't add, *and not nearly as self-sufficient as he'd like to pretend.* "Now what did Josh tell you about Sean that he didn't tell me?"

Danny laughed softly and kissed Felix's palm. "Oh, let me tell you the tale. The tale of a faithless hipster who liked to chase tail."

"No!" Felix shook his head. He'd *liked* the quiet young beat cop with the sly sense of humor. "Habitually or one bad mistake?" He tugged, and Danny followed him down the stairs and across the foyer.

"One bad mistake is what it sounded like," Danny said.

"Ah, youth." Felix felt better. If it had been a habitual thing, he would have doubted his instincts. Anyone could fall, but fixing that flaw in yourself, that's what you did as you matured.

"I believe it was an ex-girlfriend, doing the kitten-in-the-rain thing," Danny agreed. "But he hurt Josh badly, and for that I shall never forgive him, regardless of whether I met him or not."

Felix paused before opening the door, thinking about all the dangers out there: the people who were after Danny, the people who would like to see Felix burn in hell for something he hadn't done.

He squeezed Danny's hand, stepped out into the brisk breeze of the cold spring, and turned his face to the sun. Crocuses and pinks—winter flowers—filled the breeze with incense, and the pollen of blooming trees thickened the air. Danny sneezed, and Felix produced his preferred allergy medication and a bottle of water from the pockets of his fleece.

"Thanks, Mom," Danny said before washing the one down with the other. He looked down the quarter-mile driveway to a block filled with enormous houses and vast yards. "You kept the landscaping," he said softly.

"It has our tree," Felix said, nodding to an oak tree he'd had planted in the front yard before Danny had even arrived from Europe. He'd envisioned a lot for that tree—tire swings, a treehouse, carving his and Danny's initials in the trunk. He'd known so little then. It had taken twenty years for the tree to get big enough for any of those dreams, and now Josh was too old for tire swings.

But Danny was here, and they could still carve their initials.

He was planning again.

Spun-up

DANNY'S APARTMENT was actually three floors below Marnie's, which made Felix scowl a bit, but Danny had simply picked the first available apartment. Felix had grown up with money. He'd spent a long time trying to explain the nuances of different kinds of rich when they'd been younger, but unless Danny was trying to convince someone he was a lost prince from a long-dead country, he really could not see the difference.

There were the rich who enjoyed their money and lived kindly, and there were the rich who craved their money and lived cruelly. The one type of rich was hands off; the other type was hands most definitely on.

The rest was costume and character, really.

Danny's apartment was—as Felix had pointed out—so bare as to be almost sterile.

Or it had been before Josh and his friends got hold of it.

Someone had bought or stolen art for almost every corner of the place: cityscapes for the pillars by the windows, country sketches for the softer colors of the tan-tiled, open-air kitchen, and a series of watercolors featuring muted people in the foreground and the streets of Chicago blended into the back, for the bedroom. As Josh and Stirling double-checked the monitoring system and the earbuds from the desk, Danny wandered restlessly around the bedroom, peering at the pictures on the wall.

"Josh?" he asked, puzzled. "Who painted these?"

Josh glanced up and cocked his head. "Wait, Stirling, did Papers do those?"

Stirling looked around and nodded shortly. Stirling didn't do one word when none would suffice.

"Papers," Josh said. "He was by this morning when Dad was here."

"Papers," Danny said flatly.

"Yeah, you know. The guy who gave us the provenance for all the art we stole?"

"We gave it back," Danny said, because they had. They'd put every piece back in the secret safe—or, rather, the replicas they'd paid half of Felix's fortune to have made so quickly while they kept the originals. What Marnie *thought* were the originals, anyway, since she apparently didn't know real from fake. The only exception was the Pontalba jeweled comb; they had the original of that one.

But that wasn't what Danny was looking at now. "He's really stunning," Danny said, studying the

composition and the originality. "Does he do art forgeries too?"

"Sometimes," Josh said. "He's never sold them,
though. I think he just likes to count brush strokes."

"Well, I don't need to worry about the provenances, then," Danny said, chuckling slightly. "And I guess
I can stop traveling to Prague to get my passport done."

"Mm," Josh said, his voice so noncommittal that
Danny looked up.

"What's that noise?" he asked suspiciously.

"You'll have to ask Dad," Josh murmured. "Grace,
take the tiara off. Talia's going to be here any minute,
and she doesn't need your thief cooties all over it."

Grace stopped primping in front of the mirror on
the back of the bathroom door. The door was closed.
This was a system's check of the coms too. "I do not
have thief cooties." His voice rang perfectly clear in
Danny's earbud. Grace did a shuffle and a flourish that
they could see on Stirling's monitor as Grace's reflection in the mirror. "I have *dance* cooties!"

"You've got douche cooties," Stirling muttered. "I
think you knocked the camera loose. Get out here and
let me look."

"None of us have douche cooties," Grace said,
emerging from the bathroom with the tiara in his
hand. He was wearing black tights, black rubber-soled
shoes, and a black turtleneck, because there wasn't a
store open with a neon T-shirt with Cat Burglar written
across the front in sparkles. "We're all gay." He handed
the tiara to Stirling with a little bow, and Stirling rolled
his eyes, unimpressed.

"I had a bi moment," Chuck said, surprising nobody. He was in the living room, checking the monitors there. They'd put cameras in the hallway leading

to Marnie's apartment, and Chuck was overseeing who came and went. As far as the people in the apartment knew, there was only one public way in or out, and Chuck could see everyone who went that way.

"I had an entire bi year in high school," Hunter said sarcastically, and they could see him on Josh's monitor, looking around to see if anybody could hear him. Hunter was in Marnie's kitchen. Phyllis had talked to Marnie's housekeeper and gotten two of them in as catering help, just in case things got a little bit tricky when Marnie lost her shit.

"And still there's not a single straight guy for me," Molly muttered next to him. They were filling trays with canapes that the actual caterer had taken from the oven. Danny wondered if they'd had real experience in food service or were, like Josh himself, just damned quick and able to adapt.

Maybe both.

"Well, you could troll the party, but remember, most of the guys there are douchebags," Josh told her cheerfully. "Sorry!"

"You all suck," she countered in disgust. "When's Grace making the switch?"

"Everybody's getting dressed now," Josh told her. "Mom and Dad are getting here with the costumes, and Talia and Grayson are about half an hour out. We want to wait until Marnie's entire attention is taken by the drama in the front room. But he's got to get in and out super quick. Chuck, did you put your pitstop on?"

Chuck snorted. "I shaved, waxed, plucked, and gelled, little man. I'm a hottie magnet."

At that moment there was a burst of feedback in everybody's earpieces as two more people entered the apartment. Josh adjusted the feed, and Grace set the tiara down on the dresser. "That was pleasant."

"Well, it's like backstage for a musical here," Josh retorted. "Something huge, like *Les Mis* or *Hamilton*. Everyone needs to get dressed and go be pretty."

"And to that end…," Felix said, entering the room with two garment bags over his arm. "Everyone but Josh and Danny needs to clear out. You can have your toys in a moment, gentleman, but right now…."

Stirling stood gracelessly, almost knocking over one of the two laptops on the desk. "Sorry, Mr. Salinger," he said.

"Stirling," Danny interposed, shooting Felix an exasperated look. "These earpieces are top notch. Excellent job on the tech, my boy. We'd be lost without you."

Stirling let a small smile escape. "Thanks, Uncle Danny," he rasped before turning to flee.

"On that note," Josh muttered. "Coms going off for everyone but Molly, Hunter, and myself. Grownups need to talk. In five, four—"

"Can I take it out of my ear?" Grace asked, and Josh stopped tapping on the keyboard long enough to stand up from his chair and smack Grace on the back of the head.

"No. For the five-hundredth time, no! Everybody else knows to leave the damned things in your ear because they are super damned fragile but you?"

"So that's no," Grace said.

"Get out. Go get something to eat so your blood sugar doesn't go tits up when you're in the damned ventilation system, and try not to piss me off."

Grace smiled toothily, letting them all know that his intention had been to get under Josh's skin, and hey, achievement unlocked.

"Grace!" Hunter barked, and Josh paused with his fingers over the keys again.

"Sorry, Hunter," Grace mumbled. He stuck his tongue out at Josh, who flipped him off.

"So coms off in five, four, three, two, one." Josh hit a key and waved Grace out right as his mother walked in.

"How are we all doing?" she asked with a gracious smile. She'd obviously had her hair professionally done, swept into a complicated twist to one side with a place for the comb to go over her exposed ear. Her beauty would be accentuated, and the comb would be showcased. Win/win! Her makeup had also been professionally done, and Danny understood that women were using lip dye and airbrushing these days, but he was pretty sure Julia was that flawless. Of course, the exquisite makeup wasn't for any of the people she loved—probably not even for the hairdresser she was sleeping with.

That sort of makeup was almost exclusively applied when a woman was doing battle.

Danny clutched at his chest. "Oh, Julia," he breathed. "You are the only woman I could ever love, and you have shot me in the heart with your beauty."

Even her cackle was glorious. "So many lies, Danny. Don't ever stop. Felix, I'll take my bag now." She grimaced and put her hand to her stomach. "I ate a light supper," she murmured. "So these must be butterflies and not blood sugar."

Felix kissed her cheek. "Remember," he said softly, "if all you do is show up and make everybody jealous because you're the prettiest, you have done your job."

Her eyes narrowed. "I am far more than just the prettiest," she said, the core of steel that had kept her alive and away from her father's brutal hand showing in her voice.

"Then you're unstoppable," Felix told her, winking.

She took her garment bag and flounced into the bathroom, leaving Felix, Danny, and Josh.

"Son?" Felix asked, a pained look on his face. "Can you move your monitor?"

Josh grimaced. "Sorry, Dad. Really can't. I'll just sit here and pretend to be paint on the wall."

"Dammit."

Uh-oh. "What's wrong?" Danny asked. The past two days had been a lot of frantic activity as Felix had activated all his contacts and Danny had worked with the crew to put everything in place. They'd had time for some more lovemaking, hurried and intense, but since that glorious afternoon on which Felix had taken his hand and they'd gone on a simple walk, Felix waving to neighbors, introducing Danny as his "old friend," nothing more had been said about their relationship or about that most frightening of words: forever.

"Nothing's wrong," Felix told him now, giving a soft smile and striding forward to touch his wrist. A simple gesture of calming, of kindness, but gah! Felix was so good at it. It was like having allergy medication in his pocket or worrying about not connecting with Josh's friends. If Felix couldn't make it better immediately, he was always working on ways to make it better eventually. Danny should have trusted him, should have been stronger when they'd been together. Felix would have found a way to kiss his temple, rub his back, make Danny visible when that was what Danny had wanted so very badly.

Or maybe he would have just held Danny when his loneliness cramped his stomach. Sometimes that quiet understated touch had been the thing Danny had missed the most about having Felix in his life.

"If nothing's wrong," Danny asked, trying not to let his mind wander, "why did you try to kick our coms director out?"

Felix's eyes darted left, which was a tell that said a blatant lie was coming up, and they both knew it. "There's a problem," he said. "With Chuck's tuxedo. We, uh, Julia, I mean, got the measurements wrong."

Danny narrowed his eyes suspiciously. "And the person this tuxedo would most likely fit would be…?"

Felix's smile showed all his teeth. "Benjamin Morgan," he said.

Danny blinked. Felix's middle name and "Morgan? As in 'morganatic'?" he asked, his suspicions in full swing.

"Why, yes," Felix said, smiling prettily. "Exactly."

"Felix, 'Benjamin Morgan' doesn't have any identification or background. Dammit, I need… provenance!"

"You're an art dealer who spends part of his time in Europe and most of his time here," Josh said, keeping his eyes on the monitor. "Your middle name is Daniel. Your parents died in a car accident when you were young, and you went to stay with a distant relative in Des Moines. You have an art degree from NYU, and you have a job interview at the Art Institute as an assistant curator in two weeks."

"I'm sorry?" Danny said, that last part surprising him. "How in the—"

"I called a friend," Felix said like this wasn't one of the most coveted positions in the art world. Human provenance was relatively easy to forge—if you had a computer and some imagination—but real human contacts? That was risky.

"But what happens when I don't show up?" Danny asked, stunned.

"What happens if you do?" Felix said, and his body language—shoulders back, hands in his pockets, casual smile on his face—all said this was no big deal. But his voice had the faintest quaver in it, the faintest insecurity, and in a way, Danny was relieved, because this *was* a big deal and Felix got that. "You might just get the job. But don't worry about that now. Now you need to dress and go as Julia's swain. Don't forget to flirt shamelessly with Marnie, even if it turns your stomach."

"*Fuck* Marnie Courtland!" Danny snapped.

"Not on a dare," Felix returned with a completely straight face.

"Why are you doing this to me?"

"Because now you have an identity in this community," Felix said, and only the faintest tremor in his voice betrayed how nervous he was. "You have a person to be. You have a way to move about in this world and stay."

Danny flailed. "I've only been back for five days!"

Felix's eyes, when they met his, were red-rimmed and as intense as the blessed fires of the gods. "You've only been a hole in my life for ten years. We need someone to go out there with Julia. You can go and make an impression and then leave, and nobody will be the wiser. Or you can go and do the same thing and stay, and everybody will know who you are and that you're mine. The only thing that's really changed here is now you have a choice—that's all."

Danny glared at him, feeling trapped, although this was the opposite of that. "You should have asked me," he snarled.

"And give you extra time to set this up and run?" Felix retorted. "Not on your life."

"I can't be here permanently. Not out in the open!" Danny flailed, not sure if he could make this clear. "I'm wanted by Interpol, Felix. That doesn't go away."

"Well, they've been on your ass for twenty years. That's not new! This is a new identity. One attached to me."

"That's right. It's attached to *you*. You could go to *jail*, Felix. You could lose *everything*—"

"I've already lost everything," Felix retorted. "I lost *you*. And now that I've got you back, I'm taking measures to keep you as long as humanly possible. Do you mind?"

Danny gaped at him, the air whooshing out of his lungs. God, it was everything he'd ever wanted in his *life*.

"Well," Felix said, voice gentler now, "do you?" He took a few steps forward, and Danny's resistance crumbled.

"No," he muttered, and Felix closed the gap between them and wrapped his arms around Danny's shoulders.

"Good," Felix murmured into his hair. "When Julia's done, go make yourself pretty and try on the tux. I brought your good shoes from your closet. Had Phyllis give them a bit of a shine too." He paused. "Also, grab those cufflinks that used to belong to Fitzgerald. You know the ones."

Of course Danny remembered. They'd been a gift to show him Felix had never forgotten.

Danny let out a broken laugh. "God, you're manipulative."

"Am I?" Felix smiled, looking pleased. "I only learn from the best."

"Shut up." Danny leaned his face against Felix's shoulder and breathed in, trying to center himself. What he got was a lungful of Felix's cologne, of his soap, of the particular cedar/bergamot smell that was Felix's alone. The smell hit him like the resonant note on a tuning fork, and his entire body quivered, completely in tune with the man holding him.

Felix was trying to offer him forever. Danny didn't have to take it *now*, but he had to be aware that it was there for the taking.

They both heard the front door open as Torrance and Talia walked in.

Later. He had to make this decision *later*.

They separated, and Danny shook his head. "It's a good thing I showered after we went running," he said with a sniff. "I came this close to smelling like gym shorts."

"You weren't around when Josh's body odor took on a life of its own," Felix said, not-so-surreptitiously wiping under his eye with the back of his hand. "Just him walking through the door used to make our eyes water. I wouldn't even know if you forgot to wash your pits."

"Thanks for sharing that with the coms off, Dad," Josh said cheerfully from the monitor. "Happy to throw my dignity under the bus for the two of you. Should we turn the coms back *on*, and I can tell everybody about the time I tried to lose my virginity and it didn't pan out?"

Looking over his shoulder at the monitor, Danny saw Hunter and Molly trying desperately not to lose their composure.

"I suggest you don't," Danny said dryly, "or your friends are busted. Give me the tux, Felix. I can change in here and do a water comb when Her Nibs is finished."

"Fine. I'll go greet—"

Danny had just shucked his slacks and toed off his battered loafers when the door opened and Torrance Grayson walked in. Ah! Gods! Five feet, nine inches of black-haired, blue-eyed perfection—Danny hated that Felix even knew him.

It helped that he only had eyes for Josh.

"Oh!" he said cheerfully. "Sorry about that, uh… uh…."

"Benjamin," Felix supplied, looking directly at Danny. "Benjamin Morgan." His eyes softened, and Grayson all but disappeared. "He's—"

"Everything," Grayson said perceptively. "I get that now." He looked at Josh and tried a smile. "So, what's doing here? It looks like a production room, but…." He stilled. "Wait. It *is* a production room. That's Marnie. That's… that's her apartment."

"Active coms in three minutes," Josh said. "Anything special going on?"

Danny couldn't hear the reply, but he saw Josh nod and look up at Torrance with patience. "Yes, I would avoid picking your nose in the bathroom mirror tonight, just so you know."

"And I'll definitely wash my hands," Grayson said, looking a little shaken. "Is this legal?"

Josh gave him a side-eyeball scowl. "Was it supposed to be?"

Grayson blinked and turned toward Felix. "This isn't legal?"

Felix grimaced. "Is this going to be a problem?"

To his credit, Torrance Grayson thought about it carefully. "Will *I* be doing anything illegal?"

"No!" Josh answered, patience snapping. "And believe me, you'll be glad we're here. Put this in your ear—" He handed Grayson a com. "—and give this to your date." He handed over the tiara. "Don't tell her there's a camera on it. It makes people self-conscious if they don't practice."

"Then how am I supposed to convince her to wear it?" Danny had to hand it to Torrance Grayson. He really knew nothing about women.

"Oh my God, Gray! Do I really get to wear that?" A stunning—and stunningly fit—woman rustled in wearing a satin off-the-shoulder gown that befitted the goddess she was. The warm earthy bronze of her skin glittered with gold powder, and her eyes—tip-tilted and made up for battle, just like Julia's—were wide, deep brown, and only a little sweet for Danny's taste.

He knew now why Josh wasn't telling this woman she was bugged.

"Yes, precious, it's all yours for the night," Grayson said, shooting Josh a grim look.

"Here, my lovely," Felix said, stepping forward to block Danny as he hurried up and finished changing. "Let me set this… just like this."

"You said you were going to send it to the house," Talia admonished. "I was so disappointed when it didn't show!"

Danny winced. He'd been the one who'd suggested bugging the garnet hanging down the center, but those things take more than a minute to set up, if they're done right.

"We were getting it cleaned," Felix lied blandly. "I do apologize." He gently but firmly placed it on Talia's head, making sure the combs slid into her intricate coif. "Now, remember, Marnie is going to freak out a bit when she sees this. Are you okay with that?"

"Why?" Talia asked, eyes wide. It was easy to see that she adored Felix; he made a good big-brother/father figure. Danny remembered he'd always attracted followers the same way heavy cabbage roses attracted lazy bees.

"Well, she might think it's hers," Felix said, smiling ever so slightly. Danny could tell he was enjoying this, but he was torturing Talia with a little bit of relish.

Talia clapped her hand over her mouth. "Is it?" she asked, both horrified and excited.

"Not legally, no," Felix replied. He gave the tiara one last little adjustment. "But she won't know we know that. Until you walk in wearing it, of course."

Talia gasped, her eyes wide. "What will she do?"

Danny manfully suppressed his grin and allowed Felix to keep answering.

"Well, I suppose she'll run to her vault in the study to make sure the pieces are still there." His eyes slid toward Danny's. Danny gave him the thumbs-up—he'd had two days, and he knew jewelry forgers like Felix knew paper forgers.

"Are they going to be there?" she asked. She made as though to rip off a gel-nail and Felix stopped her.

"They've been there for quite some time," Felix said. Well, two hours. They'd had them just long enough to commission forgers to do their best, even though some of the pieces were forgeries themselves. They put the duplicates back in the safe before the party and kept the real ones. "It's the provenance we'll be replacing while you're at the party."

"Why are you replacing the provenance now?" Talia asked, her eyes charmingly wide.

"Well, we wanted her to believe her provenance was the right one when it is, in fact, outdated."

It was Torrance who put an end to it. "Oh, for chrissakes, Felix, don't keep us in suspense! What does the provenance say?"

Felix's chuckle warmed Danny's stomach. He still loved "adventures," as he called them—and so did Danny. But only when Danny was committing them with Felix.

"I can tell you this," Felix answered. "These pieces are mine, legally and proprietarily. So when Marnie starts foaming at the mouth, you need to make her present you with those papers. And enjoy the show."

And that right there was the truth. Felix had spent two days photographing, authenticating, and purchasing the seven stolen items they'd found in Marnie's safe. The papers Marnie would find were photocopies of faxes indicating the pieces had changed hands. Oddly enough, not one of the museums missing the items were aware of the theft—even Julia's comb had been taken off display some time before the item had disappeared. They'd been more than happy to allow Felix to purchase the items, particularly since he'd made a deal with the museums to return the pieces for display in the following months. Felix now owned everything Marnie had once possessed in her safe.

And Marnie had forgeries in their place.

Marnie might indeed foam at the mouth—but all that would get her was a whole lot of publicity she wouldn't particularly enjoy. And watching her come unglued would hopefully give Danny and Felix the nails for her coffin.

Grifting was as much art as it was science; they could set up the perfect sting every time, but how the mark would behave? That was unpredictable.

Of course the fun part would be putting the provenance of the stolen items in the safe *after* the party began so she didn't have a chance to look at it beforehand. People tended to wear their sparklies at parties—that was what parties were for—and they didn't want her tipped off.

That's what Grace was waiting for. Marnie would greet Talia and Julia, run back to her safe to check on her items, and when she left the room again, Grace would replace her forged provenances with the actual provenances featuring Felix's name.

Elaborate, yes, but also disorienting. Not the sort of thing a woman who promotes herself as bright, trendy, and cutting edge would do.

It would be so satisfying to watch.

And again, so ripe with opportunities to exploit. A woman who promoted herself as progressive would have been just shown to possess jewelry stolen from the man she was supposed to be discrediting.

It would throw her credibility into doubt and plant the seeds for showing her perfidy to the public.

At that moment Julia swanned out of the bathroom, resplendent in a sapphire-blue satin evening gown that not only showed off her toned shoulders but also showcased her slender, fit body. She wasn't the stunning athlete Talia was, but her poise and quiet beauty had its own presence. As she emerged, she and Talia engaged in girl talk about their sparkly bangles and their general goddessitude. Danny enjoyed that. From what Felix had told him, Talia had experienced a setdown of confidence, and Julia, who had climbed out of a hole of abuse with grit, cunning, and a willingness to do what it took, was one of those people who could boost the young woman's self-esteem and give her a taste for a little blood.

And women who loved sparkly things were a particular delight.

Still, when Felix turned away from the two of them to put a discreet diamond tie clip on Danny's sapphire tie, the busyness and excitement faded, and Danny was next to Felix, who was dressed in his own silk suit and smelling... ah! So good. Danny resisted the temptation to bury his nose against Felix's neck and toss the whole enterprise in the trash. They were there to save Felix's ass—that was important. Danny *liked* that ass, even if Felix hadn't given him a crack at it yet.

"You reading that, Josh?" Felix asked, looking deeply into Danny's eyes.

"Sure am," Josh said happily. His screen showed eight revolving pictures side by side, and given that two of the pictures came from this room, looking at it gave Danny vertigo anyway.

Being lost in Felix's eyes seemed the perfect place to be.

"What's your name?" Felix murmured.

"Benjamin Daniel Morgan," Danny said back. "Went to NYU. Hated the winters, loved swimming on the Jersey shore during the summers, master's in art history, doctorate in the evolution of objets d'art." He smiled faintly, Felix's body so close to his, their heartbeats almost twinned.

"Nice embellishments," Felix murmured. "When did you swim on the Jersey shore?"

"Before I made it to Europe," Danny said, referring to the brief summers when he'd hustled for his sugar daddy on the beach. "Before I met you. Do I have a resume to study, or did you just pimp me out?"

"I told the directors basically what you just said," Felix said, a faint smile on his face. "You really do have the equivalent of a doctorate, Danny, but you're self-taught and very... hands-on."

Danny's cheeks heated. "I have an interest," he said with dignity.

Felix leaned forward and kissed his forehead. "You don't have to be anything but Julia's window dressing," he said softly.

"I know how to play a part." Danny's mouth thinned. "I'm not the one you have to worry about here. We've got civilians on the floor."

Felix framed Danny's cheeks with his hands and pulled Danny into a very *un*civilized, very *carnal* kiss, and when he pulled back, he said, "What's your name again?"

"Goddammit," Danny muttered, and the curse word knocked his brain back online. "Danny—Benjamin Daniel Morgan," he snapped. "I don't see you kissing me in the middle of Marnie's apartment, so none of that counts."

"Dad," Josh interrupted. "Uncle Danny? It's about time to go."

Felix took a tissue and wiped Danny's mouth. "Talia, Gray? This is Benjamin Morgan. He'll be Julia's date for the night. Be kind to him. He's been out of the country for a bit. He might seem a little lost."

Danny glared daggers at him. "I will get you for that, Felix Salinger."

Felix gave him a smug smile and a nose wrinkle. "Now go wet comb your hair. You look positively disheveled."

Danny stalked away, muttering, "I'll kill him, Julia. You and I can raise Josh just fine. Why would we need that bastard?"

Josh hollered, "I'm grown, Uncle Danny!" before Julia's tinkle of laughter followed him into the bathroom.

A few moments later, he and Julia were following Torrance and Talia down the hall of Marnie's floor. She must have primed all her neighbors because the hallway itself was pretty crowded, but Danny didn't see a single open door or so much as an acknowledgment that Marnie had turned her apartment and the hallway into the equivalent of a red carpet to the Emmys.

A murmur went through the crowd, and people turned toward Julia in her strapless sapphire gown, with the jeweled comb placed just so in her hair. She looked delectable, but more importantly, she looked *happy*. Not angry, not vindictive, but carefree and joyous. Of course she and Danny kept up sly banter, not only with each other but with the audience they knew was listening from Danny's apartment.

"Ooh," Felix said in Danny's ear, "is that Thomas Helmsley?"

"Big chap, dark blue double-breasted?" Danny murmured back. "Jailbait trophy wife?"

"Jailbait trophy *mistress*," Felix returned. "She's his daughter's best friend from college. Because he *is* that much of a douchebag."

"That's special. Want me to do anything to him?"

"We can save him for another evening," Felix murmured. "Let's stick to the job at hand."

"Oh, darling, please let Danny lift his wallet," Julia begged. "Pretty please? The things he's said to his wife are just horrid."

Danny made a slight deviation from course and knocked into the portly man a bit. "So sorry," he said, smiling charmingly. "And you, my dear, didn't mean to impose."

Helmsley smiled and clapped him on the back, and the girl—wearing something au courant and ugly, with fake-fur embellishments and too many big rhinestones—simpered. Danny inclined his head and slipped Helmsley's wallet into the small strappy handbag at Julia's side.

"There you go, sweets," Danny murmured. "But that bag's not big enough for more than two of these, so pick your next mark carefully."

"Oh God, Danny, I'm so glad you're back."

He patted her arm. "I missed you too."

"Can we focus," Felix growled, but Danny felt much better now that the first crime of the night had been committed.

"We're almost at the entrance," Danny said cheerfully, just as Felix said, "Shit! Wait! Who's that?"

"Julia!"

Danny looked up to see Marnie Courtland herself, decked out in an ice-blue sheath dress with a delicate spill of diamonds at her throat, smile dangerously in greeting.

She was wearing her forgery of the comb of Micaela Almonester Pontalba.

Just as Danny schooled his features to adjust to the game at hand, Felix squawked, "Cocksucker! Warning, Danny. Cocksucker!" over the earpiece, and chaos erupted in the tech room.

Rookie Moves. Plural.

DURING THEIR prolonged stint in Europe when Josh was seven, Danny acquired a shadow.

Younger by about five years, Carl Soderburgh only seemed to run into Danny when he was alone. When it had first happened, in London when Danny was out getting the family coffee and scones for breakfast, Danny had been flattered. But Danny was always cautious, and after a conversation during which Felix was sure he'd been charming but aloof, he'd written the boy off as a chance encounter.

When it happened again, in Dublin, Danny had grown suspicious.

When it happened once more, in Edinburgh, Danny had taken the boy to tea and flirted with him shamelessly while passing his wallet to Julia, who texted his passport number to Felix, who used a then-vulnerable internet to do some research. And the name he came up with was not Soderburgh.

In fact, their young friend was Carl Eugene Cox—poor boy—and he'd been working as an investigator for an insurance company.

An insurance company *very* interested in how the statue Danny had recently "acquired" from a private collector had ended up in the hands of the museum from which the statue had disappeared some months before.

The collector had been appalled—oh no! Forged provenance! He had been *fooled*! The insurance company had not been so fooled, but they'd needed a scapegoat, and young Carl had been put on Danny's tail.

All of this, Danny had put young Carl wise to—using entendre and innuendo, what else? Carl had smiled politely, bid them good day, and left.

They'd thought to be shut of him, but he'd shown up again in Tuscany... and Rome... and Madrid, and throughout it all, Felix had never been sure. Was he just that loyal to an insurance company that did not actually give a rat's ass *who* had stolen the statue, as long as they could pin it on someone? Or had Danny become his obsession?

Carl the Cocksucker—as Felix affectionally called him, his jealousy making a full-fledged appearance as it so rarely did—left them alone when they returned to the States, but Felix had kept tabs on him. He still worked for the same insurance company, doggedly, persistently, with the loyalty of a spaniel and the determination of a rat terrier.

He'd been married—to a woman—once, and had a number of liaisons with either sex throughout the years.

And he had dropped completely off Felix's radar until his dark blond head crossed through Felix's vision from the back hallway, searching the crowd with wide green eyes just as Marnie said Julia's name.

The next few minutes played out in living color on Josh's and Stirling's monitors, set up side by side. Felix used to work this part when Danny was their grease man, and he was adept at translating the separate pictures on the screen into one continuous narrative. That's what he did now, absolutely certain that when it popped up in his nightmares in the following years, he'd be seeing it in real time.

"Cocksucker! Warning, Danny. Cocksucker!" Felix cried out just as he saw that Marnie was *wearing* the comb they had put back in her safe.

Shit!

Danny first.

"Molly, Hunter, see that big blond guy heading for the door? Stop him."

"How?" Molly said, moving through the crowd. "Flirting? Jujitsu? What?"

"You flirt, I'll do jujitsu," Hunter said, casually heading toward Carl.

"Grace," Felix snapped urgently, "get in there *now.* She's going back for the provenance in five minutes or less."

"Holy cow! You still want me to replace the provenance, right?" Grace asked, grabbing the two small black bags he'd prepped.

"We have to try," Felix said, "but be careful."

"Gotcha."

Grace dropped to his knees so he could crawl through the ventilation shaft and Stirling squawked, "Wait! I'm not into the security system yet!"

Grace tapped his ear. "Well, tell me when you get that taken care of!" Then he disappeared.

"Shit!" People were talking, and Felix was trying to listen to three conversations at once. He studied the monitors fiercely, watching as—

"Oh!" All of them cried out at the same time.

"And the quarterback is *toast*!" Josh exclaimed as Molly "tripped" over her own feet, took Carl Cox down with her, and landed right in his lap.

"Oh my God," she burbled, as brainless as a burb. "I'm so sorry! Oh no. Please don't tell Miss Courtland. She'll have my job."

Molly brushed ineffectually at Carl's suit with her napkin while Hunter—who had been hot on her heels—bent to scoop the tray she'd mashed up against his chest and the canapes she'd dropped with it from the superpricey peach-colored carpet.

"Oh, she will?" Carl asked, his voice making it clear that he'd be happy to get this adorable girl fired if he could.

"She needs the job to pay her tuition," Hunter rasped, giving a smile that looked more like a threat. "Don't. Do it."

Carl raised his eyebrows. "Okay, I won't. But if you will excuse me, I need to go see someone at the door."

Hunter stepped aside, and as Carl swept forward, he stuck his foot out, pulling it back as Carl went sprawling.

Molly took the tray from his hand and disappeared as Hunter started to pick Carl up, making apologies and checking to make sure he was all right.

"We want him delayed, not dead," Felix muttered.

Hunter's eye roll didn't need a com link to speak volumes. Felix ignored him and went back to watching Marnie and Julia.

And Danny.

"Julia, you look stunning!" Marnie said, her eyes darting to the comb in Julia's hair.

"Thank you, darling. You look nice too."

Felix sucked air in through his teeth. Brutal. Simply brutal.

"And is this your date?" Marnie batted her eyes at Danny, who smiled smoothly back.

"A friend of the family," Julia said quickly, and not even a flicker in Danny's eyes showed that he was surprised by the change in the script.

"Benjamin Morgan," he said, taking Marnie's hand and kissing her knuckles, European style. "So nice to meet you, Ms. Courtland." He cast her a smoldering look through his lashes, and Marnie pretended to fan herself.

"Well, I'm delighted, Mr. Morgan," she said, biting her lip provocatively. For a moment, she was completely distracted, but only for a moment.

"Julia, I see you have a replica of an object d'art belonging to Micaela Pontalba."

"Oh, not a replica, darling," Julia returned, smiling with her teeth. "This would be the real thing."

Marnie's eyes flashed. "I'm sure you're mistaken. My art procurer assured me that mine was purchased from the museum itself."

"Well, they must have been in possession of a replica," Julia said with a shrug. "Benjamin—" She batted her eyes. "—tell Marnie here how she's mistaken."

"Lucky for me," Grace murmured, pulling a small box out of his pocket, "I had it imprinted." He pulled out a small sleeve of rubber meant to feel like real skin. He'd been in and out of Marnie's apartment over the last four days, and he had the perfect set of fingerprints pressed onto five little finger caps. He slid those on now and went to work. First, he opened the large safe, which, as Stirling said, had already been released. Then he slid his hand in and gave his fingerprints to the side panel while Stirling recited a string of digits—Grace had done this once before, but there was an algorithm that changed the code every day. Stirling's help was much appreciated.

One held breath later and he was in.

And that's when Marnie saw her chance. There was a gap in the line of entering guests. She turned to Brittney Porter, her aide de camp, and murmured something before slipping away, leaving Brittney to take over.

"Shit," Josh said.

"Shit," Felix said.

"What else?" Danny asked. "And where's Carl?"

"Carl is by the bathroom—he was heading for the entryway, but now he's going for the kitchen. Jesus, Danny, this guy's got a thing for you."

Maybe it was the way his face didn't change expression over the cameras, but Felix got a sinking sensation in the pit of his stomach.

"No," he said, fighting the urge to go out and strangle Carl "Soderburgh" Cox with his own entrails.

"Now is not the time," Danny all but sang. "What's wrong?"

"Marnie's headed for the den already, and Grace isn't out," Felix muttered.

"And the bars are fighting me every fucking step of the way!" Stirling snarled.

Danny's eyes went wide. "Can we keep them from closing?"

"There's a manual release on the outside," Stirling said. "If someone holds that down for ten seconds, there's a thirty second window to get clear."

"What constitutes clear?" Danny asked, weaving through the throngs of people. He deftly used a group of young party girls as a veil to cover him as he crossed the hallway in front of Carl and Hunter, and Felix had to admit—he hadn't lost a step.

"The turn at the end of the room?" Josh hazarded, and Felix swore.

"Grace, hold tight," Danny murmured. "I'm coming."

Felix and the others watched breathlessly as Grace made the swap—the jewelry Marnie procured for the replicas they'd made—and Chuck wandered up behind them.

"Oh, hey," he said. "Carl. Good guy. What's he doing here?"

"At the moment? Trying to track down Danny," Felix muttered. "How do *you* know him?"

"He was undercover, going for a job as a baby driver." Chuck's mouth twisted. "I got the job, but I gave him a few pointers about how not to look like an obvious company plant."

Felix yanked his eyes off the screen. "Why would you do that?" he asked.

Chuck gave him a toothy, unashamed grin, and Felix had to do the math. If Chuck was about ten years Josh's senior, he was about five years Carl's junior, which made the age difference between Chuck and Carl the same as the age difference between Carl and Danny and….

"Oh my fucking God," Felix muttered. "I hope that man has a two-pronged horse cock and a prehensile tongue because his sex life is going to imprison us all!"

"You're the one who wanted to share a cell," Danny muttered. He got to the study and pulled a set of lockpicks out of his pocket that Felix didn't even recall seeing him put there.

"Where were you keeping those?" Felix asked in horror.

"They're the ones you gave me—platinum, indestructible, so many, many different prongs." It wasn't an answer—but then, it wasn't important. They watched as Danny looked up to where he knew the camera was and winked, and then he appeared in the study just as Grace finished closing the safe.

Danny locked the door, then pulled out his lockpicks and made sure it was *extra* locked.

"Are we set to go?" he asked. Grace nodded, pulling out a microfiber shammy and a small bottle of dusting spray to wipe down. Felix had a heartbeat to admire the guy's professionalism before he realized that Chuck was stripping down next to him.

"The fuck are you doing?"

Josh sputtered. "Dad, you have got to pull it together."

"What the fuck is he doing?" Felix repeated and then turned to Chuck again as he pulled up the extra garment bag that Felix had brought in case Danny had turned him down.

"This is the suit Julia had fitted for me, right?" Chuck asked, pulling the pants on quickly.

"Yes. It was sort of a decoy."

Chuck slid on the shirt. "Yes, she told me. I cleaned up just in case Danny flat-out refused. Anyway, I told her I'd never had a bespoke suit before. She seemed to think that was a shame," he said, buttoning up with lightning speed. "If Hunter and Grayson can hold out just a minute longer, I can jump in the race."

And with that he slid on his jacket, shoved the tie in his pocket, and slid his shoes back on in the space it took Felix to blink. He was out of the apartment before Felix could even turn back to the monitor.

"Where did you meet him?" he asked Josh.

Josh just laughed. Things were happening on the monitors again.

Julia saw Marnie heading for her study and stepped smoothly forward to intercept her. "Oh, honey, it's not necessary to go get your papers. Benjamin was just showing off."

Marnie narrowed her eyes. "Who is he, anyway?"

"Friend of the family," Julia said again. "Felix knew him before he met me. They were knocking around Europe together before Benjamin finished his education."

Ah, Julia. Remembering Lying 101. It was always easier when you stuck to the truth.

"Well, he does know his jewelry," Marnie muttered.

"He knows his *art*," Julia corrected. "It's his passion—always has been. He's interviewing at the Art Institute in two weeks. I bet you could interview him for your 'Hello, Chicago!' segment, do you think?"

Everyone in the control room sucked in a breath.

"All right, *Mom*!" Josh said with a fist pump.

"Julia, I love you so much," Felix murmured.

"She's fucking diabolical," Danny said from the study, where he was fumbling for the security button on the molding around the ventilation shaft. "Here you are, you little bastard."

"What a lovely idea," Marnie said, reaching for the study door. She frowned when she realized it was locked but produced the key in short order from the bodice of her dress.

"Classy," Josh muttered.

"Well, if you're going to lock one room in your apartment during a party…," Felix replied.

"Obviously not gonna be the bedroom," Stirling said, and Josh and Felix both stared at him in surprise.

Stirling scowled back. "That place is never locked," he said. "I've seen that woman have sex a *lot* in three days."

"With who?" Felix asked, keeping his attention on the monitors by discipline alone.

"Her assistant, Brittney—she's a total bitch to her in bed, by the way. And that guy in the corner of the kitchen watching Carl, Hunter, and Grayson like they're mice."

Felix caught his breath. "I didn't even see that gentleman, did you?"

"Jesus, no," Josh said.

"Molly, do you see who he's talking about?"

Molly had made it back to the kitchen and was busy setting up another tray of canapes. "Creepy little fucker, too much hair grease, and the mustache? God, he needs to go out more often. He's practically transparent."

Pale, dark hair, dark eyes, and as she said, a neatly trimmed mustache. Felix regarded the man and shivered.

"Either one of you got a second to spare for some facial recognition?" Felix asked, not liking the feeling in his stomach one bit.

"I'll capture him now but run him later," Stirling promised.

"Danny, are you almost clear?" The ventilation shaft was partly hidden by the desk in the study.

"Grace is caught on something," Danny muttered. They watched as Grace struggled to get his ankle through a difficult angle.

"Danny, did you let go of the button?" Felix exclaimed in alarm.

"The bars come down in twenty-nine," Stirling counted. "Twenty-eight."

"Grace, goddammit, move it! Felix, what's clear?"

"I have no idea. Josh, what's clear?"

"Ten feet down the shaft, maybe. Oh God no, Danny. Fuck—"

Danny glanced up to hear Marnie jiggling the door and then followed Grace down the ventilation shaft.

"Oh fuck," Felix muttered. "Fuck. Fuck. Fuck."

Marnie entered the study abruptly, having jiggered her way through what was now a broken lock, just as the cover to the ventilation shaft settled into place.

"Fifteen," Stirling whispered, and Felix wanted to kill him at the same time he listened for that clock in his head to tick down to the time when the bars crashed down, either trapping Danny and Grace or killing them.

Danny and Grace were moving in silence, and for a moment, time stopped as everybody with a mic listened to them breathe.

Julia paused at the door to the study; Torrance and Hunter abruptly stopped talking to Carl the Cocksucker; Molly stopped loading her tray and stared off into space; and even Chuck, who had just burst into the party and was shouldering his way through the crowd toward the bathroom, stopped in his tracks, eyes locked on Torrance's across the room.

"Five," Stirling said. "Four, three, two, one—"

Through the mic in the study, they all heard a soft mechanical ka-chunk as the array of iron bars in the ventilation shaft locked into place. The sound was so smooth, so oiled, it could have been a heater.

Or it could have been instant death for two people, one of whom held Felix's heart.

"*Danny!*" he cried out, and Josh fumbled sideways to take Felix's hand.

"Shh," his son whispered. "Give them time to get here. Nobody screamed. They can't talk in the shaft, and they have to go down three floors and across the building. Give them time to get here."

Chuck seemed to take a breath, and with only the smallest hitch in his stride, he walked up to Carl, Torrance, and Hunter.

"Heya, Carl, howyadoin'?" Chuck said, giving that good ol' boy smile that would warm the coldest heart.

Carl regarded him with icy green eyes and what was obviously thinning patience.

"Chuck," he said. "Good to see you." His eyes slid sideways to Hunter, who looked impassively back, and then to Torrance, who smiled cheerfully. "See you're running with a new crew."

Chuck bobbed his head. "Oh, these fellas? We don't hardly know each other at all." He winked at Hunter, who rolled his eyes back. "But I sure am surprised to see you in these parts."

Carl made a move toward the study, Chuck countered with a smooth slide of his hips, and Carl shook his head and put his hands over his eyes.

"Look, guys?" he said, a note of pleading in his voice. "If I promise I'm not here to bust Lightfingers, do you think you might let me go do my job?" He glared at Hunter, who gave that same narrow-eyed stare back. "And maybe not kill me while I'm doing it?"

"Depends on what your job is," Chuck said, just as Felix heard the scuffling in the ventilation shaft that in a worse apartment building might have indicated rats.

His heart was thundering so loud in his ears, he *almost* missed what Carl said next.

"Well, I'm here to bust Marnie Courtland's art procurer."

"And not Marnie?" Torrance asked, looking affronted.

"Hey, all we know is she said, 'Ooh, pretty, mama want!' And then this guy, Bertram Talbot, goes to get mama whatever she wants."

The three men regarded him with unfriendly eyes.

"And Marnie gets off scot-free," Torrance said flatly. "This doesn't work for me."

"Nope," Hunter said.

"No, I'm sorry. Please find another objective," Chuck said, keeping his voice friendly.

Carl pinched the bridge of his nose. "Guys, guys, I'm not here to bust Marnie. That's not my job—"

He kept talking, but Felix was distracted for a moment by Grace and then Danny slithering out of the ventilation shaft at their feet.

All thoughts of jealousy—and seriously, Carl Soderburgh Cox?—disappeared, and he hauled Danny up into his arms and crushed him, so tight neither of them could breathe.

"Felix!" Danny choked.

"Don't fucking do that to me again!"

"Felix, gotta get back to the—"

"Swear!" Felix took him by the biceps and shook him a little. "Holy fucking Jesus, Danny, you scared the crap out of us."

"I'm fine, thank you!" Grace said, grinning and brushing dust bunnies from his black outfit.

"Glad to hear it," Hunter said sotto voce.

Carl, Chuck, and Torrance all looked at him, and he smiled sheepishly. At that moment, Marnie—whom they had largely ignored once the ventilation shaft had closed—came tearing out of her study, practically plowing into Julia.

"What in the fuck is this?" she demanded, charging into the middle of the party floor.

Julia, who had been standing near the men cornering "Soderburgh," turned to Marnie and allowed her eyebrows to rise. "I give up," she said, the definition of ingenue. "What is it?"

"These papers! The provenance! Did you do this, Julia? How did this happen?"

Julia gave her an appropriately baffled look. "Marnie, you'll have to fill us in. What on earth are you talking about?"

"These say my art—*my entire collection*—belongs to Felix!"

"Oh for fuck's sake," Carl muttered. He glared at Chuck and the others. "You guys, really?"

"Well, it does," Julia said, dimpling. "Felix purchased everything, free and clear." Julia touched the comb in her hair. "It's one of my most cherished gifts."

Marnie was busy riffling through the papers. "But... but... this is impossible. This says that the purchases were made for...." She stopped and raised her head. "No."

Julia tilted her head ever so slightly, and Danny took that opportunity to start dusting himself off.

"Did Grace get everything?" he whispered. "Do I need a lint roller?"

"Here," Felix said, mostly to buy time to look at him, *touch* him, before he had to run back to work. "Let me."

Felix dragged the lint roller and a damp cloth over Danny until his tuxedo was spotless once more, and while he was doing that, they watched the entire play unfold.

"No, what?" Julia prompted, and the irony was delightful. Marnie's beloved objets d'art had been purchased as recovered artifacts. Those papers gave proof that the items had been *stolen*, then *recovered*, and then purchased upon recovery. With the exception of the provenance for the comb, which Papers had forged perfectly. *That* gave the date of the comb's purchase as the date that Danny and Felix had stolen it, some ten years before.

But even that didn't matter. If Marnie accused Felix of theft, she'd have to reveal herself as a felon as well. And if she didn't, she'd have to forfeit all of her "sparkly" treasures, with some explanation of how they came to be in her safe.

"I...." For a moment her chin wobbled, and Felix thought she was about to cry. Then her jaw squared and he could see the icy resolve in her eyes. "I have no idea how I came to own a forgery of your comb," she said at last with dignity. "I'll have this one destroyed at once."

"She'd *better* not!" Danny squawked, moving out of Felix's arms.

Julia's eyes widened fractionally. "Oh, I think that's a bad idea."

"Why?" Marnie demanded.

"Why is that a bad idea?" Julia gave a forced laugh. "Why *is* that a bad idea?"

"You'd better go," Felix said reluctantly.

Danny gave a short nod and stepped back long enough to kiss his cheek before striding through his apartment. They could hear him over coms feeding lines to Julia.

"Oh!" Julia looked startled. She focused her attention on Marnie again. "That," she said, "is a bad idea because forgeries have their place in history. Forgeries make the original item more valuable because they show that the item was coveted—and because the artist who forged the item put considerable care and materials into the forgery." Her eyes went round, as though pleased. "I'd be willing to buy that forgery from you at a very good price," she added—her idea, since Danny hadn't said anything about that. "This piece is dear to my heart."

"I *don't* need Felix Salinger's money," Marnie spat, and Julia's eyes sharpened.

"You wouldn't need to accept it, darling. I have plenty of money of my own."

Marnie's lips parted, and she realized she'd just committed a rather brutal faux pas. She gave a brittle smile and inclined her head in an act of submission that obviously cost her.

"Of course, Julia. Forgive me. I didn't mean to imply—"

"Of course you did," Julia said, her voice warm and kind. "It's why you invited me, isn't it?"

Marnie appeared genuinely surprised and a little alarmed. "Oh no! Just because Felix has revealed himself to be less than a gentleman, that doesn't mean

I wish to alienate myself to everybody at the head of the network!"

"Mm," Julia said, and her lips had thinned, a spot of temper appearing on her cheeks. "You know, after twenty years of Felix and I working elbow-to-elbow to make this network profitable and progressive, I find it odd that nobody else has come forward to proclaim Felix 'less than a gentleman,' don't you?"

Shit. She'd just put Marnie back on her home turf. She smiled condescendingly. "The wife really *is* the last to know, isn't she?"

"Ex-wife," Julia corrected. "Facts matter."

"I trade in facts, Ms. Dormer—"

"Salinger. I still love Felix, even if we're no longer married."

"Then this must be hard to hear."

"Don't do it," Felix murmured into the com. "Darling, not for me—" But Julia's fury had been too long contained.

"*Real* facts often are," Julia countered, and her tone was escalating.

"Are you insinuating I deal with false information?" Marnie practically purred.

"I'm not sure," Julia said, choosing her words with precision, "if you want to—"

"Hello," Danny said, stepping into the frame. His cheeks were flushed—he must have *flown* up the three flights of steps, because there was no way he could have gotten there that quickly using the elevator. "Did I miss anything?"

Julia and Marnie were still smiling daggers at each other, their color high, their eyes forged into emotional katana blades.

"Yes," Torrance Grayson said, beating Carl by about half a step. "Perhaps you can answer a question for us, Benjamin. Marnie here discovered that her comb was, in fact, a forgery, and Julia's was the original. She offered to destroy it."

Danny feigned surprise. "No! No, my darling." He patted her hand. "It's still a work of art. And it adds to the story!" He smiled charmingly and delivered the cut with such precision, Marnie probably wouldn't feel the blood until the next morning. "And you're the only one who knows which is the original."

Felix snorted, and so did Josh.

Stirling's lips moved. "I know that was really mean," he murmured, "but I'm not sure how."

"That's why we let Danny and Julia do that work," Felix replied. "They're masters of the art."

Unbidden, the memory of his and Danny's last fight flashed in front of his eyes, and he wanted to hang his head in shame. Yes, Danny had hurt him, but Danny could have *decimated* him. He'd pulled his punches, and Felix had never realized it until this moment.

Sure, Felix, let's fuck. It's the only thing you ever wanted me for.

Painful, but he could have said so much more—and all of it would have been true.

Danny had wanted to make Felix mad enough that he'd kick him out. But he hadn't wanted Felix to hate him. Not forever.

Felix had almost lost him tonight. Again.

Never again.

At that moment, Brittney—a petite dark-haired woman a little past thirty who was just pretty and self-possessed enough to be invisible in a room full of peacocks—rushed up to Marnie.

"Ms. Courtland, I'm sorry—the sommelier needs you," she said, which was a perfect excuse. Marnie gave them all a thin smile and excused herself, leaving Julia and Danny to take a deep breath.

"Sorry about that," Julia murmured. "I swear I almost stabbed her with my comb."

Danny's smile went radiant. "I would have covered for you. 'Oh no, Your Honor, she *fell* on that thing. It was a total accident. She toppled over and landed on it, eyeball first, ten times.'"

Julia's laughter—rich and throaty—rang through the room, and Felix scrubbed his face with his hands.

And at that moment, of course, Carl "Soderburgh" Cox had to step forward, Hunter and Gray at his heels, and ruin their glow. "So, Dan—"

"*Benjamin*," everybody growled at once.

Carl blinked and rubbed the back of his neck. "Of. Course. My apologies. Benjamin…?" He held out a hand.

"Morgan," Danny said, shaking on it. "Benjamin D. Morgan."

Carl's jaw grew, if anything, even harder. "Of. Course." He took a deep breath. "You may tell Felix that you all cost me six months of work tracking down those items. The insurance company won't give a shit now that they're purchased and accounted for, so, uhm, fuck him, and fuck you all very much."

"You may tell Cocksucker that I'll strangle him with his tie and make him eat his own dick if he doesn't back away from you," Felix said, obviously directly to Danny.

"Felix sends his regards," Danny said blandly.

Carl rolled his eyes. "Of course he does." His jaw softened, and his mouth quirked sideways. "Tell him he was a fool to let you go. I heard that Benjamin Morgan is up for a job at the Institute. I hope you get it. I know I'll be seeing you to consult."

"Tell him—" Felix began, but Julia, bless her, stepped in.

"We would love to discuss anything you wish," she said. "But don't worry, nobody will be letting Benjamin Morgan go anywhere anytime soon. Chicago is going to be his permanent home."

Danny gave her an exasperated look. "With the occasional trips to Europe, of course."

"During which time you'll be accompanied, I'm sure," she said, and Felix read the sadness in her eyes. God, they'd both missed him. He could never forget that.

Danny pinched the bridge of his nose, but everybody saw him surrender. "I wouldn't desert my family," he said soberly and then looked Carl in the eye. "And they are all, of course, right here."

Carl's eyebrows went up. "And the boy? Your son?"

"Tell him he'll recognize me three days after his wallet disappears," Josh said, with the cockiness of the young.

"Says hello," Danny said. "Uhm, do hang on to your valuables while you're in this town, though."

Carl put a hand to his vest and glared over his shoulder at Hunter, who held up his hands in a not-me gesture.

"Don't look at me," Torrance told him. "I have no idea what you're talking about."

At that moment Molly passed behind Chuck, who held up the wallet for Carl before Carl even registered she was there. "I found this on the floor," he said blandly, and Carl snatched the thing from his hand.

"That's handy," he muttered. He leafed through the wallet and sighed. "Cash is gone, cards are still there. Should I even bother to use this ID again?"

"No," Molly's voice came in through the coms as she continued to pass out canapes. "Tell him that Carlos Carter is a really dumb name."

Danny raised his eyebrows. "You've been asked to change your pseudonym," he said. "There have been complaints."

"It was a company decision," Carl said through gritted teeth.

Danny snorted. "Them again. Figures."

And for the first time, an unfiltered expression crossed Carl's features. "Well, they cost me you. Where else was I going to go?"

And Danny's expression became sorrowful and completely unguarded.

Carl closed his eyes and held up a hand. "Don't say it," he begged.

Danny nodded. He didn't have to say it. Felix had seen it in his face, in his apology, in his guilt.

Danny had never been his in the first place. Just like with Felix, that chip had been cashed in long ago. The two of them had needed to reclaim it, that was all.

At that moment, Talia walked up, unaware of the undercurrents. "I've got to tell you all, this party sucks. None of these people are smiling, everybody looks like they want to slip a knife in your back. The best part was hearing Benjamin talk about jewelry!"

Julia grinned at her. "What do you say we take it back to my place, then? I have comfy clothes, good wine, ice cream, and a big-screen television with all the movie channels." She paused and bit her lip, uncharacteristically diffident. "Or, since we're all dolled up, would we rather go out and dance?"

"Your house," Talia said with a sigh. "I hate tight shoes."

"Definitely our house," Josh chimed in. "And that's a second from Stirling."

"Yay! Can Hunter and I quit?" Molly begged.

"I'd give us twenty minutes to leave," Danny told her, "but sure."

"Woohoo!" Molly chimed. Then, "Wait. Is Mr. Company Man coming? Just so I know whether or not to brag about that wallet, because that was a *sweet* lift."

"You're invited," Danny said to Carl.

Carl grimaced as though he were about to say no, but Danny met Julia's eyes.

"Please come," Julia said. Her voice dropped with sympathy. "How exciting *is* your hotel room?"

"Not very," he said with an incline of his head. "Are you going to have to put a hood over my head and knock me out so I don't remember the way?"

Julia's laugh tinkled. "Of course not, darling. Our mansion is public record, after all. Glencoe is hardly a government secret. Okay, then, everybody brace yourselves. We're going to be saying our goodbyes to the hostess— "

"Except she's in the locked study with her 'procurer,'" Felix said, noticing for the first time. "Son, can you record that conversation?"

"Done," Josh said with a keystroke. "Why?"

"Let's just call it a parting gift for Carl the Cocksucker." He sighed, hating how mean-spirited that sounded. "Fine. We'll call him Soderburgh. Anyway...." He brightened. "Since he didn't get Danny, I think it would be a perfect trinket, don't you?"

In the study, Josh pulled up the feed, just as Marnie snarled, "You told me those pieces were real!"

"They were real."

"But the provenance said—"

"You didn't specify the provenances. You just said to have it. I had it!"

"You had provenances that said it was *stolen*!"

Her procurer, the "creepy little man," bared his teeth at her in an almost feral growl. "You *knew* it was stolen."

"Yes, but I didn't expect proof that it was stolen right where it could incriminate me!"

"That was planted in your safe, you fucking ignorant cow. Look at those dates—*look at them*. I brought you those things over the last three years. Do you think they'd all have yesterday's date on them if they'd been in your safe that long?"

Marnie stopped short and opened her mouth and then glanced around her study in consternation. "Someone's been in my study," she said, as if it had finally hit her.

"My God, you're stupid," the procurer said, like this had just hit him. "You made an idiot of yourself with that art dealer, by the way. He had you dead to rights as the social-climbing bimbo you really fucking are."

Marnie's eyes narrowed. "That art dealer...." She looked around the study again. "Do you think he was the one who switched the papers? He knew an awful lot about my fucking jewelry." She chewed on her lower lip. "And Felix's wife seemed to know him awfully well." Her mouth thinned and curled up in the kind of smile cartoon villains wore. "I think I *will* have Brittney give him a call. I think Mr. Benjamin Morgan *does* need to be on my show. I think we need to nail his sleazy thieving ass to the wall!"

"Whoa." Josh could make the sound, but Felix could hardly breathe.

"Oh my God," he murmured finally. The chance to make Marnie's criminal activity—and her lack of trustworthiness—public. By her own invitation. This could not have gone any better.

"Hello," Danny said, and when Felix checked on him in the monitor, he realized the party was exiting the apartment, Soderburgh included. "What's going on?"

"Dad and I are having griftergasms," Josh said, voice breathy and excited. "Danny, we've got her. She's in. She's going to have you on television. She wants to nail you to the wall."

"Whoa." Danny shuddered. "Congasm achieved."

Felix looked at their faces as they passed from view and saw the same vengeful light in everybody's eyes.

They were *in*.

FELIX SENT Torrance and Talia with Carl and Julia to go get ready—and also to easily sidestep the part where Carl got to see Danny's apartment.

Danny, Felix, and the kids cleaned up the apartment, but since they were leaving the monitors there with the cameras—and the bugs, as long as the batteries held out—there was minimal breakdown.

Danny was in the shower—Grace having gone first—because in their words, it was hotter than the devil's bowels in the ventilation shafts. Felix smiled a little as he zipped up Danny's garment bag. The new suit was soaked through to the jacket. They'd be lucky if he could wear it again.

Felix didn't care. He'd frame it for his own personal museum, because Danny was right. The value was in the story.

"We're ready to go," Josh said. "Will you and Danny be following?" He gave his father a significant, adult look, and Felix's cheeks warmed.

"Maybe after the first movie," he said. "We, uh, have things to talk about." He looked around the apartment and grimaced. "But I *really* don't like this place, so we'll definitely be coming home."

Josh laughed softly. "He was amazing tonight, you know?"

Felix nodded. "Well, we all were. Too bad we weren't fighting crime or saving the world. We're aces at it."

Josh grinned and then nodded. "I've got some ideas," he said, then held up his hand. "But first I'd better get down to the car so Chuck and Grace don't kill each other—or get on Stirling's last nerve."

"Are Hunter and Molly out yet?"

"They left just before I pulled everybody's coms. They're on the way home." He paused, frowning. "Which reminds me. I think, uh… I think Stirling and Molly might…. I think they miss family. We've got rooms, right?"

Felix saw it then. That acknowledgment that family was what you made it. Felix and Danny and Julia had forged their own family with Josh. Josh wanted to do the same.

"We do indeed. Ask them. Anybody in the crew is welcome." He grimaced. "And my God, we could literally put a person in every room."

Josh laughed. "I don't think it will be that bad." He bit his lip. "But I do think our study is going to be full from now on. I hope that's okay."

"It's been quiet since you left for school." He knew Josh had taken part of the semester off when Felix's news had hit the fan. "Which reminds me. When are you going back?"

Josh winked. "Later, Dad. Later."

And Felix was just going to have to leave it at that. Josh was more than capable. He'd proved that tonight—as if Felix had harbored any doubts.

The door closed, and Felix wandered into the bedroom. The monitors were still set up, but the activity on them had thinned. They were recording, so he turned them toward the wall for his own peace of mind and started to undress.

His skin ached with the need to hold Danny.

What had it been? Three minutes? Maybe four, between the time they heard the bars come down to the time they heard the scuffling in the ventilation shaft? Four minutes. For four minutes Felix thought he'd lost Danny Mitchell all over again. This time forever.

The white-tiled shower was steam-filled and close when he walked in, but it had the comforting smell of Danny's shower gel and shampoo from his shaving kit. Danny was leaning against the far wall of the shower, letting the water pound him on the back, head resting against his arms in a curiously unguarded pose.

Felix's hands were shaking as he slid open the shower door.

Running the Carnival

D ANNY FELT the burst of cooler air when Felix entered the bathroom, but the hot water felt so good, he didn't move. The shower door opening surprised him, though, and he dropped his hands, preparing to jump on whatever adrenaline ride Felix had in store for him this time.

But Felix just draped himself over Danny's back, wrapped his arm around his waist, and held on tightly, his entire body shaking against Danny's back.

Danny clasped the hands at his waist and squeezed gently. "Felix, baby, what's wrong?"

There was no answer except Felix's cheek resting against the back of his head. Danny turned carefully in his arms, and Felix buried his face in the hollow of Danny's neck and shoulders, and shook.

Oh, baby. Danny soothed him, cupping his neck, his cheeks. The shower plastered his dark gold hair against his head, and his full lips trembled. He looked young, like when they'd been kids and had gotten caught out in the rain once when riding one of the damned Vespas through the streets of Rome.

But Felix had been indestructible then. Now he was vulnerable and shaken, and Danny couldn't touch him enough.

"Hey, hey, hey—it's okay. What's wrong? What's—"

"I almost lost you," Felix gasped. "I almost lost you. I almost—"

Danny pulled back and tried to smile. "We were *way* down the shaft, I swear. I know it probably sounded scary but—"

"Not just then!" He was overwrought, and Danny reached out and made the water hotter, because Felix's teeth were chattering. "All of it. Ten years. Ten years of hoping you'd come home. Ten years of thinking about how to get you back, and I… I almost lost you a thousand times. Gangsters and insurance agents and iron bars and—" His voice was pitching hysterically, so Danny kissed him.

Hard, relentlessly. He took Felix's mouth without hesitation, pushing him back against the wall of the shower and grinding against him, grounding him, pulling him out of the spiral of what-ifs and might-have-beens.

Felix groaned and opened his mouth, accepting, and for once he didn't try to turn the kiss, didn't try to take over. He let Danny comfort him, take *him* over, and Danny was hungry to do just that.

Ten years since he'd taken this body. Ten years since he'd had Felix pliable and needy under his hands.

How could he have stayed away for so long?

He broke away from Felix's mouth only to feverishly kiss down his jaw and nibble on the side of his neck. Felix tilted his head to give him access and moaned.

"Need you," he begged, and Danny reached out to turn off the water.

"Bed," he panted. "Now."

He stepped out of the shower and toweled off, doing the same for Felix when he emerged. Danny took extra time on his erogenous zones, his nipples, between his cleft, his groin—he was going to taste this time. He'd needed this, needed to show Felix he wanted to be there, needed to win Felix over the same way Felix had been trying desperately to win Danny.

They'd both been responsible for their catastrophe. He needed to be there to fix their ship.

When they got to the bed, he tore down the top covers and turned to kiss Felix again. These kisses were gentler, less out of control but no less powerful. He claimed Felix's mouth; he dragged his nails across his skin. When Felix gave a breathless moan and collapsed on the bed, Danny pushed him backward, kissing him until he groaned, and lifted his feet to the edge of the bed, splaying his thighs, welcoming Danny to explore.

Danny didn't want to explore so much as he wanted to reconquer his home country. Felix thought he had something to worry about in Carl Soderburgh? Soderburgh had entered the art world like Danny had. His father painted houses, and his mother cleaned them. Soderburgh had gone to junior college, then state school, all in the quest for an art degree. He was loyal to his job because it made him money, and that was the only way he'd learned to give value to things. Danny understood men like Soderburgh, but they didn't stir his blood.

Felix stirred his blood. Felix, who attracted the rich and the powerful because they didn't scare him. Danny had to worry about Torrance Grayson, about men who were born into money, about men people expected to know a Renoir from a Vermeer. All Danny had ever wanted in his life was to be surrounded by art, and then he'd met Felix, and Felix *was* art. Not just his looks but his manners, his kindness, his touch, and his charm.

Danny needed to take him, to glut his hands upon his skin, to taste his sweat and his come. Danny needed to feel the clasp of him around his cock, needed to bury himself inside Felix's willing body, needed to release the tension born of need.

He nibbled his way down Felix's throat and sucked a nipple hard enough to make Felix cry out and arch toward him. Felix buried his fingers in Danny's damp hair, wordlessly begging him to suck harder and then urged him down.

Danny left his mark—little nips along Felix's rib cage, along his stomach. But when he got to Felix's cock, erect and dripping, he paused with a bit of appreciation.

"All that for me?" he teased, sticking his tongue out and lapping at the head.

"Nobody else," Felix told him, eyes wide and ingenuous across his own body.

Danny could believe him. Yes, there may have been some squatters touching this body in the last ten years, but this was Danny's home, and he was taking it back.

He swallowed Felix's long, thick erection in one smooth gulp, pulling it to the back of his throat, tasting the sweet/salty tang of precome as Felix gasped. Danny worked his throat, milking him, until Felix tugged on his hair enough to pull him off.

"Inside me," he whispered. "Please, Danny. I'm so cold without you."

Danny fumbled for a sachet of lube he'd snagged from his shaving kit in the bathroom and set by the edge of the bed. Then he shoved Felix's thighs up, separating his cheeks with his thumbs.

His. His territory.

He licked fiercely, softening, slickening with his tongue, until Felix squirmed. "Danny, please!"

Danny broke the top of the sachet and squeezed some slick on Felix's opening, then penetrated him slowly with his thumb.

Felix's long, fine body arched off the bed, and he cried out, arms spread, thighs parted lewdly, open and vulnerable, a being meant to be used and taken. But only by lowly Danny Mitchell, who had never seen a piece of art so fine in his life.

But first, he needed one more taste. Wrapping his lips around the bell of Felix's cock, he sucked hard, and before Felix could process Danny's mouth, Danny drove himself up and into him, his feet still on the ground, Felix sprawled beneath him like an offering from the gods.

He penetrated slowly, not sure when Felix had last done this. Danny had never minded bottoming, but Felix—Felix had loved to top. Felix moaned, reaching for his cock, but Danny got there first, stroking long and slow as he pushed forward.

Finally, finally, he popped in, thrusting more until he was all the way inside, and Felix moaned, hard and low in his throat, body flushed and shaking with desire.

"Please, Danny," he croaked. "Please."

Danny pulled back and slammed forward, and Felix screamed, "Yes! More!"

And Danny gave.

More and more and more. Hard, fast, and absolutely unmerciful, Danny fucked himself into Felix's body, wanting to penetrate more than his ass. Danny wanted inside him again, inside his skin, inside his life. Inside his heart.

Felix kept begging, kept needing, Danny's name coming from his lips in hard little sobs as Danny fucked him with the pent-up longing and frustration and yearning of ten years apart—and ten years together—and twenty years of wanting every part of Felix Benjamin Salinger but never being able to get it.

Until now.

"Yes! God yes! I'm coming, Danny. Keep fucking me… please. Forever. Fuck me forever. Oh God—now. More. Please!"

Danny's hips rocketed, and he wrapped Felix's hand around his own cock so Danny could hold his thighs up higher. Felix's hand blurred, and suddenly, time stopped.

Felix's body gave a long, slow contraction, and his back arched off the bed again, his hand stilling on the end of his cock as he milked it hard. The first white strip of come shot up to Felix's chin, and Danny yearned to taste it, but his body was still working, still—ah! Oh God! Felix's asshole gripped his cock and squeezed until Danny saw stars.

"Felix," he cried, his voice breaking, and the wave, hard and powerful, broke in his body at the same time, crashing, flooding him with ecstasy, with power, with *Felix* inside his heart now more than he had ever been.

Danny moaned and rutted, spurting come in the haven of Felix's body, watching as Felix's face went slack, his eyes half-closed, spent, Danny's completely, in body and soul.

He collapsed, his toes barely keeping purchase on the floor, but he didn't care. That white stripe of spend lay spattered across Felix's collarbone, and he stuck out his tongue and licked it off before kissing Felix's mouth with come on his lips.

Felix kissed him back, carnally, demanding everything Danny had left.

The kiss ended when Danny's feet slipped, and he fell out of Felix trying to stand up. Felix laughed and scooted so his head was up on the pillows, and Danny followed, flopping on the bed next to him.

"Oh my God," Felix mumbled, pulling until Danny's head was on his shoulder.

"Oh my God," Danny repeated. His brain was a spinning a wheel of stars, and his breath was not getting enough oxygen to his brain.

"That was… that was everything," Felix panted, dropping a kiss on the crown of Danny's head.

Danny gave a quiet, silly grin. "Told you I could run that game," he said.

Felix managed a soft laugh before wrapping his arm around Danny's sweaty shoulders and squeezing. "Danny?"

"Yeah?"

"I love you. Don't ever leave me again."

Danny closed his eyes, thinking, *Those are the words. Those are the words we didn't say enough, because we thought we each knew. And we didn't say them enough, and we forgot that they existed.*

"I love you too. I won't. I can't leave again. It'd kill me. I barely survived the first time." He smiled sadly. "I hope you're ready to have me in your life for the rest of it." His throat tightened. "I don't give a shit about Dublin or Prague or Tuscany. I swear to God, Felix, I've got nowhere else to go."

"Good," Felix said, his own voice thick. "Because this is where you belong. With me. With your family. You're home."

And then Felix broke again, and he cried quietly as Danny rubbed his hand on his chest and calmed him down.

When he could talk again, he murmured, "You know, you're right. I really should let you run the circus more often. It's not every day that the ringmaster gets to fly through the air."

Danny laughed softly, but he had no words. The important ones—*I love you*—had taken all the banter out of him.

Eventually, he knew they would get up and leave, leave the city, drive to the suburbs, sleep in their own bed.

But first he had to stay there, listening to Felix's heartbeat, and believe, truly *believe*, that he was home.

THEY GOT to the house as the first movie was ending—something sweet and romantic and melancholy—and they sat down on the couch and ate popcorn for the second movie, which had more explosions and pretty boys with good hair.

Danny sat with Felix on one side, Julia on the other, and Josh down on the floor by his feet. Josh had his friends sprawled on him as well—Molly, Chuck, Grace—and Carl and Hunter sat friend-close on the floor in front of the love seat. Talia was *on* the love seat, dressed in Julia's sweats, her feet in Torrance Grayson's lap as he kneaded them.

Stirling took up the recliner, arms around his knees, eyes focused on the screen hungrily. He seemed lost in the fantasy, and Danny made a note to watch these kinds of movies often.

And for Danny's part, he leaned against Felix, half-somnolent, content as he hadn't been in a long time.

His family. *His.* He'd left before because he could never be theirs in public, because he could no longer grift to be with the people he loved.

But now, the chance was right there. Interview, take the job at the institute, get to know Pablo Picasso like he was a new best friend, and only grift on the weekends.

His eyes wandered the room, where a group of twentysomethings who should have been grown were gathered together in Felix's den. They'd been so excited to work together, and so much fun to work with. Maybe he'd take the occasional job on the weekdays too. It was a thought.

He snuggled his cheek into Felix's chest and cut his mind loose. So much to do. So much to think about.

Later.

After the movie, the twentysomethings decided to start another one, Torrance left with Talia, Julia set Soderburgh up in a guest room in her wing of the house, and they let Josh make sure everybody else had a place to sleep or a safe way home.

Danny called Stirling aside for a moment and pulled him to the back of the den.

"Has Josh shown you this?" he asked, opening a door to a small bedroom with an attached bath. The room itself was plain—the walls were painted off-white with blue trim, and the bed was bare, although there were linens in the closet. He knew Josh had set up a gaming console in there when he was in high school but had broken it down when he'd gone to college. The room's biggest feature was the multiple outlet strip on the floor near an adult-sized computer desk and an ergonomic chair.

"Nice!" Stirling said softly, eyes darting to where everyone was debating the next movie. There was something yearning about the glance. He wanted to be part of that, Danny guessed, but he didn't have the people skills to ask for his choice.

"Thing is," Danny said, "I know you and your sister have an apartment in the city, but your work means you only have to be on-site every so often, am I right?"

Stirling nodded. He designed the lighting and sound system for the productions, went in to help install it, made sure it worked, saw opening night, and was already moving to the next job.

"Well, Felix and I thought maybe you could set up shop here if you like." He smiled gently. "The city is a good place, but it's loud. Someplace quieter does us good sometimes. And this way you could still spend time with your sister when you're needed."

Stirling glanced around. The bedroom was bigger than Danny's garret in Rome by about twice the floor area, but Danny knew sometimes the personal place wasn't in the floor space but the head space.

"Yes," he said, voice raspy and thick. "I…." He looked at Danny nakedly. "You'll be staying, right? It won't be just me and Mr. and Mrs. Salinger?"

"I'll do my best," Danny said. He wanted to say yes unequivocally, but Stirling knew better than anybody that sometimes life took turns people didn't expect. Still, Danny was determined to make a go of it here—he'd meant every word he'd said to Felix about not going anywhere. Stirling seemed so badly to need someone. Danny and Felix had turned to each other when they were this age, and they had made so many mistakes and had felt so alone. Josh knew he had three parents to turn to when life got confusing, but Danny'd had none. Stirling, who he had a feeling had finally learned to trust people before his foster parents died, needed him. And God, Danny had been so lucky. He had the scars of near misses on his body, on his psyche.

He felt like this was what he owed the universe, and he was happy to do it.

"Can I bring my stuff tomorrow?" Stirling asked.

Danny shrugged. "Sure. But, uhm, everyone else might want to sleep in."

And he saw an amazing thing. Stirling's smile. "That's fine. I may want to be here for breakfast anyway."

Danny winked and left then, bidding the younger people good night before following Felix up the stairs to the ground floor and then up more stairs to the bedrooms.

He went to turn right into his room, but Felix took his hand and tugged.

"No," he said softly.

"Okay, your room tonight," Danny said, rolling his eyes.

The mansion had light runners up the stairs and along the hallway, and Felix's expression was easy to read in the semidarkness; he wasn't kidding around.

"This room, our room, every night," he said, his voice intense. "This isn't a drill, Danny. I wasn't fucking around. Josh is going to *expect* to find us in the same bed every morning. My room has two walk-in closets, and one of them has linens. Tomorrow, it will have your clothes, and the day after that, it will have *more* of your clothes, and that fucking suitcase is going in the basement in the storage room next to the bedroom."

"I gave that bedroom to Stirling, by the way," Danny said to distract him.

Felix stared at him. "You are deliberately changing the subject."

Danny tilted his head. "Well, yes," he admitted, and blew out a breath.

Felix recoiled in betrayal. "You said you would stay—"

"Well, yes! I want to. Do you think I don't want to spend every day for the rest of our lives together?" Danny was forced into honesty here. "But there's mobsters. And Interpol. And I'll go straight as Benjamin Morgan—I will. I will do Marnie's interview, and I will catch her like the spider she is. But…." He looked at Felix helplessly. "There are things in my past I can't undo, Felix. No matter how much I want to." He scrubbed his face with his hands. "And there are things I long to do, but I can't."

"Like what?" Felix asked, pulling his hands away.

"Promise you that Kadjic won't come for me," Danny said, "if he gets wind I'm alive… and here. Like promise Stirling that I'll never go away. Like pinky promise to Interpol that I'll go straight, I swear I will, if only they'll let me have a normal life with the man I love."

Felix looked stricken for a moment, and then he let out a breath.

"If Kadjic comes for you, we've got a crew who can deal," he said calmly, and the bottom dropped out of Danny's stomach.

"Felix, I will *not* expose these kids to that madman!"

But Felix just shook his head. "Your ex-boyfriend is sitting on my couch downstairs because he picked up pointers from one of our son's friends. He's got a bruised face and a cut on his chin because another one is an enforcer, and he's short cab fare and identification because everybody decided that they were going to pick on him because he was making eyes at you. I know this Kadjic guy's dangerous, but Danny, so are we."

"But—"

Felix held up a hand. "And as for Interpol? Well, if they come knocking, we've got lawyers. I can't promise much, Danny. But I can promise that what we have is worth a fight. And now that you're back to help me, I've got an army to help you. Will that do?"

Danny sighed. "For tonight. But this isn't over. Fox, we need to prep the kids. We need to work with them so they can spot Interpol. We need to—"

Felix chuckled tiredly. "We need to sleep. And we need to live our lives. And you need to prepare for your interview with Marnie. And your interview with the head curator of the Art Institute. But first—"

Danny yawned, making his point for him.

"Sleep," Felix told him gently and held out his hand. "In our bed. Come on, baby. It's been a long time coming."

They undressed, Danny leaving his clothes neatly draped over the chair by the dressing table as always. Down to their boxers, Felix slid under the covers and pulled them back to invite Danny in.

Without even thinking, Danny turned to his side and backed up to Felix, welcoming his arm around Danny's waist. It was how they always slept together, the only time in his life he ever remembered waking up feeling safe. The last few days flooded back to him—the feverish lovemaking, the constant planning. This was the first time in ten years he'd crawled into bed next to the man he loved *just* because he was the man Danny loved.

Danny let out a grunt.

"What?" Felix murmured, nuzzling the back of his neck.

"I hate it when you're right."

"Excellent. How's that working for you."

"Shut up." But his voice lacked heat, and Felix laughed softly, kissing his bare shoulder.

"Danny Lightfingers Mitchell, I love you. Someday we'll be married. And I don't care what your name is going to be on the wedding certificate, you'll know who you belong to. I'll know who's in my arms. You'll see."

Everything he'd always wanted—and Felix knew it.

"It's hard to tell you no when you talk so pretty."

Felix laughed again, but Danny was already mostly asleep.

For tonight, they had some peace.

Enter the Clowns

THE ALARM went off at about 5:00 a.m.

It wasn't a clumsy, loud screech—no. Felix's phone buzzed particularly vehemently, and so did Josh's and Julia's, because that's how Josh and Stirling had programmed them less than a week ago.

As Felix scrambled to sit up in bed, Danny at his side, his phone lit up with a map of the house and a red dot entering his study.

Felix pulled a stun gun from his desk drawer and turned to Danny to order him to stay back because Felix had a weapon, but Danny was already out the door. Felix ended up hurrying to catch him before he hit the ground level.

Danny was too fast. He slid in through the study door, and Felix heard some body blows, a crash to his desk, and an "*Oof!*" before he turned on the lights and saw Danny, knee to the back of a very familiar-looking scumbag.

"Felix," Danny said through gritted teeth while holding the man's wrists together behind his back, "is there any way you could get me some zip—"

"I've got handcuffs," Carl said, coming in through the door of the study with what sounded like a crowd behind him. He was semirespectably dressed, in boxers and an undershirt, and Felix tried not to hate him. He was helpful, he had handcuffs, and he didn't look like he'd been getting laid under Felix's roof. And Danny had been in *Felix's* bed when the alarm had gone off, and that counted for something.

"Kinky," Chuck drawled from the doorway, looking at the cuffs. "No, everyone else stay back. That room is pretty crowded."

"Felix, who broke in?" Julia demanded, sidestepping Chuck neatly.

"Hey!" Grace's voice chimed.

Chuck replied, "She owns the place, moron," right before Josh appeared under his arm.

"And so does he," Chuck said with a sigh. "But that's it, folks."

"Look who we have here," Carl said happily, kneeling by Danny. "And caught red-handed!"

Danny slid the cuffs on the guy with ease, and Felix noted the intruder was wearing the same sort of outfit Grace had worn to crawl through the ventilation shafts.

"Who is this guy?" Danny asked. Said guy gave a wiggle, and Danny dug his knee into his back. "Stop that. I'm not usually violent, but there's a couple of people here who could probably kill you using their thumbs, so maybe you should calm down."

"Marnie's procurer," Felix reminded him. "Talbot? Carl said it, whatever it was." He brightened. "But we do have him on record talking about getting Marnie a bunch of stolen objets d'art, so that's something."

Carl scowled at him. "We sat and watched movies all night, and you didn't say a word about that?"

Danny grimaced. "Sorry, Carl, Felix and I had some shit to sort out. I swear we were going to give you the thumb drive before you left. What's his name again?" The guy bucked some more, and Danny called, "Hunter! Hunter, we need your expertise."

Hunter slid in past Chuck, all fluid muscle, predatory darkness—and Spongebob pajama pants. He took Danny's place at the guy's back and applied just the teensiest bit of pressure at the base of the spine. With his thumb.

The would-be burglar cried out and burst into tears.

"Now don't move," Hunter told him firmly.

"Whoever you are," Danny added and then stood shivering, dressed only in his boxers. Julia stepped forward wearing Felix's old sweats and a graceful peignoir.

"Carl," she said, her voice authoritative, "*who* is this man on my carpet?"

"His name is Bertram Talbot, ma'am," Carl said respectfully. He grunted. "What exactly did he say on that tape?"

"Here," Josh said. "Chuck, let me through. I'll go get it."

He was back in a moment, and Hunter used that time to haul Talbot up by his armpits and shove him onto Felix's office chair. For his part, Talbot glared at the ring of faces hovering over him, wearing a scowl. Not for a second did Felix trust him not to wreak harm on his family should he get free.

Josh slid behind the desk, typed all three of Felix's passwords, and inserted the thumb drive. Felix gave his son a level look.

"What?" Josh asked irritably. "If you'd wanted them to be a secret, you would have used an encryption key."

Danny shook his head and *tsk*ed. "Pitiful. Just pitiful."

"You hush," Felix muttered, embarrassed. Fine. So his skills were rusty. But Josh was sort of a prodigy, wasn't he?

"Okay, here we go," Josh murmured and turned the monitor to everybody else. The conversation between Marnie and Talbot came through loud and clear, and Carl narrowed his eyes.

"Felix, do you have the original provenance?" he asked.

Felix opened his mouth to say "What on earth do you mean?" but Carl gave him a droll look.

"Just don't argue," he said. "I'm trying to nail this guy to the wall."

"He's wearing too many clothes!" Grace said, his voice loud enough to carry.

"And he's not my type," Carl retorted, and Felix gave in. Fine. Whatever. They trusted Carl the Cocksucker Soderburgh now. He was fine. It was fine. Everything was fine.

"I'll go get them," he muttered. He slid away, sharing a look with Danny before he went. Danny knew where the safe was, and Josh and Julia, of course, but he wasn't sure if the others knew that he'd secreted the papers in a safe installed in the subflooring below the bar while he'd been microwaving popcorn. He may have been *old* compared to this group, but he still had a few tricks up his sleeve.

He padded downstairs, shivering in the chill, and had just removed the sliding panel that gave him access to the safe when he heard footsteps on the stairs. He looked up in time to see Grace holding out the black velvet bag with the expression of a Labrador retriever handing someone their own chewed-up tennis shoe.

"Sorry," he said, shrugging. "I was going to put it back in the morning."

Felix took a deep, restrained breath. Grace only stole from people he really hated or really loved—but maybe it was time he refined that habit. "And you felt the urge to steal it because…?"

"You wanted it hidden," Grace said, looking embarrassed. "Like I said, sorry."

Felix snagged the packet from his hand. "You're forgiven, Dylan, on one condition."

Grace cocked his head, adding to the impression of a watchful Labrador. "Yes?"

"You don't steal from your crew permanently. I get that you're good—"

He nodded and smiled, tongue practically lolling.

"—but your worth as a thief isn't equivalent to your worth as a friend or member of the family."

Grace tilted his head again, eyes moving quizzically. "I… I never thought of it that way."

"Well, consider it." Felix gave a shiver. "It might save us time wandering around in our underwear after the heat's gone off, for one thing."

Grace nodded in agreement and pointed to his own bare chest. "My nipples could cut glass."

"Absolutely. Now could you close up here? They need these."

Grace looked at the exposed safe and then at Felix. Felix kept a number of things in there, as Grace had probably known for years. Jewels—legally and illegally obtained—and passports and pseudonyms and birth certificates, the real ones. Leaving him here to close up was an act of trust, but it was also an acknowledgment that Felix and his family were vulnerable to a good thief.

If Grace passed the test, Felix would know he could trust the young man, and the young man would know he'd earned it.

"Absolutely, Mr. Salinger," Grace said soberly. Then he added, "Josh and I, we were thinking of moving back here for the rest of the semester. And maybe take next year touring Europe. And doing… things, with the crew. Would that be okay?"

Felix laughed a little, wondering if this was what Josh had wanted to put off. Leave it to his friend to address it *now*.

"That's fine," he said. "Honestly, Grace, we're fine with it. Stirling's got the basement, though. Danny promised."

Grace's face lit up. "It'll be like a den of thieves. Or Professor Xavier's mansion. Or, like, the bastard love-baby of them both with Phyllis to cook!"

"Which reminds me, she's going to need help," he murmured. "Now if you'll excuse me—"

"Oh yeah," Grace said. "Things. We have things to do." He waved his hand as though he were the one who had to give the order. "Also, don't trust that guy you just caught. I may steal your signet ring while you sleep, but he'll drip poison in your mouth because he can."

Felix coughed out a laugh. "Warning heeded. Thanks!" He headed up the stairs, velvet bag in hand, not sure how Grace had learned the revolving keycode to the safe, but pretty sure he didn't want to know. It was like running the network. You hired good people who knew what they were doing and let them do their jobs.

He got to the top of the stairs and handed Carl the provenances they'd gotten from Marnie's safe. He inspected them, mouth tight. "Felix, do you mind if I ask? The papers Marnie pulled out of her safe today—"

"Absolutely real," Felix said. "They were copies, though. We have the original ones here." Hopefully, if he'd been right about Grace.

Carl nodded. "So, Bertie," he said thoughtfully, "were *these* real when you gave them to Marnie Courtland?"

Bertram Talbot looked pained. "Mm...."

"So, you stole those items for her."

Talbot gave a grimace—perhaps he was a superlative thief, but he couldn't lie for shit. "I acquired them," he said with dignity.

Carl looked at Danny. "Do you all know where they were from?"

"Well, *duh*," Felix said. He had a right to be grumpy. He'd held Danny for a grand total of *two hours* before this bullshit had begun.

"And that is...?" Carl had obviously not gotten *his* sleep either.

"Oh, I'm sorry," Felix pinched the bridge of his nose. "From the museums in which they were last reported to reside. We were aware the items weren't legitimately acquired, so we purchased them from the museums after reporting them located."

Carl just stared at him. "You can do that?"

"You can do anything if you are given a big enough inheritance and some functioning businesses and don't squander it away," Felix said primly. And then he felt some honesty was required. "And you know how to grift and can turn a rather lucrative and yet legal profit."

"*That* I'll believe. So the museums think you have the original items—"

Felix cleared his throat.

Carl's eyes widened. "So you *have* the original items, and Marnie has—"

"Wait a minute," Talbot interjected. "I stole those pieces straight from the museums!"

"And some of them were real," Felix said shortly. "Until we purchased them and… reclaimed them."

Carl started to laugh. "I've got to hand it to you. I was pissed, at first. I thought you'd completely undermined all my work, but given this recording—" He gestured to the computer, where he'd obviously watched Marnie and Talbot discussing art theft. "—and this guy's readiness to talk, I think I can arrest *both* of them for theft." He let out a sigh. "Or, well, I could if my insurance company gave a damn anymore."

Danny cleared his throat. "I, uhm, may have a contact for you," he said, giving Felix a sideways glance. "And a plan. But we would need to find something to do with *this* gentleman for… how long would you say, Felix? A week? Two?"

"Until when?"

"Until Marnie interviews me for her show."

Felix frowned. "Danny, this is it. This is revenge. This is Marnie locked up in jail for a long time, or at least her reputation shattered."

Danny shook his head. "No, no it's not. This will go right over people's heads. You know that, right? Art theft? Forging provenances? It will be like politics. People will take sides and argue and eventually forget her. She might even get a lawyer to argue her time be served in a women's country club, and that's not fair. She didn't just discredit *you*, Felix. She undermined the stories of every person who ever came forward and was dismissed. This will be embarrassing for her, but it's not going to be humiliating. I want *abject* humiliation. It needs to be public. I can't even explain to you in words how much I need to hear her hated by the people who sing her praises right now."

He was practically transcendent with fury, and Felix had a moment to wish they were half-naked but *not* surrounded by a group of college students who wanted them to be parents. What he was feeling for Danny right now didn't have a damned thing to do with being a father and *everything* to do with making up for the last ten years with the love of his life.

"But we can't guarantee that will happen," Felix said, chewing his lip.

Danny gave him one of those looks, the kind of look he gave right before he was about to steal something nobody thought could be stolen. The kind that made him unbearably sexy, like a puckish god.

"Trust me," Danny said, nodding his head.

Okay, fine. "If you trust me," Felix told him. "Interview for that position. Be an assistant curator in your dream job."

"I already told you I would," Danny said, sounding bored, which probably meant he'd been working on ways to wiggle out of it even in his sleep.

"In front of everybody here," Felix said. "I'll let you set up Marnie's spectacular flameout if you get a fucking legitimate job."

Danny rolled his eyes. "What if I see something I want to steal?" he goaded. "Like, it *needs* to be stolen."

"Give it up, Danny. The only things you ever think *need* to be stolen *need* to be stolen so you can give them to a museum. This just cuts out the part where you break into the museum." Felix crossed his arms. "Is it a deal?"

Danny shivered. "Fine." He glanced at Carl. "If I hook you up with Interpol—and give you a chance to put on some clothes—can you find somewhere to stash this cockroach for the next two weeks?"

Carl looked around the room and then back to Felix.

"No," Felix said, appalled.

Carl did it again. And this time, he focused on Julia.

She rolled her eyes. "I have a walk-in closet with an adjoining bathroom that is much more accommodating."

Carl smiled grimly. "Danny, if you give me your Interpol contact, and we stash him here, it's a deal."

Danny grunted. "Stirling, how awake are you?"

"A case of Red Bull and I'll be fan*tastic*."

God, only the young.

"Are you awake enough to make an electronic thingy that will fit in a bauble that our man can't disable?"

"Definitely. Give me about half an hour." Stirling slumped determinedly away.

"Grace, can you design some sort of manacle that's Grace-proof?"

Grace hummed. "Why Grace-proof?" he asked, and Danny rolled his eyes.

"Because if you can't get out of it, this guy can't." He glared at Talbot. "You woke us up, you turdjacket. Do you realize how long it's been since I've gotten a good night's sleep? You didn't even have the decency to sneak in and steal our stuff. You had to be an incompetent asshole and get us all out of bed. Buddy, you are going to wish you were back in bed with Marnie, that's all I've got to say."

Talbot looked faintly nauseated. "Please," he whispered. "God, please no. I… I mean, I was working for an employer, right? That's what you do. But God. That woman." He shuddered. "It was like sticking my dick in an ice maker. So… cold…."

They all shuddered, because yes, it did sound like a fate worse than death.

"Yeah, so don't dick with us," Danny said and then yawned. "Hunter?"

"Yessir." Hunter all but saluted.

"Can you secure Mrs. Salinger's closet with the adjoining bathroom? Make sure there's nothing there he can use to get out?"

"You can't just keep me here," Talbot said, suddenly realizing what was happening. "You can't imprison me against my will."

"Buddy," Danny told him, "you are going to have three squares, a nice mattress, your own bathroom, and time off for good behavior. Felix has a full cable package. Even a weight room if that's your thing. It will be like an extended vacation compared to Interpol prison, I'm telling you right now."

"How would you know that?" Felix asked, suddenly aware that he only knew of about two years of Danny's absence.

"That's another story," Danny said. "But one that only lasted about a fortnight."

"I paid for his bail," Carl muttered "But he'd already escaped when they went to get him. There's money I'll never see again."

"I told you I didn't need rescuing," Danny said mildly.

"Oh, I think you did." Carl gave Felix a significant look. "I just wasn't the man to do it."

Danny snorted. "Okay. Chuck, go get dressed, then come back and spell Carl. Hunter, go secure Mr. Talbot's demesne. Stirling will be back in half an hour, and we can set up a guard rotation in the morning. Are we good here?"

"What do you want me to do?" Molly said, yawning.

"Go sleep, precious," Danny said, smiling gently at her. "You and Josh are up for guard duty after Interpol gets here." He yawned. "And those bastards always take their own sweet time."

"I'll set up a schedule tomorrow," Julia said, yawning too. "If anybody needs anything, wake me and leave Danny and Felix alone."

"Thanks, darling," Felix said, taking her hand and kissing it.

She bussed him on the cheek and wrapped her peignoir tighter around his old sweats.

"Come along, Hunter. I'll show you where we need to set him up. It used to be my father's safe room. It's double-enforced steel, with a sliding door and a heavy-duty ventilation system. And of course, a bathroom."

"Oh my God, and it's a walk-in closet now?" Hunter said, respect in his voice.

"Well, my father was sort of a bastard. I thought painting it pink and stowing my winter wardrobe in there would have him turning over in his grave," she said. "Josh, if you'd like, you can help us move things to my bedroom."

"Sure, Mom!"

Josh winked at Felix and Danny and took off, leaving them and Carl in the room with Talbot. Danny leaned forward and put his hand on Talbot's thigh, squeezing.

"Bertram," he said, getting the man's complete attention.

Talbot swallowed. "Yes?"

"I need you to know that the lot of us can be a fun group. I'm not lying about having all the cable stations. This is *such* a better place than an Interpol prison. And it has the advantage of getting you away from Marnie and having her go down in very public, very humiliating flames. Carl here can probably get you off in, what—two to five?"

Carl nodded. "I'll go to bat for you," he said, obviously seeing where Danny was going with this.

"On one condition," Danny said. "I dare you to guess what it will be."

"Don't fight you," he mumbled.

"Indeed." Danny smiled thinly at Carl. "I'm going to put a number in your phone and then disappear into the house. However you and the people from Interpol interact, you must not, under any circumstances, *mention my name*."

Carl grunted. "I'll be back in two minutes."

Well, of course. The poor man wasn't wearing any pants.

"Felix," Danny said, gesturing to all of them in their underwear. "Could you do something about this?"

"After he gets back," Felix said. "Carl, go get your phone, then I'll go get you sweats. There need to be two people in the room with this man at all times."

Danny nodded and sighed. "I was so looking forward to the next two weeks," he said tiredly.

"It won't be so bad," Felix said. "There's enough of us. We should get whole days off without guard duty."

"Well, Interpol will be here too," Danny said. "They usually send two people on principle." He grimaced. "We really *will* have to get Phyllis some help." He yawned again and looked in apology to Carl. "I'm sorry."

"No, no. I'm guessing this must have been quite a week." Carl gave him an almost whimsical look. "You know, I think I really *could* use the lot of you in some undertakings that are, say, less than straightforward."

"Did you hear that, Felix?" Danny said. "I got us *all* jobs."

Carl laughed and went to fetch his pants.

All in One Tent

ALL IN all, it took another hour before they got to return to their beds, secure in the fact that two very bemused Interpol officers were ensconced in Julia's father's safe room, complete with a couch, two twin beds, all the snacks in the world, and an intercom straight to Carl, who had opted to go back to sleep himself.

Everyone else had crawled back into bed with an injunction to sleep for at least another six hours and a plan to meet for brunch around noon. Julia had texted Phyllis—who had slept through the entire thing—and told her to hire two more people for the foreseeable future and to send them shopping for an army in the morning.

And then Danny and Felix had gone to bed and slept like they'd been shot.

Danny woke up to the thin sunlight of midmorning and Felix making an ungodly racket in his closet.

"The fuck you doin'?" he mumbled, rubbing sleep from his eyes.

"Unpacking your suitcase," Felix said. "I don't trust you yet."

Danny thought about how many times he'd tried to back out so far. "That's fair. Why are you doing it now?"

"Because if I hide it while you're still mostly asleep, you won't be able to find it and you won't be able to go."

Danny yawned again. "If I don't put up a fight and let you do this, will you come back to bed when you're done?"

Felix yawned too. "God yes. I'm *wrecked*. Remember when we used to be able to stay up for forty-eight hours at a time and then fuck like lemmings?"

"Yes. I can't believe we wasted those days on Josh. He's obviously self-sufficient and didn't need all that attention when he was teething. Who knew?"

"Right? That kid probably could have fetched his own ice and taken his own acetaminophen if we'd just given him the chance." Felix shoved the last pair of clean underwear in a drawer and took the nice little netted bag of laundry and dumped it in the hamper in the bathroom. Then he grabbed Danny's trusted, if battered, giant suitcase and the matching carry-on. "If I'm not back in ten minutes, Interpol failed, that little cockweasel in Julia's safe room got away, and you should ditch us all and save yourself."

Danny yawned and closed his eyes. "Sure. I'll do that."

When he woke up again, he was snuggled warmly against Felix, and it was still nowhere near brunch time.

"Felix?" he mumbled.

"Yes?"

"I'm home."

"Good."

THEY WOKE up again to a gentle tapping on their door. When Felix gave a sleepy hello, Julia entered, looking well rested and showered and made up and even dressed nicely in a tunic and leggings.

"You're disgustingly perky," Danny said, yawning. "Felix, if you had to have a wife, did she have to make us look like slobs?"

"Yes," Felix said, stretching as he sat up. "She gives us something to aspire to. Good morning, my dear. I trust nobody's escaped, been murdered, or needs bail?"

"No, not so far. But I think you two will be wanted downstairs shortly, and I wanted to head you to the shower."

Felix nodded and then pulled his arms around his knees. "Come here, sweetheart. Sit."

Julia did so, resting her arm on Danny's hips as he turned to the side. "What's up?"

"Are you okay with all of this?" he asked seriously, and Danny's heart cramped just a tinge. These two people had ten years to establish a routine, a way of living that did not include chaos and did *not* include him.

She turned toward Danny and stroked his cheek with a cool hand. "Are you really coming back?" she asked. "For good?"

He captured her hand and kissed the knuckles. "If you really want me to."

She flicked his ear. "My God, you're dense. Yes. I've been begging you to come back for the last week." She looked at Felix and smiled. "All the people in the house—all these *young* people. It's amazing, isn't it?"

Felix nodded, and Danny pushed up to lean on him a little. "You two, this could be our lives. You realize that now. You'll have day jobs—"

"As will you," Felix reminded him.

"But the kids, they seem to want to… to do things. As a group. Not quite legal things. Things that could get sticky."

"Exciting things," Julia said throatily. "Things that make me feel young again."

"Things that make me feel useful," Felix said. "Taking Marnie down—that's a good thing. Can you imagine how many good things the lot of us can do?"

"Good, slightly illegal things?" Danny said with a faint smile.

"Mm." Felix gave him a stern look. "All your talk about Interpol and you had a contact on the inside?"

Danny gave him a level look back. "Did you notice everybody has explicit instructions not to mention my name? Even Talbot thinks I'm Benjamin Morgan, museum curator in the background." He'd made that clear before the guards had arrived.

"Yes, but you went to bed before they got here," Felix said with a snort. "You didn't see the looks they shot me when I mentioned 'Benjamin Morgan.' I don't know who you talked to, but someone there wasn't fooled for a damned minute."

Danny shrugged and then decided they'd trusted him so far, he might as well tell them the truth.

"Somebody had to pull me out of the gutter and take me to the hospital when Kadjic was done with me," he said softly. "Turned out there was a *very* young Interpol agent who'd been sort of"—he grimaced—"making me his hobby. Much like Carl had, really."

"And you never really explained that." Felix looked grumpy, and Danny had to laugh.

"I'm getting there. Anyway, young Liam Craig saved my life and then shoved me in a rehab facility with someone he called an old friend."

"Carl?" Felix asked, surprised.

Danny nodded. "We bonded over wanting another fucking drink, Felix. Don't be jealous about that."

"Why didn't he arrest you?" Julia asked. "I understand prison dries you out very quickly."

Danny gave her a brief smile. "Right? It's a wonder I never tried it."

But Julia didn't laugh, just regarded him with sober blue eyes.

"Anyway, apparently he'd been studying me—studying *us*—since he'd come up through the ranks as a young detective. Youngest in his borough, I guess, and was recruited by Interpol. He noticed, as nobody else seemed to, that we tended to rescue as many paintings as we stole, and that intrigued him. So he sat by my bedside as I healed and asked me about…." Danny looked away.

"About us?" Felix asked, because he was perceptive like that.

"Yes. And instead of drinking, I spent three days telling him about *us*. And about how I'd left my family behind and…." Danny's eyes burned. "I missed you all so bad, that first year especially. He urged me to stay in Josh's life, you know. I guess Liam's father left when he was a kid, and he sort of made me promise not to ghost our son like he'd been ghosted. He's a good young man, really." Damn. Must be the sunlight through the shades. Danny wiped under his eyes with his palm. "Anyway, when I *did* end up in Interpol lock-up, it was sort of by his request. He, well, he had a job for me to do."

Felix was looking at him with a sort of hero worship. "You're not just going to leave it like that, are you?"

Danny gave him an embarrassed smile. "But I just told you the most interesting parts of a ten-year absence. You want me to give you all my stories now?"

"But why are they still after you?" Felix asked. "Tell me that, at least!"

Danny laughed. "The arrest was legitimate, although I had to pretend to be a bull in a china shop to get their damned attention. Liam made sure I'd end up in a part of prison where... well, he suspected crooked guards, and he was right. So I set the guards up. He was going to help me get out—clear my record for service, that sort of thing—but I was in a bit of danger, so I just escaped, left the guards in a pickle, and sent him a post-card from Prague."

"So your record was never cleared, but it *could* have been?" Felix asked, appalled.

"Well, yes." Danny gave him an abashed smile. "But then I'd be a thief with no provenance. Who wants to employ a thief who's not wanted by Interpol? I would have lost thousands of dollars!"

Felix groaned and buried his face in his hands, and Julia shook her head.

"It's a good thing we love you," she said.

He showed all his teeth in return.

"No, I'm serious. It's a damned good thing we love you as much as we do. You're worse than Josh, you know. You have given me more fine lines than my *son*, and that's saying something," she continued.

Felix cleared his throat. "And speaking of our son giving us wrinkles…."

They looked at him.

"He will *not* be returning to school this year."

Danny rolled his eyes. "I'm stunned."

"Shocked," Julia said dryly.

"I feel chest pains coming on," Danny added.

"I may succumb to the vapors."

Felix glared at them both. "I'm going to go take a shower. You two can sit here and bathe in your self-satisfaction now. That's fine."

He stalked off, and Julia arched an eyebrow at Danny. "You're not going?"

"In a minute." He regarded her soberly. "This was probably not what you had in mind when you said you were glad I was back."

She cocked her head. "Not *this*, exactly. But I had *something*." She rose and kissed his temple. "For ten years, Felix and I have been settling into middle age quite comfortably. But we've been *settling*." They both heard a thump from somewhere downstairs, followed by a clatter and three voices, in chorus, screaming, "*Grace!*"

Danny put his face in his hands. "Sorry," he mumbled.

She smiled and waggled her eyebrows. "Don't be. This isn't comfortable, and it's not middle-aged. This is *young*. And it's *fun*. But this time we've got enough common sense to do it right."

He smiled at her a little. "You know you're the only woman I could ever love, right?"

"Of course I am," she murmured, standing to exit. She paused at the doorway, though. "Danny, please make this forever. I...." She held her hand to her chest. "You, Felix, Josh—you're my heart. I may never fall in love with a man the way you two love each other, but knowing that kind of love is around, that it's in my home.... It's everything."

"I told him it would kill me to leave." He gave half a shrug. "Everything else is nerves." He took a deep breath. "I keep getting afraid that ten years, it's such a huge hole in our lives. But Felix, you, Josh you were so much in my heart that whole time that it's been like you were there. I just have to tell you the adventures to remind you."

She dashed her hand under her china blue eyes. "Today," she said deliberately, "in the afternoon, after we have everybody scheduled and our plans all synchronized, you and I are going to sit down with Josh's photo albums—"

He held up a hand and stood. Felix had put it on top of the dresser and hadn't said a word.

He handed it to Julia: a bound volume of photos. Josh had sent them as computer printouts, but Danny had them processed onto photo paper so they'd last. Each one was backed with Josh's letter, each letter obviously read until the ink was faded in places.

Julia took it and opened to the first page.

> *Dear Uncle Danny—I missed*
> *you so much. I started real school this*
> *week and I hated it. Grandpa makes*
> *me go to the one where I have to*
> *wear the tie and the shorts. Mom tells*
> *me that it's because I'm smart and*

*Dad tells me it will give me access
to things like drama and computers.
I miss you telling me that it's a big
scam, and the best I can do is fake it
until I find out what's in it for me. The
only kid I can stand is Dylan who I
knew from trying school before. This
week I taught him how to steal the
mean kids' lunch money. He's going
to use it to buy a new mirror for his
dance instructor. He can stand on his
toes all by himself.*

She closed the book then and shook her head, holding her hand in front of her mouth. "Oh, Danny. I... I...."

He put his hand on her shoulder and kissed her temple. "Read through them yourself," he said softly. "In your own time. He was my own little conduit to your world."

"We really were with you," she murmured. "Josh kept all your letters, you know. Felix and I knew them by heart."

He shrugged. "I'll be honest, Julia, I don't know how much of them is real. I mean, I may say 'I visited the Louvre again today,' but that may or may not mean after hours when I was there to collect something that didn't belong."

She sputtered laughter. "Just stop. I need to go read these and cry, but later. Go shower with Felix. We need to eat. It *was* ten years, but the love has obviously always been there." She tucked her lips into a thin line, which meant she was controlling her emotions. "That's more than any of us had when we started. It's going to see us through."

She left the bedroom then, and he went into the ginormous en suite bathroom. He stripped and dropped his clothes in the hamper and then climbed into the shower with Felix.

"The water was getting cold," Felix said, sounding sulky.

"It was not." Danny took the shower puff from him and squirted soap on it. "I was talking to Julia. She needs us."

Felix tugged gently at the shower puff and started to wash Danny's shoulders. "I could have told you that."

"Yes, but Julia and I never put it into words, you know. The two of you had ten years, a lot of it alone together, to realize you loved each other like brother and sister. I didn't realize it until I thought I'd never see her again."

"Then you were stupid," Felix said, voice thick.

"I am aware."

Felix didn't answer, just kept scrubbing him—pits, creases, chest, and neck—like he could wash all the sorrow away. Danny was glad he couldn't. Sorrow was something you learned from.

He'd learned that his family was worth keeping. His family was worth fighting for. Everything else he could deal with, as long as he remembered that one true thing.

THAT EVENING they took over guard duty from Hunter and Grace, who had taken over from the Interpol agents, who were currently eating dinner downstairs. Phyllis, ever efficient, had hired three other people—all of them students, as far as Danny could tell—to help her take care of the army that had invaded the big, once-empty mansion.

They were currently trying to pick Bertram Talbot's weaselly little brain.

"So, were you her only procurer?" Danny asked as Talbot shoveled a mouthful of truffle risotto into his mouth.

Talbot rolled back his eyes and held up a finger. "This is amazing," he said. "I will give up my life as a thief to live here."

"Which is just as well," Felix said in a burst of ill temper, "because you weren't that much of a thief. Three forgeries. You stole *three* forgeries and passed them off to Marnie as originals."

Talbot huffed. "Yes, I know that. Wasn't my fault someone got there first, and Courtland was too dumb to tell the real from the fake." He sniffed. "She didn't actually care when it came down to it. You realize that, right? She. Didn't. Care. All that art," he said, sulking. "All those lovely things she paid for me to get, and really, she just wanted to say she had them."

Danny frowned. "Was she working from some sort of list?" he asked, suddenly curious. "I was familiar with most of those, but I have a"—he glared at Felix—"*major* in objets d'art from the seventeenth, eighteenth, and nineteenth centuries. I'm familiar with a lot of small items."

Talbot frowned. "Actually, she *did* have sort of an agenda. When she first hired me, it was on the pretense of being on the up-and-up. She said she wanted that comb you made such a big deal out of, and when the museum wouldn't part with it for her price, she told me to do whatever I had to. I took her at her word. But it went that way with most of the items. I'd get back, she'd add the thing to her collection, and then she'd send me out for something else."

Danny and Felix met gazes. "That sounds unusual," Felix murmured. "I wonder if there's any way we can find out where that list came from."

Danny arched an eyebrow. "I. Wonder."

Talbot finished his risotto and begged them to tell the cook that he was madly in love with her and would visit as soon as he was done with his sentence, and then the three of them settled into a cutthroat game of cribbage.

Honestly, Talbot wasn't so bad, once you got to know him. Yes, you had to search a Paris sewer to find his moral compass, but it was in there. Somewhere. And his fingers were extraordinarily quick.

If he hadn't been playing against Danny and Felix, he might have won a game or two.

"Fine," Talbot muttered after an hour of play. "You two win. I don't have any money, and you won't let me have matches. What exactly are we playing for?"

"More information," Danny said.

"I've told you *everything*."

"Mm." Danny shuffled the decks ably, the cards flying back and forth between his fingers. "Have you, though? When did the sex start? And did she expect it?"

"She made a show of seducing me," Talbot muttered. "It was pretty clear it was part of the contract." He gave the two men a covert look. "You're not going to call me a whore?"

"I've known some whores," Danny said, thinking of Rome. "Been one once or twice. What you do to feed yourself or pay your rent is your business. No. I'll be frank—we've been recording you. Not porn style, but we got the idea. You weren't shitting around about sticking your dick in an ice maker. But you didn't get the half of it. She was hell on her assistant, I'll tell you that."

Talbot grunted. "Yeah. She fancies herself a man-eater, but she hates women most of all. Ten minutes with her and I realized all sex was to her was power."

"Did her assistant know that?" Danny asked, thinking about the girl's half-worshipful, half-afraid look as she'd called Marnie away.

Talbot shook his head. "We weren't supposed to talk, but I got the idea that Brittney thought she and Marnie were an actual thing, not just a weekday workout." He sighed and looked away, his ridiculous mustache quivering. "Poor kid. She probably thought it was true love, that she was the only one who could tame the savage beast."

"Interesting," Danny said. "Felix, isn't Brittney the intern who refused to back Marnie up?"

Felix nodded. "I wonder how that played between them."

"Not well," Danny murmured. "I think the noose might have gotten just a little bit tighter." He sized up Talbot. "So, if we put you on national television, do you want your face blotted out and your identity hidden, or do you want the full frontal, look at this man's creds, don't you want to break him out of prison so he can steal for *you*?"

Talbot thought about it. "Can you leak just enough so the *right* people know it's me?"

Danny looked at Felix, who nodded his golden head. "Oh yes, that's no problem. A hint of hair or mustache perhaps?"

"Absolutely." He looked wistful. "If I get out in less than two years, is it okay if I look you guys up? This has been the best jail time I've ever served."

Aw. That was sweet. Danny patted his shoulder. "Sure—but I'd rethink breaking in. If you think this place was airtight now, you have no idea what's been done to it in the last twenty-four hours."

Talbot nodded. "It's a class act. Sacrosanct. I'll tell my friends." With that he yawned and told them that he'd spent part of the day in the weight room, and he approved heartily, but he was ready for bed now. They couldn't turn out the lights or leave him alone, of course, but they could watch television quietly in the background until the next guards were up, and leave the plotting until after their shift was over.

Shopping and Lunch

FELIX WATCHED as Danny deftly handled Stirling and wondered how anybody thought Felix himself had patience or a way with people.

"Mm, yes, that's good. Maybe a twitch more mustache," Danny said, looking over his shoulder at the monitor.

"But it doesn't make any sense!" Stirling wailed. "Why would you *want* him to be recognized?"

"Well, he didn't get busted stealing the things, did he?" Danny asked. "No, he got busted because his *employer* was a dumbass. He can't help that. The fact that she employed him to go get the original provenance was a gauche move on her part but, again, not his fault.

So no, he did some solid thievery here, and he deserves some solid contracts."

"Fine," Stirling grumbled. "Why am I doing this again?"

"Well, our Mr. Talbot is going to appear on screen with her Royal Twatwhistle herself, so I think it's only fair he gets his say about who gets to see him and how. There. No, that's perfect. And listen to the way she talks to him before he finally snaps. Yes, I'd break this man out of jail to hire him. Good."

"But didn't he try to rob us?" Stirling asked, completely bewildered.

"Yes, but it wasn't personal, my boy. I'm not saying *I* want to hire him. But I don't mind giving him a reference."

Stirling huffed out a breath. "Who *are* the good guys, Uncle Danny?" he asked with an agonized wail, and Felix's heart stopped.

"Have you ever tried to hurt someone from pure viciousness?" Danny asked after a moment.

"No," Stirling murmured.

"Have you ever stolen from someone who hadn't deprived someone else of their dinner?"

"I don't really steal," Stirling told him. "I have a trust fund. Mostly I just… I don't know. Troll. Like that senator who was getting his dick sucked by an eighteen-year-old while he was going on about how homosexuality is going to kill us all."

"Which one?" Felix asked, curious.

Stirling thought about it. "The one that *just* got outed. Like three weeks ago. With video. To six internet outlets."

"That was you?" Felix asked, delighted.

Stirling nodded, with just a hint of pride.

"Well done," Danny said with a gentle squeeze to the shoulder. Not a clap on the back—Felix noted—because that would startle him. "See? Think of us in terms of gods of mischief. Not Loki. The Norse gods were horrific and fucking mean. The Navajo god, Coyote, perhaps. He bothered people and he wrought some mischief, but he also did the great god's bidding and helped people and eventually was depended upon to save many of them, if I remember correctly. It might have been at the end of the world." He gave an apologetic shrug. "I'm sorry. Most of my schooling has been in European art. Other stuff? It's a failing."

Stirling laughed—*laughed*—and said, "No, I remember this. Coyote was a trickster. His job was to test the boundaries of order and to give the bad guys comeuppance." His face went grim. "He didn't *like* people who preyed on children or the innocent."

"No, he did not," Danny agreed. "So that is who we'll be. Talbot is an unknown quantity. We push the boundaries of order and chaos barely on the side of order. I don't know if he's on the other side of that line. But we will respect him as a fellow boundary pusher and bank a little goodwill, given that we're sending him to prison and all."

"Understood," Stirling said with a nod. He swallowed and held out a thumb drive. "Thanks, Uncle Danny."

Danny winked and took the thumb drive. "Any time, young man." He turned to Felix. "Are we ready for our big day out?"

"Are *you*? You're the one who made all the back-and-forth motions about the job."

"Well, yes, but if I'm going to get it, I should have the wardrobe." He made a face. "Am I going to have to wear tweed jackets with patches on the elbows?"

Felix recoiled in horror. "Dear God, no." He paused. "Maybe. I understand you'll be working in the archives. There will be a lot of dust involved."

"Mm... well, a few more suits, I suppose." He arched an eyebrow. "Seeing that I have a closet here and all."

Felix nodded. "You don't fill enough of it. We need more clothes. And more. And more."

"Are you planning on making me want to stay or heaping them on top of me until they find my shriveled body underneath many years later?"

Felix pursed his lips. "It all depends on what sort of commitment you're willing to make."

"I committed to interview for the job. Also for the con. Two different interviews. I think you may buy me clothes and still let me live."

Felix grabbed his hand and hauled him up the stairs to the foyer. "You say that, but I'll believe it when I see the clothes in the closet."

Danny just laughed, but he let Felix pull him outside, into the chilly spring day and the shopping district, which were two things Felix very much wanted to do.

Time with Danny that wasn't fraught with the job; time with him that wasn't as emotionally intense as their lovemaking had become. Could they do that?

Oh they could! And it was delightful.

Saks was a riot. Danny picked the pockets of six people who were being insufferably snobbish. He ditched the ID and shoved the cash in the purses of people who were shopping in the clearance racks for job interviews, or underwear that wouldn't disintegrate with the first deep breath. The sixth time, Felix made him stop and get down to work, picking everything from shorts and madras shirts for outings, to slacks and button-downs for in-between times, to three very snazzy bespoke suits, one for each interview and one for a night on the town.

"Do people even dress nicely for dates anymore?" Danny asked. "I remember it was a thing when we were young, but you've seen all the young people at our house. They seem to think black trousers and black turtlenecks are a uniform."

"That's because they're thieves, Danny. I've seen Josh dress very nicely when he's going out on the town."

Danny laughed, and they'd presented their list of purchases to the young woman behind the register. Their arms weren't laden with packages—those were being delivered to the house as soon as the alterations were complete, along with everything from underwear to pajamas. Danny pulled out his wallet to pay—and Felix had no doubt he could, under whatever name was on his ID—but Felix beat him to it with Benjamin Morgan credit cards and an impossible-to-fake Illinois driver's license in the same name.

Danny eyed the ID, and his eyes widened. "My birthday," he murmured, after their purchases had been rung up. "My real one." None of his fake IDs had his real birthday—Felix had known that when they were younger, but he'd wanted as much as possible to be real this time.

They headed for the elevator with their dress shoes ringing sharply on the tiles while Felix searched for words.

"I looked it up," Felix said as they drew near. He bit his lip. "I... I didn't know where you were at the time, so I checked out where you'd been as a kid." He swallowed. "There was so much you didn't tell me." His heart ached with all of it. Danny had said his step-father had died—but not in a knife fight in front of Danny's parents' apartment when Danny was three. His mother had gotten sick, and Felix had read the terrible history of someone whose hospital bills had almost rendered her homeless, until she'd had to turn her son over to the foster care system just so he could have a roof over his head.

The first time he'd run away—at age fifteen—had been to attend her funeral.

Felix had read all the way to seventeen, when Danny had disappeared one night with all of his foster parents' money, after sending a thumb drive to social services with recordings of the two of them beating the hell out of the four kids in their care.

Danny had taken a lot of the beatings to spare the younger kids, but nobody could find him to try to make it right.

At seventeen, Danny Mitchell had fallen off the map, only to resurface in Rome after hopping a ride with a couple of sugar daddies to get as far away from Des Moines as he possibly could.

And here he was, back in Chicago, Peter Pan eyes alight with mischief, the maturity of more than twenty years not sitting heavily on him at all.

Until this moment when he glanced away, his painful past sitting between them.

"Wasn't a pretty story," he said, trying to shrug.

"It was a boy, looking for a home," Felix said, his throat tight. "And I didn't realize in a thousand years how much it must have hurt you not to offer it to you permanently."

"You were a kid too, Felix," Danny said. Always so generous. He smiled, pulling that sunshine moment back just as the elevator doors opened. "Come on, let's go eat and then stop by the studio. You know we have a little bit of work to do today."

Lunch—deep dish pizza with everything at Lou Malnati's—and they were both very proud of not getting a single spot on their shirts.

"God, do you think that comes with practice eating?" Danny asked, admiring his pristine tie.

"I'm just glad something good comes with age," Felix said.

And then Danny broke his heart and remade it in one moment.

"Love," Danny said. "I am more in love with you now than I was twenty years ago. That's got to be worth it, you think?"

Felix couldn't think. He couldn't speak. He couldn't breathe. He closed his eyes against the burning behind them and nodded, then snagged Danny's hand and kissed his knuckles and couldn't say a single word for a long while. They had just enough time to walk to the Dormer-Salinger Network building. It held an open-air studio on the ground level for their morning show segments, and people always gathered to look inside at the set.

The person they were going to meet was already standing out to the side, near the smaller entrance to the building itself, a slim, neat figure wearing a deep-sapphire-colored topcoat, nervously smoking a forbidden cigarette. Felix knew for a fact that Marnie disliked smoking intensely. He wondered if Brittney had picked up the habit before or after she and Marnie had become lovers.

God, Danny, could you cool it on the scotch? It's starting to ooze through your pores.

Oh, you don't like the scotch? Maybe I'll switch to vodka instead.

The flashback hit him so hard he almost vomited, and in a burst of clarity, he knew why Danny had asked to arrange this meeting.

"Felix," she said, throat working. "You... you look really well. I didn't expect to see you today."

Felix inclined his head. "Well, since Julia scheduled Mr. Morgan's meeting, I thought he and I could make an afternoon of it." He looked up into the sky, which may or may not have been about to dump hail on them, and drew his topcoat around him, resisting the urge to fuss with Danny's scarf. "The morning *was* bright." Chicago could have three seasons in one day, and locals either embraced that or moved. "But it's been a delightful day."

Danny grinned at him. "It has! So, Ms. Porter, I understand you're supposed to prep me for my segment next week?"

She nodded, her limpid brown eyes brightening fractionally. "Do you want to come in and see the facilities?" She cast an apologetic look at Felix, one he understood immediately. He was persona non grata; it was almost liberating in a way.

He and Danny made eye contact, and then he leaned forward and kissed Danny on the cheek. "I'll busy myself with a walk along the river," he said, and Danny winked.

Of course he would.

Brittney's eyes widened as she took in their show of affection, and Felix saw Danny's eyes do that foxlight thing.

"Surprised?" Danny asked.

Brittney nodded. "I... we didn't know he was... I mean...." She shook her head. "It's a stupid assumption to make in this day and age. Bi and pan are everywhere—"

"Except here!" Danny laughed. "Oh no, sweetheart. Felix and I are Rock Hudson-grade gay."

"But... but...." She glanced from one of them to the other, Felix's very public marriage—and obviously amicable divorce—sitting between them as a matter of record.

"Twenty years ago was a long time," Felix said. "And you should never underestimate what people will do when they're desperate." A con man's biggest tool was what people thought they knew. Brittney would write a story from those words that would explain everything but only touch lightly upon the truth.

"I'll be by the river," Felix said. "Unless, of course, the weather turns vile, in which case I'll be at the Dunkin' Donut on the corner."

Danny looked affronted. "Then you'd better buy me a strawberry sprinkle."

"Done," Felix said. Another buss on the cheek and he turned to leave. As soon as he hit the cross street, he turned his face to the wind coming off the lake and put his earpiece in.

He knew Danny was wearing his, and Stirling was back at home recording them.

"So, my dear," Danny was saying, "why don't you tell me why you look so sad."

Brittney's forced laugh almost cracked Felix's earpiece. He kept his eyes on the streets, and as rain began to bullet down (it never pattered in Chicago—there was some sort of rule), he pulled his umbrella out of his pocket and listened to his lover do what he did best: gain the confidence of the people around him.

"No particular reason," she said and then broke the rhythm of her speech. "Marnie, this is Benjamin Morgan. Remember, we're having him on the show next week?"

Marnie paused a moment. "Is someone smoking?" she asked, her voice taking on an unpleasant buzz.

"Not in the building, Marnie," Brittney said, all false brightness. "But you know, outside—can't stop people from doing what they do."

Marnie wrinkled her nose. "Don't patronize me, Brittney. It's a legitimate complaint."

"I am aware," Brittney murmured, and Felix heard the same sound he'd heard in Danny's voice when Danny had been desperately unhappy. "But Mr. Morgan doesn't smoke, and he's here to see what the segment will be like, and—"

"Not much to talk about," Marnie said, a calculated combination of smarm and dismissiveness. "Did you see the studio downstairs at the window?"

"Yes, but that's not normally where you film your 'Hello, Chicago!' segments," Danny observed. "Is there some reason we're not going to be in a closed studio?"

"No reason." And Felix could picture her shrug. "It's just been so beautiful outside. I thought I'd try something new."

It didn't take the heavens opening up at that moment and pissing hail on the heads of all pedestrians to make Felix think she was full of shit.

"She thinks she's got something on us," Felix murmured. "Be careful."

"You're not trying to make me uncomfortable, are you?" Danny asked, and Felix could imagine his eyes twinkling. "That would be a very poor way to accommodate someone who was asked to be on your show."

"No," Marnie said. "I just want all of Chicago to see you, that's all."

Danny laughed softly. "I don't fool myself that I'm particularly handsome, Ms. Courtland. And I am very aware that my fondness for old junk isn't a passion shared by many. Are *you* sure you want so much attention upon *you* as you give a boring interview to a middle-aged museum employee with no particular social standing? I mean, how embarrassing."

There was a click, and Josh came on the line. "Not handsome? Is he kidding me?"

"Shh! It's probably the only reason he came back to me," Felix murmured. "Don't tell him now."

Josh's laughter, warm and wry, was kind, but Felix knew the truth. He was lucky—damned lucky—for his second chance.

"Well, you were certainly excited to share your passion for 'old junk,' as you call it, on Friday," Marnie said, and it wasn't Felix's imagination—a caustic edge had crept into her voice.

"I was," Danny said. "And I'll be happy to do so again. In fact, if you like, I was thinking we could do a demonstration. You provide the pieces, and I'll do an analysis. Let's see how close I get. Make sure Brittney here holds the provenance, though. That's only fair."

Felix sucked in a breath and tried not to crash into the person who'd stopped at the crosswalk in front of him. The hail was becoming increasingly heavy, so he *did* take that turn into the nearest Dunkin' Donuts and tried not to put a hand out to hold himself up.

"You'll do *what*?" Felix choked.

"He'll do *what*?" Josh demanded.

"Yes!" Marnie crowed. "Now *that's* good television. I think that will make for a very interesting segment, don't you?"

"I'm on the edge of my seat," Danny said. "And you have to admit it will be a definite show of my professional grace, don't you?"

"Yeah, yeah, we got it, Danny," Felix muttered. "Josh, is he at the house?"

"*Grace!*" Josh hollered, loud enough to make Felix cringe, and he hoped Josh kept his feed to Danny blocked. "He's coming. What am I having him do, Dad?"

"I don't know yet," Felix said. "Let me think. There were seven pieces in the safe. Three were forgeries, one of which we provided, right?"

"Yeah," Josh said, obviously thinking.

"I need very careful, very detailed pictures of all of them," Felix said after a moment.

"Why?" Josh asked.

"Because this is our trap," Felix said. "I know she hasn't forgotten her provenances are in our name. If Danny says they're forgeries and she says they're not, he can produce the provenances and tell her we've caught her 'art procurer,' and he's told us everything. But she must have something in mind."

"What if she says they *are* forgeries?" Josh said.

"We need the histories of each theft *before* Talbot got his hands on them," Felix decided. "We knew she was working from a list. She obviously thinks she knows something we don't."

"What if she doesn't use her pieces?" Josh asked, just as Marnie's voice chimed in on Danny's earpiece.

"I have just the items for you to assess," she purred.

Felix's eyes narrowed. "Josh?"

"Yeah?"

"Have Stirling check her apartment specs for another safe."

Josh sucked in a breath. "I could swear we—"

"Yeah, but *that* note in her voice says she's got another source. We need them all, son. Danny needs to be able to do what he does best."

"Got it."

And then the two of them sat back to listen to him work his magic.

Kindred Hearts

DANNY LISTENED to Marnie spill more candy-coated malice and tried to decide which she was most likely to do when they were actually on camera—pretend the items were forged or pretend they were real and the provenances were forged. Didn't matter; Danny was ready. Felix was going on in his ear about a hidden safe and maybe some items that he didn't see. If Danny could talk, he'd tell Felix to ask Talbot, but he figured he'd get there eventually.

Danny's mission here was something else entirely.

He finished up with Marnie and asked if Brittney could direct him to the bathroom. When he got there, he mumbled, "Ask Talbot, you ninnies," and heard Josh and Felix swear.

"I was getting to it," Felix said with dignity.

"You always over plan," Danny said. "But don't worry. And take the pictures and forge the real pieces if you like. If it makes you feel better. But give me a moment here and you'll see why that might not be necessary."

"Icing on a cake isn't necessary," Felix replied tartly, "but it does make your birthday more of an adventure."

"Fine. Just make sure we don't end up with shish kebab of Grace and I'll be fine. Now if you lot could stop panicking in my head, I have another thing to do."

With that he washed up and went back out to smile at Brittney. As he'd suspected, the girl's shoulders had drooped, and her eyes were red-rimmed when she looked up. He gave her a gentle look and took her hand.

"My dear, do you have an office of your own?"

She shook her head. "No, I'm sorry. I share a desk with someone else in the newsroom."

He glanced around the utilitarian corridor, wondering if all studios were built like this—white tile, tan walls, and black-carpeted production rooms that put the gorgeous "don't you wish this was your living room" film sets in stark relief.

"Well, then, why don't you accompany me downstairs and maybe even come get a donut with me. You look quite like you need one."

The girl nodded dispiritedly, and Danny was silent as they took the elevator down. There were a couple of executives in the elevator having a tense conversation in undertones about how the board didn't know their ass from a hole in the ground without Salinger's input, and Danny hoped Felix was taking note. He was needed. This place had been a worthy institution. Felix had believed it when he'd sacrificed time with them in order to build it up, and Danny still believed it. News—good, fair news was important. So was quality arts and literacy programming, which was another of the channels, and so was classic movies, which was the third. Dormer-Salinger Network was a thriving entertainment business. One Felix could be proud of.

"Why isn't Julia running things?" Danny asked, almost to himself.

"She does," Felix replied through the earpiece. "She just hates fighting all of that fucking misogyny bullshit, so she and I make a lot of decisions, and I walk in and pretend to be captain of the universe. It's a solid con. Has been for years."

"Mm…." Danny looked at Brittney's air of exhaustion and sadness. "Maybe ask her if she feels like being more hands-on."

"What?" Brittney said, seeming to snap out of her own head.

"I'm sorry, just making notes to myself." Danny smiled. "But you do seem distracted, my darling."

Brittney made to turn her head away, but he stopped her.

"It's hard, isn't it. Being in love with someone who can't give you the same in return?"

Brittney gasped, and the elevator doors opened to street level. They spilled out, and Danny made her pause while he fished his umbrella out of his pocket.

"You took your coat off upstairs, didn't you?"

She nodded, teeth chattering, and he shrugged off his topcoat and draped it over her shoulders.

"There you go, my dear. How's that?"

"Warm," she mumbled, bringing to mind Bertram Talbot's line about sticking his dick in an ice maker. Poor kid, she was suffering hypothermia of the heart.

"It was definitely a little chilly upstairs," he said, thinking about Marnie's bitter rant against smoking. "I, uh, couldn't help notice how that hurt you."

"It's stupid," Brittney said, wiping under her eyes. "I'm doing it to get attention, and I know it will just make her mad. But… but I feel like I'm just… just a lay to her and not a real part of her life."

"That's a shame," Danny said, his throat aching with compassion. "When you start hurting yourself to get what you need from a relationship, that's a sign that something in you is bleeding."

She gave a choked little sob, and Danny put his arm around her shoulder. "It is," she confessed brokenly. "And I don't know if I have the strength to leave her. It's so stupid. I know she has other lovers and I'm just… just a toy but…."

She broke, and Danny paused under an overhang so he could push her face against his shoulder and let her cry.

"You're not just a toy," he said softly. "And you shouldn't be used like one. Sweetheart, if this relationship is hurting you, it's time to make a clean cut and bandage the wound."

"But…." She sobbed, and sobbed again. "But every time I try, she seduces me or *blackmails* me or…. She threatened to tell my parents, and I'm not out yet, and…."

He rocked her for a moment in the anonymity of the shopping district while he held an umbrella over her head and kept her warm. *We all need that sometimes*, he thought. Sometimes a stranger's good graces—or an Interpol agent's or an insurance investigator's—were the only thing that got you through the act of picking up the pieces and putting together a person who could go out and love again.

She eventually quieted, and he laughed a little. "Sweetheart, I'm going to reach into the pocket of my coat and get my handkerchief. Is that all right?"

She nodded, and he pulled it out, along with the thumb drive he'd taken from Josh. After he was done mopping up her face a little, he gave her a smile.

"Better," he pronounced. Above them, the hail lightened up, and he turned and offered his arm. She took it, and he continued down the street toward the donut shop, patting her hand. "So," he said. "I'm afraid Marnie is right about something."

"What's that?" she asked, her voice clogged.

"I am, in fact, more than what I seem. You didn't mention to her that Felix and I are together. Was that on purpose?"

Brittney nodded thoughtfully and, with a kind of freedom in her movements, liberated her frazzled bun and let her dark hair spill down her shoulders. She really was quite fetching when she did that. He wished for her a person who could really appreciate all that she was.

"I just… it seemed personal to you. And she's so awful to me. I thought, 'Fuck it. Let her get blindsided. I don't care about the show—she's already gotten rid of the guy who runs the place. Are we going to have to deal with her as our boss for the rest of our lives?'"

She stopped and put her hand to her mouth.

"Finally occurred to you, didn't it?" he asked.

"Yes!"

"You're planning to quit."

"Yes!" she said. "Oh my God, yes. Quit the station, quit her. Oh my God. I'd move back into my parents' house just to start over again."

Danny smiled inwardly and tucked the thumb drive into her palm. "My darling, I'm giving you a great trust here. It's something Marnie doesn't want us to know, and now you'll know it too."

Brittney looked at the thumb drive with horrified fascination. "Will it make me care for her less?"

Danny paused. "Make no mistake, sweetheart. This will make you hate her."

Brittney's face stilled and then curved into an evil smile. "What... what do you want me to do with it?"

"Well, Marnie wants me on display while she tries to trap me on national television, right?" He wasn't a moron. She wanted to intimidate him with the crowd outside while she sprang an unpleasant fact on him, possibly from his past.

"Yes." Brittney sighed. "I didn't know she'd planned to do that to you. I thought you were nice."

"Well, I can be," he said diplomatically. "But don't worry about her trapping me. I want you to find your favorite part of this little recording, and when I say, 'Okay, darling, could you play that clip I gave you?' go ahead and play it." He grimaced, remembering how crude Talbot had gotten in his description of Marnie. "Have your finger on the bleep button, though. You'll know the places."

"Okay," Brittney said. She swallowed. "What if... what if I chicken out?"

"Just tell me you're having technical difficulties," Danny said with a light shrug. "I'll understand. All I ask from *you* is that you don't warn Marnie. Can you do that?"

"Yes," she whispered.

"And if she does get hold of it, a heads-up would be appreciated." A change in plans would definitely be in order. Maybe he could convince Felix that Dublin was superb this time of year?

"It can be our secret," she said softly. They neared the donut place, and Danny held the door open for her. Felix was inside with three steaming cups of coffee and two dozen donuts—probably planning to take them home.

"Did you get my pink sprinkles?" he asked, bending down to kiss Felix's cheek.

"Of course I did." Felix smiled, his eyes soft and sad.

"Sit down with us," Danny said. "Let's talk about the weather if you like. Or the Cubs this year, or the Bears last year or—"

"Or how the Art Institute will be lucky to have a new assistant curator," she said, her voice taking on fond overtones.

"Ooh, I like that," Felix said. "So, Benjamin, what would *you* add to the museum's collection?"

Danny smiled and mentally started cataloguing his dream pieces. "Maybe a display dedicated to true love, do you think?"

"Rubies and garnets and carnelians, oh my?" Brittney asked, taking the coffee from Felix and sniffing appreciatively. "I'd visit it every day." Her voice was hoarse, but she had every appearance of someone who was willing to sit and enjoy pleasant company for a moment and think about the consequences later.

And with that, Danny began to spin a pretty fantasy of what he would do if he had jewels enough and time. Next to him, he could hear Felix practically humming with the promise of it all.

EVENTUALLY THEY escorted Brittney back to her job and then walked to fetch their car from the parking structure near Saks.

As Felix piloted the big rich-man's SUV through Chicago traffic, he pulled his earpiece out, and Danny did the same.

"What you said to Brittney," he began, and Danny winced.

"You're not going to hold it against me, right?"

Felix shook his head. "I've fallen in love with you over and over again in the last week and a half. I just… I need to tell you. I know why you left. If you ever feel that way again, tell me. Tell me before the first drink. Tell me before you look at the bottle. Tell me before you know yourself. I let you get away—"

"Felix, your network building is really beautiful. You're the kind of boss that inspires loyalty. You made sacrifices to take care of your employees—"

"You shouldn't have been one of them."

Danny smiled, holding that to his chest and enjoying it. "We both had to grow. I promise to tell you if my life hurts too much to deal without alcohol."

"I promise to make time—lots of time—to be your partner and not the CEO of DSN."

Danny had to laugh. "That's good. Because I have so much I want to do with you. Do you know there are ossuaries all over Eastern Europe?"

Felix gaped for a minute. "And an ossuary would be…?"

"Chapels made of human bones. Can you imagine the story behind those?"

Felix was clearly brought up short. "That sounds, well, grim, sort of."

"They're beautiful. Oh, Felix, you should see one. They're just this amazing piece of art that's been created with the bones of the faithful."

Felix laughed. "So definitely a tour of chapels of Eastern Europe. On the bucket list."

"There's also a penis museum in Finland."

Felix's laughter nourished Danny's soul. He made sure to make Felix laugh all the way home.

BERTRAM TALBOT earned a year off his sentence by telling them that Marnie kept a second safe in the pedestal of her bed. Felix was so pleased it had panned out that he had Phyllis cook a prime rib for everybody for dinner that night and let Bertram—and Interpol—come eat with the family. Before he sent the officers and the prisoner back to the safe room with a bottle of port after dessert, he asked if Bertie alone could sit in on the evening planning and the speculation about what Marnie was going to spring on Danny during the interview.

"What if she brings up something from your past?" Felix asked, and Danny thought he was very dear when he was worried.

"Like what? That I was a foster kid from Des Moines? Lucky for me, I know someone who cooked up a very nice backstory that explains all that. 'Raised by my aunt' could very well be 'fostered by my aunt.' The rest of it—well, only a real cunt would rip *that* scab off in public, and she'd pretty much sign off on that

Miss Adorable Newswoman trophy if she did that. And we *still* would have won."

Felix scrubbed at his face with his hands. "What about the… the…?"

Danny rolled his eyes. "Hopped a plane with a sugar daddy to Europe? Please. The fun part about Benjamin Morgan is that he could be as gay as he wants to be, and he's not a public figure. I can play the coy reprobate to my heart's content." He batted his eyelashes.

"What if she knows someone you've stolen from?" Josh asked.

Danny flashed his eyes to Talbot. "I don't know. Bertie, how well known *am* I?"

Bertram Talbot mulled it over. "Not… not well. 'Lightfingers' is legendary. You? Mild-mannered little guy who looks twenty but talks like he's sixty? Not so much."

"Did you hear that, Felix?" Danny said archly. "Bertie wants to get into my pants."

Bertram rolled his eyes. "I'm serious. You do what thieves *should* do. You don't steal from anyone to hurt them. You don't steal from someone who can't afford it. You lay low. You don't destroy anything. There should be a difference between thief, vandal, murderer, and thug. It should be a matter of professional pride. You make that difference."

Danny's entire body washed warm with the compliment; there was nothing like hearing your life's work validated by a fellow professional. "That's kind," he said with dignity. "But would Marnie Courtland know who I am?"

Talbot snorted. "She barely knows how to test for real gold."

Danny's eyes narrowed. "Really. What *does* she know?"

"Well, she kept wanting to do nitric acid, 'cause it looks super cool in the movies," Talbot said, disdain evident. "I tried to show her how to weigh it in water for specific gravity, but too much math makes her brain hurt."

"It's hard to hurt what's not there," Julia said disdainfully.

"You're not kidding," Talbot muttered. "Anyway, I had to tell her that dunking an item that wasn't pure gold in nitric might ruin it, and if the piece's value was in its history and not its materials, she'd destroy her work of art."

Danny grinned. "Oh. Oh that's good."

"In what world?" Felix asked, appalled.

"In the world where we're trying to trap her. I shall have to purchase a testing kit. And a jeweler's monocle, just to look the part." He pondered for a moment. "And maybe an XRF analyzer. Dammit! I didn't bring mine with me. I have a perfectly good model in Prague, but they're so hard to get through customs. Everybody thinks they're weaponry." He looked at Grace. "Did you take pictures of what you found in her pedestal safe?"

Grace nodded. "High res camera too. We're printing it out on photo paper so we can enlarge the pictures without pixilation."

"What was it, mostly?"

"Little teeny coke boxes," Grace said. "Ivory with gold filigree."

"Coke boxes?" Felix stared at Grace, and Danny rolled his eyes. Oh, he loved the man, but had he ever grown middle-aged quickly.

"Snuffboxes, Felix," he explained patiently. He cocked his head. "Did one of them have a miniature portrait of a young woman, done in pastels, on the inside lid?"

Julia caught her breath. "Do you think…?"

Felix's eyes grew huge. "How would she know?"

That first Rosalba Carierra snuffbox Julia had stolen to present to Danny as a gift because she'd wanted his help. He'd fenced it, in the end, and gotten enough money to send Julia and Felix to Chicago to set up housekeeping without her father's knowledge. They'd sent him money when she'd gotten control of her trust fund, but he'd been too busy—and missing Felix too much—to go looking for it again. He'd considered it a good trade-off for the big score they were about to make: money, security, the good life.

He'd do it again, of course. In a heartbeat.

But someone had done it for him.

Danny swallowed. "What else was in the safe?"

"A few other pieces and a hand-written list," Grace said. "You were right, Danny. Somebody had given her a treasure hunt."

"Send the list to my phone," he said, thinking hard. Kadjic? But how would Kadjic have known? Danny had treated the man like a mark—hadn't told him anything about his family, about his life. Kadjic had wanted to carve his initials into Danny Lightfingers. He hadn't known a damned thing about Danny Mitchell or Felix Salinger or Julia Dormer. Even at his drunkest, Danny had kept them close, and his quarters in Monaco hadn't had a single personal item. He'd made sure of it.

"What are you thinking?" Felix asked.

"That this is a mystery for another time," Danny decided. "It could be a coincidence, but it doesn't feel like it. It feels very… measured. To get me back here. To make me expose you and Julia and maybe even Josh to danger."

The thought made him sweat, but then Felix let out a rather predatory laugh.

"Well, joke's on them, I suppose."

Danny squinted at him. "I beg your pardon?"

Felix glanced around at the group of friends Josh had assembled, who had all taken to being parented by Felix and Danny like ducks to water.

"I think we're a pretty dangerous bunch, don't you?"

Talbot nodded. "Seriously. Most of the criminals I know would think twice if they knew about all of you."

Danny and Felix blinked at him.

"Which they won't," Talbot said.

They continued to stare. "Just Lightfingers," he said. "It'll make him look like Superman."

Danny burst out laughing, but Felix looked rather pleased. "Did you all hear that? I'm sleeping with Superman."

The table broke up into general laughter, and Talbot went back to his room shortly after that. When he was gone, Danny turned to everybody there.

"You know, this could get risky," he began.

"Shut up," Josh said, snagging a chocolate from the middle of the table.

"Don't want to hear it," Molly told him.

"Don't," Stirling rasped.

Hunter rolled his eyes.

Chuck laughed appreciatively. "Beats driving a getaway car for assholes who got nailed *inside* the damned bank."

"What did you do?" Stirling asked, eyes wide.

Chuck winked at him. "Drove the fuck away. Changed cars. Kept driving. Ended up in Chicago. Enrolled in theater 'cause I was bored between jobs. Met Josh last year."

"We haven't really utilized your talents, have we, Chuck?" Danny asked.

Chuck shrugged. "You fed me," he said. "I'd move in, but I really do have a cat."

"A cat?" Julia said, enchanted. "What kind of cat?"

"A nimble little black cat who likes to talk to me when I'm home," Chuck said, smiling at her.

"Could he talk to *me*?" she asked, batting her lashes prettily.

"We can get you a cat, Mom," Josh said.

"Then Chuck's cat will have company," his mother told him. She turned her attention back to Danny. "So, it's decided. Whoever this new threat is, we'll deal with them when they reveal themselves. And as for Marnie...."

"I'll be on her show next week," Danny said. "And interviewing for the Art Institute the day before."

"Then you should do your homework," Felix murmured. "What do you say we check out the institute tomorrow?"

"I also need to read some books," Danny said thoughtfully.

Felix's smile went nuclear. "That's even better."

IF DANNY had ever allowed himself to dream of home during the past ten years, the next week and a half would have been that dream.

Except better.

There were no lonely silences while he waited for Felix and Julia to come home from their days being visible and productive. There were no sudden adrenaline-ridden moments of "Holy shit! Is that Hiram?" There was no trying to remember who he was supposed to be and whom he'd met before under what alias.

Everybody in the house called him by his real first name.

Everybody outside called him Dr. Morgan.

He went to Felix's bed every night—after holding Felix's hand in public, meeting his friends, knowing what his life was like and who he knew outside of their little bubble.

He met Julia's lover, who was a little young and a little puppyish and not quite bright enough to realize there was more to his girlfriend than met the eye, and he got to know Chuck's cat. Julia's lover may or may not have been a long-term thing, but Danny definitely fell in love with Cary Grant, the highly nimble black cat Chuck had found at a rescue center. And with the companion black cat, Logan Lucky, that Julia had adopted as well.

Something about having all of the company, the camaraderie, the excitement around her, had revitalized Julia. She kept saying it was because Danny was home, but Danny thought it was more that her family had grown and she had an active part in it.

When they weren't invested in thievery—or guarding Talbot—the crew managed to find things to do. Josh, Molly, and Stirling were all involved in a show that would open in a couple of weeks. Grace was rehearsing for a recital of his own. Hunter worked out at the gym and worked as a bouncer, mostly for fun.

Chuck worked out with Hunter, ran errands around the house, helped where he was needed, and…

"Chuck, what *do* you do?" Danny asked two days before the Art Institute interview. He was sitting in the upstairs living room, surrounded by library books and about half a truckload of Amazon.com merchandise, giving himself a refresher course on every art period in European history, including materials, political movements, and innovations in technique. His tired brain was trying to decide if El Greco had been in favor of the Spanish Inquisition or not when it suddenly dawned on him that Chuck was the only one who didn't really have a job.

"Not much," Chuck said mildly. "I actually sort of reject the Puritan work ethic that says you have to have a goal or a purpose to make your life interesting and productive."

Danny took a minute to process that. "Don't you get bored?"

Chuck shrugged. "Hey, you practically gave me a master's course in European history and artwork just mumbling to yourself." He pointed to his own stack of books—Danny's castoffs—and smiled. "And that shit is incredibly interesting. How can I be bored?"

Danny grinned at him. "I'm impressed."

Another shrug. "Besides, remember that job where I just drove away?"

"Yes?"

"Turns out, the head of the crew was going to turn on everyone else and take the payoffs for a string of jobs we'd all helped with. I drove away with the payoffs when I was escaping—and that's a shit-ton of money. So I've been investing. Etrade. It's better than gambling if you do your homework. I, like, quadrupled the original amount."

Danny's mouth dropped slowly. "Uh… but won't…? I mean, how long will he be in jail?"

Chuck's eyes went grim. "Buddy, I don't desert a person until his body hits the floor, whether or not he's a scumbag who plans my demise."

"The whole crew?"

Chuck shuddered. "Two guys had wounds that got better in prison. I set them up bank accounts and sent them the access codes for when they get out. The rest of that shit is up to them, but they should be okay. The lead guy—the guy who was going to turn on us all? He got what was coming to him." Chuck's mouth softened. "This crew here? It's like being back in school again. Thinking all your buddies got your back. After that bullshit, I could use some goody-two-shoes, let's spill no fuckin' blood kind of thinking, you know?"

"Yeah," Danny said. "And I could see how some time spent in reflection would be good after that."

"Yup. So tell me what you're studying. What the fuck is 'rococo,' anyway?"

Danny grinned. "Well, it's a time period known for its extreme, painful artifice in fashion, and it's very structured art. But since everything was so structured, it has this intricacy that requires great skill, so it's sort of fascinating."

Chuck grinned. "I think so. Teach on, sensei, I feel a rococo jones coming on."

"Oh, Chuck, the art we can steal…."

"Righteous."

THE JOB interview was held in one of the Art Institute's small offices on the first floor, behind the public area of the Burnham Library. First, of course, they had to walk past the grand entrance, past the famed lions, who were dressed dapperly for the Bulls.

Danny took a deep breath as they entered the library itself, with its archways and muted lighting.

"Open to the public, Felix," he said.

"I know."

"It's such an amazing trust."

"Yes."

"You don't understand. All these books, some of them quite old. They have special cleaning rooms so the paper doesn't disintegrate, and I could—"

"You could touch history." Felix's hand, warm and supportive in the small of his back, was the only thing that kept Danny from hyperventilating. Felix had needed to put the knot in Danny's tie that morning because his hands had been shaking so hard.

"What if I don't get it?" Danny asked, his voice small. In his entire life, he'd never had a thing he wanted so badly that he couldn't steal—except love.

"Then we find a smaller museum and start there," Felix told him. "Come on. David is a friend of mine. We don't want to be late."

David Fielding was a pleasant, rather distracted man in his fifties, with a slight paunch, a ruddy face, and thinning hair. His desk—in an office cluttered with boxes of antique pins, glass cases of little-known paintings, and the occasional loose piece of jewelry that probably belonged in a catalog box—showed pictures of his family. Three daughters, one son, and a plump wife with a winsome smile and graying hair that looked like it never behaved.

Danny liked him on sight, and they spent a pleasant time engaged in small talk about art, about the difficulties of procuring it, about how to display it effectively, and what security meant in this day of technology and savvier and savvier thieves.

After about forty-five minutes, Danny remembered himself and asked when the interview started.

David laughed and pushed his glasses up the bridge of his nose. "Oh! Look at the time. Yes, well, Felix gave us your resume, and I'll tell Eleanor to start the paperwork. You can sign it on your way out. I assume you have your ID on you?"

"Uhm, yes. Driver's license, passport—"

"Good. We'll need copies, and there's some background checks and clearances, but Felix gave us most of that information when he proposed you for the position. Anyway, it'll take about half an hour." He paused, appearing disconcerted. "We may not have too much for you to do at first. You'll be an assistant curator, part-time. That's not a problem, is it?"

"No," Danny said, still stuck on the part where he got to sign paperwork. "I... I'll fill the hours."

David laughed. "Excellent! Miriam, our head curator in European art, is getting a little old. You'll be helping her. Anyway, I'll see you back here on Monday morning. It's been a wonderful conversation. I look forward to many more."

Danny gaped and allowed himself to be escorted out of the office and brought face-to-face with Felix.

"So?" Felix said, vibrating with anticipation.

"I got the job."

"Yes!"

Danny found himself hefted into the air and whirled about once before he made Felix put him down so he wouldn't wreck his back.

"I have to fill out paperwork," Danny said, trying not to be anxious. "It's a good thing I brought my ID."

"It is," Felix said, "Benjamin."

Danny smiled, his stomach lit up with butterflies. "Yes."

"It's going to be a good life," Felix murmured.

"Hasn't started yet," Danny warned him.

Felix shook his head. "You've got a job. Revenge is secondary."

Exasperating man. "My life isn't the point here!"

But Felix was adamant. "Oh, Danny, you're wrong. It's high time my life took a back seat to yours. Tomorrow is simply icing. It's great on a birthday cake but not really necessary."

"For me," Danny said soberly, "it is."

BUT FELIX didn't let Danny's concern over the next day stop them from celebrating his new job—and their new lives. Danny had to admit milestones were a lot more fun with a house full of people to share them with.

He caught himself drinking sparkling cider by the window in the foyer, looking out across the front lawn, which was growing bright with the promise of spring.

"You're missing your own party," Julia said softly.

"Feels premature," he said, casting her a sideways glance.

"Are you worried about tomorrow?"

He thought about it. "Not particularly. I…." He grimaced. "Okay. Fine. I am a little." He sipped at his cider. "I spent so long being his dirty little secret. If this is going to be my public introduction, I want to make him proud. And I want the person who hurt him to suffer." He took another, bigger gulp. "Is that too much to ask?"

She laughed. "Not from you. Come on. Everybody is about to try to teach me poker. Josh hasn't said a word, and you can watch me take them for all of their disposable cash."

"Oh my!" His worry fell away. "Darling, you always have the best ways to pull me from my funk."

She squeezed his hand and sobered for a moment. "You are absolutely everything he's ever loved about you. The man you've become in the last ten years is even more than you were before you left. You couldn't let him down in a million years, and if this goes tits up and she blurts out your real name and real history on a national broadcast, he will leave his life behind to follow you into the aether. So don't worry about it. It's going to be fine."

He chuckled. "You'd come with us, right? Into the aether?"

She squeezed his hand and tugged. "You couldn't shake me. I'd be the barnacle on your ass, Lightfingers. Don't doubt it."

He followed her to the killing fields, heartened.

Looking at the worst thing that could happen—and then figuring out how you'd live through it—was always a good way to deal with butterflies.

Ten years ago, he'd lived through his breakup with Felix, and the sun had risen again. He'd get through this too—regardless of what happened.

The Payoff

"Do you have your testing equipment? Do you have your earpiece?" Felix asked for the thousandth time.

"Yes, Felix. Do you have yours?" Danny's voice was supremely patient, but he was doing that thing where he held his elbow and chewed on his thumb as they drove.

"Both of you calm down," Julia said from the back of the vehicle. "Everyone is in place: Josh and Molly are in the production booth, Grace is backstage, Stirling is next door on coms, and Hunter and Chuck have security. Felix, you need to back off, or he's going to fritz out like a microwave with a gold bracelet inside."

Felix's brows drew tight, and he could feel Danny's puzzlement.

"That's a really odd simile," he said after a moment.

"Right?" Danny asked. "I mean, it's better than 'Pomeranian in a microwave.'"

"Oh my God, and so much better taste."

"But I've never heard that before."

"I'll beat you both with a stick while you sleep," she said pleasantly. "Here, Felix, let us off here, go park, and I'll be downstairs to let you in."

"It's my own goddamned office suite," Felix muttered to himself.

"Yes, it is, precious, and your boyfriend is going to go win it back."

"Fine." Felix pulled up next to the curb in a loading zone, and Danny grabbed his metal case full of expensive gadgets and tiny chemistry sets before sliding out.

"Wait," Felix croaked.

Danny paused and turned to smile at him. "It'll be all right, Fox. You'll see. You trust me, right?"

Felix took a deep breath. "With all that I am."

Danny grinned. "Excellent. I'll see you there, right?"

"Wouldn't miss it."

Danny slid out, and Felix gasped as the door shut.

"Wait," he whispered. "I needed a kiss for luck."

Julia let him in through the entrance in the parking garage, smiling winsomely at Hunter and Chuck, who were both wearing security-guard uniforms.

"What did you do with Joe and Chris?" Felix asked, hoping the men weren't locked in a closet somewhere.

"Gave them the day off," Hunter rasped. "With pay."

"Cash," Chuck said. "But I'll tell you, they weren't going to take it until they found out it was to et you back in charge. You have some good people, Mr. Salinger."

"And apparently we owe our security staff a raise," Felix said mildly. "First thing on my list when I get back in charge. Are Josh and Molly in the studio?"

"Yes, and Stirling is in my office, running coms." Julia was still trying to be patient.

"What about Grace?" Felix asked, tapping his earpiece to activate the mumble of the commlink.

"Grace is in Marnie Courtland's office, rearranging her bobble-head dolls and touching all her sanitary products." Grace spoke sotto voce, which added to the picture of the young, slender man in a darkened room, doing furtive, illegal things.

"There's an image," Felix muttered. "Are you doing anything that, say, can help Danny as he stares the entire city of Chicago in the face?"

"There's a bra in this drawer," Grace said, sounding surprised.

"What size?" Julia asked curiously. "There should be a tag on the back."

"You're asking me to touch a thing that touched boobies!" The horror in Grace's voice was unmistakable.

"Deal with it," Hunter growled over coms.

"Forty D," Grace squeaked, and Felix wondered for the hundredth time about the strange power Hunter seemed to have over the unknown quantity that was Josh's best friend, Dylan.

Then the number sank in. "Marnie and Brittney are both extremely petite," he said, looking at Julia in confusion.

"Satin, cotton, or Lycra?" Julia asked.

"This is scarring me for life."

"*Grace*!" Hunter growled, and Grace blurted "Cotton! It's cotton. Pretty blue flowered cotton. Sturdy, double-stitched, reinforced cotton!" almost on his heels.

"Rebecca Oswald," Julia said promptly.

Felix looked at her, surprised. "And you know that how?"

"She's about that size, and she works fifteen-hour days, Felix. When you can take the damned thing off in twelve hours, you can do underwire and satin, but if you're running your ass off, you want something supportive that breathes."

Felix gave her the once-over. Her figure, slim and willowy as always, didn't seem to need something with double stitching and structure. "So, uh—"

"A lady never tells," Julia said with a catlike smile.

Felix laughed softly. "So, Rebecca is going to be back in the production booth, is she?"

"Yes," Julia said.

"Do we return her undergarment, or perhaps ask around to make sure it's hers?"

What he was *really* asking was whether she thought Rebecca was being blackmailed or was complicit in Marnie's activities voluntarily. Julia would know, in the same way she knew the brassiere was Rebecca's.

"I say we ask around," Julia said softly. "It will end up in her hands eventually."

So Rebecca was Marnie's friend. Good to know.

"Perhaps we should start with Brittney, then," Felix said. "She might have an idea of what to do with it."

Julia nodded. "Indeed she might." They had gone up the stairs to studio level, and Julia pulled Felix into an alcove behind the cameras, where he could see out onto the set, but nobody could see him. The lights in the

...udio were harsh enough to create their own blinders, so Felix wasn't worried, although he did wrinkle his nose at the dust.

"We need to check this spot out once in a while," he muttered, pulling out his handkerchief.

Julia backed away apologetically. "I need to be in front of people, Felix. I'm sorry, but here you'll have a view, and you're back behind the microphones and acoustic curtains. Nobody should hear you on coms."

Felix nodded and gave her a hopeful smile. "There's still time to run away to Dublin. You know he's got an apartment there. We can share."

She rolled her eyes. "It's going to be fabulous, Felix. Have a little faith in him." She sobered. "He's due."

Felix nodded and tried to make himself invisible as the production crew hustled around his hiding place.

"I'm in the green room," Danny said over his com. "Waiting to be called. Everybody doing okay?"

"Two guys have tried to enter, claiming to be Marnie's assistants, but they didn't have ID," Hunter muttered. "Professional muscle but low-rent."

Chuck's laugh crept into the coms like an evil soundtrack. "*So* low-rent."

Hunter grunted. "How low-rent *were* they, Chuck?"

"Their suits squeaked on the pavement when they hit the ground."

Felix squeezed his eyes shut as he tried not to groan.

"That's terrible," Danny said lightly. "I approve entirely."

"Of the joke, or the sound they made when they hit the ground?" Chuck asked.

"Both. Everybody else?"

"My mom just handed me a bra," Josh said, sounding stunned.

"With instructions for what to do with it!" Julia muttered.

"Bras aren't catching," Grace told him, but it sounded like the desperate reassurance one friend might offer another after a rough night partying.

"So you say," Josh said, and then he was speaking to someone else in the room. "Brittney?"

"Yes, new guy? Sort of busy here."

"Yeah, uh, Julia Salinger asked me to give you this." Oh, the disgust in his son's voice! "We, uh, found it in Ms. Courtland's office."

"That's not mine," Brittney said, her voice flat.

"I swear to God, I don't know what to say."

"That's…." Brittney trailed off, and Felix could picture the girl's eyes narrowing. "Oh. Okay. Tell Ms. Salinger I know exactly what to do with this."

"I'm glad someone does," Josh said diplomatically. "'Scuse me, I'm going back to my station."

"Wait a minute," Brittney said. "You're working video feed?"

"Yes."

"And the new girl is working sound?"

"Again, yes."

"Do either of you have any *training* doing that?"

Josh's laugh was, eerily enough, echoed by everybody on coms.

"Enough," Josh said mildly, and they heard the sound of his footsteps as he apparently found his spot.

In Felix's com, he heard Danny say, "Yes, thank you, I'm coming." The stage manager stood in front of the cameras, which were lined up between the great plates of plexiglass that opened out onto the Chicago

...reets and the couch and love seat of the morning-show set. The furniture was tan leather, and the coffee table was white. Everything was spotless, although two bright red coasters sat on the table, one with Marnie's bottle of water and one with whatever Danny had requested in an orange mug with a Hello, Chicago! logo. The rug was orange and gold, and the draperies hanging in the background were red, orange, and gold. Everything looked so bright and shiny that Felix, from his hiding place beyond the black drapes offstage, felt a headache coming on.

"Okay, everybody," the stage manager—a spry man in his forties with frazzled brown hair and a puckish face—called. "Places!"

There was a last-minute scurrying as the four cameras aimed at the people on set—and the one aimed over Marnie's shoulder at the crowd—were positioned and focused. Through his intercom, Felix could hear Josh giving instructions on his job mic.

"Camera one, we need more light. It's still pissing rain outside. Camera two, nice, but raise up a little. We need some red in the shot. Three, four, and five, you're fine. Geordie, we're a go."

Then Molly's voice came on. "Okay, everybody, testing, testing." Suddenly her tone lowered as she spoke directly to Felix and company. "Stirling, adjust the feed in Danny's earpiece or he's going to give us feedback." Then she was giving directions to the people on set.

"Are we good?" Geordie, the stage manager, said.

"Is Marnie in place?" Rebecca asked, and Felix turned to the side and got his first good glimpse at Marnie Courtland since that terrible moment when he'd looked her in the eyes and she'd mussed her hair and spread her mascara into her red-rimmed eyes befc running out into this very studio to tell everybody tha he used intimidation to silence the truth.

Then she'd loomed so much bigger—a titan, covered in warts and scales, monstrous in his mind as she was in her own heart. But now she was just… a woman. Petite, pale, and pretty, with a coy look in her blue eyes that she'd cultivated for her thirty-odd years on the planet and a way of tilting her head that she knew to be adorable. She was decently talented, ambitious, and deeply, deeply amoral. But none of those flaws showed up on her person.

Today she was wearing a turquoise skirt suit that added to the perkiness of the set and a pleasant, relaxed look on her pointed features that didn't quite match the tension in her shoulders.

She was anticipating this interviewee to be tougher than an assistant museum curator should be, but she could be wearing a cast-iron girdle and she still wouldn't be able to get the better of Danny.

"Marnie, are you ready?" Geordie asked.

"I'm good to go," she said, and it was on.

"Okay, everybody, places. We are good to go in five, four, three!" Two fingers, one finger, and it began.

Marnie smiled.

First she introduced the show, then she introduced the segment, and then she introduced her guest.

"So our guest today is Benjamin Morgan, and he's applying for a job as a museum curator at our very own Art Institute of Chicago. Welcome to the show, Mr. Morgan."

"Doctor," Danny said, walking onto the set with his hand extended. She offered her hand in startlement, he shook it before taking his seat. "Doctor Morgan. have a PhD in European Art History from NYU."

"My apologies," Marnie said brittlely.

"And I actually got the job!" Danny grinned at the cameras and gave a little wave to the crowd that had inevitably gathered outside the window. The crowd responded wildly, and Marnie blinked.

"I'm sorry?"

"You said I was applying for the job, but I start Monday." He wrinkled his nose. "And I'm so very excited to be here."

She took a sip of her water and composed herself. Wrong twice in the first sentence—nicely played, Danny!

"Well, congratulations. So, Dr. Morgan, we first met at a party at which you identified some of my jewelry—"

"Well, not yours," Danny said, and Felix watched her teeth grind together.

"No," she murmured. "As it turns out, I hadn't realized the jewelry hadn't been rightfully purchased when I came by it, or even that some of it was forged."

"Well, they do say the value is in the story," he said. "You just had some *very* interesting pieces."

"I did," she conceded. "And they're even more interesting now."

"Yes," he agreed. "As soon as they're returned to their rightful owner, of course."

"Well, I think that's a little matter for Interpol to decide," she said, her smile tightening.

Danny nodded in complete innocence. "Well, as soon as they've spoken to your jewelry procurer, I am sure they'll know the entire story."

For a moment, she was on top again, and her lips curved upward into a real smile. "Unfortunately, he seems to have disappeared. I've told the police I have no idea where he's gone, but as soon as he shows his face again, I'll be very excited to have him apprehended."

"I have no doubt you will be," Danny said, his eyes practically glowing. "That would certainly be newsworthy."

For a moment, Marnie paused. Something in his voice, or maybe it was the unhidden glee in his eyes, put her on alert. Felix wanted to chortle. Interpol had, in fact, left the house with Bertram Talbot that morning. He'd been a little bit fatter, a little bit more relaxed, and very charming as he'd been carted away in cuffs. The two guards given the detail had been complimentary to the accommodations as well, both of them promising to send flowers in thanks as soon as they were able.

They were probably *very* entertained by the broadcast at the moment, given that they were standing in the wings.

"But that's not why you're here," she said, trying to regain control of the conversation. She turned to the crowd. "I was so impressed with Mr.—I mean, Dr.—Morgan's ability to look at a piece and ascertain its history and even its composition that we've set up a little demonstration for him so you all could see how very, very much he knows."

"Yes," Danny said, eyes twinkling gently. "It shall certainly be entertaining should I get the piece wrong. That is guaranteed."

Oh, he had people laughing with that one!

"Well, yes. I have some pieces you might not have seen yet," Marnie told him. "And we have the provenances here run on chyron as you examine the object."

"How very high tech," Danny said. "And to that end, I've brought some gadgets myself. I hope you're okay with that?"

Marnie's lips tightened. "You're not going to ruin my objets d'art, are you, Dr. Morgan?"

"Oh no, not in the least. I mean, I do have nitric acid to test for real gold, but I have some very noninvasive equipment. I think you'll be particularly impressed."

Marnie's eyes widened fractionally, and Felix caught his breath.

He smelled fear.

Marnie and Danny made small talk for a moment and then faded to a commercial break. Both of them turned then to a production assistant, who returned shortly with two cases.

Danny's case was metal, with foam inserts to keep his equipment intact, and the production assistant was a sober-countenanced, dancing-eyed Grace.

"Thank you," Danny said, giving the young man the side-eye. "Too kind."

Grace smirked and winked at him and all but danced away, leaving Danny to unpack his kit so it would be displayed by the time the commercial break ended.

Marnie was doing the same, but as she opened her case she gave a startled little gasp. Everybody on set looked at her in time to see her pull out a brightly flowered cotton bra—one definitely *not* her size.

Danny glanced up and hid a smile and then studiously attended to his own task while Marnie desperately shoved the thing in the corner of the couch.

In the production booth, Josh said in all ingenuousness, "Rebecca, you may want to tell Marnie we can still see that."

There was a pause—probably Rebecca actually *looking* at what was happening on the stage—and then a "*Shit!* Geordie, go get that thing out of the picture!"

The wiry little stage manager ran like the wind, diving in and out of the camera's range just as another voice said, "Coming back from commercial in five, four, three!" And Geordie stuck his hand in front of the camera and counted off the last two, and they were live again.

In the sound booth, there was a moment of absolute horror. "How in the fuck did that happen?" Rebecca muttered.

"That's what happens when you sleep with the boss," Brittney replied pleasantly.

"Everybody duck," Josh murmured. "It's knives out."

"How would you know I slept with the boss?" Rebecca sounded horrified—and not particularly adept at the game.

"Fellow sufferer," Brittney told her, her voice hard. "Apparently it's how she rolls."

Rebecca gasped, and the sound had tears in it. "That bitch," she whispered.

"Don't get mad…," Brittney said.

And Rebecca filled in the rest. "Get even. Metcalf, move!"

"Who's Metcalf?" Felix asked.

"Chyron tech," Josh murmured. "This should be good."

But it couldn't possibly be as good as what was happening onstage.

"What the hell is that?" Marnie asked, sounding rattled—and she might well have been. The gadget Danny had pulled out of his case looked a little like one of those hand scanners used in the grocery store, out with more bells and whistles. "That's not danger-ous, is it?"

Danny gave a practiced laugh, and Marnie's eyes twitched as she realized how off balance she'd sound-ed. "Not unless it's aimed at a fraud, my dear." He held the thing up like a ray gun and pretended to aim it at her. "It's only dangerous if it pings."

Marnie's mouth worked, and Felix wondered if her past hypocrisy was coming back to bite her. Or maybe it was her criminal misdeeds.

"But…?" She swallowed. "But what does it do?"

Danny grinned. "So it essentially shoots a very mild X-ray in a focused beam down this tube," he said, pointing to the little barrel. "The X-ray bounces back, and the radiation signature is measured by the fluoro-scope to indicate the composition of the elements it's aimed at. Each element has its own frequency, which registers as a color. Since gold is frequently mixed with alloys, I'll get a readout on this screen that tells me which elements are mixed in. Is it *barely* gold, like in much jewelry that's gold plated? With this—" He pointed to the nitric acid kit still in the case. "—I'd have to scrape off a little bit of the gold to see how it responded to the acid, and that would degrade the item, even if only slightly. This way I don't have to take even a scraping."

"Oh!" And to her credit, Marnie sounded interest-ed. "Were many items left with little scrape marks on them from the nitric acid test?"

"Oh yes. That's one of the benefits of prove-nance—if it describes the item having the scrapings, then that too becomes part of the story. And most pieces have some sort of inscription on them, usually with a rating out of twenty-four. So eighteen parts gold out of twenty-four parts gold becomes eighteen carats, and pure gold becomes twenty-four carats, and so forth."

"Are they ever marked with more than just the carat rating?" Marnie asked curiously, and for a moment, Felix was saddened. This woman, at the moment, was neither calculating nor evil. She was simply curious, a reporter doing her job and doing it personably and well. He wondered if a moment like this, a moment of being interested in the world and bringing other people's interest along with her, would have ever been enough for her. Because the scheming, the thieving, and the fraud, all of it, was going to lay waste to what was—even he could admit—a lovely natural talent.

He'd spent so much time hating her, he'd forgotten how much he'd enjoyed grooming someone for her job. He wondered if Torrance Grayson would be willing to come up the ranks.

"Yes indeed, they are," Danny said, pulling his attention back to the scene while looking up at Marnie prettily. "Do you have an item there? Here, let me get my magnifying glass."

She pulled out an object from her case, which was littered with pretty, sparkly things held secure by foam now that the bra was out of the way, and Danny regarded it without surprise. Grace had provided him with detailed pictures, of course, but Felix thought it was from more than that.

"That, my dear, is a signet ring worn by Charles the First. Royalty wear them, of course, because see the coat of arms there? That's exclusive to Austria, and that picture was used to imprint a 'signature' on hot wax or clay. In the time before widespread literacy, the signet ring was used to give a seal of authenticity to official documents." He remembered to look up and smile.

"That's why they're usually worn on the little finger. It's easier to imprint in the wax that way."

"But how do you know it belonged to Charles the First?" Marnie asked smugly. Danny's eyes widened a fraction, and Felix's mind raced. This would have been part of the same collection Talia's tiara had been included with. They must have been stolen at the same time. So *this* was the trap she had laid for him. If he mentioned the tiara—and the collection that hadn't been displayed—Danny would reveal himself as a thief.

Fortunately Danny was a very clever thief.

He smiled. "This particular one is seen frequently in photos." He held his hands up to his chest. "The double-breasted suit, you know. But also," he said, pointing to something that Felix couldn't see. "These small stones here—garnets. Bavaria was famous for them. And here…." He flipped the ring around. "Charles's family frequented this jeweler. The quill is his mark, and it's imprinted on the inside of the ring."

Marnie took the jeweler's monocle from him and examined the ring on both sides. "It says fourteen carats," she murmured. "Not twenty-four."

"Well, this was a working piece of jewelry. It was probably alloyed with something a little stronger so it would maintain its shape."

Marnie took the jeweler's loupe off and shook herself, as though coming out of a moment in which she and Danny were friends. "So it's real?"

"Well, offhand I'd say probably. But you can't bring a ray gun into a movie and not shoot an alien, right?" He turned and waggled his eyebrows playfully for the camera—and for the audience gathered outside—and they laughed. "Besides, signet rings used to be a form of identity theft. Getting hold of one—or replicating the design on one, particularly if there was something clever about it—was a way to steal power. So yes, it looks like it could have been a signet ring belonging to Charles the First, but maybe it was a signet ring designed by somebody in the last sixty or so years and then added to the collection because somebody thought it would look amazing." As he was speaking, he took the XDF and aimed it at the piece, and when he finished speaking, he smiled in a way that still gave Felix shivers up his spine. "As this one was."

Marnie gasped. "Really?"

"Oh yes. Look at these readings. Do you see the level of radiation? This spike here? This can be found in objects created after nuclear testing. Fallout really is everywhere, my dear. So it's a forgery, but it's a clever one, and one, I think, done for perhaps an historical purpose."

"Really?" Marnie repeated, and for a moment she seemed captivated completely by the story. "What purpose might someone have to forge something from that time period?"

The corners of Danny's mouth curled up. "It's quite a long story, and I understand you have other pieces you'd like me to look at?"

Marnie's eyes darted to the clock above the set, and she gasped. "Do we have time for one more piece?" she asked.

"Two, if he's quick," came the reply through Josh's com.

"Oh! I had such hopes you'd get to do them all," Marnie said, her voice taking on a hint of desperation. So every piece had its little trap, laid out on the supposition that Danny was either a thief or a liar. Interesting. But as Danny had already proved, hardly effective.

"If I may," Danny said, looking Marnie in the eye, "may I take a look at that piece?"

He gestured into the case, and Marnie lifted the item out curiously. And then her attention sharpened. "That piece? Why?"

Felix thought he'd been prepared to see it again, but setting eyes on the magnification of it on the screen overhead brought it all back. That lonely figure, fighting his way up the hill in a storm. Julia giving him a small gift, something she had stolen from her father. Danny hadn't forgotten. He'd recognized it from Grace's description. But something had clicked for him—Felix could see it in the softness of his face, in the way he took the piece from Marnie reverently in his gloved hands. He laughed softly.

"Tell us about that piece," Marnie said, and she'd remembered they were in the game now. She edged forward on her seat, her hands clasped in her lap.

"It's an original Rosalba Carierra," he said, almost absently. "She was a rococo painter who made her name on miniatures and wrecked her eyesight. The outside here is gilt—gold plated—and the box itself is made of ivory. It's the inside that's the true treasure." He gave a little laugh, and Felix heard him murmur, "I'd forgotten," under his breath.

"Tell her its provenance," Marnie ordered, her smile carving a snarl from her face.

Danny paused to regard her, not as though afraid, but as though he were a cat, toying with a mouse.

And Felix realized he himself had the power to free them all and bring Danny's paw down on Marnie's head.

"Tell her," Felix said clearly on the coms.

"Tell her," Julia said. "Josh and I can take it."

"Tell her," Josh said. "Don't hold back for me, Uncle Danny. This one's for you and Dad."

Danny hovered over the piece for a moment and then looked up at Marnie, a tear of joy shining clearly on his cheek.

"Well," he murmured, "the provenance of this particular item is unremarkable in history. It was in a French nobleman's collection, carried in a sack to England when the revolution started and used to finance a new start with the other emigres. Bought by an Englishman—a member of the House of Commons who liked to make himself look more important by taking snuff from this little piece—and from there it stayed mostly in his collection in their villa in Rome, until his family went bankrupt after the Second World War. After that it was picked up by an American entrepreneur as part of the estate. This American was a coarse, illiterate businessman who liked to make himself look more important, much like the Englishman, by having priceless objets d'art in his home to throw at his daughter and his wife if they displeased him."

Marnie caught her breath. "Oh!"

"Oh, indeed," Danny said, looking her in the eye. "He was a right bastard, if I say so myself. And when his daughter found herself pregnant, she was terrified. But then a young man who'd gotten lost knocking about Europe came along. He'd had a fight with his lover, you understand—" Felix's breath caught at that one lie, and so did Julia's. "—but before they could make up, the young man was taken in by the young woman's father. She knew he was in love with someone else, but she was desperate, and she offered the young man's lover the snuffbox as recompense for getting her out of her jam."

"Did she take it? The young man's lover?" Marnie asked, mesmerized.

"Oh, make no mistake, Ms. Courtland, I took it. I took it, and I sold it and used the money to spirit the two out of Rome. Hiram Dormer was a *very* dangerous man."

Danny met her eyes, and her face drained of color. "*You* owned that box?"

"For a very short time," Danny said. "But I examined it before I sold it, and I discovered a little hiding place right here." He set his hand to his own kit and produced a pair of tweezers. "See? There's a false bottom. It was, in fact, made for smuggling love notes. I never had time to figure out which people in its history would want to smuggle such things, or if it was only an affectation in the end. But when Felix Salinger and I were together, I'd made a list of pieces I'd like to see one day. They weren't the biggest or most expensive pieces in the world, but they meant something to *me*. When I realized that our plans had been derailed, I put the list in the bottom of this box before I sold it. I suspect I was being young and dramatic, but I didn't see myself as being able to go out in the world and find all of that art again."

He looked her directly in the eyes. "And you found this piece when you were visiting Rome… when? In college? Last year?"

"Three years ago," she said, her voice rusty.

"And you found that piece of paper and decided it was antique or important, and you hired an art thief to steal every piece."

His voice hardened, and Marnie flinched back as though struck.

"He was a legitimate procurer!" she said defensively.

Danny's look became feral—this man *could* be the cool-witted thief who had outwitted Interpol and lived despite being tortured by a jealous mobster.

"Are you sure about that?" he said. "Do recall that I know your history of claiming things that aren't true."

"Go!" Brittney snapped over coms, anticipating his cue by a hair. She was followed hard by Josh, who he'd lost track of during the last few drama-filled moments.

"Watch the screen, Dad."

And up on the screen was the film taken from Marnie's study, of her and a blurred-out Talbot talking about how much she didn't care if her art collection had been stolen.

Underneath it ran the chyron: Brittney Porter, Marnie Courtland's Assistant, and Rebecca Oswald, Producer of Courtland's News Shows, are Suing Courtland for Sexual Harassment at the Workplace.

Again and again and again.

While Marnie confessed on camera to paying someone to steal for her.

Danny broke off eye contact with Marnie to watch the screen, and then he flicked his eyes back to Marnie.

"But…," Marnie said softly. "But why would you do this to me? He… he married Julia!"

Felix stepped out from behind the curtain, and Julia entered the stage from the side.

"*Benjamin*," Julia enunciated carefully, "is like a brother to me. And so is Felix. Their dedication to my son and me kept us both safe when my father's legal team could have ensured both of us would stay with him until he killed us all. I'll love them until I die, but it's time for them to be in the sunlight."

"Just because he's bi doesn't mean—"

"Gay," Julia said firmly. "In the last twenty years, they have never loved anyone but each other. Through separations and reunions, it has only been them. Felix has earned his title here with blood, sweat, and sacrifice, but the one thing he's never sacrificed was his integrity. He wouldn't steal a story or ask you to lie about it, and you knew that when you accused him so publicly." Julia's eyes went to the screen. "But your word on the matter is hardly reliable now, is it?"

"This proves nothing," Marnie snarled, eyes focused on the screen like she could melt it by will alone.

"Well, no," Danny said, "but the whole world just heard you say you had no idea your procurer used thievery, and there you are saying he wasn't good enough at stealing because your pieces were forged. I think Interpol will be very interested in the difference between your story and his."

"But he's disappeared!" she said triumphantly.

"Yes, right into Interpol's hands," Danny said with one of his scalpel smiles. "As will *you* disappear, in just a moment."

Felix had heard Chuck and Hunter welcome the two Interpol guards as the drama had gone on in front of the cameras, and watching them come onto the stage and flank Marnie was almost all he could have asked for.

"Wait, no!" Marnie cried as one of them pulled her hands behind her. "Wait. I'm a US citizen—"

"And we're acting with permission of the FBI and Homeland Security," said one of the guards. He grinned like he knew he was on camera. "But we'd do it for sheer pleasure. Mr. Salinger there is the nicest man. What you did to him is a damned shame."

"That's kind of you, John," Felix said sincerely. In his ear Rebecca said, "So, commercial?" in the shaky voice of someone who had detonated her own career and wasn't sure whether she was happy or sad about it.

"Wait," Josh said quietly. "Dad?"

Felix stepped forward and held out his hand.

Danny stepped forward as well—down off the rise of the stage, but they were both still in view of the cameras. He took the offered hand and smiled shyly at Felix.

"Well done," he murmured, then, sotto voce, "Fox."

Felix grinned and pulled his knuckles up to kiss. "Marry me, Benjamin. I don't want to lose you again."

Danny smiled at him and looked away.

Then he turned back. "Yes."

Felix kissed him then, in front of the gathered, cheering crowd, in front of all Chicago, in front of the cameras.

In front of the world.

Sure, there would be jobs in their future, and gangsters and shadows of their past—but big things leave big shadows, and nothing, it turned out, was bigger in their lives than the two of them.

"Aw…," Josh said softly.

In the background, one of the Interpol officers said, "Wait a minute, where's her case? The one with all the bling in it? We were going to use that as evidence!"

"Shit," Josh murmured. "We had the cameras on the two of you."

"Well, who took them?" Danny murmured under cover of the kiss.

They all heard Hunter in their earpieces, exasperated as hell, shouting, "Goddammit, Grace!"

Then Josh said, "*Now*, Rebecca. *Now* fade to commercial."

Temporary Sunset

"NOW DO you feel like celebrating?" Julia asked as they gathered back home again. In deference to all of Phyllis's hard work, they'd brought Lou Malnati's out from the city, along with a case of sparkling cider and one of champagne.

"Every day," Danny said, smiling. The kids were downstairs, reveling in the play-by-play—Chuck and Hunter's exploits with the low-rent security Marnie had hired was part of it, but so was everybody chewing Grace out for stealing the case of evidence on camera.

"I gave it back!" Grace said, but he didn't sound repentant in the least.

Here, up on the main floor, where Danny could look out on the grounds from the sitting room window, all of that excitement permeated the house but left Danny feeling strangely mellow.

How was a man supposed to feel when he'd achieved his life's dream?

"So what was the story?" Julia asked. "The one about the forgery of the ring?"

Danny felt a happy little flutter in his stomach that she'd remembered. God, he'd forgotten what it was like to talk to people who lived for the story.

"Well, Franz Ferdinand had that politically embarrassing marriage—"

"The morganatic one," she said meaningfully, since that was his name now.

"Yes, exactly. And while I don't have confirmation, I do believe one of his children tried to claim they were an heir to the Hungarian throne. But remember, Franz and Sophie had both formally renounced their offsprings' right to the throne itself, which meant the only way to lay claim to being heir to it would be to say Charles the First gifted them with the title before he was dethroned. One of the best forms of proof for that would be possession of Charles's ring, so—"

"They forged the signet!" Julia sounded delighted and sad at the same time, which was just how Danny felt.

"Indeed. Interesting concept, right?"

"That you have to fabricate a truth to expose one?" Julia asked.

"Yeah. Makes us almost… you know. Legitimate."

Her laugh tinkled and broke the spell of melancholy that threatened.

"God forbid! Has it sunk in yet?" Julia asked, leaning her head on his shoulder.

"Give it time," he said, dropping a kiss on the top of her hair.

"I plan to," Felix said, coming up on his other side.

"And that, gentlemen, is my cue." Julia kissed his cheek and then Felix's, then went downstairs, hopefully to participate in the excitement.

"Should we join them?" Danny asked, but Felix was taking his goblet of cider from his fingers and setting it on the windowsill.

"Not yet," Felix murmured.

"No?" Danny soaked in his warmth, his nearness, and the way the light from the setting sun cast no shadows and showed no lines. Felix was ageless, the boy he'd fallen in love with, the man who'd come forward to claim that love today.

"No," Felix said and then kissed him. Danny opened for him, allowed him in, this kiss for them and them only in the setting of the sun.

As Felix's heat soaked into his senses, Danny thought dimly that there would be a sunrise, one showing them naked in each other's arms. And another sunset, revealing the two of them actively involved in mentoring their happy, adrenaline-chasing batch of great thieves.

And truly good people.

But right now there were only the two of them, *this* kiss, *this* sunset, and Danny was going to enjoy every moment.

He and Felix knew, of all people, that the perfect moments weren't like art. They weren't held forever in gold or ivory or oils or canvas.

Perfect moments were kept safely only in the hearts that treasured them.

Danny would never let his treasures be unguarded, unwanted, unloved, again.

Choose your Lane to love!

Orange
Amy's Dark Contemporary

See what happens next in the series!

A LONG CON ADVENTURE

The Muscle

AMY LANE

A Long Con Adventure

A true protector will guard your heart before his own.

Hunter Rutledge saw one too many people die in his life as mercenary muscle to go back to the job, so he was conveniently at loose ends when Josh Salinger offered him a place in his altruistic den of thieves.

Hunter is almost content having found a home with a group of people who want justice badly enough to steal it. If only one of them didn't keep stealing his attention from the task at hand....

Superlative dancer and transcendent thief Dylan "Grace" Li lives in the moment. But when mobsters blackmail the people who gave him dance—and the means to save his own soul—Grace turns to Josh for help.

Unfortunately, working with Josh's crew means working with Hunter Rutledge, and for Grace, that's more dangerous than any heist.

Grace's childhood left him thinking he was too difficult to love—so he's better off not risking his love on anyone else. Avoiding commitment keeps him safe. But somehow Hunter's solid, grounding presence makes him feel safer. Can Grace trust that letting down his guard to a former mercenary doesn't mean he'll get shot in the heart?

www.dreamspinnerpress.com

Prologue
Broken Steps

DYLAN LI sat on the worn and warped wooden floor in the fifth-story dance studio a little off the Loop in downtown Chicago. He hugged one knee to his chest and leaned against the mirrored wall behind him, watching Tabitha Marie Mikkelnokov dance the final scene of a student-written, student-produced contemporary version of *Cinderella* that she had choreographed.

She was sucking big balls at it too.

Normally Tabby was like a gymnast's ribbon—her body moved through the air like silk. She was a tad too tall to make it in the big ballets, but the Aether Conservatory, the school Tabitha's grandfather had put together with grit and most of his savings, had made it policy to take the dancers who worked hard, the ones who loved dance with all their soul, and to make allowances for things like standard height and even—on the odd occasion—ability. One of the best teachers at the Conservatory, Rudy, was a young man who would only ever perform with their adult education classes because his body was simply not that of a dancer, with tight sinews and slight congenital deformities that wouldn't allow him the fluidity of movement a dancer needed.

Artur Mikkelnokov kept Rudy there because his heart was consumed with the dance, and he passed this passion on to his young students. They learned to love the joy and pain of it because Rudy did.

Tabby didn't have such problems. Even with those extra inches, she could have performed in some of the top ballet troupes of the country, although she would not have gotten the lead because her partner would have needed to be nearly six foot three to stand even with her when she was en pointe. Aether was one of the first studios in the area to start considering how a dancer looked performing, how they made the audience feel, instead of how the dancer conformed to an almost impossible ideal of beauty.

Dylan—who stood shorter than her at five feet, seven inches tall—loved being partnered with her and loved watching her dance.

Except today, when an epileptic donkey would have been more graceful on the floor.

Dylan couldn't take it anymore. "The actual fuck, Tabby," he burst out in the middle of a plaintive violin solo.

Tabby whirled, coming down from a clumsy en pointe and almost stumbling to her knees. "Goddammit, Dylan!" she snarled. "I was trying to concentrate!"

Dylan leaned over to hit Pause on the sound system so the strains of plaintive violins stopped bouncing around Aether's biggest practice room. "You were failing! The fuck is wrong with you? I've seen my housemates' cats dance better!"

Tabby glared at him and then dropped her eyes. Dispiritedly, she padded across the platform to fall into a crisscross-applesauce sit-down at Dylan's side.

"Sorry," she said miserably, and then like she knew him—they'd been paired together since they were twelve years old—she leaned her head against his shoulder.

He looked at the top of her head, baffled. Her hair, toffee brown with tiny crinkles that were a result of her mother's Russian ancestry and her father's African-American family, sprang up from the usually merciless bun she pulled it back into and tickled his cheek.

"We're doing this now?" he asked. Usually he'd be acerbic or teasing or even somewhat of an asshole, but this was Tabitha, and if he'd ever had a sister, he wouldn't love his sister this much because she'd probably be too much like him. But Tabitha was earthy and honest, and she ignored seven-eighths of what came out of Dylan's mouth and listened, instead, to the things he actually did.

He gave her tiny earrings every birthday—real gold or silver, real semiprecious stones—and she wore many of them in her ears every day. He never told her that he often stole them from the jewelry boxes of the girls who'd made fun of her in high school. His baby-thief training years, as it were. He would enjoy that little bit of irony all by himself.

"Yes," she said, her voice clogged from tears she was obviously trying not to shed. "You are my emotional support animal, whether you want to be or not."

He sighed and looped an arm around her shoulders. "Fine. Under duress." He gave her a little squeeze, and she let out a laugh.

"Good emotional support animal," she praised, and he dropped a kiss on the top of her head.

"You gonna tell me what's wrong?" he asked softly.

"I can't," she said, and her voice broke.

He rocked her for a few moments and then asked, "You're not pregnant, are you?"

"No!" She laughed through her tears, which looked really hideous, in fact, but he preferred it to the hopeless sobbing. "You ass, I am not pregnant! Jesus. Why would you ask that?"

"Because I want to keep dancing with you," he told her, because, duh! "And I was sort of hoping you weren't knocked up. You can call me your emotional support animal all you want, but we both know I'm a selfish bitch, so you can't be all that surprised."

She sputtered, wiping her face on the loose T-shirt that hung over her leotard. "Dear God, Dylan Li. The things that come out of your mouth. Don't!" She turned to him with horrified eyes; he'd been known to blurt out uncomfortable things about his sex life at the merest provocation. "Don't even go there," she told him sternly. "If I have to hear about some guy's come that tasted like cinnamon gum, I will vomit. I don't have to be pregnant to have standards."

Dylan chuckled appreciatively, although, point of fact, there hadn't been a guy or a hookup or whatever for a couple of months now. He refused to dwell on why that was because then he might have to put a name to….

He wasn't going to do it.

"Well, fine," he told Tabby, suddenly grateful she had problems for purely selfish reasons. "I won't tell you about cinnamon come, but you *will* tell me why you're dancing like shit. We go live with this show in three weeks, babycakes. You can't afford to suck donkey balls now!"

She let out a shaky breath. "Except it might not," she whispered, and Dylan's heart froze.

"What?"

"Oh, Dylan. It's awful. My grandfather might lose everything. His lease on the studio, his performance contracts, *everything*. It's not fair! And there's nothing I can do about it. Nothing!"

Dylan took a few deep breaths and tried to center himself. "Aether Conservatory?" he asked, just to make sure. His parents traveled the globe, mostly looking after their financial interests in Hong Kong. Dylan had been left alone with nannies and housekeepers at a very young age. He tended to be destructive when bored or lonely, and only two things had kept him from flaming out in a big ball of drugs and id.

His best friend, Josh Salinger, was one of them, and dance—specifically dancing at Aether Conservatory—was the other.

"You will explain that," he said to Tabitha, needing to hear the details.

The more she spilled, the longer she spoke, the more he realized that maybe the gods of chaos really were looking out for him.

Because Dylan Li, and his friendship with Josh Salinger, might be the only things to save the dance company that had saved his life.

Predatory Animal

After Paulie, Before Josh

"*PAULIE!*"

Hunter Rutledge woke up sweating, shaking, and cold. God. Fucking dream. Why? Why did he have to remember it? Keep remembering it for the past eight months?

Him and Paulie, outside their employer's mansion in Arizona, scanning the dusty confines of the compound with restless eyes.

"Did he say why we're going now?" Hunter asked.

Paulie shook his blond head grimly and arched a mischievous brow. "I know his timing could have been better," he said dryly, and if Hunter had been anyone else, he would have smirked.

Paulie Claymore had a slender, tight little body and was one of the sweetest assholes Hunter had ever had the privilege to plow. He and Paulie had been *off duty* when the phone rang in their guest quarters. It had been their boss, telling them they were on emergency duty because the guys who were *supposed* to be on shift had gone into town for....

Yeah. There was no reason. The guys had just flaked.

Hunter had been a mercenary for three years after his six-year stint with the corps—bodyguard work mostly, with a few stretches of industrial security. He knew what good logistics were and he knew when things were fishy—and this was definitely fishy. But, well, he and Paulie had a job to do.

They'd been guarding Ronald Pinter, industrialist, ex-cattle-rancher, and entrepreneur, for the past three months, and the guy had "paranoid drug user" written all over him. Hunter hated the job. Pinter refused to tell his people what he was so afraid of, and every time Hunter saw him, with his wet eyes and red, runny nose, he expected Pinter's brains to explode.

The job was sketchy, and after three months, Hunter wanted out. But first he wanted Paulie to come with him.

He and Paulie had been hired at the same time, both of them referred by a mutual military contact, and when they moved together, Paulie was like the extension to Hunter's shoulder he'd always wanted. Off duty, they'd run evacuation logistics, beefed up Pinter's security, and practiced their marksmanship as synced together as the parts of a well-maintained engine.

The sex had been inevitable.

Paulie had been willing, excited even, to hook up with another man on the job. Usually, he'd told Hunter, his hookups were guys he met in the club scene or people he dated through mutual friends. Being with someone who knew what he did—and what he was capable of doing—was a rush for Paulie, and he loved Hunter's cock as much as Hunter loved his ass.

It wasn't true love. It wasn't even friendship. But Paulie was a brother-in-arms with a unique place in Hunter's life, and he didn't want to leave his fuckbuddy to the wolves.

Fucking is where they'd been when they'd gotten Pinter's call.

They were *barely* dressed now. Hunter could still smell Paulie on his skin, still feel the silk of his body gripping Hunter's cock.

Still remember Paulie's ecstatic smile as Hunter slid into his ass.

And Hunter was having a hard time getting his head in the game. Where in the fuck did the other team go again? Chancellor was in his fifties, hot in a silver fox sort of way, and Creighton was built like a gorilla—Hunter regarded them with intense dislike, but they seemed to be Pinter's favorites. Lacking in humor, both of them, but they had a sort of brutish, impersonal competence that made them easy to work with. But not trustworthy—and definitely *not* friendly. Hunter was just as glad Pinter had taken a liking to the two of them, giving them the plum assignments and the trips to Cabo and giving him and Paulie time to get busy.

"We should put him into the car while it's in the garage," Hunter said seriously. "You go fetch him and start the engine. I'll keep lookout by the gate."

Paulie nodded and winked. "Taking point, as always."

Hunter nodded soberly. He didn't engage in a lot of banter or play, but he enjoyed that Paulie did. And Paulie's boyish smile hid the heart of a tried-and-true soldier. "Protecting my people," he said, smiling slightly when Paulie gave a little hop as he turned toward the garage.

Hunter pulled out his radio and called the gatehouse to tell them to be ready for the limo to pull through and got only static in return. His stomach churning, he jogged the two hundred yards or so to the small building that stood guard between the two lanes of the driveway to see why Stanley wasn't answering.

He was twenty yards away from the gatehouse, searching for the retired cop's jowly face through the white-bordered window, when he realized that all he could see was a crimson stain against the back wall.

Fuck!

He pulled out his radio again and hit Paulie's code. "Paulie, they're inside. Double-check everything. The gatehouse has been compromised. Dammit, Chancellor and Creighton must have set us up!"

Hunter had no idea why—hell, he really didn't know his employer's occupation beyond "retired tech magnate." All he knew was that a month ago, Pinter had taken the four of them to Chicago. Paulie and Hunter had waited with the car inside a parking garage while Creighton and Chancellor had gone to some sort of public function on Navy Pier, after-hours. Pinter's behavior had gotten more and more erratic since that trip—and the nose candy had been flowing like water.

Then two weeks ago, Creighton and Chancellor had escorted Pinter to a swank hotel in Guadalajara for a good meal and a trip to a strip joint. They'd come back two days later with a tan. When Hunter had asked if they knew why they'd taken the trip, both guys had shrugged, not even curious.

"*He* did something," Chancellor, the silver fox, had said. "He went downstairs without us and came back, put a thing in his suitcase, and said it was time to party. So we went and partied, hookers on him."

Charming.

Chancellor didn't remember anything else, not even what the thing was that Pinter had put in his suitcase. All Creighton could talk about was the hookers. The hookers grossed Hunter out, frankly, because Creighton sounded like he'd treated them like shit, and ever since then, Pinter had been even more weasel-eyed than before. Hunter's instincts had been screaming GTFO at top volume.

But Paulie had wanted to wait it out. This had been an easy gig—Fat City, he'd called it. He was so excited not to be tramping through a desert or a jungle, and he had a guy and was getting some on a regular basis. Why would he want to leave now?

And Hunter? God help him, he hadn't had a real boyfriend since he'd left the military for mercenary work. If they could get clear of this job, perhaps find a different gig, a better one, maybe he and Paulie could actually talk—maybe even connect emotionally and not just physically. But they had to be in a place that didn't make his intestines itchy, where he and Paulie didn't have to hook up on the down-low.

Or be prepared to see a sweet old retired cop's brains splattered against the gatehouse wall.

"We're loading into the limo now," Paulie said over the radio. "Pinter's a wreck. Had to fish him out of a bowl full of blow. Fucking Jesus!"

"I'll be by the gatehouse. Standing by."

Hunter watched as one of the doors of the four-car garage attached to the side of the house opened, his eyes moving constantly, gut muscles pulled practically to his spine. Oh, he didn't like this, didn't like this—

Flames first.

Orange and billowing, blowing out of the garage with the force of the concussion that hadn't yet rocked him.

By the time his feet had started to move, the blast was tearing through the garage, through the back portion of the house, through his soul.

There wasn't enough left to identify in the end, although DNA had confirmed both Paulie and Pinter. But that's not what Hunter saw in his dreams. In his dreams, he saw skeletons, scorched and shaking, sitting in the burned-out husk of the limousine, jaws locked open in an endless scream.

That had been eight months ago, and Hunter was beginning to realize he wasn't ever going to shake that vision, not even in sleep, and his class on computers in criminal justice wasn't much of a motivation to roll out of bed. But Hunter had depended on routine and order to get him through the last eight months, and today was no different. He sat through the lecture, making the occasional note about something that had been changed from when he'd gotten a similar course in the military, then all but sleepwalked back to the parking structure that held his car.

Where he saw another one.

God. These fuckers. So transparent. Watching their victims—usually females but sometimes a smaller, skinnier male who looked defenseless—waiting for a chance to strike. Sometimes it was just a purse snatching or a mugging, but others? Hunter was pretty sure he'd stopped something else entirely when he took those guys out.

Because when he saw them, he always took them out.

Award winning author AMY LANE lives in a crumbling crapmansion with a couple of teenagers, a passel of furbabies, and a bemused spouse. She has too damned much yarn, a penchant for action-adventure movies, and a need to know that somewhere in all the pain is a story of Wuv, Twu Wuv, which she continues to believe in to this day! She writes contemporary romance, paranormal romance, urban fantasy, and romantic suspense, teaches the occasional writing class, and likes to pretend her very simple life is as exciting as the lives of the people who live in her head. She'll also tell you that sacrifices, large and small, are worth the urge to write.

Website: www.greenshill.com
Blog: www.writerslane.blogspot.com
Email: amylane@greenshill.com
Facebook: www.facebook.com/amy.lane.167
Twitter: @amymaclane